ABOUNDING WITH THANKSGIVING

A Future Novel of a Past Time

Donald Bowers

TMS Press

ISBN: 978-1-7322850-4-0

Cover design by:Ellen Anne Eddy
IFrontis illustration by: Mark Baker

Printed in the United States of America

Foreword, Acknowledgements,
and all those other things we write at the beginning

This story is the product of much research, serious thought... and some borrowing.

The characters visiting 1926 from far time, including the Baughmans and Nymans, and the Johnson family, along with the non-human characters of the ruBracks, cyber-intelligences Sherry, Peter, and Fred, and the Woogies (by reference), come to this book from the historical Lane Johnson novels of my oldest friend Marvin Reem, and the Christian science fiction novels of his pen name and alter ego, Ward Wagher. They appear here by kind permission of Marvin/Ward, with many thanks. And he does know where the bodies are buried in three universes!

His book websites:
http://www.wardwagher.com/
http://www.marvinreem.com/

Places and businesses in uptime Galesburg exist, and you may visit Pizza House, Calico Cat, and the Landmark restaurant if you visit our town. Coney Island is still here too, on Cherry Street as it was in 1926. And the Inn at Union Pier still uses those Swedish fireplaces!

Gator Sauce, the condiment that wins Mimi's heart and taste buds is very real and exactly as advertised. You may try it for yourself by visiting Dave's Autobody in Galesburg or visiting http://davesgatorsauce.com/

The image of the bottle is used by permission of Dave Dunn, owner and purveyor.

As always, I owe a tremendous debt of gratitude to my relentless and remorseless editor and cover illustrator, Ellen Anne Eddy Bowers. Any improvements in readability and emotional impact are due to her kind but firm redirection of my copious written hot air. She has finally convinced me that these books are not only Christian historical alternative universe fiction, but also romances. You may find her novels and other books on Amazon under Ellen Anne Eddy.

To all the other folks I have known, past and present, who contributed their personalities to characters in this book I say thank you, and hope I have done justice to your person or your memory.

Don't
Peek!

All things work together for good,
Those are the pieces.
To those called according to God's purpose.
That is the picture.
Whether or not we let God assemble the pieces
Determines whether it will be a picture or a puzzle.
God sees the picture from the beginning,
You won't see it till it's finished,
Don't get lost among the pieces.

Vance Havner

As ye have therefore received Christ Jesus the Lord, so walk ye in him: Rooted and built up in him, and established in the faith, as ye have been taught, abounding therein with thanksgiving.

Colossians 2: 6 and 7

PROLOGUE

Healey Willan: Friday, February 26th, 1926, 10:30 AM, A little wedding music

"I so hope I'm not intruding on your enjoyment of this day, Lucille," I said as Lucille Rochlus Foster climbed aboard the organ bench with me.

"Not at all, Healey," she replied, "I couldn't sit with my husband anyway because he's in the swords detail. I'm glad to turn pages and help manage this beast."

"I do appreciate that," I said, "Missing the connection in Chicago yesterday put us here late last night. I'm so grateful you and Gilbert waited for us."

"Our pleasure," the dark-haired musician said softly. "I got to practice a little, and we ran through his songs while we waited."

"Did I hear Gilbert sang to you at your wedding?"

"He sure did! He told me he was going to sing *O Promise Me* but then the stinker comes out with *Che Gelida Manina*!"

"My word! And he got through it?"

"Like a pro! He says after that one singing *The Call* today will be a snap."

I nodded as I watched the amber lights by the power switch turn to green. "Thank you for accompanying him this morning. I didn't get time to practice that one."

"I was going to do it anyway. Gil wants me to."

"Of course."

A bald middle-aged man in a semblance of a polo shirt approached us on the platform. He wore an odd combination headphone and microphone and carried two of the same.

"Hi, I'm Rick Meath," he began, "We met the Monday after you became a partner."

"Indeed, and good morning Rick. Have you something there for us?"

"I do," Rick replied and gave a headphone set to Lucile and me. "These are set to only work between you two so you can communicate. If you need to say something to others on the network just push the red button on the side of the earpiece." He showed us on his set.

"Thanks, Rick," Lucille said, "What if you need to talk to us?"

"The voice will come over the headphone. Just reply normally."

"Normal? Today?" Lucille retorted.

Rick laughed. "Today is anything but normal! Now I'm heading back to the booth. With everything going on today we'll be a little busy." With that, Rick retreated up the aisle.

I took out my pocket watch and checked it with the small clock on the console. "Shall we begin?"

"Sure," Lucille replied, "Do you want me to keep quiet while you play?"

"Not at all! It will be a pleasure to converse softly with these gadgets while I'm playing. At Saint Mary Magdalene I must manage the choirs and organ alone. I may ask you about some of the people though."

"Fine, Healey, I'll tell you whatever I know."

I opened to the first page of Charles-Marie Widor's *Fifth Organ Symphony*. I checked the time again, then launched the almost playful first movement.

"I'm so happy Gladys found someone to sit with," I remarked.

My assistant grinned. "Sitting between Helen Smiley and Deborah Kittridge they'll keep her laughing."

"Nobody but Company partners were invited to this wedding,

correct?" I asked.

"Right. We had to do that because Jackie's getting married in uniform and that would tip people off they're not from here."

I nodded and continued playing. "I have this symphony mostly memorized, so if you're late with a page turn that's all right."

Lucille gave me an old-fashioned look. "Sir, I know what can happen during a performance, and I'll turn on the mark for you —oops!" she quickly flipped the page of the score. "Mostly."

I grinned. "Not to worry. But who is that tall woman with the headphones bustling around the platform? I don't believe I've met her."

"I've only met her once myself. She's Kathy Trainor, in charge of the Company office in Galesburg uptime. She's Apostolic Christian, very nice—and supremely competent from what I've seen. She's the stage manager for this wedding."

I glanced over at Lucille as I played. "I've never seen a wedding require a stage manager."

"Trust me. This wedding does!" she said with a giggle, "Rehearsal yesterday was a scream—literally!"

"Are they aware of their cues for the processional?"

"They know how long they have to get down here, and that the music will be loud. Otherwise, only Rick and I know what you're playing. We timed the march down yesterday and it'll work out. If they get here early, they just stand and wait till you're done."

"I am happy to be able to watch the platform without using a mirror," I added.

As I bored my way through the first movement, I noticed several men and women moving around rolling tripods with what appeared to be large shoeboxes mounted atop them. "What are those tripod things?" I asked.

"They're called video cameras. I'm told they make those videos we watch on the laptop computers. Everybody with laptops gets a copy of this wedding, especially those who couldn't be here. Wow! Two months ago, I would've thought I'd spoken Chinese if I said that!"

"And one month ago, I would have thought the same," I replied, "I find the laptop interesting, but Gladys is enthralled by it. Our friends here are sending her a steady stream of videos and music to play on it."

"They aren't stingy about sharing things from uptime," Lucille replied, "There's a lot of bad things to see from then, but much good too."

"So I've noticed. Overall though I feel massively blessed, especially with access to what the other Healey wrote. I've begun using some of it here."

Lucille turned another page. "Did it feel funny hearing the music the *other you* wrote in that universe? How does it feel to put music out now, long before you would have if you'd written it here?"

"My dear, you've asked a very serious question on this pleasant Friday morning. Let me finish up this first movement and I'll answer you."

"Of course, Healey."

The crescendo to the end of the first movement occupied me for the next three minutes. I let the last chord echo through the hall for several seconds before beginning the second movement—and answering Lucille's question.

"It did seem very odd indeed at first. I was consumed with questions. Would I have written the works the same way here? Did they express something I wanted to say here but just hadn't gotten around to writing yet? Would using these pieces quench my drive to write new music different from what I now have access to?"

"You think they'll stop you from composing?" Lucille asked as she turned a page.

"That's the oddity of it. I don't think they will," I replied, "I played several of the shorter pieces for Gladys. She affirmed they were definitely in my style. I have limited time to compose between my teaching duties and work at Saint Mary Magdalene. This last month I've spent a portion of my free time editing the works Don has given me. I spent the rest composing at a leisurely pace rather than staying up all night writing something under a deadline. That practice creates a merry havoc in class the next day!"

My assistant nodded. "It sure does! I find myself staying up later since I've been married, and I feel it in the afternoons, especially lately."

"There is a time and place for every activity," I said softly. I noticed Lucille's blush before I continued.

"Anyway, I find what I'm writing now seems fresher, less mundane than it tended to become before. The masses require an inordinate amount of music, and the members are used to hearing new music to fit each segment of the liturgical year. Now I find I can mix the *uptime* music with my new work, provide things the *other* Healey never wrote, and expand the body whole. And my publisher is quite taken with the additional output."

"So having the uptime work is a blessing?" Lucille asked.

"So far, most certainly. Gladys thinks it has improved my mood also. I'm not as tired as I was before. And Don tells me I will feel even better after another trip to Hoople this summer."

"That's what Gil tells me. He's been there, I haven't yet."

I came to the end of the second movement and Lucille queued up the third. "Shall we give them a little oompah music?" I asked.

Lucille's answer was a giggle.

I glanced out into the audience and saw a couple and adolescent boy being hugged by Helen and Deborah and introduced to Gladys. "Who are those folks with Deborah?" I asked.

Lucille looked. "Fred and Violet Johnson and their son Pacey. They farm out by Appleton, and they're in charge of the school board out there. They're partners, just found that out. Their younger son and daughter are in the wedding party."

"Oh," I replied, then spied a very thin woman with long blonde hair wearing a suit and pants sit behind my wife's party, and Deborah introduced her around. "And who is that woman behind my wife?"

Lucille looked. "Her name is Kimberly Baughman. She's the wife of the Company's coordinator of far time operations, about five hundred years in the future in a different universe."

"I still find it hard to comprehend life that far in the future," I commented. Kathy the stage manager walked over to us. I turned slightly so I could hear her over the organ.

"Everything is on schedule Mr. Willan," Kathy announced quietly, "Do you have the order of service?"

Lucille showed her the small card she held in the pocket of her dress. "We've gone over it. If the party gets down here on time, we're fine; if they don't we're still fine. They ought to be able to get down here in six minutes flat!"

Kathy chuckled softly. "That mob? We'll see how close they come. And thank you for the beautiful prelude, Mr. Willan."

"You're welcome. Call me Healey, my dear," I said as I finished the third movement.

"Of course, Healey," Kathy said, then pushed a button on her headset. "Affirmative Rick, final check of the lineup in a moment, out."

As Kathy walked quickly up the aisle of the hall Lucille put up the next movement. "Now for the gentle set-up to the processional," I remarked, and launched.

Precisely on time came the last whisper of the next to the last movement of the symphony. We'd save the final movement for the recessional, as the couple requested.

"You didn't tell them what the processional would be, did you?"

"No way, Healey! They surprised me enough at my wedding; now it's payback time."

"Musicians have long memories," I remarked with a smile. I glanced at the back of the hall, then pushed the four presets for the various divisions and launched the *Grand Chœur Dialogué* of Eugène Gigout.

"People jumped," Lucille said softly through the headset. I nodded and smiled. This piece is loud enough to discourage conversation, and I did not stint on the volume. I secretly hoped to shatter a light bulb backstage.

Slowly through the doors to the hall began a very slow and stately procession reminding me of our processionals at Saint Mary Magdalene, but almost Catholic in its complexity. "If you would tell me who is in the procession as they get to the platform, I would appreciate it."

"Sure. Although I've only just met some of them," Lucille replied. We could hear each other quite well through the headsets.

Leading everyone came Pastor Kittridge in uniform.

"He's a Commander in the Navy Supply Corps Reserve," Lucille supplied before I asked.

In step behind Pastor walked a small boy in a suit. "Who's he?"

"Lane Johnson. He stood up with Luther and Syl at their wedding last December. He's got the rings today."

Following Lane came a big man with graying black hair in a Navy captain's uniform.

"Matt Plotczyc, He manages transportation for Wain Engineering," Lucille spoke before I asked, He is leading the swords detail."

Following Matt, two by two, slow marched the arch of swords detail. They were to stand on the platform with the wedding party. Each wore a sword at their waist and white gloves. Beyond that, the uniforms were an incredible mixture from different times and different places.

The first pair were Luther Barlow in his Marine uniform and a tall, erect elderly man in a strange blue uniform. "I know Luther. Who is the other man?" I asked.

"Earl Heckel. Both men hold the American Medal of Honor. Luther won his in the Great War, and Earl won his in the American Civil War!"

"Right for them to be in front," I replied, then caught sight of the two men following. Both wore berets; I did not recognize one uniform but the other I did. "Whoever are they?" I asked, "One of them is wearing the Victoria Cross!"

I could hear the uncertainty in Lucille's voice. "That's Dick Meriden, Don's second-in-command. He won the V.C. in the next world war in the other universe. I'm still having trouble saying that."

"Next, you'll tell me that other man ran a whole planet."

"Wha—how?" Lucille's calm demeanor cracked asunder at my idle comment. The pair were almost to the platform before she could reply. "That's Frank Nyman. He and his wife are retired and live in Chicago. Don's vague about it, but he supposedly did just that in the far time universe before he retired. I don't know anymore."

"I was joking, Lucille. But around here reality is no joke."

"You said it!" Lucille replied, then steadied down for the rest. "The next pair, the older woman's name is Fleur; she's Frank Nyman's wife. She was a doctor in whatever military he was in and consults with our people in Hoople. The other woman you know. Amy Lansdale served in the Navy and some other service, and as a lawyer."

"She is striking with that long blonde hair," I remarked, "and quite an array of medals."

"She won't talk about how she got them. I think that time bothers her."

The two ladies were stepping onto the platform before Lucille continued.

"The next two. The one closest is my husband Gil. You've met him. He's still in the Air Service Reserve, just made Major. The other gentleman is Sergeant Major Chuck Simmons, retired. He just got brought into the family, so to speak."

"I see," I said, "and the others?"

"Bringing up the rear are retired Army captain Paul Sherwood, Edna Kimpton's new husband. They got married last weekend. Finally Master Chief Sammy Allen. I think you met him when they showed you the second balcony."

"Oh, yes," I replied, "Brilliant man. And we have just a couple of minutes to go. Can you see if the guests of honor are coming?"

Lucille turned a page then craned her neck around. "Yep, here comes Don, white gloves and all!"

I glanced up the aisle. There indeed came Don, in full dress uniform but hatless. "Harder to kiss with a hat on?" I asked.

Lucille blushed. "With both him and his wife wearing hats it was impossible! They tried it at rehearsal. It did not end well."

I chuckled, then, "Who is that portly balding gentleman escorting him?"

"Don only introduced him as Marvin at the dinner last night. Said he performed his and Pam's ceremony many years ago, and Don talked him into being best man at this one."

"Does he know where the bodies are buried?" I asked with a smile.

"Both universes," my assistant replied with a snort.

The groom and escort arrived at the platform just before I began the final booming section of the piece. Above the organ, an amplified voice rang out, "Attention on deck!"

"That's different," I remarked.

"Worked, didn't it?" Lucille replied as the audience stood.

At first, I could only see one head bobbing at the back of the hall. Then as they got closer, I could see a small girl in a peach-colored dress, walking slowly and carefully strewing rose petals from a basket.

"Sarah Johnson, daughter of Violet and Fred, sitting with your wife."

"Right."

Behind Sarah stepped Jackie, resplendent in her Naval officer's uniform. I could see her gold Naval Aviator's wings above her medals, and another badge below them. Next to her walked a tall elderly woman in a blue dress. Lucille anticipated my question.

"Lillian Taylor, our boss in the School District. She's got cancer, retiring at the end of this year. Uptime meds help control her pain."

"Can't the wizards at Hoople help her?"

"No, the cancer is too far advanced. Lillian chose not to have surgery and just manage the pain."

"How awful," I said.

"Lillian's OK with it, says the surgery would be worse and not solve the problem. I don't know if I could make that decision."

"Let us pray you never have to."

The bride and her escort moved into place on the platform with thirty seconds to spare. The party stood motionless while I blasted out the final chords of the work on that marvelous, unique organ.

The wedding service resembled those at Saint Mary Magdalene, except no Eucharist was offered. About one third through Lucille nudged me and I shifted to the left side of the bench. She took over, and the simple accompaniment of Ralph Vaughn Williams' *The Call* echoed through the silent hall.

Lucille's husband Gilbert turned from his position in the formation and sang that song with a clarity and intensity only one who has experienced life can muster.

Come, my Way, my Truth, my Life:
Such a Way, as gives us breath:
Such a Truth, as ends all strife:
Such a Life, as killeth death.

Come, My Light, my Feast, my Strength:
Such a Light, as shows a feast:
Such a Feast, as mends in length:
Such a Strength, as makes his guest.

Come, my Joy, my Love, my Heart:
Such a Joy, as none can move:
Such a Love, as none can part:
Such a Heart, as joys in love.

Lucille had told me of the day he trusted Christ, as his aircraft was falling in flames after being shot down by Ernst Udet the German ace. Gilbert's miraculous survival and later career showed the hand of Our Lord indeed. Tears were flowing down Lucille's face as she finished. I offered her my handkerchief which she took with a sniffle and nod.

A few minutes later the ceremony approached its end. Pastor Kittridge gave the couple leave to kiss, and they took full advantage!

As the audience clapped and whistled, I spoke to Lucille, "Ready for the postlude?"

"Ready to roll," she replied, "I'll leave the headset with you when he's praying."

"Very good. Have fun!"

The couple eventually broke the kiss, and Pastor turned them around to face the audience. "Now, before I introduce you, let us pray."

As Pastor prayed Lucille took off her headset and slipped off the bench. She took an object from behind the organ console and stepped quietly over to the bride. She put the object into Jackie's hands behind her back, then moved behind Pastor. Gil and Luther switched places in the swords group, and he and Lucille stole a quick kiss.

Pastor finished praying. He stepped to the side of the couple and spoke.

"And now it is with the greatest pleasure that I present to you Vice Admiral and Captain, Jackie and Don, Mr. and Mrs. Donald Wain!"

The audience applauded. Don started to take a step forward, but Jackie stopped him. She held up one finger, then walked swiftly to the side of the party. Jackie handed a gaudily decorated fore-and-aft hat to Gil. He put it on and gave Lucille his Air Service hat. Jackie returned to a puzzled-looking Don.

As Jackie performed these moves, I began to play a single repeated phrase, doubled on the great and swell keyboards. Pastor put up his hands and the audience quieted quickly. I then launched into the introduction for music I knew well: the double-header of *I am the Sovereign of the Sea and When I Was a Lad,* from *HMS Pinafore* by Gilbert and Sullivan. I had directed this operetta in Toronto the year before, and it was a favorite of mine. These two songs chronicle how a less than competent officer became '*ruler of the Queen's navee.*' A grand hilarious parody, and a complete surprise for Don!

Gil sang the part of the Admiral to perfection that day, with all the appropriate mannerisms. Lucille sang the replies to his lines, and cued the chorus: the entire wedding party, including the bride! The chorus sounded a bit ragged, but it didn't matter. Gil and Lucille made every syllable crystal clear.

The audience laughed and howled. Don just stood there. He turned red and shook but I couldn't tell if he were in a rage or laughing hysterically. Eventually, Jackie had to take hold of his arm and turn him a bit; then I could see him both laughing and crying.

Mission accomplished, I thought.

The song ended to a storm of applause and bows from the singers, then I launched into the real postlude, the last movement of the Widor symphony.

The wedding party strode up the aisle and the crowd started to get up to leave. I finished the Widor then launched into an improvisation on themes from *HMS Pinafore*. After ten minutes I ended the improvisation, turned off the organ, and made my way to the stairs backstage to get to the lobby through the basement. I knew Deborah and Helen would have Gladys there to meet me.

*****

Amy Lansdale, 5:05 PM, the Auditorium office, wind down and debrief

"Now that was a day," Matt Plotczyc remarked.

Elwood and I just groaned in reply.

The wedding, reception, luncheon, and arch of swords were finally history. Matt and I had changed out of our uniforms and now slouched in jeans and sweatshirts in Don and Jackie's office chairs. Elwood lounged in my chair, still dressed in his stained shirt and bow tie. During the wedding he had taken a station in the Broadview's kitchen, helping restaurant manager John Wright and his cooks prepare the meat for the luncheon. As usual, the guests acclaimed the results as fantastic. And none of us had the energy to go home just yet.

"I've never seen Don so surprised as when Gil sang that song," Matt said.

"Whose idea?" Elwood asked.

"I guess Healey and Slap Happy started talking during his physical out at Hoople during the blizzard."

"Doctor Happy. It figures," Matt said.

"Yeah," I continued, "They found out each liked Gilbert and Sullivan operettas. Old Happy wondered if those songs wouldn't fit to twit Don somewhere in the proceedings. Sunday after the blizzard the cyber-intelligences arranged a 3-way conversation with Jackie here and Gil and Lucille in Chicago. Jackie loved it, and the rest..."

"...Was logistics," my two associates said together.

"See it on the vid later," Elwood added.

"Gil could be a professional," I said, "and the chorus didn't do too badly either."

"How they learn it?" Elwood asked.

"We had vids of the songs," Matt said, "The far-time folks had never heard of 'em, but they caught on all right. Fleur Nyman asked for copies of all the operettas we could find so she could learn them."

"Quite a lady," I added, "I hope to see more of them as we get our jazz group set up."

"Frank plays bass, right?"

"Yes Matt, first chair in the symphony. He says it was his hobby when he was where he retired from. He has a real feel for jazz. Elwood and I are going to have a blast playing with him."

"Where did the two go?" Elwood asked.

"I can answer that," Sherry replied through the speakers, "They went uptime with Kathy Trainor. She made reservations for them somewhere, even I do not know where. If we really need them, I will call Kathy."

"Fair enough," Matt said, "We can handle things here, and call Dick in Peoria if we have to."

"Won't have to," Elwood pronounced.

The telephone rang; I picked up the receiver. "Yes, Sherry?"

CHAPTER ONE

F. Lillian Taylor: Friday, February 26th, 1926, shortly after 5 PM, her house on South Street

I did not stay for the arch of swords or the couple's departure. After the physical stress of the wedding and reception, I came home to my Tramadol, a hot bath, and a long nap. I found when my back hurt, sleeping in a chair helped ease my discomfort.

A light but insistent knock at the front door roused me from my nap. I walked slowly to the door and looked out the peephole. I quickly opened the door.

"Mimi, please come in! Let me help you."

A younger woman with unkempt black hair stepped slowly into the house. She leaned heavily on a cane; I was shocked how emaciated she had become. Her voice came in a whisper.

"Thank you for letting me come in, Lillian. I have a problem, and do not know where to turn. I hope you can help me."

Another surprise. So far as I knew this woman had never asked for help from anyone in the fifteen years I'd known her. I took the arm opposite the cane and led her slowly to a chair. She sat down with a thump.

"You're exhausted! You will stay for dinner, and no backtalk."

"I couldn't talk back even if I wanted to."

I got a better look at my guest in the light from the lamp and immediately shifted to my professional persona, this time to hide the shock and horror I felt at the appearance of the woman who had been the most competent young principal I had ever worked with. *Lord, what does she need? Use me to help her!*

I poured my guest a cup of tea and set it on the table next to her. I returned to my chair, watching my guest carefully.

"What is the immediate problem, and the need, Mimi?"

Mimi slowly pulled an envelope from the pocket of her dress. She placed it on the table next to her tea.

"First, Lillian here is a letter from me, resigning as Principal of Silas Willard, effective immediately. I'm not getting better fast enough, and I will not try to do that job unless I am fully restored to health. This I fear will not occur."

Mimi Conger was one of the finest young women ever to graduate from the teacher training program. She was cut from the same cloth as Helen Smiley and Edna Kimpton, and after two years of teaching had been advanced to building Principal. Mimi had managed Silas Willard since 1917 until she fell ill the previous November. She had required the same surgery Sylvia Barlow had, but the recuperation had dragged on. Looking at the once vibrant, charismatic young woman I realized she was at the point of collapse, maybe death. I made two decisions in the five seconds between the end of Mimi's statement and my reply.

"Mimi, I regretfully accept your resignation. However, we aren't done yet. First, who is your doctor, and when did you last see him?"

"Doctor Sandburg. I think I saw him in January sometime. I really cannot afford to see a doctor right now."

Not that quack. No wonder she's like this, I thought. "Mimi, you can't afford not to, and right now! I'll cover the cost. Tell me the truth: Are you out of money?"

A tear coursed down Mimi's cheek. "Yes, ma'am. I cannot afford to pay the March rent on my apartment."

I was not surprised. All teachers saved what they could toward a rainy day, but no teacher could survive without income for very long. Mimi had been more prepared than most.

"You're still in the Park Apartments, right?"

"Yes, apartment 3."

"Not for long. You'll be living here, effective immediately!"

"But...."

"Would you like to dispute me, Miss Conger?"

A moment. "No, ma'am. I don't have the strength anymore."

"Good," I replied. Now for the first call. *Lord, please let John be home!*

Doctor Bohan was, and said he'd be right over. I next called *fifteen thirty-one blue*, and Sherry answered.

"Sherry, this is Lillian Taylor. I need to speak with someone over there immediately. *Flashlight.*" I spoke the code word Don had given me to declare an emergency requiring Company resources.

"Roger, copy. I have people on-site. Connecting." The cyber intelligence replied, and I heard the phone ring once before it was picked up.

*****

Amy: The Auditorium office

"Yes, Sherry?" I said into the receiver.

"Lillian Taylor is on the line. *Flashlight Alert*," Sherry announced.

"Roger copy," I replied as I pushed the speakerphone button, "Amy Lansdale here, Lillian. What's up?"

"Mimi Conger, former principal of Willard just came to my door. She's been sick, had surgery, and she's near collapse. I called and Doctor Bohan's coming but I need backup over here. Can you help?"

Even in extremis Lillian keeps her cool, I thought, then "The three of us will be right over! See you in ten."

"Thank you," Lillian said and hung up.

We stood up to leave. “Let's take Don's Wills. It has more room. I'll drive.” Matthew Plotczyc, retired Navy captain, transportation specialist, and Company jester, was all business.

*****

Lillian: A few minutes later

“This is Doctor John Bohan, the best doctor I know. He’s going to check you over.”

“Can’t afford it.”

“I’m affording this, Mimi,” I intoned. “You’re in bad shape, and we need to find out why and fix it if the Lord allows.”

“But....”

Mimi barely got the word out. “No buts. Be helped, that’s an order!”

“Yes, ma’am,” she whispered.

Three others stepped through the front door: Amy Lansdale, Elwood Foutch, and Matt Plotczyc. “Status?” Amy asked.

“Doctor Bohan is just about to check her,” I replied.

Mimi Conger began to sweat as Doctor Bohan moved to check her. She jerked and winced as he touched her left middle abdomen.

“Something’s inflamed in there,” he announced, “We’ll have to operate, right now. Got to get her to Cottage. Mimi, can you walk?”

“I...I don’t think so, Doctor. I barely made it here.”

“OK, we'll get you there. Anyone up for a carry?”

“Right here, Doc,” Matt said quietly.

Matt walked over to where Mimi slumped in the chair. He slid his arms under the dreadfully thin form and lifted her out of the chair. She winced, but then put her arms around Matt’s neck.

“Thank you,” the faintest whisper.

"Someone get the door please," Matt said. I moved to open it.

"Cottage, right?"

"Yes," John said.

"I'll drive," Elwood announced.

"OK. Amy, please help me in the back seat."

"Sure, Matt," she replied, and they began to lever Mimi into the car.

"Please come with me, Lillian. I need to ask you some questions about her."

"Of course, John," I locked the front door and followed Doctor Bohan to his car.

*****

Amy Lansdale, 7:30 PM, Cottage Hospital, the wait ends

The waiting area of Cottage was well lit but quiet, empty except for Kristen the night supervisor working behind the front desk, and the four of us sitting there, waiting. Gloria Hodges, the Director of Nursing had been talking with Kristen when we came in; she hustled upstairs to help Doctor Bohan with the surgery.

In the corner closest to the elevator Matt sat in a single chair, alternately bowing his head and staring out a window at the half-light of Seminary Street. In the other corner, Lillian sat in a single chair, dozing. Elwood and I sat on what may have been a love seat in some Victorian parlor, but now was a threadbare scuffed relic of its former glory. This hospital spent nothing on furniture.

We sat and occasionally shared a word or two, but no conversation. We would have plenty of time to talk the next day, as the Company partners were engaged for a moving marathon, shifting Pastor and Deborah, and Luther and Syl into different houses in Galesburg. Elwood, Matt, and I had organized the festivities and lined up folks to help; all we had to do was show up the next morning and move stuff.

Plus, Lillian asked us to empty Mimi's apartment and move the stuff to her house since she would be living there when she recovered. We all recognized the implied *if* in that statement. Jackie and Don had been deliberately kept out of the moving arrangements. *They have more important matters to discuss,* I thought with a grin.

So, I sat there thinking, and as often happens thinking leads to *thoughts*. I realized even in spite of the life or death reason for our presence here this evening, I felt more comfortable just sitting next to this short, taciturn, amazing man than I had ever felt with anyone except my beloved Pat. I had a hunch Elwood was thinking the same thing. He said nothing, did nothing overtly affectionate, but I just felt *something* around him. and it just might be love. I decided if Elwood wouldn't say anything, and I knew he wouldn't. then I would. My father always said, "*When you get a hunch, bet a hunch.*"

I turned slightly toward Elwood. "The time has come, the Walrus said, to talk of many things:"

Elwood was right on the mark. "Of shoes—and ships—and sealing-wax—Of cabbages—and kings—"

We turned to look at each other as I continued, "And why the sea is boiling hot—And whether pigs have wings."

Instead of delivering the next line, Elwood looked me square in the eye. "Have you ever thought of getting married again?"

That surprised me, but I was ready. "I'd like to marry you."

Elwood's expression didn't change. "OK."

"When?" I asked.

"Saturday a week," Elwood replied, "OK?"

"OK."

We sat there staring at each other. Finally, I spoke, "You know what we need to do now."

Elwood's answer was to take me in his arms for a long, steamy kiss. *Long, steamy, and wonderful!* I thought.

When we broke the kiss, we both had to catch our breath. "How did you learn to kiss like that?" I asked.

"Just because it's never happened to me doesn't mean I don't know about it," Elwood replied.

"You said that at lunch the day of Pastor Ward's funeral!"

"Still true," my betrothed replied, and we resumed the kiss.

*****

Gloria: During the surgery

"Gloria, you see what I see?"

John and I were in the middle of emergency surgery on Mimi Conger. Sarah the nurse minding the anesthetic had to step away for a few moments and I took over for her while assisting the doctor. None of my friends had ever expressed a desire to watch over my shoulder during surgery; I always found it fascinating.

I peered into the open uterine cavity. "Yep," I said behind my mask, "Sandburg should have gotten that with the *D and C* but didn't."

"Among other things," John muttered, "We say nothing to anyone about this. Her business. Doesn't matter now. Everything has to go and we pray she survives. *In nomine Patri et Filii et Spiritu Sanctu Amen,*" he finished with the verbal expression of the Sign of the Cross.

"My word, I will not disclose it," I replied.

Sarah returned to the operating theatre and took over the anesthetic.

*****

Amy: 10:15 PM, Cottage waiting room

Once again, two exhausted figures, doctor and nurse, exited

the elevator. Lillian stayed seated while the rest of us stood round her.

“Does Miss Conger have any family?” John Bohan began.

“None living that I know of,” Lillian replied, “I guess I'm closest to her, and the others here.”

“If she had family, I'd call them in,” John continued, “I don't know if she'll survive this, to be honest.”

“How bad was it?” Lillian asked.

“First, Doctor Sandburg was her attending, right?”

“That's what she told me, John,” Lillian replied.

“This goes no farther than this room, but he started a dilation and curettage, or D and C, on her but never finished it! He cut out some of what was in there, but not all of it. What was left no doubt continued to cause her pain. Also, he nicked several areas of the organ, and they kept up a steady slow bleed. That gave her anemia and fatigue. Finally, I think there was an encapsulated infection in there that burst, spreading the infection she now has. We got all of it we could see, but the infection is still throughout her body. She came through the surgery, but she may still die of the infection. The next forty-eight hours will be critical. that's all I can tell you, folks.”

We all looked at each other. Matt looked at me and mouthed a phrase, ABT, antibiotic therapy; I nodded my head. I couldn't withhold treatment which could save her life at a time like this, and since I was acting Commanding Officer when Don and Dick were gone I made the call.

“Doctor,” Matt spoke formally, “Do you still have the package labeled E-pack one we gave you a few months ago?”

“Yes,” John replied, “I have it in the refrigerator as Don directed.”

Matt put on his imaginary Commanding Officer hat and continued, “Please take that package, open it, and follow the directions inside to deliver its contents to Miss Conger. It is experimental antibiotic medication from our researchers at Hoople, kept here in case one of the company partners has need of it. We authorize you to treat Amy with it." Elwood and I nodded in agreement.

"I'll do that immediately, Matt. I had no idea what was in that package. Gloria, could you bring that package up to Mimi's room and we'll see what we have."

"Of course, Doctor," Gloria replied, then flashed us a smile and a wink before she strode off. As of two weeks before, Gloria became a partner in Wain Engineering, and had been briefed on the package.

"Thank you so much for your work with Mimi tonight," Lillian said as she slowly got up, "I want you to know I am paying for this surgery and her hospitalization."

"No, Lillian. I'm paying for it."

We all looked at the man with the graying black hair and command presence. "You?" I asked.

"Yes, I must do this. Please." Matt Plotczyc said almost plaintively.

"So you shall," Lillian breathed, and the rest of us nodded.

Elwood took my hand. "One other thing," he said.

We dropped Lillian off at her house before Elwood and I spent a few pleasant minutes in my driveway.

*****

Lillian: just before midnight, in bed

I lay awake, very tired but unable to sleep, listening to the occasional car pass on South Street. The deep covering of snow still muffled the usual sounds, especially the railroad yard.

Normally Friday nights at Knox College across the street brought out groups of students parading around campus and downtown, seeking whatever food, drink, or what other mischief they could find. The blizzard put a stop to that, at least temporarily. Losing eighteen of their classmates in the storm also tended to dampen their enthusiasm. A dozen were still missing in the mountainous drifts, all from the *TKE* and *BTP* fraternities just across the street. I figured they would be in mourning until spring when the bodies reappeared as the snow melted.

I lay in my bed, my pain dulled but not eliminated by the Tramadol. Don had told me he would be able to provide more potent medication when I needed it, but I wanted to hold off as long as possible due to the side-effects. Tonight, though, the pain wasn't the main problem.

I thought about the situation, in turmoil once again. *Can it get any more tangled? Now I need a permanent replacement for Mimi —she won't be back after she resigned, even if she recovers. Sylvia's doing fine at Willard, but what about Ayers? Do I have any more rabbits to pull out of the hat? And how much longer can I go on— I know my body is getting weaker by the day, and the pain is definitely increasing. What am I to do?*

My reverie, or whining, same difference, was interrupted by a comment by the *still small Voice*. Once again, very clear and to the point.

Oh...I haven't, have I? How could I be so stupid? I'm almost seventy-six years old; I'm supposed to have quit making mistakes like this! Of course, Lord, I'll rectify this one right now!

For the next five intense minutes, I prayed as I was prompted. I prayed first for Mimi Conger, for her recovery and her salvation. I also prayed for guidance, and for the first time in a long time intervention, in the situations at Willard and Ayers...and for my own physical condition. I hadn't prayed that way for myself before; I knew what I had, knew what would happen, and accepted it. But that was part of the directive, so I obeyed.

When I finished I lay back and sighed. I was now completely confident the Lord would work out all the problems I faced... even in my body. As I faded out, I noted my back did not seem to hurt as much as usual.

CHAPTER TWO

Healey: Saturday, February 27th, 1926, 6:00 PM, New China Cafe

"Looks like they've weathered a hard day," my wife Gladys whispered to me.

"Indeed, my dear," I replied, "They've usually not this knackered."

A bedraggled group gathered in the back room of New China that Saturday evening. The group included those who helped move but were not being moved themselves. The *movees*, as it were, stayed in their respective new homes and tried to sort out the incredible confusion even the most orderly move generates.

So Gladys and I witnessed another side of this normally vibrant lot. Sitting around the long table with us were Matt Plotczyc, Amy Lansdale, Elwood Foutch, Gil and Lucille Foster, and Evelyn and Jeff. Someone I hadn't met sat with Amy and Elwood. They introduced him as Don's friend John, nicknamed Slim.

Jackie and Don were off on their honeymoon, of course.

Matt said the blessing for the food then the proprietor's daughter brought out the bowls and platters of food.

"These are genuine Chinese dishes," Gladys remarked, "not like what we get in Toronto."

"This lot insists on the real cuisine, seasoned properly," I replied, "the proprietors are old friends of the Wains."

As the group ate they began to perk up. All except Lucille. She barely picked at her food and said nothing. Not like her at all.

"That woman's Lucille Foster, correct?" my wife whispered.

"Yes. She seems unwell."

"Unwell? Don't you remember me looking like that, three times?"

I smiled and nodded. "I do indeed, dear! I had forgotten."

"What was that, Healey?" Amy asked.

"My wife was just reminding me of a forgotten memory," I replied. I didn't feel that was the moment to embarrass poor Lucille, particularly if she didn't know what was happening yet.

"So how did the move of Mimi Conger's things go?" Evelyn asked.

Amy raised her hand a moment while she swallowed. "Sad, but no real problems. The landlord came by and asked what we were doing, then called the police on us."

"Rather cheeky of him," I remarked.

"Oh, yeah," Amy frowned, "The police all know us. They checked our story and strongly suggested the landlord stop bothering us. He wasn't happy, but he left. I think he figured he could get the stuff in the apartment when she couldn't pay the rent and sell it. I saw 'em try that in Chicago when I worked with Maggie B."

"Good," Elwood declared, "How is Mimi today?"

"I called at noon," Matt reported, "She's still unconscious, Gloria says she could be like that for several days. So far, they haven't had to take her back to the operating theatre. In fact," Matt looked at his watch, "I need to be going. I'll let you know more at church tomorrow."

"Sure, Matt. G'night," Amy said as Matt left the room quickly.

The rest of the group looked at each other.

"I guess we now have a Manager for *Project Mimi Conger*," Gil said what everyone was thinking.

"Why is he so interested in her?" I asked.

Gil wiped his mouth and put down his napkin.

"Here's the story, and please keep it to yourselves. Don's known Matt since he and Pam, er, were in California. He worked with Matt in several billets and eventually they both ended up in DC."

Amy had told us Slim wasn't a partner yet; Gil remembered in time. I nodded, and Gil continued.

"Pam was especially close to Matt's wife, Grace. Matt married her when he was stationed in the Philippines. Short lady, thick accent, sweetest Christian you'd ever want to meet. But she had tuberculosis, not of the lungs, but in her spine."

"How awful! I've seen that before," my wife interjected.

"It was every bit as bad as you can imagine, Gladys. She managed to stay out of the Sanitarium, but her condition became more painful and debilitating. Matt ended up being her caregiver for the last few years. He accepted a desk job in the Navy Department, knowing it meant he'd never make Admiral, to be with her."

Lucille suddenly got up and walked quickly to the washroom. We listened as Gil continued.

"Then the skipper of the collier *Cyclops* went bonkers, and Matt, as Inspector of the Naval Auxiliary Service, had to go out to the ship and send the guy home in a straitjacket. The ship's company was in chaos, but the ship was desperately needed for the fleet train in the Atlantic. He ended up having to skipper the ship for five months until the Bureau of Navigation could shake loose another Captain to take over."

Gil looked toward the washroom, wiped his brow with his handkerchief, and carried on.

"He got back to Washington in time for her funeral. Pam Wain stayed with her the last month, and her other friends made her end-time blessed, but her husband was not there. Matt's never gotten over it. So, like several others in the Company, he decided to retire and come work for Don. He's always been a jokester, and he's adopted that persona to help hide his pain, his grief. He's the best at what he does, but he always carries with him the guilt of *not being there.*"

Amy wiped her eyes. "I've noticed he's very private about that stuff. I've never heard that story before. I wonder if he sees in Mimi Conger someone he can help, and maybe make a difference where he couldn't before."

Elwood put his hand on Amy's. "Won't tell us what's going on in his head. For now, posit you're right. Lillian said Mimi is not a Believer. Need to pray for that first, also she recovers."

"Could we pray right now?" Evelyn asked.

"Of course," Amy replied, "Let's pray around, I'll start. You folks may pray silently if you'd like," she added, looking at Gladys and me.

"I believe I'd like to join in vocally, if I may," my wife said, and I nodded. Lucille did not return until after we had prayed.

*****

Gloria: 6:50 PM, Cottage Hospital

Another hour, I thought with a sigh.

Since our night shift charge nurse resigned to go to St. Mary's hospital, the middle of the month my assistant Kristen and I had pulled watch and watch twelve-hour shifts managing the hospital. We were both constantly tired, but we had no choice until our newly hired replacement, Agnes, would be ready in another month.

Time didn't drag, though. My work filled the available time, divided into the usual nursing formula: One-half time paperwork, one-half time staff supervision, and one-half time patient care. Medical Director John Bohan, like all the rest, never learned to add.

To his credit, John never begrudged the time I spent on our

patients. He didn't even mind that I prayed for them as well as gave good nursing care.

This night I was most concerned about Mimi Conger. Considering the mess we had to clean out the night before, I marveled she survived long enough to seek help at all, and then survive the surgery. I was sure she needed the uptime antibiotics from the Wain emergency stash to recover from such a massive infection.

Most of all she needs the Lord, I thought. I prayed for what we call positive outcomes in both her physical and spiritual states.

So I alternated between my paperwork and making the rounds of the patients, checking vital signs and looking for hints of trouble. My nurses did this too, but I retained a strong streak of look for myself gained from twenty years at Cottage and ten as head nurse.

A beefy man with graying black hair and a slight smile on his face entered the waiting area.

"You're up late tonight, Matthew."

"You seem to be keeping the same hours, Gloria."

Matt and I had been friends since he'd retired from the Navy and moved to Galesburg. Friends, nothing more. I knew he still grieved over his wife's death while he was at sea. I also knew he had cried with joy when I trusted Christ a few weeks before.

"Come to check on Mimi?" I asked.

"Yep. How is she?"

"Still unconscious. Getting fluids by IV and the antibiotic from the Company stash. Hasn't needed oxygen yet. We just wait to see what happens."

Matt nodded. "So she's not been conscious since before the surgery?"

"No, but that's not surprising," I replied, "Sometimes they'll go a week or two before coming around. They're in there, healing quietly, then eventually they wake up and continue, or they don't."

Matt winced but nodded. "May I see her?"

"Sure, I was just going to take vitals. You can help."

I picked up my blood pressure cuff and walked with Matt down the quiet, darkened hall. "I wish you had time to volunteer here like you used to. You're almost as skilled as a nurse."

"Thanks, Gloria," Matt said softly, "Wish I could too, but the Company work has just piled on. I have the time, but I don't have the brain to do it right."

We left unsaid how he gained that skill nursing his wife over the years.

We stopped at a door. I knocked softly and walked in.

Mimi Conger lay in bed on her back. Fluid dripped slowly from a bottle on a pole through tubing to a needle inserted in her left forearm. She slept on, oblivious to us.

Matt turned away while I checked Mimi's incision for infection. "OK, you may turn back. Please take her blood pressure while I draw up the next dose of antibiotics."

"Sure," Matt replied. He set up the cuff, pulled a stethoscope over his ears, and performed the procedure with the same care he used testing errant cars. He wrote the numbers down on the chart and showed them to me.

"Pretty good," I said, "just what they were last hour. She's showing remarkable resilience, considering what happened to her."

We finished and tucked Mimi back into the covers.

"Mind if I sit for a while, Gloria?"

"No, that's fine. I'll tell Kristen you're in here when I relieve."

I turned to leave, then turned back to Matt. "You're taking this one personally, aren't you?"

Matt looked at me; his eyebrow twitched. "I guess I am."

"She's not Grace, Matthew."

"I know. And I don't want her to become Grace, either."

I pointed my index finger at the retired Captain. "And another thing, she's not a Believer. She and I have talked before. She grew up in the Universalist Church."

Matt took out his handkerchief and made a pass at his eyes. "I know that too. Just have to pray, be the example, and watch for an opening to witness to her."

"Like you did for me?"

Matt grinned. "Like a lot of us did for you."

I grinned back. "Well, I'm sure glad you did! It's in the Lord's timing, though. He knew what it would take to break me, and He provided it, a little at a time. His way is still perfect."

Matt turned back to the chair by the bed. "That's sure true. I'll just sit and watch and pray awhile."

"OK, Matthew. I have to go relieve off. Yank the cord if anything happens."

"Sure. Good night, Gloria."

Kristen said Matt finally left around one in the morning.

CHAPTER THREE

Sylvia: Sunday, February 28th, 1926, 6:30 AM, first morning in our new house

"Another Sunday morning, My Love…rise and shine!"

The blond breathing machine next to me in the bed opened one eye a little. The light of the just-rising Sun pouring in the east window shone right in his eye. He opened both eyes and quickly shut them again.

"What is that bright light in my eyes?"

"That, Mister Barlow, is called The Sun. We have an east window in this bedroom that lets the wonderful light right in. I think it's beautiful."

From the look on his face, my husband thought something different. "Uh, where are we?"

"We are in our new house on Johnston Street in Galesburg, my love. The house Pastor Ward's widow gave to us for *free*, in case you've forgotten! So we could give Edna and Paul my—*our* old house. Look at it this way, husband mine, you don't have to wear your robe to go to the bathroom anymore! We don't have anyone living with us in this house!"

Luther sat up in bed and looked around without a word.

"Still wondering where you are?"

"I know where I am, Love. I'm just not sure where anything else is."

I giggled. "Oh, you'll figure it out eventually. Just follow your nose…"

"I believe I will," he said as he bent over to kiss me.

Several pleasant minutes later we remembered what we

should be doing.

Luther reached for his prosthesis. "I'll be right back, Love. Time for the bathroom!"

He strapped it on, got out of bed, put on his slippers, and walked to the nearest door. He opened it and walked into...the closet.

He shut the door. "Have you figured out where you are yet?" I called.

I heard mumbles and shuffling noises, then the door opened and he came out. "Strangest bathroom I ever saw."

"Luther, you didn't!"

My husband looked over at me and grinned.

"Stinker!" I threw my pillow at him.

The resulting activity made us later than usual, but the shorter distance to drive to church made up for it.

*****

Pastor A.P. Kittridge: same time, a house about four blocks away

Is there a woodpecker in here? My first conscious thought that morning made no sense until the rapid-fire tapping sound started again. Then I remembered where I was...and I wasn't in Appleton anymore.

In the diffused light from the window, I looked over at the other side of the bed and did not see Deborah. I heard her though, tapping like mad on the Blick Electric typewriter. I'd fallen asleep many nights to the sound of that typewriter, but this was the first time I could remember waking up to it.

I got up, put on my slippers and robe, and moved to the nearest door. It opened to a closet.

Oh boy, this is gonna be fun! I thought. I closed that door and tried the other one which led to the short downstairs hallway and a bathroom.

Ablutions complete, I followed the sound of the tapping into the living room of the new house and up the stairs to the partially finished second floor.

In one corner of the large room, Deborah sat at her desk, typing vigorously. A notebook lay open on the desk at her side, and several sheets of paper littered one end of the desk.

I stepped over and put my hand on her shoulder. She stopped typing and we kissed. I moved over to the closed hide-a-bed next to the desk and sat down.

"I can't remember you waking me up with typing before."

"First time I ever tried it! I had a half dozen plot twists come to me in the middle of the night and I had to see if any of them made sense enough to use. So far they all have!"

"So this move has stirred up your writing?" I asked.

"Looks like it. And this is a wonderful place to write, dear. It's so bright, so open, and it smells like new wood."

I closed my eyes and sniffed. "Like being in a forest."

Deborah stopped typing and joined me on the hide-a-bed. "So shall we call this house *The Hollow Tree*?"

"Sounds good to me, Deborah. And how will this place affect those books you write, I wonder?"

Deborah cuddled up to me. "Like those cookies, they served at Don and Jackie's wedding I think they'll be *uncommonly good*!"

We looked at each other, then I understood and snorted. "Like on the packages: *Keebler elves*. Is that where you got the name for the house?"

"Maybe, maybe not."

"Right," I whispered, "I never realized this old hide-a-bed was so comfortable."

"It's early, AP..."

"So it is."

The distance from the house to Chambers Street Baptist was about the same as from our former home to Appleton Baptist, but it seemed shorter this morning.

*****

Luther: after Sunday School

After checking with Syl I walked up to the organ, turned on the blower, and made my way to the Pastor's study for the morning meeting. Lucille was already there, along with Amy Lansdale.

"Hi, folks. Any changes in the music?"

"Nope, as written unless something goes wrong. I'm leading, Amy here is playing piano with you."

"I didn't know you played, Amy," I commented.

"What I do," the lithe middle-aged blonde replied.

"Now you're starting to sound like Elwood," Luce remarked.

"Nice way to sound," Amy countered.

Lucille smiled, then grimaced like something was bothering her. "Are you improvising in the offertory today?" she asked me.

"I thought I would, if nobody minds."

"I guarantee they won't mind," Lucille replied. "They just love to hear that thing playing again."

"They don't know it'll be silent for the summer while we work it over."

"That reminds me, Luther," Amy said, "Several of us have to go up to Chicago to take care of some business on Wednesday. Don and I wondered if you'd like to ride along, practice with the Symphony, and maybe visit John Wick. He'll be in their Chicago office this week. We'll be back mid-afternoon Friday."

"I think I can shake loose. But will that interfere with getting ready for you and Elwood's wedding?"

"I don't think so," Amy replied, "We want it very low-key, not fancy. Almost like Paul and Edna's, except more onlookers."

"OK. Count me in. How are we getting there?"

"The Dash 3. You and Syl flew in it out to Hoople, didn't you?"

"Right, Amy. I slept most of the way through."

"You can do that this time too if you feel like it. I might too—rest up, you know."

Lucille and I produced raspberry sounds at that crack.

Our conversation was interrupted by the arrival of the other attendees at the meeting: Pastor and Terry Fensterer, the Deacon of the Day.

"All right, folks, let's get down to it," Pastor Kittridge said, "Anything unusual with the music today?"

"Nope," Lucille replied. "Harold's singing a good one this morning-Don keeps coming up with these gems. Luther's improvising for the offertory, everything else normal."

"Thanks, Lucille. Anything unusual with you, Terry?"

"Everything's nominally nominal, Pastor."

Lucille and I looked at each other, and she rolled her eyes slightly.

Pastor and I prayed, and we took our places on the platform.

The service proceeded as usual. Amy Lansdale played the piano very well, no fancy embellishments, just a good solid accompaniment. I wondered why she hadn't displayed her talent earlier.

For once I knew what I was going to improvise on for the offertory this morning. While I was carrying boxes into the house the day before, the Gospel song *Nearer, Still Nearer* kept running through my head. At first, I thought it was some subconscious wish for the moving to be nearer its end, but then I realized it was something I should be praying in my heart all the time.

From there the tune went 'round and round in my head, and

later that evening I played it a bit on the Bösendorfer. As usual, I had no idea how the improvisation was going to turn out, but I figured something would happen, and as Pastor prayed, I prayed the Lord would use it as He wished.

Pastor finished. I began, soft as I could. This organ had a fine swell chest, if one knew its little tricks. The mechanism opened the swell doors much faster than it closed them, so I had to plan ahead. If you tried to open the doors too quickly the mechanism would make a loud snapping sound as it responded, and occasionally the sound would be accompanied by a jammed door. We would definitely fix that when we rebuilt this organ.

As I wound the improvisation to the usual climax, I found another tune insinuating itself into the flow—*Nearer My God to Thee.* The ideas were similar, but I wasn't sure how the melodies would play together. I found they did fine, but I could not predict how the variations developed.

I glanced in my mirror as the piece wound down. I saw the ushers had finished passing the plates, but I knew the congregation didn't mind if I kept playing for a while. I noticed someone had come in to sit with Elwood, Don's friend Slim. I had noticed Elwood was keeping an eye on the doors in the back; they must have been expecting him. He was a thin fellow, tall for his age; I knew Don and Jackie were friends of him and his family.

I finished the offertory, as softly as I started it. Lucille came up and announced the last song before the message—*He Leadeth Me* by Gilmore and Bradbury. I noticed her voice had an odd twist in it, one I couldn't remember hearing before.

The song finished, Amy and Lucille went down to sit with their respective gentlemen. Harold Coupland came up for the special. I marveled at the lyrical quality of his voice, even at his age. Don knew the repertoire of Gospel songs from this period and *uptime*, and he'd come up with another beautiful one, well-suited to Harold's voice, called *Grace Abounded More.* I had seen the copyright date on the sheet music before Don erased it. It was 1960.

I was able to keep the reed chorus muted, ephemeral in the background. This was one song I did not want to overpower! At the end, Harold repeated the last line of the chorus and took the last three notes in an ascending scale instead of descending. It was gorgeous, and I almost started to cry as several recent examples of that truth flashed through my mind.

I canceled the presets and went down to sit with Syl as Pastor Kittridge began the message. Syl had been crying, and we held hands and smiled at each other.

*****

Amy Lansdale: the rest of the service

In all honesty, I can't remember much of Pastor's message that day. I know it was good, that it touched my heart, but it didn't stick in my conscious brain. That happens sometimes...and I find later that I've learned something new about the Lord. I can trace it back to a specific message, but not to anything I could remember was said. It happens sometimes.

I sat there in the pew, holding Elwood's hand, and smiled at him. Maybe my mental block was brought on by all the crazy changes in my life the past few months.

Pastor closed the message, and as he prayed Luther and Lucille went up to the platform to begin the invitation.

The invitation hymn that day was a fairly standard one—*Grace Greater than Our Sin.* Luther began to play, the congregation began to sing, and immediately I sensed motion to my right. Matt Plotczyc walked quickly down the aisle and knelt in front of the front pew. He appeared to be crying, but when Pastor went down to check on him, he whispered something and Pastor backed off. I wondered if the situation with Mimi Conger had anything to do with it.

Then Elwood and Slim got up and walked to the front. Pastor

met them and talked with them for the better part of a verse. He then turned to Lucille and Luther and gave him the signal to stop after the verse they were on.

When the music stopped, Pastor spoke.

"John here comes forward to report he trusted Jesus as his Savior yesterday while helping Amy and Elwood during the moving operation. He'll be baptized this evening, Lord willing."

Pastor continued, "After I pray, Luther will play the postlude and you'll be dismissed; there will be no 'last song' this morning. Let's pray."

*****

Luther: surprise at the end

As Pastor prayed, I quickly decided to convert the last song into a modified postlude. The last song today was *Lord Dismiss Us With Thy Blessing,* a well-known tune played in a sprightly manner for these words. However, the tune is used in other forms, as a Christmas carol, and as part of the music for the Catholic liturgy. The other uses gave me an idea, and as Pastor finished I pushed two presets and launched.

I played the first verse of the song as everyone expected, light, lilting, bright. The next time through I shifted to the minor key and intertwined several compatible figures into the fabric of the song. Then I opened up the swell, cut the speed by more than half, and started to play embellishments to the tune quickly in the pedal. My prosthesis was surprised by this development, but I figured I could get away with the exploit before it retaliated.

Finally, I shifted back to the major, punched the full organ preset, and let loose with a majestic rendering of the song, using whatever of the other figures I could find a place for in the tapestry. I shifted back to the faster speed for the coda and ended with everything the organ had.

CHAPTER FOUR

Don: Sunday, February 28th, 2019, 3:30 PM, The Inn at Union Pier, Michigan, news from home

My new bride and I lay on the huge bed in the brightly decorated room of our honeymoon destination. Once we arrived back uptime, we set out for the resort Kathy Trainor had booked us into. We stayed Saturday night at a hotel along Interstate 80, selected for peace, quiet, and a charging station for the Company's Chevy Bolt.

Later Saturday morning (no hurry, indeed!) we made the rest of the journey through northern Indiana and into the western coast of Michigan. This inn is delightful even in winter, not least because of the Swedish ceramic fireplaces, called *kakelugns,* gracing every room. Jackie had run into these fireplaces before and had ours burning merrily before I could even find the wood box. For the record, I did learn how to feed the thing before we checked out!

Snow covered the landscape, but the roads were clear, and we had just returned from a nice pizza lunch up the road a ways. This was time to rest, relax, get to know each other in a pleasant environment, and...yes, that activity too!

"Love, I'm going to call in and see what's going on. Do you mind?" Jackie asked.

I turned and gave her my best version of The Look. "We're supposed to be getting away from all that by being out here. Do you really want to hear it now and get all worked up about stuff you can't do anything about?"

"Don't you trust our friends to keep a lid on it while we're gone?"

She had me. "Of course I do, Precious, it's just that's so far away right now."

"Only about two hundred fifty miles and ninety-three years away in a different universe," Jackie replied and started pressing buttons on her cell phone.

"Whatever," I mumbled and put my headphones back on. I was listening to Ralph Vaughn Williams' *Third Symphony* and starting to get drowsy. For some reason, I felt really tired...

I snapped awake as Jackie leaned over to kiss me. "Wha?"

"You're so articulate when you're asleep," my bride said as she finished the kiss.

"I was asleep?"

"Hour and a half," Jackie replied, "Look at the light outside."

I pushed myself up on my elbows. "Yeah. That late?"

"Some of it. Lake effect snow coming in. Eight inches by morning. The proprietors called to say they'll serve all meals tomorrow while we get dug out."

"Like we need more snow after last month," I was starting to wake up.

"The roads will be cleared and the walks shoveled. We can get it off the car easily enough," Jackie replied, "Want to hear the news from Lake Woebegone?"

"I'd rather hear it from Galesbu...." I began, then we were otherwise occupied for a few minutes.

"So what's new in 1926?" I asked, several exhilarating minutes later.

Jackie faced me under the covers. "A few things. The moves went fine yesterday. Pastor and Deborah, and Luther and Syl are all moved in. The principal of Silas Willard, Mimi Conger, came to Lillian's door Friday night, nearly dead! Lillian got Doctor Bohan and Matt, Amy, and Elwood to help and they took her to Cottage for emergency surgery. Terrible infection, touch and go."

"We should release our antibiotic stash for her, shouldn't we?" I asked.

"Amy and Matt already did. Doc said she'd probably die without it. That's why we have the best folks minding the store while we're gone."

"Right as usual, Precious. What else?"

"Well...it looks like Matt's taken a personal interest in Mimi Conger's recovery. He's paying for her care. She's out of money. He went forward at Church this morning in tears about something."

"Maybe he sees her as someone he can help, since he couldn't be there for Grace."

"I dunno," my bride replied, "we'll see when we get back. Next item: Amy and Elwood are getting married next Saturday."

I sat up and kissed my bride. "All right! You win, Love. You saw it coming. Any details?"

"None yet," Jackie replied, "Amy just said they decided to do it while they were waiting for Mimi's surgery to finish."

"Good for both of 'em," I said, "Do we know if Mimi's a Believer?"

"She's not. I've talked to her," Jackie said, "She was raised in the Universalist Church, went to Lombard. Have to pray the Lord gets hold of her."

"I'm sure Matt's praying that. I wonder if that was a part of this morning?"

"Could've been, Love. Next item: confirmed Hugo will be in Chicago for our meeting Wednesday afternoon, plus Thursday and Friday morning if we need it. Amy says he wants to *talk turkey*."

"His companies are in a mess, aren't they?" I asked.

"Definitely," Jackie replied, "He wants out of Germany badly, and it sounds like he's ready to accept our terms to move the plant to America."

"That's great news, Love! The devil is in the details though."

"As always. But Hugo's ready to call it *Junkers-Wain* and see what happens. Amy says he's very interested in our ideas for the *Jumo* engine family."

"Wait'll he sees the turboprops, and the *Deltic*," I chuckled, "That means we travel home Tuesday and fly up Wednesday. Will the Bolt make it all the way home on one charge?"

Jackie nodded. "From what I saw coming up here we should be fine if we stop for lunch where there's a charger. Won't be running the air conditioner so that should help."

"What about the heater?"

"You brought a warm coat, didn't you?"

I shivered, prompting a kiss from my new wife.

"One last item, you want to hear it?" Jackie asked.

"Why not, Precious? Hit me with it!"

"Amy and Elwood had Slim helping them move people yesterday. They led Slim to the Lord and he walked the aisle with Elwood this morning. Being baptized tonight."

The lights faded again, and I was somewhere else.

Jackie tells me I spent the next five minutes with my head in her lap, crying like a baby. My recollection of that period is a long series of memories of my father as I grew up and afterward, all the memories until the morning he passed. My thoughts became more lucid as I swam slowly out of the reaction.

"You seem to be back with me now," Jackie said when I opened my eyes, "Would you like to talk about it?"

"I would, but I'm not sure what happened myself," I replied, rolling to sit up in bed. "Would you pass me some tissues please?"

Jackie reached over and handed me the box. "Thanks, Love."

"You've never cried like that since I've known you. Slim's salvation is great news, but what made you lose it like that?"

I wiped my eyes and face while I considered Jackie's question.

"I think," I finally responded, "that something in my relationship with my father just resolved there. I know this Slim isn't my real father; he has the same basic genes my Dad had, similar personality and upbringing until now, but he's not the same person as the one who fathered me uptime. I've always known that intellectually; now I *feel* it. Does that make any sense?"

Jackie grasped my hand. "It does, Love, but I think there's more. When did your father uptime trust Christ?"

That stopped me for a moment. "He had a certain set of stories he'd tell about his life before the War. Some from growing up. The Boy Scout streetcar one for example. I knew he worked for Lee Wright from the early '30s. He rode motorcycles and met my Mom just before the War. Otherwise, he said almost nothing about his teen years and afterward until he enlisted after Pearl Harbor. He just never opened up."

Jackie bent over and we kissed. "A lot of young men from that time just sort of wandered through the Depression," she remarked, "until the War gave them something big to do, an anchor to their lives. That's what happened with my own father."

"That could be a big part of it," I replied, "but that doesn't speak to your question. They never started attending church until I graduated college and married Pam. Just started coming one Sunday morning, biggest shock I can remember up to that time. They weren't anti-Christian before. I wasn't living at home by then, but I think some folks from church had been talking to them over several months. They never explained what happened."

"I wonder if you're thinking, deep down, your father wasn't converted until later in life. Now in this universe, he is."

I stared at my new wife. "I think that's it! A lot of it, anyway." Another memory came to me. "I just remembered, only one time, after I was grown and married, he talked about his life in the mid-thirties. He mentioned the girl he was seeing at that time and implied they were quite *busy*."

Jackie snorted. "I get it, Love. Anything else?"

"Never another word about it before or after, and I didn't want to pry and breach his reticence. He was utterly faithful to my mother after they married, so it was a moot point."

Jackie nodded. "So, whether he had trusted Christ by then or not, his behavior didn't necessarily follow along."

"Right. But the matter was settled, as far as I can ever know, uptime...and now appears to be settled here." My eyes started tearing up again, and as Jackie wiped my eyes and kissed my face another memory popped into my frazzled mind.

"Here's something else, Love," I began, "One of my earliest memories, had to be when I was three or four, my mother put me down for a nap in my toddler crib in the bedroom. Of course, I didn't go to sleep, but stood by the rails of the crib and looked over at the tall dresser at the other side of the room. I was just able to focus that far away and saw the picture of a man that hangs in the den of our house on Broad Street. Handsome face, blond hair just starting to recede a bit. I realized that was my father. But he had hair! I never saw him but what he was bald as a cue-ball."

Jackie giggled at the reference, then sobered as I continued.

"I started to cry and wail like I was dying! Mother came in and tried to comfort me, but I was inconsolable. I pointed to the picture, and to my head. She figured it out, explained that was his senior picture from High School, and he went bald a few years later. I finally calmed down and have kept that picture ever since."

"Change?"

Jackie had it. "Yes, Love! That was the first time it dawned on me that humans change, age, and I had to learn to deal with it. I couldn't have articulated it then of course, but that's what it was. I understood it better as time went on."

I embraced my bride. "Now this Slim gets to face the future with its challenges and change, with Our Lord instead of all by himself. He's way ahead of the Slim uptime, and although he won't know it, I will, and that's where the tears of joy are coming from!"

"And I think there's even more," Jackie said, "You know how devastatingly limited the world was during the Depression in our home universe. The other Slim had real limits to his opportunities. He overcame some of them himself but being poor added more limits. We all have limits; we all have opportunities. If what he needs is more opportunities to grow in the Lord, are you the answer to your prayers for him? Is our mission here to provide the answer to your prayers for opportunities for him?"

"You're starting to sound like Tasker there... *Eeep!*"

"Well..." I murmured as we lay there a few minutes later, "I think that is a part of our mission as I understand it. Not just for him of course, but for anyone else the Lord sends our way, besides the larger organizations. In the end, helping this society should end up helping the humans in the middle of it."

Jackie tapped the back of my hand. "Remember, his life won't turn out as your father's did. This is a different world, especially now, and he is a different man."

"I know, Jackie, but the Lord will have a say in it if Slim will let Him. So," I kissed my bride before I finished, "we'll provide whatever opportunities we can for him to come out a little different too."

"Your father flew, didn't he?" Jackie asked.

"Yep, but never could develop it like I knew he wanted to because of lack of money. And that," I added as we changed subjects, "may not be a hindrance this time."

Jackie smiled without speaking as we moved on to other matters.

****

Gloria: 4:15 PM, near the end of a split shift

I sat down at the desk after finishing my last round of patient checks. Kristen and I split the Sunday day shift so we could each attend one church service. Since her church only had a morning service, I took the first split. When our new night shift supervisor was fully trained in about a month our schedules could return to their normal ten-hour grind. We were both ready and then some.

I was happy to see Mimi Conger continue to improve. She hadn't regained consciousness yet but her vital signs looked good. I paused a moment to pray for Mimi—her recovery and her salvation both.

As I started to record my observations in the log, I thought of the interesting couple who stopped by just after lunch. The woman was a doctor, her husband a physical therapist. He looked like a football player. They were looking for Doctor Bohan, but he was out of town until Monday morning. The doctor said he had invited them to come out to Illinois from the east coast if they ever thought of relocating. *Sounds like John,* I thought, *always on the lookout for new talent.*

I was surprised when the doctor asked if I knew of a good church that had Sunday evening services they could visit. I surely did! I explained about Chambers Street Baptist and also worked in my testimony. The couple were both Believers too. I arranged to pick them up from the Custer, where they were staying. They said they didn't mind squeezing into a Model T coupe—I supposed she could sit on his lap if need be.

This will be interesting, I thought as a petite woman with platinum blonde bobbed hair wearing a nurse's uniform came into the hospital.

"Hi, Kristen, ready to relieve?"

"Guess so, Gloria. What's new with our patients?"

CHAPTER FIVE

Luther: Sunday evening service with a twist

We arrived at church about 5:30 that evening. I had just enough time to turn on the blower and cancel presets before two other couples came down the aisle.

"Hi, guys!" Syl chirped at the newcomers.

"Hi back," Edna replied. "We were visiting my folks and thought we'd stop in here tonight."

"Great! Maybe we can grab a bite to eat afterward."

"I don't know, Syl, Edna's been needing a lot of sleep lately... *Eeep*!"

"Philistine," Edna muttered toward Paul, "We'd love to do that!"

While Edna was instructing Paul, I greeted the other couple.

"Hi folks! How's the other end of Florence Avenue?"

"Just fine Luther, except for the constant tapping noise from next door."

I winked. "Woodpeckers?"

"Deborah," retorted Lucille, "Actually, I've only heard her a couple of times. Nice to have some life next door."

"Hey Luther, did Don invite you to fly up to Chicago with us Wednesday?" Gil asked.

"Yes, he did. Should I bring anything special?"

"Just a couple changes of clothes—we're staying up there two nights. Your baton, if you use one. We'll supply the barf bag-s....*Eeep*!"

"That's two Philistines," Lucille remarked to Edna, who nodded.

I saw Gloria Hodges, along with a strange couple, come in the back doors and start down toward the front. I froze. *No, it couldn't be. But who else could it be?*

"Hey Paul, does that couple look familiar?"

Paul looked, looked again, and stared, eyes bugging out and mouth opened. "Ye-ye-ye—"

While Paul continued his imitation of the Chrysler's starter, I saw the couple stop, stare, and then the woman started running toward us!

"Luther! Paul!"

Somehow she managed to sweep up both of us in a bear hug. Our wives and friends just stood there staring as her husband and Gloria walked up to us.

"Don't worry, ladies, she just gets a little emotional when she gets a big surprise. She wasn't expecting to see two of her patients here at one time."

"Patients?" Now it was Gloria's turn to stare.

The large man explained in a soft voice. "She's Doctor Jennifer Setterdahl, and I'm her husband Keith. We are...were, rather, head of the orthopedics department and prosthetics fabrication lab, respectively, at Johns Hopkins Hospital in Baltimore. She and I keep those two gentlemen happy, healthy, and walking."

"Oh...now we get it," Edna remarked as Jennifer finally let us go.

Paul and I looked at each other. I nodded to Paul—I was still out of breath.

"OK, I'll start, and you finish. You three know who you are. This is my wife Edna, Luther's wife Sylvia, and our two close friends Lucille and Gil Foster. There'll be a bunch more people coming in here to introduce you to, but that'll do to start. Luther?"

I had my breath back. "This is Doctor Jennifer Setterdahl, Orthopedist, and her husband, Keith, the man who built the prostheses Paul and I depend on!"

"What are you two doing here, though?" Jennifer added. "Last we heard you were both someplace called Galva. And married?"

"A long story," I replied, "which we can fill you in on if we all go out to eat after church. And why are you two here, pray tell?"

Jennifer sobered. "Short story, hospital politics. We were both turned out of our positions. The administration wanted Ivy League Men in there. They got them, and we're out hunting for someplace to land. Doctor John Bohan recruited us."

"You know John?" Syl exclaimed.

"Yes, we met him at a conference a couple of years ago. He said to contact him if we ever wanted a change. We need a change, so we contacted him. He's expecting us this week."

"He's the best—saved my life a couple of times. He's a doctor for all of us, right?"

The group nodded.

"We'll have to talk more when church is over," Lucille said. "Here comes Pastor and Deborah, and the mob's right behind them!"

We quickly introduced the newcomers to Pastor and Deborah, then I hustled up to the platform to start the prelude.

*****

Luther: after the service, American Beauty Restaurant backroom

"So that's everything that's happened up to now," I pronounced.

"No, you missed the Earth cooling....*Eeep*!"

I couldn't let Syl get by with that remark.

The church service had gone well. Slim was baptized, the family stayed for the whole service, but none of the others came forward.

Afterward, we scooted over to the American Beauty in time to get dinner without annoying the irascible kitchen manager. Paul Poulos greeted us and showed us to the back room.

While we waited for the food and ate, Paul and I caught Jennifer and Keith up on our crazy lives since we'd seen them last. Our wives, Lucille and Gil, Gloria Hodges, and Pastor and Deborah, all contributed to the flow of the narrative. I think we could have filled at least three books with the result!

Finally, we got to dessert, and the end of the stories.

"And you may come here to practice?" Edna asked.

"Doctor Bohan wants us here badly," Jennifer replied. "He says my specialty is desperately needed in this part of Illinois. He mentioned one case in particular, where a man was caught under a steam traction engine that had broken through a bridge into a creek. He said our skills could have cut his recuperating time in half, and greatly eased his discomfort."

"We know that man," Syl said. "The steamer broke through about a mile from our former house east of town. He goes to our former church in Appleton. Had a real struggle."

Keith continued, "Besides Jenn's skill in orthopedics, Doctor Bohan tells us there is absolutely nobody south of Chicago who can even try to make a prosthesis, let alone a good one. He says we would have all the trade we could handle in about six months from start."

"I believe it," Gloria interjected. "I see so many come through Cottage you folks could help, and I'm sure that's true at Saint Mary's too. Doctor Bohan is the best, but one man cannot know everything."

"In your opinion, would Doctor Bohan be able to help us get established in this area?"

Gloria replied with a small smile. "He is president of the Illinois

Medical Society, after all."

So There! I thought.

*****

Luther: Later, in bed

"Are you still going to be able to come over to school tomorrow, Love?" Syl asked.

"I think so. About ten?"

"Right. We'll meet in my office and the anteroom, if no students are in there."

"Another incentive to get that new lid put on, eh?"

"You said it, Love!"

We were in our new conference room, discussing the day past and the day to come. The architect and general contractor for the construction at Silas Willard were coming over to brief Syl on the plans and timeline. She wanted me there to help interpret, and keep them honest.

"Syl?"

"Yes, Love?"

"Will Jennifer and Keith be brought into the *Company* now that it looks like they'll be living here?"

Syl shut her eyes for a moment while she thought. "They very well might. They're Believers, top in their field and the Lord's brought them our way. He seems to like to plant people here so He can use them."

"For sure," I replied, "and once Jennifer tries out the Auditorium organ she'll know it's not ordinary. She might figure them out the way Healey did."

Syl touched my nose with her index finger. "I wonder if Jackie and Don will have dreams about it. They've never met Jennifer and Keith, and don't know they're coming."

"Guess we'll see, Love," I replied, and kissed the outstretched finger.

"So we will. I guess we should go to sleep, Love."

I looked at my beautiful wife in the light of the night lights.

"...or not," I countered.

CHAPTER SIX

Jackie: Monday, March 1st, 2019, 7:20 AM, The Inn at Union Pier. Business intrudes on the honeymoon

So this is how it's going to be, I thought as the dream ended and I started to ooze out of sleep.

This made even less sense than the dream with Pam, I continued my slow climb to awake and what passed for alert.

I opened one eye. Bright sunlight streamed through the curtains of our honeymoon room. The Swedish ceramic fireplace with the name Don couldn't pronounce had gone out and left the room chilly. I heard several snow blowers clearing the wooden walkways between the buildings.

I continued to remember the dream vividly. I decided to visit the bathroom before waking my new husband.

Don was taking off his CPAP mask when I returned. "Good morning, love of my life," he mumbled.

"Good morning yourself," I replied and slipped under the covers. The CPAP stowed, our hands found each other.

"Anything new?" I asked.

"Uh oh," Don replied, "Dream?"

"Roger that. You?"

"Uh-huh," Don mumbled through a kiss, "Should've brought the cloth square."

"We'll manage," I said, "Go tend to your business and I'll set it up."

"Okay," he said and shuffled toward the bathroom.

I pulled a pad of *Union Pier* notepaper and a pen from the nightstand and quickly scribbled a few sentences. I tore off the paper and folded it. As Don got back into bed, I handed him the pad and pen.

"Thanks, Love," he said. He scribbled and folded his paper. "Trade?"

We traded papers and read. "No doubt about this one. Any idea who's getting let in?"

"No clue, Love," Don replied, "I don't know anyone like that couple—short woman doctor and a big, quiet man. We'll know 'em if we see 'em, that's for sure."

"Like Saul getting directions to go find Ananias in the book of Acts," I said.

"Or vice-versa." Don looked at his watch. "Too early to call the office and ask. We have an hour and a half to kill."

I snuggled closer to my preoccupied husband. "I think we can manage that."

Adding in breakfast, it was closer to two hours later when I phoned home.

*****

Luther, 10:30 AM, Principal's office, Silas Willard School

"Well, Love, I think they got it right this time," I remarked.

"I'm glad to hear that. Still going to be a mess of a summer, though," my bride replied.

Syl and I were enjoying a cup of tea in her tiny principal's office after the meeting with the architect and contractor.

"These one-story buildings were overbuilt with just this idea in mind," I continued, "The plans were made for expansion. They put the second story on Farnham School last summer and it worked fine. This building's a bit larger, but the same principles apply."

"I hope they stay on schedule," Syl said.

I sipped my tea and nodded. "This building has to be usable when school starts, and if it isn't Gunther Brothers are in deep trouble. The penalties in the contract for late completion would ruin 'em."

"So much for our summer vacation," Syl added.

"At least I won't have to go out to Baltimore to get my stump checked."

"No, Love. I think Jennifer and Keith are going to land here. I wonder...."

The telephone interrupted Syl. "Silas Willard School, principal's office, Mrs. Barlow speaking."

I got a little thrill when Syl answered the phone with her new name.

"Oh, hi Sherry...Yes, he's right here, do you need to speak with him...Oh, OK, we were wondering if that'd happen. I'll tell him. I'm sure he'll be there. 'Bye."

"Well, Mister Barlow, you are summoned to meet Jennifer and Keith, and someone from the Company, at Coney Island around 11 AM for lunch. After that, you're going back to the Auditorium to watch them get brought in. Jackie and Don had the dream."

"Well, what do you know?" I said, "I'm just in awe over what the Lord's done around here the last couple of months!"

"You can say that again, Love!"

"I'm just in awe..."

"Very funny, Luther Barlow. So where are we taking them for supper tonight?"

I stood up and set the teacup on a tray. "I figured New China."

"Sounds good. Now get outta here so I can get the next class in the anteroom!"

"Right. See you later, Love!"

I bent over to kiss Syl, but she pointed to the door where three small faces were plastered to the window.

*****

Doctor John Bohan, 10:15 AM, his office on Main Street.

"So what do you think?" I asked the couple seated across the desk.

"We love the area!" Doctor Jennifer Setterdahl declared. "We already know so many people here."

"Like who?"

"Luther and Sylvia Barlow, and Edna and Paul Sherwood. Luther and Paul were both patients of ours out at Hopkins."

I slapped my desk. "I should have guessed that! I knew Luther went out to Hopkins every year for a tune-up. They both saw you?"

"Right," Keith Setterdahl spoke softly, "Our late mentors, Doctor Bill Raichart and Steve Mason, originally fixed them up. I've always built their prostheses."

I smiled. "I've known Sylvia since 1918, and Luther since they got engaged. I also know Edna well...and she's meant a lot to me over the years."

"Who does her braces? And it's polio, isn't it?"

"Yes, Keith, age ten. Her parents sent her up to a children's 'hospital' in Chicago, brought her home a few weeks later, but not before the swine gave her an unauthorized tubal ligation!"

How awful!" Jennifer exclaimed, "and how typical."

"Indeed. Her parents didn't tell her until she brought Paul home. Paul's a gem. He put them all at ease, and showed them his prosthesis."

Jennifer nodded. "And the other question?"

"Her braces come from a clinic in Chicago. Not the highest quality. Her family doesn't have much money. You saw them. Can you improve them?"

Keith Setterdahl grinned, "I think we can do something about that."

With a short knock my office manager, Mrs. Hall, entered the office. She dropped two message papers on the desk in front of me, then turned about and walked out without a word.

"Don't mind her," I remarked, "She's not very social, and she's annoyed because I made her change her typewriter ribbon this morning."

"No kidding?" Jennifer said, "And was that a quill pen in her right hand?"

"It was," I grinned, "She keeps the office running smoothly, but she's just a little old fashioned. She's retiring this summer."

"I haven't seen a quill pen since grade school," Jennifer said with a snort.

I looked at the messages. For all her irascibility Mrs. Hall knew when to interrupt me, and this was the time.

"First, for you two," I announced, "around eleven two friends of mine from Wain Engineering nearby will meet you here and take you to lunch at Coney Island. I eat there often; I think you'll enjoy it. They will bring you back to a special meeting at the Auditorium Theatre on Broad Street. Luther will be there too."

We're meeting Luther and Sylvia for supper tonight at a Chinese restaurant," Jennifer said.

"Ah, New China," I replied, "best Chinese restaurant I've ever eaten at." I looked at the other note. "Usually I'd eat lunch with you, but I've got an urgent request by one of my dearest friends for a consult just after eleven. I'll be at Cottage Hospital this afternoon; maybe we can meet there after your meeting."

"Did they say what the meeting with these Wain people is about?"

I shook my head. "No, the message doesn't say. Wain Engineering consults in many areas. They've provided me experimental medications that have really helped folks. They have a research facility out in North Dakota; their headquarters are in a building on the square, and that rebuilt theater. Fine people! I think you'll like them."

"We met several of them at church last evening," Keith remarked, "seemed very nice, competent."

"They are," I added, "Now let's talk about the logistics of getting you two set up here."

*****

Lillian: 11:10 AM, the same office

"Something good is happening to me, John. I can feel it."

"What do you feel, Lillian, and when did you start to feel it?"

"It was last Friday, after we brought Mimi Conger in. When I got home the pain had spread up my back, much worse than usual, even with the Tramadol."

My doctor and friend nodded, "Go on please."

"I felt worse than I ever had that night—not only because of the pain but thinking of what happened to Mimi. I did all I could to help her but it wasn't enough. With that and the pain I was at the end of my rope, in a way I never thought I would be."

I stopped, took a deep breath, and continued, "At that point, my Lord reminded me I had not asked Him point-blank to help me. What I counsel my staff to do I had not done myself! I corrected the sin of omission."

"And?"

"John, from the moment I finished praying the pain in my back has steadily decreased. I have not used the Tramadol yet today, and I feel better than if I had. What do you say, John?"

John Bohan looked at his hands for a moment, then looked out the window. He returned his gaze to me.

John took a deep breath, then another, and made the Sign of the Cross.

"We need to do another X-ray of your pelvic area, to see what the tumor is doing. We can do that this afternoon if you will meet me over at Cottage. What grows in a body can also go into remission; I don't know how, I can't predict when, nor do I know for how long. But I have seen it happen."

"When should I be there?" I asked.

CHAPTER SEVEN

Gloria: Monday, March 1st, 1926, 1:15 PM, awakenings

I sat at my hospital desk again. Monday after the weekend always seemed to drag, especially since Kristen and I hadn't had a day off since we lost our night shift supervisor. I was happy she got a better job, but until our new supervisor was ready all I could do was pray for strength and sleep when I could. As my mother said about nursing in the old days, *It's a great life, if you don't weaken.*

One of my floor nurses came to my station. She spoke quietly, "Gloria, Mimi Conger is starting to wake up."

"OK, Thanks, Sarah. Let's go." My knees creaked as I stood up. *Too much hospital floor*, I thought.

We walked quickly down the hall to a room on the right. I knocked and opened the door partially.

I turned to my nurse. "Sarah, go on about your work please, but call fifteen thirty-one blue first and ask for Matt Plotczyc to report here. And if I hit the call light, come running."

"Got it," Sarah said and hustled back up the hall.

I walked into the room.

Mimi lay in bed, as she had since she arrived from surgery the previous week. She had been carefully rolled and propped on her side consistently to avoid bedsores and kept clean. But she hadn't regained consciousness. Until now...

I bent over the young woman. Mimi opened her eyes, blinked a couple of times, and spoke. "Gloria...where am I?"

"You are in Cottage Hospital, Mimi. You were very sick and had major surgery. How do you feel?"

"Very...weak...but no...pain. I had...pain...all the time...before."

"No pain is very good. It will take you a long time to regain your strength. You can rest here for as long as that takes."

"Gloria...I felt...so...alone."

"You are not alone now, Mimi. Lillian's been here several times; your friends who brought you in here have visited, and that big man who carried you in here has sat with you every evening since the surgery."

Mimi frowned as she spoke. "I thank...them...for doing that. But...I still...still feel alone."

I smiled. "I think I know what that is. The last time we talked, in November, I felt the same way. I didn't show it on the outside, but I felt dreadful—I dreaded what was to come when I died."

Mimi nodded slightly. "Yes...that is...how I feel...I came so close...and I can't face...dying." Mimi turned her head toward the door; her face showing anguish. "And...and I killed another person! In me...the operation...all for that. What...am I...to do?"

I felt my eyes well up. "Mimi, Doctor Bohan, and I know what happened; we will tell no one. It's over. What you need now is forgiveness, just like I did. Now I can tell you about the One who forgives us all. I can answer that question. I couldn't the last time we talked."

Lord, please give me the words to say! I prayed.

*****

Luther, 1:40 PM, the Green Room, fun to watch...

The video ended. Matt pushed a button on the remote and the screen on the wall went dark. Another push and the wooden panel slid over the screen.

"And that's the story," Amy Lansdale said, "Please take care not to say anything about what you have learned today to anyone who is not a partner; we'll give you a list of partners. Gloria Hodges is; Doctor Bohan is not. He knows we do medical research out at Hoople, but nothing more. We'll get you both out to Hoople to meet the team there as soon as we can. Do you have any questions right now?"

"Will we be able to watch any more of those movies, er, *videos* you talked about?" Jennifer asked.

"Yes," Matt Plotczyc replied, "We have laptop computers like the one Amy is using you can watch videos on here at our offices. We'll give you one of your own, and access to our network, sometime this week. This will make more sense as we go along."

"And the newlyweds—Don and Jackie—are in charge?"

"Right, Keith," Amy said, "He's a retired Navy Vice Admiral, she's a retired Navy captain from *uptime*, Naval Aviator. Women could do that there. I'm a retired Navy Commander, JAG Corps."

"Lawyer, right?" Jennifer said, "I met some of them at Base Hospital Eighteen during the war."

"Yes. I did other things in the Navy, and a related agency, but retired as a Navy lawyer. I came out here and got a big surprise!" Amy reached over to Elwood sitting next to her, and they kissed.

"And how did you get involved, Luther?" Keith asked.

"I was in the wrong place at the wrong time," I said, to snorts from the others. "I supervised the installation of the Wicks part of the organ upstairs. Don and his late wife Pam had one of their dreams, the Lord telling them to bring me in. Like what happened for you this morning. So here I am. Syl was brought in earlier."

"Wow," Jennifer breathed, "This is gonna take some time to digest. Could we see the organ now?"

"I don't see why not," Amy began, then another voice interrupted.

"Pardon me, but I have a message from Cottage Hospital for Matthew. Gloria says you should get over there as soon as possible. Good news. I suggest you take Jennifer and Keith with you to see the hospital, and Luther can pick them up for dinner later."

"Thanks, Sherry, I'll leave immediately," Matt said, then stopped. "Jennifer and Keith, the voice is Sherry, the company Class-A Cyberintelligence."

"The WHAT?" Jennifer and Keith spoke together.

"A nearly human-acting computer from far in the future, installed here to help the humans in any way I can," Sherry replied, "You'll get used to me eventually. Everyone but Donald has. He is fun to annoy."

"What we do," Elwood remarked with a chuckle.

"Let me give you a ride, folks. We need to get going," Matt announced, and bounded up the stairs two at a time.

"Don't worry, he'll wait for you," Amy said as Jennifer and Keith followed Matt's trail of dust.

"I wonder what he'll find?" I asked.

"Lord's Will. We'll see." Elwood pronounced.

****

Gloria: 2 PM, Cottage

Doctor Bohan greeted Jennifer and Keith and ushered them into the elevator for the ten-cent tour.

I faced the big man with stooped shoulders. "She woke up shortly after one, Matthew."

"How is she?" Matt asked.

"Very weak...groggy...and very scared. Scared of dying. She realized how close she came. She felt lost."

"With good reason, I guess. What did you say to her?"

"I told her I had the same fears when I talked to her when she was here last November, but between then and now my fears had gone. I then told her why."

"What happened?" Matt looked like he was going to faint.

"Mimi trusted Christ, Matthew. I saw the glow on her face. I think she meant it."

Matt said nothing, but reeled away from the counter and collapsed into a waiting room chair. He put his face in his hands and wept. His tears started to soak his clothing.

I brought a towel and laid it in his lap. Matt looked up and nodded, continuing to cry. I just sat across from him, watching. *The work can wait a few minutes,* I thought.

Finally, Matt pulled a handkerchief from his pocket and wiped his reddened eyes. He looked over at me watching him.

"I guess I ought to explain why I lost it there," he said.

"Only if you want to," I replied. A moment, then...

"When we brought Mimi in that evening all I could think of was how pretty she was, and how sick she was, and how I had a chance to do for her what I could not do for my Grace. I wanted to help her so much...but the more I prayed, the sicker she got. I didn't understand how the Lord could do that to me again."

I nodded. Matt continued.

"Finally, in church yesterday He got through my thick skull that He, the Lord Himself, was in control of this situation, and I had been agonizing and praying for my will to be done, not His! I had to give the situation, and her, over to the Lord...and at the invitation I did. And He said to me, in my heart, *Thank you, Matthew, now stand back and watch Me work! I'll let you know when I want you in on it."*

"And here we are."

"Yes, Gloria, here we are. May I sit with her for a while?"

"Sure. I'll take you down and introduce you in case she's forgotten that night."

"Thanks, Gloria. And—would you please keep this confidential? I haven't told anyone else about this, not even Don."

"Sure. Thanks for entrusting it to me. We all have secrets we must keep." *Especially in Mimi's case,* I thought as we started down the hall.

*****

John Bohan: 2:25 PM, X-ray laboratory, Cottage Hospital

"There are the two films, Lillian," I announced as I clipped the large films to the backlit viewer on the wall. I took a pencil out of my pocket.

"There is what the mass looked like in the middle of January," I said, pointing. "Three inches around and growing about a half-inch a month, beginning to impinge on the organs around it."

I pointed to the other film, still damp from the developer baths. "Today the mass is about one half the size it was the middle of January. We'll want to keep track of it more closely. However, based on what I see, and what you report to me, whyever, however, and for however long, that cancer is going into remission."

Lillian had asked Jennifer and Keith to join us in the lab, and they grinned along with my patient.

"Praise the Lord," Lillian breathed.

"Amen," Jennifer added.

Gloria stepped into the room. "Oh, glad I caught you," She started, then looked on the wall. "Lillian, is that your tumor?"

"Yes, it is."

A huge grin now split Gloria's face. "Praise the Lord! What a day this has been." The four hugged each other, then hugged me. I couldn't remember Gloria ever doing that.

"Doctor, I came in to tell you Mimi Conger has awakened and is asking for you," Gloria said after we were through hugging.

"How is she?" I asked.

"Well, she says she feels weak but has no pain. She was very concerned that she nearly died and wasn't ready. We had a chat. I don't think she'll be afraid like that again, praise the Lord!"

"What a blessing!" Lillian breathed.

"Amen!" added Jennifer. Keith grinned but kept his arm around his wife.

And I just stood there. I was thankful for Lillian and Mimi's improvement, but there was something more. *What have my esteemed colleagues, and the lady I hold the most respect for in this world, outside of my wife, got that I haven't got?* I wondered, then filed the question away for later.

"Let's go, folks!" Lillian led us out of the X-ray lab.

A large man I knew well stood by Mimi's bed.

"I think we all know Captain Matt Plotczyc, United States Navy Retired," Lillian said as she shook Matt's hand. "Mimi, I'd like you to meet Doctor Jennifer Setterdahl and her husband Keith. John's recruited them to practice here."

"I guess I'm the guest of honor; Pardon me if I don't get up."

Lillian grinned. Welcome back, Mimi. You are sounding like your old self."

"Thanks," Mimi replied in a soft, slow voice, "I want to say something while I have the chance. Lillian, thank you for being there when I came to your door. I was too far gone to realize how close I was to dying. You made me accept…help. Doctor

Bohan, thank you for coming to see me and saving my life. And thank you, Gloria, for caring for me, and telling me what you just did."

Mimi blinked slowly, took a deep breath, then continued. "And thank you Matt...for being here when I just woke up again. Now if you will excuse me..." She shut her eyes.

Mimi drifted off, a group of weeping people in her room.

*****

Matt: 10:30 PM, Mimi Conger's room, Cottage Hospital

"Are you still here, Captain?"

I startled out of my stupor at the soft, clear voice coming from the bed. "Y-Yes, Mimi, I am. Can I get you something?"

"I'd kind of like a steak, but I doubt if I'd be able to chew it yet."

Just how Lillian said she'd respond, I thought. "I'd get it for you, but I agree we ought to wait a while."

Mimi looked out the window into the dark. "What time is it?"

"Ten thirty in the evening."

She looked back at me. "Why are you still here, Matt?"

She doesn't beat around the bush. "I guess I just couldn't leave until I heard your voice again."

"If a man says that he's *interested,*" Mimi said quietly.

I started to reply but couldn't think of what to say.

"Don't try to explain, Matt. I understand," Mimi frowned, "but I can't have you—us—start something without telling you why I'm in here."

"I think I know why, Mimi," I finally put the words together.

"Do you?" Mimi sounded like a Principal facing a naughty child. "So tell me what I'm going to say."

"Pain wasn't the only reason for that first surgery."

Mimi's head jerked back, then she winced. "Can't move that fast," she said, "Did someone tell you what happened?"

"Nobody," I replied, "At least, nobody human. "My late wife had to have the same surgery. She was pregnant and too sick to carry the baby. We had to do it to save her life."

A tear coursed down Mimi's cheek. "I wasn't sick, just foolish. I had a man, another principal I was seeing in Rock Island. We were going to get married after school was out in the summer, he told me. I got myself in trouble."

"Did you tell him?"

"I called him. He told me he had a wife, and we were through. Hung up on me. Waste of a long-distance call."

"So you arranged the procedure."

"What else could I do? You know what would happen if the school board, if Lillian, found out!" Mimi took two deep breaths. "Now I'm out of a job anyway, out of money, out of hope...until this afternoon." She smiled and cried at the same time.

I took tissues from the nightstand and began to wipe Mimi's face.

"Thank you," Mimi said after a moment, "I can't use my arms right now—I'm sorry."

"Nothing to be sorry about," I said, "I knew you were too weak to move. And about that other business," I started to put my imaginary Captain's hat on, then set it aside.

"What you did is in the past. Jesus forgave you your sins when you asked Him this afternoon. All of 'em. We've all had to get to that point and surrender. I sure did. It really is a new life, one He controls, not us. It might not seem full of joy at the moment, but it will down the line."

Mimi stared at the ceiling for a moment, then turned her head toward me. She smiled.

"Thank you, Matt. What you said makes sense now; it wouldn't have when I woke up. I have a long way to go, but now I know I will have friends to help me. Will you be with me?"

"Where else would I be?"

CHAPTER EIGHT

Deborah Kittridge: Tuesday, March 2nd, 1926, 10 AM, Pastor's Study, Chambers Street Baptist Church, counseling session

What a contrast, I thought as the lithe blonde and her gnome-like fiancé sat down with us in AP's study. They had asked me to join in this pre-marital counseling session; AP normally did these by himself.

We had gotten to know and love the couple during our short time at Chambers Street Baptist. They both retired here from uptime, Elwood from a civilian logistics career, Amy from a Navy career with a side-journey in the *Naval Investigative Service*. She hadn't told me much of that life, but she'd said enough.

When we were comfortable AP prayed for the meeting, then we got down to business.

"Thanks for seeing us on short notice," Amy began, "I have to fly up to Chicago tomorrow with Don and Jackie and won't be back till noon Friday."

"Do we have enough time for the rehearsal?" I asked.

"We're keeping it very simple, and informal," Amy replied, "We'll be back in town in time for the rehearsal late afternoon Friday."

"Simpler than last Friday, for sure," I chuckled, "OK AP, you're on."

AP gave me his excuse for The Look and began.

"Thank you for agreeing to this session," he began, "I know you're solid and established in your Christian walk and Chambers Street Baptist, but I promised the Lord I'd counsel with every couple who comes to be married, and I need to fulfill that promise."

"OK," Elwood said.

"Amy," AP continued, "we heard your testimony when you joined the church. I asked the deacons for their testimonies when I came aboard here last month, so I heard yours then, Elwood."

AP took a well-worn sheet of paper out of his pocket and unfolded it. "Now, I have this list I always use for pre-marriage counseling. I find it keeps me on track and makes sure I don't forget to ask something in the heat of battle, as it were."

"And gives him something to wave as he capsizes and sinks."

"Deborah, was that crack really needed?"

"For these folks, yes," I retorted, "This is due diligence, not a personnel inspection! They've not only seen the elephant, they've danced the Charleston with 'im! Besides, you don't outrank them. That way, anyway."

"Is that why you wanted Deborah here for this, Love?" Amy asked Elwood. He half-grinned and nodded.

"Are you through, Deborah?" AP asked.

"For now. Go on."

AP looked at his paper. "Do you know where you're going to live yet?" he asked.

"We're going to stay in Elwood's apartment for now," Amy replied, "He has it fixed up nicely, and all his musical gear is there. That'll save the South Street house for Ev and Jeff when they get married."

"You play music, Elwood?" AP asked.

"Some," he replied, "Jazz drums, some keyboard. Hobby, what I do."

"I never knew that about you, Elwood," I said.

"Don't know everything," Elwood fired back.

AP snorted. "Next question. Have you two discussed family finances once you're married?"

Amy looked over at Elwood. "Yours"

"We have pensions. Don pays us well. Don't spend much. Cheap to live here. We'll do OK."

I relished the next ten seconds while AP realized that was all he was going to get and fumbled with his paper.

"Next question. What do each of you feel is the other's habit or trait that bothers you the most?"

"Elwood talks too much."

"Amy's delicate."

The couple smiled and held hands while AP and I tried to stop laughing.

I recovered first. "Forget AP's paper! Have you two talked about how you'll handle things as a married couple?"

"We've talked about what we do well and what we have trouble with. I'm going to handle the social interaction as the spokesperson for the operation. Elwood *does* things. I'm going to help him do what he does and explain him to folks who don't know him well. I won't cook, and he won't recite poetry, except for me!"

"Poetry?"

"Right, Deborah. When the tornado flattened the Square a month ago we dove under the table in the operations room."

"We've seen the room," AP said.

"Anyway," Amy continued, "While the tornado wrecked things Elwood started to recite a Shel Silverstein poem. I knew it, and we traded lines. We were both comforted, and we realized we might be compatible in other ways."

"There's a polar bear in our Frigidaire," Elwood announced.

"He likes it cause it's cold in there," Amy added.

AP and I just sat there while they recited the poem. "That's cute!" I said when they were through, "I've never heard it before."

"That's because Silverstein wrote it in 1981 uptime," Amy replied, "Besides music, we both read poetry as a hobby. Gave our minds something to think about besides work."

"One more thing," Elwood added, "We both made decisions in our work uptime. We do it here. Marriage, we'll ask the Lord, then decide things together. Worked so far." Amy nodded, then kissed Elwood.

"All right Deborah, I'll take over now," AP announced. "I know this issue won't affect you directly, but it's on the list so I should ask it. What do you think about having children?"

"Dunno, haven't asked him," Amy replied. She turned to Elwood. "Dear, how do you like children?"

Elwood shrugged. "Broiled or fried, whichever."

I chuckled but AP frowned. "You do realize you already have a child living with you, don't you?"

"Jeff is not a child," Amy began, then stopped. "Oh."

"You are right," Elwood added, "Very unusual, but a child."

"What are you talking about, Elwood?" Amy asked, "He lives in the other apartment, I see him whenever I visit. We never speak."

I spoke up, "Remember, that's because he *can't* speak, except when he's feeling strong emotion or someone is in danger."

"Doesn't live in the other apartment when you're not there," Elwood added.

"I know he has some special needs," Amy admitted, "but I've never asked what's wrong with him."

"Nothing's *wrong* with him," I began, "He has Asperger's Syndrome, also called high-functioning autism. Jackie and Syl have briefed us in detail about the condition. The brain has trouble taking in sensations from the environment and communicating back through that environment to others. Although he has trouble speaking, he remembers everything he reads. He understands it all too, from every test Syl and Helen have given him. Some folks communicate with him using few words; I don't know how they do it, but it works."

"Evelyn, Mrs. Hastings and me," Elwood added, "Never think about how. Just do it."

"That's never worked for me," Amy said.

"Doesn't work for us either," AP replied, "but when he types out his thoughts on the typewriter, he shows true genius. I've never met anyone with as clear a grasp of complex technical information as Jeff, anywhere."

"Still needs growth, help in activities of daily living," Elwood said, "I do that now, we will do that when we marry. OK?"

Amy looked like she was going to cry but didn't. "All right, folks, I think I understand now. I never gave Jeff that much thought before. And yes, I'll be happy to help you raise Jeff. Just remember I didn't have a *normal* childhood either. This will be as new to me as it is to him. OK?"

Elwood looked at Amy, then leaned over to kiss her. "OK. Next question."

I was enjoying this meeting more now that I saw the couple realized they didn't know everything. I noticed AP had the little eye twitch he got when he became rattled. Even more fun.

AP took a deep breath and trudged on. He looked down at his paper. "I'm almost afraid to ask this, but have you two discussed what happens after marriage? *Conjugal relations*, I mean."

"Sex? We're familiar with it," Amy replied, and Elwood nodded solemnly.

Since AP looked like a gasping fish on a trawler deck I took over. "I can understand that from you, Amy—you've been married.

But Elwood?"

"Just because it's never happened to me doesn't mean I don't know about it," Elwood replied.

"The subject is taught in public schools uptime," Amy added, "and you know how television and movies are back there."

"Does *anyone* stay chaste uptime?" AP finally ground out.

"We did," the couple replied together.

AP looked at his paper, then put it in his pocket. "I think you two will do fine. Maybe we ought to have you two counsel *us*."

"Ok," Elwood said, "AP, how do you feel about Deborah making more money than you?"

"Yes, how about that?" I turned to my husband.

"It doesn't bother me at all. The Lord gives us our jobs, and enough money to get by on. Hers just happens to pay more—so what?"

"That's what he's always said, and he acts as if he believes it; that's good enough for me," I added, then blew AP a kiss across the room.

After Amy and Elwood left I motioned for AP to come sit with me on the love seat. "Is that how all your counseling sessions end up?" I asked.

AP wiped his brow with his handkerchief. "Not at all, Deborah! Not even Don and Jackie's session was like that."

"Oh? Jackie told me you tried those questions with them. She said Don just kept mumbling and she provided the answers—in Chinese!"

AP put his head in his hands.

*****

Matt: just after noon, Cottage Hospital

"Haven't I seen you someplace before?" A hint of a smile crossed Mimi's face. *Good sign*, I thought.

"Perhaps. I've brought you your lunch. I thought maybe you would like me to serve you this magnificent repast."

"Is that gruel?"

"Yes, but only the best gruel. We left out the Tabasco sauce this time."

"Love Tabasco, but not now. I'm sorry I can't sit up to eat this."

"No problem," I said as I pulled up my chair, "May I feed it to you? Very slowly, carefully. You concentrate on swallowing, OK?"

"You do your thing, I'll do mine. I know Christians pray before meals, but I don't know how."

"That's OK. I'll pray, if I may."

"You may…if you *can*."

I snorted. "Lillian said you had a mouth on you."

"She doesn't know the half of it. Please go ahead."

I prayed, then slowly started feeding Mimi, spoonful by spoonful.

"Not bad," she said, "but I have a question."

"What?"

"I keep getting…injections…in my arm. Gloria said they are from your company. What are they?"

I knew what I could say—and what I couldn't. "They are injections of an experimental antibiotic medication, to fight your infection. The company I work for is researching those medications. This one seems to work."

Mimi swallowed and paused before speaking, "I guess it does—I'm still here."

"So you are," I replied. We didn't talk for a while so she could concentrate on swallowing.

"We're almost done," I said after a while, "and before you go back to sleep, I need to tell you I have to be away from Wednesday morning till Friday supper time. I have to fly to Chicago to help Don and Jackie negotiate a deal with Hugo Junkers."

Mimi's brow furrowed. "Isn't he the German who builds airplanes?"

"Yes. We fly his airplanes and modify them. We want him to bring his company to America and build them here. Don—my boss—thinks he's ready to do that."

"Quite a deal," Mimi said after she swallowed the last bite, "So shall I see you Friday, Matt?"

"You bet, Mimi," I said as she closed her eyes, "You bet."

*****

Don, the same Tuesday, 6:30 PM, American Beauty Restaurant

"I wasn't expecting a company meeting tonight," I said as Paul Poulos opened the backroom door for Jackie and me.

"We didn't know you'd be here either," Amy Lansdale said as the assembled group stood, "but since you are, here's Doctor Jennifer Setterdahl and her husband Keith, new company partners."

"We've heard about you folks, welcome aboard," Jackie said as we shook hands.

"And we've heard about you," Jennifer replied, "We're still trying to sort it all out."

"You will, eventually," I said, "You'll have lots of help from all of us."

"So how was the honeymoon?" Amy asked as we sat down.

"Great!" Jackie said before I could respond, "The inn was beautiful, the food excellent, the snow deep."

"Snow?" Elwood asked.

"Ten inches on Monday, lake effect," I said, "We got out OK. And congratulations to you two! Next Saturday, right?"

"Right," Amy replied, "We had our counseling session this

morning."

"Did you tie poor AP up in knots?" Jackie asked.

"We did, but he and Deborah brought up something we hadn't talked about—taking care of Jeff. Got it sorted out."

"Train two," Elwood added.

While I tried to figure out what Elwood meant, Jackie asked Jennifer what she thought of the organ.

"I've never seen anything like it!" Jennifer said, glassy-eyed. "Then when I heard Marcel Dupré had played it, and what happened to him, I kind of lost it..."

"She faints when overwhelmed by good news," Keith said, "I've learned to watch and catch her. She comes to quickly."

"Have you ever had that happen during surgery?" Jackie asked.

"Never," Jennifer replied, "But I make sure my nurses know it could happen and watch. Something neurological, I think."

"And I hear you have another project cooking," I said to our Director of Transportation.

"You might say that," Matt replied. I didn't know he could blush that deep.

"Just be careful what you tell her about us until we get the word to bring her in," Jackie said, "although since she's now born-again that could well happen, under the circumstances," Jackie added with a sly grin.

"I will," Matt said, "Now since you're here I have a couple of questions about the negotiations with Hugo tomorrow—"

A chorus of raspberries and the arrival of our server changed the subject.

CHAPTER NINE

Don: Wednesday, March 3rd, 1926, way too early in the morning

The intrusive tones of our *Bose Wave Radio* playing a mazurka of Chopin blew me out of another realistic dream. I opened my eyes to darkness except for the night light. I turned off the *CPAP* and took off my mask. I could hear three others breathing nearby: Jackie and two shih tzus. Theodore and Melissa ignored us when we got home the night before but insisted on climbing into bed with us. We would have to make time for other activities without them.

Jackie opened one eye. "That music is appropriate after the dream I had," she mumbled as we embraced.

"Sure is," I said, "but I don't get the dream I had at all. We're bringing in Khatia Buniatishvili?

"Who? That name is familiar, but I can't place her."

"Uptime pianist from Georgia, old Soviet Union. Dark curly hair, pretty features, big—"

"OK, now I remember her," Jackie said, rubbing her eyes, "I saw Matt Plotczyc and the Barlows doing that for Mimi Conger! She's a dead ringer for the uptime Khatia."

I grasped Jackie's hand. "So, we both had the same dream. That makes sense since Mimi's now a Believer and is getting involved with Matt. I'm ok with it; are you?"

Jackie smiled and snuggled as much as she could with two shih tzus between us. "Yes, that's fine. She's a real character, a lot like Matt. I think they're a good fit. They can bring her in when we get home Friday."

I looked over at the clock. "It's 4:35 in the morning, Love! Did we really have to get up this early?"

Jackie shifted in the bed in a very interesting way. "We were too tired when we got home from the restaurant."

"So we were. Let me try something. Puppies Out!" I called. The dogs jumped down and ran out of the room.

"Genius," my new bride murmured.

"Waddya know, it wor...."

Some comments are better left unfinished.

*****

Luther: 11:15 AM, Frederick Stock's favorite restaurant, near Orchestra Hall, Chicago.

"So how was the flight?" Fred Stock asked Don.

After we landed the others told Don to stay away from the hotel for the afternoon while they set up the negotiations with the Junkers party. Don and I arranged to meet Fred for lunch before I tackled the orchestra. Fred said he wanted to talk away from prying ears, and that included his secretary. Don described Magda as a *battle-ax*.

"Interesting to say the least," Don replied, First, the air was turbulent, so the plane bumped along all the way up. Then four tri-motors were hogging the pattern at the Air Park, wouldn't let anyone else in. Airline test flights. Jackie politely asked to be let through—with the radio at full volume! Everyone cleared except one. That jerk said he wouldn't move for a woman, then called her a name I can't use here."

"On the radio? That's cheeky," Fred remarked.

"Yeah," Don replied, "I said something on the intercom about machine guns, but Jackie shushed me. Ended up she slipped *underneath* the other plane to land before him! We taxied into the hangar before he landed. He had other choice words for her and he bounced the landing badly."

"How do you know what he said?" Fred asked.

"Because he forgot to cut the microphone off and everything

went out over the air! I don't know what happened afterward. We high-tailed it out of there."

"Are there any rules against bad language on the radio?"

"Not yet. Next year the Department of Commerce is going to put out regs governing aviation and radio—Commerce oversees both. Until then they do what they want."

The server came then, and we ordered.

"Seafood platter again?" Fred asked.

"Yep," Don replied, "At least here I can get the things without heads, or eyes! Jackie loves to have 'em watch me."

"Is Jackie going to keep doing that to you now that you're married?" I asked.

"I dunno. She was good on the honeymoon. Actually, she was fantastic!"

I sent a little water out my nose as Fred laughed harder than I'd ever heard him.

"I didn't mean it like that!"

"Oh yes you did!" Fred said between laughs and sputters.

We finally calmed down and Fred changed the subject.

"Are you ready to try your hand at conducting, Luther?"

"I have a couple of answers for that, Fred, but I guess I'll use this one: 'Sure, bring 'em on!'"

"I probably should warn you about a couple of the young men you'll be conducting today," Fred said between bites. "They're both fine young musicians. The clarinetist is the best young player I've heard in many years. The trombonist is good too, but his musicianship is much better than his actual playing. They're both first-rate, but...they only play for us part-time, so to speak. They both play for a popular dance and jazz band in the city."

Don interrupted Fred, "Ben Pollack?"

"Why, yes."

"Benny Goodman and Glenn Miller?"

"Right again."

Don grinned from ear to ear. Fred asked the question I was thinking.

"Don, how did you know that?"

Don took another bite of scallop. He chewed a bit, then took some water to wash it down.

"I know what you're doing, Don, so quit stalling! How did you know who they were?"

Don still grinned. "Because from the middle 1930s uptime they led two of the greatest *swing bands* of the era. Benny combined band leading with classical work; Glenn died in the next war. Maybe he won't here. I'll be thrilled to listen to them this afternoon! Right now, though they're a little immature, eh Fred?"

Fred laughed. "Hit it on the head! Glenn is usually serious—delves deeper into the construction and orchestration of the music. I think he's arranging some of Pollack's songs. Benny has wonderful talent, but he plays pranks. That's fine in a dance band, but not here. Also tends to give the conductor the 'evil eye' if he doesn't get his way."

"Can't be any worse than an offended Marine Private," I remarked. "This oughta be fun!"

"How many other clarinetists in this ensemble?" Don asked.

"Only one," Fred replied, "Sharp, quiet young man named Arthur Arshawsky."

"I'll have to give Sherry a quick call to see if I'm right, but if that fellow is who I think, he'll have a top band right along with the others, as *Artie Shaw*."

"What should I be alert for?" I asked.

"Glenn won't do anything," Fred replied, "but watch out for

Benny. I've had him slip a jazz riff right in the middle of a woodwind passage and do it so subtly it takes a moment to figure out what he did. By then it's too late to nail him for it. Drives me crazy sometimes!"

"Why don't you just can him?" Don asked.

"Because he's the best young clarinet player I think I've ever heard! I just can't bring myself to do it. One of these days he'll be the most popular dance band leader in the country—or one of us conductors will strangle him!"

I never heard Fred say something like that before, I thought, *This guy must be unique.*

"Thanks for the warning, Fred. Let's see what he pulls, and what I can do to shape him up, if anything."

"May I bring popcorn?" Don asked.

*****

Luther: 1 PM, Chicago Symphony rehearsal hall, showdown time

Promptly at one o'clock Fred, Don, and I walked into the rehearsal hall in the Orchestra Hall complex. All the players I would be conducting this afternoon were assembled; those not playing in the Ives would wait while we ran through it, then join us for the *Bartered Bride Overture*.

I smiled and nodded at Bethann and Charles, and they smiled back. Fred introduced me and Don, then left as I greeted the orchestra. Don found a chair by the door and tried to look mostly harmless. I sent the players not needed for the Ives off to the side, and we got to work on *Children's Day.*

I was greatly relieved to find the actual act of conducting was not too strenuous. I was able to keep my place in the music, and thanks to Fred's trick of memorizing the recording, I was able to pick up when something went wrong and correct it easily. The players seemed happy with the faster tempo.

As I conducted, I kept an eye on the players waiting at the sidelines. I picked out our two lunch subjects easily. The young man with the trombone seemed serious, listening to the Ives as we worked through it. The clarinetist was more nonchalant, but I could see him keeping an eye on the proceedings too. He spoke quietly to the other clarinetist who nodded. I suspected they were plotting.

We ran through the Ives one last time to my satisfaction and I called the other players in for the Smetana. The *Bartered Bride Overture* is a lively work to conduct and play. It kept the interest of the players, and the way I paced it nobody fell asleep!

All was well until the middle of the piece, where there is a short development section with figures from the various woodwinds in the group. I was listening closely as we approached that section. Sure enough, when we got to the four-measure figure for clarinet I heard the second clarinet stop playing. Benny then inserted a jazz construction called a *riff*, very fast, instead of what he should have played. It was there and gone before most people would register it had existed...*heh.* I put my plan into action.

I called a precipitous stop to the music. Don said later he was watching Benny, and saw shock, amazement and a little embarrassment pass over his face while the orchestra was rumbling to a stop.

I looked over at my two clarinetists. "Outstanding riff, Mister Goodman. Please put down your clarinet, fold your hands on your lap, and sit while we take the overture from the top. Mister Arshawsky, you have the clarinet part by yourself this time."

While the orchestra shuffled their scores back to the beginning, I noticed Benny had fixed a baleful gaze upon my person. This must be 'the look' Fred had referred to. *Piker.* I sent The Look right back at him, with a slight tinge of boredom added.

We stared at each other for about ten seconds; then Benny lowered his eyes, his face relaxed and he studied the clarinet in his lap. *Not bad, but no match.* I had another thought as I lifted my baton. *If Syl had been doing this, he wouldn't have lasted five seconds!*

After the rehearsal, I asked Benny, Arthur, and Glenn to stay back for a moment. We walked over to some chairs by the door and I motioned them to sit down. They sat, and I sat in a chair facing them. Don leaned up against the wall behind them, a slight smile on his face.

I knew Bethann and Charles had told the orchestra members about me before I walked in that day. Now they knew I could conduct and catch a prank. That was enough. I silently asked the Lord to guide my lips and launched my speech.

"First off, Glenn and Arthur, I know you had nothing to do directly with what happened this afternoon. But you may find what I'm going to talk about useful to you down the line someday, so just consider this training for later. OK?"

Glenn nodded. "But Mister Barlow," Arthur spoke, "I helped Benny. I stopped playing when he asked me to."

"So you did, Arthur," I replied, "but let me ask, who is the leader of the clarinet section?"

"Benny is."

"And you're supposed to follow the direction of your section leader, right?"

"Yes, sir."

That was different, I thought. "So, you did what your section leader told you to do, correct?"

"Yes, but I shouldn't have."

"Arthur, in the context of what we're doing here you did the right thing to obey your section leader, even if you thought it wasn't right. You might have told the conductor about it, but you didn't know me and there wasn't time to tell me that anyway. So in this case, it falls to me to correct the situation with the section leader. Does this make sense?"

Arthur and Glenn nodded. Benny sat with the baleful glare he had worn earlier. I turned to him.

"Benny, I know you know why I stopped the rehearsal and had you sit out. Let me put that in perspective, if I may."

Benny kept sucking on the sour pickle in his mind while the others watched me.

"You three are outstanding musicians. You wouldn't be playing in the Chicago Symphony if you weren't. You're also excellent popular and jazz musicians. I'm familiar with your work with Ben Pollack."

That was stretching it a bit, but not much.

"All three of you are going to be leading bands yourselves in a few years, fewer years than you think. Those bands will be the best in the business, I am completely sure of that!"

Thanks to our lunch conversation I figured I could say that much about their future. Don smiled and nodded as I said it. *Now to connect the dots*, I thought.

"You'll be dealing with young musicians, brilliant musicians, with the same sort of background and attitudes you have now. You'll get to see it all again from the other side. Follow me so far?"

Glenn and Arthur both nodded yes. Benny's look slipped into a pout.

"OK. I can tell you three have a passion for the music you play, whichever kind it is at the moment. What are you gonna do when one of your young, brilliant musicians plays a prank with the music? You know there'll be all kinds of horseplay off stage—that's expected. But what if it happens with the music? What'll you do? Scream? Cuss? Fire the little twerp on the spot? Or do something more subtle to correct him, admonish him, without making him feel like dirt."

"I wouldn't embarrass him in front of the whole band," Benny muttered through his pout.

Glenn looked straight at his friend. "Don't give me that Benny. I know how hot you can get. You'd fire that prankster's ass out of there so fast they'd have to send his shoes airmail to catch up!"

Behind them, Don put his hand over his mouth to stifle a guffaw. He was the only one laughing.

Benny stared at Glenn, mouth open. Slowly he shut his mouth, relaxed his facial muscles, and turned back to me.

Benny spoke. "I think I see what you're driving at, Mister Barlow."

Light dawns on Marble Head, I thought. *Been there, done that. Time to let him back in.*

"I'm glad. And it's Luther to you three. I just gave you guys a little lesson in managing musicians this afternoon. You may choose to do it differently, and that's fine. It's your band. But as you're moving up and learning your trade, take time to think through what you'd do in the different situations you run into, or run into you. Know what you'll do before you're standing on that bandstand and one of your boys throws a temper tantrum in the middle of a song. OK?"

The three young men smiled, true smile, no fake. *Whew*, I thought.

"Thanks a bunch for the advice, Luther," Glenn said. "I hope to have my own band one day. I know Benny and Arthur do too. We'll remember what you said."

"I know you will, guys. You are going to be able to make the gig in Galesburg April second, aren't you?"

The young musicians smiled broadly. "Wouldn't miss it for anything, Luther!" Benny said.

Don kept grinning in the background.

Don drove us back to the hotel where the others had been meeting with the Junkers folks. I would be sitting in on the negotiations the next day and visit John Wick at his Chicago area office Friday morning. We'd get back to Galesburg just before Amy and Elwood's wedding rehearsal. *Three, no four packed days*, I thought.

As he drove, Don hummed and sang wordlessly a succession of tunes I had never heard before. He said they came from the bands Benny and Glenn would lead in the future. He hummed and sang quietly all the way to the hotel, and from time to time all evening. Jackie didn't try to stop him but smiled and clung to his arm.

CHAPTER TEN

Luther: Friday, March 5th, 1926, 8:05 AM, Wicks Organ Company Chicago office, Schiller Park, Illinois.

"What did you guys do, drive all night?"

John Wick was amazed to see me appear with Don in tow at his office door this early. Normally I never made an appointment at either Highland or here before noon.

"Several of us had business up here this week so we stayed in the city," Don said, "We're flying home around noon."

"Flying? The airlines haven't started regular service here yet—still testing the routes, I hear."

"Wain Engineering has its own little air fleet, flying Junkers F-13s," I explained.

Don continued. "And we came across four trimotors from four different airlines stooging around the Air Park when we came in Wednesday. My new bride had some fun bluffing them out of our way!"

"New bride, Don?" Now John looked puzzled.

Don sobered. "I'm sorry; I didn't realize you hadn't heard. You knew my wife Pam passed suddenly January seventh. In a codicil to her will, she strongly urged me to get together with her best friend Jackie, our chief accountant and Aero Club pilot. Long story, but I guess we got together."

"I need to visit you folks more often," John said, "Anything new with you, Luther?"

I smiled. "You know Paul Sherwood and I got turned out of the Coal Company. Syl got a job as a Principal at a school in Galesburg. We moved into town, and Paul and his new bride are living in our old house. She's teaching at Wagher now."

John sat down slowly in his desk chair. "Well...Congratulations on all of it, gentlemen! I guess we ought to get down to business. The Chambers Street Baptist organ, right?"

"Right. Luther's got the design proposal and our cost estimate right here. I'll back out and let you two read it."

I pulled three manila binders out of my briefcase and gave one to each of us. "Remember, gentlemen, I work for both of you. I've been as straight with these numbers as I could. Now you two have the pleasure of analyzing them and negotiating the actual price of this rebuild. Have fun!"

We all sat down to read.

"So, our friends at Saint Sulpice want the Barker machines?" John asked.

"Sure do," I replied, "They've had the roof leaking into the organ case and the Barkers. The roof will be fixed but not until June. So for now all those wooden rods and levers are warping and swelling, and they don't have enough parts to fix them. The top keyboard on the Saint Sulpice console is out of commission because it has donated parts to keep the rest of the organ going."

"Ouch! They're in dire straits," John said, "and as I read this you folks are going to dismantle and pack the Barkers, right?"

"Yes," Don continued, "we have the manpower and skill to do it. Plus, Monsieur Widor is sending Marcel Dupré over to help with the job and escort them on the liner back to France."

John nodded. "Those things would be about priceless to someone with one of Cavaillé-Coll's organs. Nobody makes anything like them these days."

"They know, so they're taking every precaution. We will too."

John read on. "Not too much alteration of the voicing, eh?"

"Augmentation, as you see, but no real altering," I replied,

"Somehow or other that collection of fifty-year-old pipes sounds very good as-is. We just need a little more power in the areas you see."

John scribbled on a yellow pad. "Hook and Hastings had some fine tonal craftsmen back then. They really did some good work, sometimes with the strangest combinations. Second-hand stuff, but good stuff."

John got to the end.

"Another excellent workup, Luther. All eminently doable. Is there anything else we need to consider as we design this rig?"

"Yes, one more thing," Don interjected. "I want everything to be designed in modules, carefully labeled, so we can easily unplug the components and move them someplace else without having to untangle spaghetti!"

John and I both stopped, staring. Don hadn't said anything about this to me.

"We can do that, of course, but it'll cost extra."

"For that feature, cost is no matter. Besides, I think I can provide you with the cables and connectors. But I want it that way, gentlemen."

"Why?" John never beat around the bush.

Don looked at both of us with a look I hadn't seen before.

"That church is bursting at the seams, gentlemen. We've even talked about going to two services. Nobody wants to do that. Sooner or later we're gonna have to get a bigger building, a much bigger building! It'll be the Lord's timing of course—a bigger building for the wrong reasons is the kiss of death for a church. But we'll have to do something. And however it turns out, I want to be able to move the entire organ with a minimum of fuss and risk of damage. I owe it to the people, and the Lord."

"Always thinking ahead, aren't you, Don." John Wick said it as a statement, not a question.

Don nodded, jaw set as he spoke. “It’s what the Lord called me to do when I started this company, and by God’s Grace I will keep doing it.”

“Amen,” I breathed.

“Would you like everything on wheels?” John asked with a twinkle in his eye.

Don laughed. “Not wheels, John. But how about padeyes at the balance points on the wind chests so we can hook on with a crane and lift ‘em out?”

John and I chuckled, then stopped. “You aren’t kidding, are you?”

“Not this time,” Don replied.

After our meeting with John Wick, we walked back out to Gil’s red roadster which we’d borrowed for our side trip.

“You drive please, Luther,” Don said, “I’ll tell you how to get where we’re going.”

I started the car. “That’s a smooth engine,” I commented.

“Should be,” Don replied, “It has a flywheel at each end of it.”

“Never heard of that before,” I said

“German aero engines were built like that during the war. The guy who designed this saw that and liked it.”

We stopped at a gasoline station to fill up. While the attendant filled the tank, I opened the hood to check the oil. I was surprised to see the name on the radiator shell: *Rickenbacker*.

“Eddie Rickenbacker?” I asked Don.

“Yep. Notice the hat-in-the-ring insignia. Gil wanted something built by his old flying buddy, and he got it.”

“Nice car,” I said, fastening the hood latches.

Don sat back up in the seat and fastened his seat belt as I got in. “Gil’s driving this back to Galesburg today. We don’t want to keep putting miles on it up here, and besides, he’s got it sold.”

"What'll we drive when we are up here?"

"Jackie and Matt picked up a couple of late-model Chrysler sedans back home. We'll put the safety updates in 'em and station them here.

I started the car and pulled away. "And Gil's decided to sell this?"

Don chuckled. "Our export manager, Doctor Art, has someone *uptime* who desperately wants a Rickenbacker Vertical Eight Superfine roadster like this. Art's pretty good at finding old cars, oddly enough. We'll send it back to him and Gil makes a tidy profit to pay off their house and buy an airplane."

"Just with this car?"

Don grinned and nodded.

I followed Don's directions through a tiny village called Orchard Place and turned into a side road just beyond a sign reading *Orchard Place Field*. We drove maybe half a mile and stopped by a small building.

Don looked around. "Nice place," he remarked, "Quiet."

We sat a few minutes enjoying the unseasonably warm day, then I felt I had to say something. "Aren't we going to be late to the Air Park? We need to get back for the wedding rehearsal."

Don took off his hat and scratched his bald spot.

"Relax, Luther. It's a nice late winter day, the sun is shining, and here comes our ride."

Don nodded off to the east, and I saw a speck which resolved into the dash3, flying low and fast.

"Giving him a flat-hatter ride," Don observed.

"Who?"

"You'll see."

The last time Don said that to me, he produced Marcel and Jeannette Dupré. This time I figured it out. "Hugo?"

"Right! I wanted him to see the site for our new airfield and his aircraft assembly plant."

"I thought he was going to set up in Nashville."

"Spoof for the newspapers," Don replied, "I bought fourteen hundred acres here last week. Jackie and I snuck up and signed the papers in a day."

"Why all the way out here?" I asked.

"Won't be out here for long," Don replied as we began to hear the turboprop, "Uptime this spot will become the busiest commercial airport in the world. Not a bad idea to own the land it'll sit on."

The dash 3 streaked over the field just above treetop height, then pulled up into a steep climb. It kept climbing until it stopped in mid-air, then pitched over sideways to come screaming back over the airfield at treetop height again!

"Bet he's never been in that maneuver before," Don remarked, "It's called a chandelle."

"Worse than a roller coaster," I grimaced.

"Got that right."

As the aircraft slowed and settled into the pattern around the field, a limousine pulled up beside us. The chauffeur opened the door and Amy and Gil got out.

"Wish you were up there with them?" Don asked.

"Naah," Gil remarked. "Let the old boy have his fun!"

The plane finally landed and taxied over toward us. The engine stopped and Matt popped out the left side door.

"How'd he like it?" Don asked.

"Couldn't stop talking. I couldn't translate fast enough on the intercom!"

Matt also couldn't stop grinning.

Jackie stepped out the door and turned to help a distinguished-looking elderly man, thin, with a handsome face framed in white hair. He was grinning ear to ear and talking a mile a minute!

Hugo Junkers strode over to us and shook our hands vigorously. He spoke and Matt translated.

"Professor Junkers thanks us for the profitable discussions culminating in the agreement of last evening. He also thanks us for the hospitality of the accommodations, and then, this morning, for the most exciting flight of his long life! He says he'll be back very soon and bring his company with him."

Don spoke a few words in German, and we all shook hands again...except when Professor Junkers got to Jackie she got a bear hug!

Hugo waved again and got into the limousine, which started up and left.

"Well, kids, let's go home," Don announced.

"In a few minutes, Love," Jackie retorted. "I want to see our new digs ...and use the loo!" She headed toward the single building on the field.

"Priorities, Don," Matt pronounced.

*****

Sylvia: 4:45 PM, Mimi Conger's room, Cottage, when it's least expected...

"Mimi, are you awake?" Matt asked softly.

The thin young woman opened one eye. "Not that anyone's noticed," she whispered. "Who are our visitors?"

Luther stifled a giggle. I kept a straight face. I knew about Mimi's barbed wit.

"You already know Gloria. If you were awake, I could introduce Sylvia and Luther Barlow. But since you're not..." Matt started to turn away.

"Snot!"

"You started it!"

The entire exchange occurred in a whisper. *Looks like Matt's met his match for banter,* I thought.

Mimi continued, still whispering. "I'm happy to meet you two. Sorry. I can't speak any louder. This is all the strength I have at the moment."

"That's OK," I said, "Will you be able to stay awake for a few minutes while we explain something?"

"Is the subject interesting?"

"Let's find out," I said, "Who gets to start?"

"I will," Matt said as he pulled a paper from his pocket.

"This better be good," Mimi whispered, "Let's hear it, Matthew."

Matt smiled as he began. "You have been selected to become a partner in the company known as Wain Engineering. Everyone else in the room is already a partner."

"Did I win some sweepstakes?" Mimi interrupted.

"No," I replied, "Don and Jackie Wain, the owner and his new wife, each had a dream that we were bringing you in. They told us to do it."

Mimi squinted one eye. "They had 'a what' and decided '*what*?'"

"Are you interested yet?" Matt asked.

"What do I win?"

"You might be surprised," Matt said, then continued.

When he had finished reading the first page Matt stopped. "Any questions so far?"

"Pull the other one, it's got bells on."

"No, Amy," Gloria said softly, "Any other time you'd be right. I couldn't believe it either when they told me. But it's true—wonderfully true."

"Gloria, I will believe you, but one other thing—What is the date today?"

"Friday, March fifth," Gloria replied.

Not All Fool's Day," Mimi whispered, "and I seem to be awake. Do you have any proof that this is all real and I'm not dreaming?"

"I think we can provide something," I said, "Luther, please bring out the laptop computer."

Luther pulled the machine out of its bag and opened it. He held it so Mimi could see. "This is a laptop computer from uptime," Luther began, "It can do many things, but one thing it can do is show movies, videos they call them, of life from both here and then. Jackie said we should play this video for you first off. None of us have seen it ourselves yet."

I picked up the thread. "She says it is of a concert pianist *uptime* named Khatia somebody and will introduce you to a little of the *technology* as they call it. Here goes!"

I clicked on the file labeled "Use Me" and we all stood around to watch the little screen.

An orchestra in some concert hall sat waiting. Then out came the conductor and a young woman in a white dress. *Yep, looks just like her,"* I thought.

"So clear, such color," Mimi whispered, then she saw the woman's face. "Is that me?" She squeaked.

"No, just someone who looks like you," I said, "Khatia. I can't pronounce her last name."

We got a good look at the woman's face before she sat down at the piano.

"Just like me," Mimi said, "but too much lipstick."

"And not enough dress," she added as the woman sat down.

Gloria moved the bedside table, so Luther didn't have to hold the thing. We watched the first ten minutes of the first movement of Schumann's *Piano Concerto.*

Mimi finally spoke up. "Guys, my head is spinning and I'm starting to doze off. Could we watch this later?"

"Sure," I said as Luther stopped the video and shut the lid. "This machine is Matt's. I'm sure he and Gloria can figure out someplace to keep it so nobody else sees it."

"Use that locker in the corner if you have a lock," Gloria said, "I'll tell my staff to knock and get permission before they come in if you're here."

"What if we're necking?" Mimi asked.

Matt's face lit red like a flame.

*****

Mimi: 8:30 PM, the hospital room.

I swam out of the latest bizarre dream. I was sitting at a piano on the stage in the third-floor recital hall of Lombard College, my alma mater. I was playing something by Chopin...in a bathrobe. Then I remembered what was playing on that little device of Matt's just before I fell asleep. *Bathrobe covers more*, I mused.

I opened my eyes and looked over to the chair. "I am glad to see you are still here, Matthew."

He looked over at me and smiled. "I had to stay here to feed you your supper. It is something different Jackie Wain sent over."

He pulled the lid off the plate with a flourish. I wasn't impressed. "More gruel?"

"Much more than gruel, milady," he replied, "It's called super cereal, full of calories and vitamins. It's from uptime."

"So, I wasn't dreaming this afternoon?"

"You were not, Madame. Gloria told me you can sit up to eat now. Did she tell you that?"

I nodded. "Yes. If you will get behind the bed and grasp me by the arms you *may* pull me up."

"I *can* do that," Matt said and moved to comply. He took my arms by the elbows in his large hands and pulled me up without straining.

"No stealing a kiss?"

He turned bright red again.

"I like you. You're fun to embarrass!"

"I am so glad you're feeling better," Matt countered.

"So am I," I said as Matt picked up the spoon. "And before I forget, please ask Sylvia to come see me when she has time. I want to hear about Silas Willard, and you."

"Me?"

"You," I replied, "Due diligence. And now may I try praying for this meal, Mister Plotczyc?"

"Of course, Mimi"

And I did.

CHAPTER ELEVEN

Luther: Saturday, March 6th, 1926, 10:15 AM, Chambers Street Baptist Church, another day, another wedding

"Looks like it's time to make my appearance!"

Amy Lansdale, shortly to become Amy Lansdale Foutch, stepped out of the Sunday school classroom dressing room and walked up to me.

"*You're* going through with this, aren't you?"

"Bet your bippy I am, Luther," Amy replied, "Do you dare to question your lawyer?"

"Uh, no."

"Good. If you did, I would have to tell Sylvia, and she would give you a good tickling!"

I was still trying to figure out what a bippy was as Amy breezed past me and headed for the stairs.

She checked her image in the mirror one last time. I'd never seen anything like the outfit she wore, but Syl said Amy was wearing a dove gray silk charmeuse drop-waist skirt and top, waltz-length, with white pearl buttons and a Brussels lace collar. It was inspired by Coco Chanel and made for her by an old friend uptime.

As Amy marched up the steps, she shot one more comment back at me, "Don't forget to have lots of tissues for Elwood!"

I shook my head at her retreating form.

Syl came out of the kitchen and put her arm around me. "Where's she going?"

"Up to start her part of the preliminaries. Do you want to watch?"

"She's always entertaining. Elwood's in the foyer, you know."

"She knows. Watch him when she starts."

"Starts what?"

"She's going to play a little piano recital for him."

"Jazz?" Syl asked.

"No. Something else. Let's go watch."

We walked up the stairs after Amy. We got to the foyer in time to see her take Elwood in tow and head down to the front of the sanctuary. We followed, passing the few guests who were milling around. *They won't be milling long,* I thought.

Amy sat Elwood down in the front pew on the piano side of the platform. She walked up to the piano, pulled out the bench and sat on it. Amy had this recital memorized, as she'd shown me the day before.

As the music rolled from the lithe blonde on the bench, a line from an advertisement for a music school I'd seen in a magazine recently came to mind. *They laughed when I sat down at the piano, but when I started to play!*

"What is that music?" Syl asked in a whisper, "It's gorgeous but so short! And the melody's wandering all over the place."

"He's a young French pianist and composer. I don't think he's thirty yet. He's one of a group of avant-garde musicians based in Paris. Amy says he's got the feel of piano music like Chopin! Sounds like Francis Poulenc knows his business."

Don and Jackie, hand in hand, strolled over to us.

"Poulenc. Figures."

"You know that composer, Don?"

"Oh, yes, Luther. I like his music; his personal life makes me ill. I thought Amy only played jazz. Boy was I wrong."

"You certainly were. Now hush so we don't spoil the recording." Jackie whispered.

Amy finished one short piece and started another; it seemed to be related to the first.

"Look at Elwood," Jackie whispered.

Even though his eyes were streaming tears, Elwood continued to stare at Amy, a massive grin plastered on his face.

"The tissues, Love," Syl reminded me.

"Yeah," I whispered, and walked down to Elwood. I tried to offer him the tissues, but he just continued to stare at Amy without even noticing me.

"Competence," I heard my bride whisper, then she came up next to me and took the tissues. "I'll handle this; go talk to Don and Jackie." She started to wipe Elwood's eyes.

Eventually, Amy finished her pre-wedding recital, bowed to the applause of the gathering guests, and left the sanctuary. Syl and Jackie tried to calm Elwood down and make him reasonably presentable. They couldn't do anything about his reddened eyes.

I went up to the organ and switched on the blower. Lucille came up on the platform behind me.

"I didn't know Amy played classical piano," Lucille said, "She's outstanding!"

"She told me she kept it secret from people after Pat died. She played for herself and the Lord, not for others. She and Elwood play jazz together. Poulenc is her favorite composer; he didn't know anything about it!"

Lucille wiped her brow. "I'm seriously impressed. I wonder if she'd like some students? I just don't seem to have the energy to grind through lessons like I used to."

"Maybe, if you ask her, Luce."

"I will, after the honeymoon. Now you're on!"

As I started the short prelude to the unusual wedding ceremony, I wondered if there was such a thing as a 'usual' wedding ceremony around here!

******

Mimi: 3:15 PM, her room at Cottage, catching up

"Come in and pull up a chair," I said, "Matt is at a wedding so it's safe to gossip."

"I was at the same wedding," Syl said as she shut the door, "He said he'd be here around five."

"That should be enough time. See, I'm able to turn on my side now. Another couple of weeks and I'll be able to wipe myself."

My guest turned red. "Lillian warned me you'd say anything in the right crowd! I am honored to be included."

I nodded as Syl sat down. "There is a certain freedom in all of this. On one hand, Jesus has turned my life around in ways I'm still discovering. On the other hand, I no longer have to measure everything I say or do against the judgment of my peers. I love Lillian. She saved my life. But it was a pain living up to her expectations."

"She's been very forgiving with me and my questions," Syl replied, "but the relationship isn't like what I had with AP and Deborah Kittridge, and the Johnsons."

"Who were they?"

"The Pastor of Appleton Baptist and his wife. They're at Chambers Street Baptist now; you'll meet them soon. The Johnsons head up the Wagher School board."

"So are you satisfied you made the right move?"

My guest thought a minute. "I think so. Lillian was in a bind after Flora Potter died. I was there to take over, and Edna Kimpton, now Edna Sherwood could take over for me. The Lord works things out like that, you'll see."

"I already have, Syl," I replied, "and I am so glad Edna has a place to teach away from that evil school board member, Hank Sloss!"

Syl's eyebrows rose. "You haven't heard about him?"

"No. I let the newspaper go when I couldn't afford it. What happened?"

"He was caught after he abducted a young boy in Peoria. Tried a shootout with Federal agents; he lost. The school board's looking for his replacement."

"Was he...," I growled.

"We think so,"

I felt my incision twitch. "I always thought he was pure evil besides his politics. Now we know. And I appreciate your candor about what happened. You say what you think, bark on. I like that—you'll do fine with the teachers at Willard."

"Thanks, Mimi," Syl replied, "So far they've been nice to me, haven't been insubordinate. I have to keep checking on them though."

"You will," I said, "They're getting more mature, but sometimes one of 'em will say or do something stupid and need the verbal woodshed. Hattie can also sneak around you sometimes —say yes to your face then go do what she wants."

"I've seen the look on her face when I've given them directions," Syl said, "Thanks for the heads-up."

"Don't get me wrong," I added, "They're a good group of girls, and that's the problem. They need to mature. They will if you'll mentor 'em like you were mentored."

I saw Syl's face twist and her eyes darken. "I didn't have much mentoring. My ma taught at Wagher, and I helped out when we reopened after the influenza in '19. That summer she died suddenly, and I took over. Helen Smiley helped me for two years before Lillian hired her for Ayers."

"I remember hearing about that time from Helen," I said, "You did a wonderful job of preparing her for Ayers. You'll do just fine at Willard." I reached out with both hands and grasped a cup of water. I brought it to my lips and drank. "Hey, I only spilled a little! Better than I did yesterday."

"Thank you for the compliment, Mimi," Syl said, "I'll trust the Lord to keep me useful over there. And you're gradually getting your strength back. That's how it was for me when I was so sick in 1918."

"Helen talked about that. Now, I have something else I want to ask you about. Matthew Plotczyc...what do you know about him?"

Syl sat back in her chair and put her index finger to her lips.

"Let me think a moment," she began, "Has he told you about his late wife Grace?"

"Yes, and where he was when she died. That's a sorrow he needs to work through. I think I might help him do that if he'll let me."

"I think he will," Syl replied, "although he's a very private man. He hides his grief behind the mask of a jokester."

"I've done that for years," I admitted, "I've always had this mouth, and I love a good prank. Ask your teachers. I couldn't do much, but every so often I pulled one off. Mention the name *George*."

"I will," Syl said, "I saw you and Matt trading quips yesterday. You two are a match for each other."

"So it seems," I said, "but I need to know: in your opinion is there anything about Matt I should know before it comes up to ruin our relationship?"

"Nothing that I know of," Syl replied, "I haven't seen much of him, but what I have seen is consistent with what others have told me about him. No skeletons that I know of."

"That's comforting. But I am confused about who is retired from where. Can you tell me where Matt came from? And when?"

Syl shrugged. "I do know he served his Navy career in this time. Several of the others are retired from uptime, or spent some time there and some time here. I can't explain it but there you are. We're gradually learning more about the company here, and life uptime. I haven't been there but Helen has—she can tell you about it. I do know she didn't want to stay there!"

"Did I hear she is getting married when school is out?"

"Right. She met Luther's best friend Jack when he came in for our wedding. Long story, but they're both pilots. He's a Marine Gunny, and is down at Pensacola, Florida, becoming a Marine Aviator."

I twisted slightly in the bed. "Ah, that's better. So Helen leaving this summer started the musical chairs?"

Syl laughed. "You might say that! Now Lillian still needs someone to replace her. I was going to, but now I'm at Willard."

I took another drink. "I'm sorry I caused your shuffle in the middle of the school year. I never figured this would happen to me."

"But it did, and look what happened to you."

"Out of a job, nearly died, broke. Although all of that was my own doing."

Syl looked straight at me. "And?"

That stopped me. I thought, and my eyes started to water. Syl reached over with tissues, and I wiped slowly.

"My friends I didn't know I had got me to the hospital, and Doctor Bohan operated to save my life. Wain Engineering gave me antibiotics to save my life again. Gloria told me about Jesus—the full story. He saved my life. And now I'm connected with a group of people from another time and universe, here to help this place. And if that weren't enough there is that big man with the smile. I understand the word is *blessed.* and am I ever!"

"Now you've got it, Mimi," my guest said and cried with me.

*****

Amy Lansdale Foutch: Sunday, March 7, 1926, 5 AM, Hotel Broadview, Galesburg

I slithered out of the mindless sort of dream I have when I try to sleep overheated. *Don's gotta get the HVAC sorted out in this place if he buys it,* my first rational thought of the morning. I saw I had kicked the covers off me during the night in the too-hot room. Then I saw the smiling face at the other side of the bed.

"How long have you been watching me?" I asked.

"An hour," my new husband replied, "Enjoy the view."

I rolled toward Elwood. "Better?"

"Better." Still smiling.

"Before we take this conversation further I need to visit the 'loo," I said, then turned to get out of bed. I reached for my robe on the chair.

"Don't bother," Elwood remarked.

"I won't," I replied, and sauntered across the room to the bathroom.

The preventive maintenance of a middle-aged woman completed, I opened the door and returned to the bed. Elwood was still watching, still smiling.

"You're next," I said.

"OK," Elwood replied.

"If you can," I added.

I didn't know Elwood could giggle, I thought.

Six minutes later the bathroom door opened and Elwood returned to the bed.

"Comments?" I asked.

"Most beautiful woman I've ever seen," Elwood replied.

"Thank you," I said, "you know how to make a woman very happy."

"What I do," Elwood said, "Prime directive."

"Now how did you learn about that?"

"Just because I've never experieeee..."

Enough talk.

CHAPTER TWELVE

Second Lieutenant Lewis Burwell "Chesty" Puller: Friday, April 2nd, 1926, 9:30 AM, Pensacola Naval Air Station

I put on my cap as I walked out of the Station Administration Building and down the stone steps into the early spring sunlight—and maybe oblivion.

I had just met with the Student Evaluation Board and I was out of flight training.

They were very polite to me. They praised my military bearing and ground school work, but... I thought. I knew all about the failings of my flight instruction—knew them intimately, as I'd gone over and over them in my mind at night. I really couldn't dispute a single one of their observations, but to hear the verdict, kind about it as they were, gave me a pain in my gut much worse than being shot at.

I don't take defeat well.

I worried about what they would do with me now. I'd only gotten my commission back in 1924, and I never forgot when I was caught in the reduction in force of 1919. *And what would Ginny say*, I wondered.

The door opened behind me. I turned, snapped to attention, and saluted. The tall, balding Marine Major returned the salute and stood with me on the sidewalk.

"Thank you for standing up for me again, Major Vandegrift."

"My pleasure, Chesty. No way to find out if this was for you but to try it."

Major Alexander Archer Vandegrift had been head of the Marine Corps mission in Haiti. He was one of the Marines lobbying General Headquarters to have my commission restored after my service in Haiti earlier in the decade. The pestering of Major Vandegrift and Sergeant Major Chuck Simmons had tipped the balance with the Commandant, and here I was. Such as I was...

“Do you know what might happen to me now, Sir?”

Major Vandegrift smiled. I’d never seen him do that.

“Chesty, you’ll go back to Quantico for a bit...and then, I think we’ve found something interesting for you to do. Please keep it confidential, but unpleasant things are starting to happen in Nicaragua. Looks like some of us are going to have to go down there and sort the business out. This will be a regular operation, not just training the police. I know you’ve got the skills for the job, and the brass agree. Figure July, maybe.”

I smiled for the first time in a couple of weeks. “That would be wonderful, Sir! I’d be honored to take that assignment.”

The major winked. “Leave it to you to be thrilled over another assignment to yet another stinking tropical country where people will be shooting at you!”

“Sir, yes Sir!” The thought of a campaign snapped me back to good cheer.

Major Vandegrift snorted, then changed the subject.

“I asked the Commander in there if I might be able to take a familiarization flight in the aircraft you’ve trained in, so I can see first-hand what they put you through. I’ve also heard the equipment is pretty bad; I want to see it for myself. The Commander said he’d call over and have a plane and pilot ready for me. Let’s walk over that way.”

“Yes, Sir,” I said, “If they want you to fly with a Marine they’ll probably send you with Gunny Jack Sewell.”

“He was your Gunny at Quantico, wasn’t he?”

“Yes, Sir. We went out to Illinois for his best friend’s wedding just before Christmas. Gunny came back at New Years with about seventy more flight hours...and engaged to his instructor pilot!"

"I heard something about that. Sergeant Luther Barlow's wedding, right?"

"Yes, Sir. Retired, lost a leg at Belleau Wood the day after Gunny was hit. Got the NC for carrying him and some others to the aid station, then got the Medal for destroying a Hun machine gun nest."

"I remember now. An organist too, if I heard right."

"Yes, Sir. Fellow of the American Guild of Organists. Married a schoolteacher who lost her husband in the Fifth at Belleau Wood. Her best friend turned out to be Gunny Sewell's fiancée and flight instructor!"

"Is that him up there by that ancient wreck of a biplane?"

I nodded, "That's him, Sir. Begging the Major's pardon, that's one of our best training planes!"

Major Vandegrift groaned.

*****

Gunnery Sergeant Jack Sewell: pilot of the hour

I stood by my aircraft and watched the two officers approach. Giving the major a flight was an honor; the vehicle, less so. I knew its history.

The flying machine I was assigned could only be called an aircraft by the loosest of definitions. Typical of the result of years of reduced funding and neglect after the war, it had started life as a collection of spare parts for various products of the Curtiss Aeroplane and Motor Corporation.

In the very lean year of 1922, the Naval Aircraft Factory had combed their collection of spare parts and constructed 33 aircraft using whatever assemblies they had. These assembled collections were given the type designation PT-1 and PT-2, depending on which Curtiss floatplane the majority of the parts had originally been built for.

The apparition on the ramp this morning had originally begun life as a PT- 1, meaning it was mostly a Curtiss R-6L. The two-seat biplane had unusually long wings and was powered by a de-rated Liberty V12 engine when it chose to run.

On the strong recommendation of the Morrow Board report, this ship and her sisters were to be replaced by new aircraft. The new aircraft were due to be procured Real Soon Now.

None of us, instructor or student, trusted this particular aircraft as it had acquired the reputation of a hangar queen, causing frequent emergency landings and constant repair. It was the only ship available at short notice, so I was stuck with it.

The two officers walked up to me and I squared off to a typically crisp Corps salute. The officers returned the salute.

"Lieutenant Puller tells me you're the pilot who's going to give me a familiarization flight this morning."

"Sir, yes, Sir! The ship is ready, if you'd like to climb aboard."

I gave Major Vandegrift a leather flying helmet and helped him into the back cockpit.

"No parachute, Gunny?"

"Sorry, sir, only rated pilots get one—some Navy reg. I'll make sure you don't need it, sir!"

The ground crew fitted the *gosport* speaking tube between me in the front cockpit and the Major in the rear. After several heaves on the propeller, the engine grudgingly came to life. I half wished it had not.

*****

Chesty: watching from the ground

As I watched the trainer fly over Pensacola Bay, I saw a Navy Commander walking toward me. I cracked off the salute in good order.

"Lieutenant, is Gunnery Sergeant Sewell flying that plane?"

"Yes, sir," I replied, "He's taking Major Vandegrift on a familiarization flight."

"Archie's here too? I guess this is my lucky day!"

"Sir?"

"I'd better introduce myself. I'm Jack Towers. Gunny Sewell and three of his associates flew with us in an airship across France in 1918, then I rode the *New Jersey* with them back across the Atlantic."

"I'm Lewis Puller, Sir." We shook hands. "Sergeant Sewell was my platoon Gunny back at Quantico. We came down here to get our wings. He got his..."

"I heard about what happened to you, Lieutenant. Don't take it personally. Some pretty competent people just can't fly one of these things. And you're competent—I heard about your work in Haiti."

I nodded, "Thank you, Sir. I do what I can."

"All any of us can do," the commander said, "I worked with Major Vandegrift a bit in DC. Good man, good Marine. Both of them up there, Lieutenant," he looked out over the water, "they'll go far..."

"My God," the commander added and pointed.

*****

Jack: In the air

"I was hoping to experience a little aerobatics up here," Major Vandegrift yelled through the gosport.

"Sorry, Sir, but this crate isn't safe doing that stuff anymore," I replied, "We have a couple of civilian Travel Airs we use for that part of the syllabus until we get the new aircraft."

"Which couldn't be too soon, Gunny!"

"You said it, Sir!"

I gently banked the PT- 1 back toward the Station field, passing over Pensacola Beach as we returned.

"Nice beach down there," Major Vandegrift remarked.

"So I've heard, Sir. Never been there. No time."

At that moment, four thousand feet above Pensacola Bay, time very nearly ran out in another way.

I heard a snapping, tearing sound from beneath my feet and forward. Then I saw the entire left-wing assembly, top and bottom both, snap and wrench upward, the top wing breaking right above my head!

The wings were now in an ever-sharpening V and the plane began a vicious roll to the left. I had no time to yell or pray. Something Helen had mentioned to me during our ten days of constant flying came back to me. As the ship rolled to the left, I added however much aileron I had left, and the ship continued to roll on its back.

As it came fully inverted, the left-wing assembly bent back to something roughly resembling normal…and stayed there!

I had no idea how long the wings would stay in that position before they finally snapped off, but as long as they stayed like they were I might have enough control to get the plane down to a crash landing. If the wings broke off, that was it, of course. *Lord, please have Your will….*

A voice interrupted my frantic prayer. "Gunny! Bale out! Save yourself!"

Major Vandegrift's order required an answer and I gave it.

"No, Sir! If I can keep control like this until we get close to the ground, I'll roll her at the last instant. We'll crash, but it won't be from so far up. If the Lord lets us, we may survive!"

At that moment the engine, starved of fuel when upside down, stopped.

I heard Major Vandegrift now, quite clearly.

"I see, Gunny. You do what you think best."

I thought of one more thing. "Yes, sir. Suggest you pray and ask Jesus to save you if He doesn't have you already."

"Er...right."

I kept the crippled ship in an inverted glide as we approached the shore and the airfield beyond. I heard ominous noises and flapping from the wings, but they held well enough to maintain the glide. If the wings stayed on we'd make the field. I fought the effect of blood rushing to my head.

Over the shore, and the field boundary. Grass coming up quickly.

"When we crash, don't release the seat belt until it's all stopped!"

"OK!" the major replied.

As the ship approached the ground, I saw two figures running toward the field. *Timing...*

Now!

I rolled the ship at the last instant toward the bad wing. Investigators said later the upper wingtip made a small furrow in the grass as it rolled past the vertical.

The instant the ship rolled far enough the broken wing folded up completely, and the machine dropped onto the field on its wheels and right-wing. I felt something hit my leg, then blacked out for a moment.

*****

Chesty: the crash scene

I ran ahead of Commander Towers and reached the crash. I found Major Vandegrift still strapped in the shattered fuselage.

"Sir, are you all right?" I panted.

"Fine, Chesty. Go find Jack!"

I ran around the remains of the plane and came to a seat, with Jack still attached.

Jack was semi-conscious, but I knew he wouldn't be for long. The ragged remains of Jack's left lower leg spurted blood like a fire hose.

I whipped off my belt, wrapped it around the remains of the leg just below the knee, and tightened it as tight as I could. The blood slowed to a seep.

"Thanks, sir. Guess that old leg's finally had it," Jack whispered.

I learned in Haiti that the best way to keep a wounded man from shock was to talk to him normally. "It has. Call me Chesty, Gunny. You've earned it and then some today."

Gunny knew the drill too. "And I'm Jack. Looks like I get the same thing Luther has."

"Guess so, Jack. Does it hurt?"

"Little bit. Hurt worse last time, at the Wood. Sounds like help's coming."

I looked up. "Yep. All sorts of gear coming."

"How's the Major?"

I looked over my shoulder and saw Commander Towers helping Major Vandegrift out of the cockpit.

"Looks like he's OK. Commander Towers is helping him."

Jack's voice was noticeably weaker. "Towers? Rode across France with him last time. Old home week here, I guess."

"Rather meet some other way though."

"For sure. Chesty," Jack's voice was fading fast. "Call back to Helen, please. Main 1758 is the school number. Tell her what happened, and that I love her very much. OK?"

"As soon as I can find a phone, Jack. Promise."

"Thanks, Chesty. You know, this seat isn't that uncomfortable..."

Jack faded out.

An hour and a half later I sat with Commander Towers and

Major Vandegrift in the spartan waiting room of the Base Hospital.

"Wretched junk piles," Commander Towers observed, "Admiral Moffett sent me down here to see how the replacement of those things was going. Answer: it's not. It will now, that's for sure!"

Major Vandegrift looked thoughtful. "Gunny wouldn't do any aerobatics in the ship. Said he didn't trust it. Can't blame him, not now." He scratched the bald spot on his head. "You know, he said he'd make sure I didn't need the parachute I didn't have, and he did! I ordered him to bale out but he wouldn't. He flew that wreck close enough to the ground that we survived. Wish he'd been able to walk away from it."

"Don't beat yourself up over it, Archie," Commander Towers replied, "Nothing you could do about what happened. Billy Mitchell may have been a zealot with an axe to grind, but he was right about the equipment we've been using."

"Just before he passed out he asked about you, sir," I said to the Major. "He was very glad he'd been able to save your life."

"And he's getting a writeup for the Navy Cross for it, too!" Major Vandegrift declared, "He ought to get The Medal, but I know that wouldn't fly in DC."

"That'd make three Navy Crosses for him, sir," I said.

"Three?"

"Yes, sir. One for charging a Hun machine gun nest the day Luther carried him back; one for saving his Lieutenant and his men on a speakeasy raid gone bad in San Pedro. He took a slug in the gut and nearly died then too."

"Things seem to happen to the Gunny," Commander Towers observed, "And we need more men like him!"

"Amen," I intoned. It seemed like the thing to say.

The door opened and the doctor on duty came out.

"What news, Doc?" Commander Towers asked.

"We have the blood flow stopped, and the worst of the remains of the leg removed. He needs skilled orthopedic surgery to shape the end of the remaining bone and form the stump his prosthesis will rest on. I don't have the skill or equipment to do that here. The nearest place I'd trust for that job is Walter Reed in Washington. He's not stable enough to transport that far yet."

"What about that unit at Johns Hopkins that did such great work in the war?" Commander Towers asked.

The doctor shook his head. "We've ended our relationship with that hospital, sir. A few months ago. they decided the orthopedist and prosthesis specialists they had there weren't *blue blood* enough for 'em so they fired them!"

"That's crazy," Major Vandegrift remarked.

"I agree, but, begging the gentlemen's pardon, the military doesn't have the corner on stupid."

"Seems like it sometimes," Commander Towers muttered, "So the plan is to get him stable, then transport to Washington? How long will that take?"

"A couple days to get him stable. He doesn't have any other serious injuries so that's a plus. Then two days and nights on a train to DC. I wish we could fly him, but we don't have anything that would make that trip."

"Obviously," Commander Towers intoned.

I got an idea. "Gentlemen, Gunny asked me to call back to Illinois and tell his fiancée what happened. I also feel I should call and talk to the people she flies for part-time. Don Wain has a reputation for being able to do some pretty fantastic things."

"As in Wain Engineering?" Major Vandegrift asked, "They've done some work for the Corps that was just great!"

"Us too," Commander Towers agreed, "especially with aviation. If anyone can get this mess sorted out, they can. We'll sit in on the calls, if you don't mind."

I nodded. "I'd appreciate that, gentlemen. Now to find a phone..."

"I used to be Executive Officer of this station," Commander Towers grinned. "I think I can manage that."

CHAPTER THIRTEEN

Lillian Taylor: Friday, April 2nd, 1926, Noon, Ayers Primary School, lunch meeting

"So how is Dorothea doing?" I asked.

"Another natural," Helen Smiley replied. "Knows her material, relates fine to the children, quiet but effective with discipline. She's a keeper!"

"Excellent!"

Mentor and protégé, we continued to eat our lunch in my office. This was a chance to get away from the commotion of the classroom and catch up on the subjective evaluations which were so important to training good teachers.

"Will she be ready to hire when she graduates?"

"I think so. She's passed all the exercises, and her classroom work is first-rate. She's fine."

"Good," I said, "I need four teachers for Willard in the fall. I want to send her out there." *I need a principal too. Lord,* I prayed to myself. *I leave it to You. Please provide as You see fit.*

Just then the phone rang.

"Lillian Taylor...Yes, Operator, I'll hold...Oh, hello, Lieutenant. How may I help you today?"

Helen was concentrating on her sandwich and did not see my face freeze into an expressionless mask.

"I understand. She is right here in my office. Have her give the phone back to me when you're finished, please. Here she is."

I handed the phone to Helen; she put down her sandwich and took the phone.

"Hello. Oh, Hi, Chesty! How are you?"

I watched Helen carefully as she listened to the Marine Lieutenant on the phone. *Another test of her composure, one I wouldn't wish on anybody,* I thought. Helen's face didn't change, but her eyes suddenly became fixed, unfocused.

"I see, Chesty. Any other injuries?...The Major's OK?...All right. When you see him tell him I love him too. I will give you back to Lillian at this time. Thank you for your report."

Helen gave the phone back to me and sat staring, lunch forgotten.

"Lillian back...Wain Engineering's number is fifteen thirty-one blue...I think they will come up with something, perhaps fly him where he needs to go...Helen and I will go to the Wain offices immediately. We will be back in contact. Thank you for your prompt call, Lieutenant. Good-bye."

I hung up and turned to Helen. "Are you OK enough to travel over to the Auditorium?"

Helen's face was still a mask, but she took a deep breath.

"I can do that. I will hold together for a while yet. Dorothea can take the class for the afternoon."

"I agree. Let's go. I'm driving. We will stop by the classroom on our way out."

We stood up and walked to the door.

*****

Luther: 12:07 PM, the Auditorium office

The office was a bit crowded this Friday afternoon. Seated among the desks and side tables in the office were Don and Jackie, Dick Meriden, Fred Stock, and two recent arrivals, Harmony Ives and Doctor Jennifer Setterdahl. I was there because I couldn't think of anything better to do before my conducting debut that night.

"I can't ever remember being able to sit back and have nothing to do the afternoon of a major concert," Fred remarked.

"Prior planning and all that," Don replied. "Plus not having to go retrieve one of the performers across Iowa."

Amy and Elwood were stationed at the Santa Fe depot to meet the special train carrying the orchestra from Chicago. This time they would be put up at the Broadview overnight. After hearing about Amy and Elwood's honeymoon there Don decided to test the management of the hotel before he made an offer to the owners. An invasion of about a hundred musicians seemed a fine way to do that. Amy and Elwood would also be managing that operation; Fred had already offered his condolences!

"This concert seems very well-organized," Harmony Ives said.

"Got you fooled!" Jackie responded. "We found early on that anything can happen, at the worst possible time, so we try to remember the Lord's in control of all of this and we're just the cogs."

"Like when a power surge blew the organ electrics thirty minutes before the school concert in December," Dick remarked.

"Or that little blizzard while you were on vacation in January," Don retorted with a little grump.

"You made us take that vacation, Don, and looking back on it I'm glad we did. Estelle and I had a second honeymoon while you all were digging out of the blizzard."

"And honestly, I'm glad I made you do it. You guys needed it."

"But we didn't miss your wedding," Dick added.

"Didn't give us a gift," Jackie chimed in.

"Are these people always this snippy?" Harmony asked Fred.

"Oh, no, usually they're much worse!"

The ringing phone interrupted the banter. Jackie answered it.

"Hi, Sherry, what's up..."

The group quieted as Jackie's face changed.

"Roger copy *Flashlight.* Stand by for some outbound traffic in a few. Put him through please."

Jackie turned to us. "It's Chesty Puller—Jack's been hurt at Pensacola."

A moment of gathering worries, then "Good afternoon, Chesty, Jackie here. May I put you on the speakerphone?...OK, wait one..." a flipped switch, then...

"Chesty, we can all hear you now, please state the situation."

We heard Chesty's voice, scratchy but distinctive, through the speaker.

"Good afternoon folks. I wish I had better news. Gunny Sewell took our friend Major Vandegrift up for a familiarization flight this morning. The plane came apart in the air, but Jack got it back to the field for a crash landing. The Major's OK but Jack has lost his left leg just below the knee. The docs here have stabilized him. He doesn't have any other injuries. But he needs to go to Walter Reed for surgery. I understand the doctor who handled this at Johns Hopkins is no longer there, so that's not an option."

"That's right, Chesty," Don Wain announced. "That would be Doctor Jennifer Setterdahl, and her husband made the prostheses. Doctor Setterdahl is sitting in this office right now!"

The quiet on the other end of the line stretched on.

"Chesty, are you there?" Don asked.

We heard something like a sob, then Chesty's voice.

"Understand, Don. That's unbelievable! Jack needs her services very badly, and her husband's too. We have no way to get him out of here quickly, either to Walter Reed or to your folks. I know you've done some pretty remarkable things out there; can you help Jack?"

"We certainly can, and we will," Don intoned. "Does Helen

know?"

"I called her first. Her principal said they were coming over to see you."

Don looked out the office window. "Yes, they're just coming in the door now. Once they get in here let's figure out the logistics of this operation. And I'll cover the expenses."

"Thank you, sir. Commander Towers and Major Vandegrift are here with me. They say they'll set things up down here."

"OK, then. Helen and Lillian have just come in, and everyone's hugging around. Let's get down to business."

*****

Jack: 3:10 PM, Naval Air Station Pensacola Hospital

"The Lord does it again," I whispered.

"What?"

"The Lord, Chesty. The surgeon I need to get my stump ready for a prosthesis is sitting in the office at the moment you called. And her husband, who makes the best prostheses around, is there too. Not a coincidence."

"I don't think I understand this," Chesty said.

Chesty was sitting in my hospital room that afternoon. He'd just explained to me how the Setterdahls found themselves in Galesburg, and what was going to happen the next day. Even though I was still groggy from the anesthetic I understood better than he did.

I had another thought. "Nothing happens by chance, Chesty. Nothing. Doctor Setterdahl gets turned out of Johns Hopkins. She and her husband remember a doctor they met at a conference and contact him. They come out to little Galesburg, Illinois. They fall in love with the place and move there...and are there when I need them."

"It still seems like coincidence to me, Jack. Look what happened to you today."

I knew Chesty didn't know how the Lord works, but I did. The occasional tear I dripped was not sadness.

"The Lord arranged today too. I was allowed to get that ship to the ground in good enough shape to save the Major's life. For some reason, He's decided to change my career. He could have done this at Belleau Wood, or out in San Pedro, but He did not. Now He has. I can accept it, and pray I do what He wants me to."

"Didn't they used to call this kind of wound a *blighty* in the War?"

"As in a ticket back home? Yeah, I guess they did. But the Lord was merciful—I get to do something else, and I can still fly if He wants me to. If Luther can manage organ pedals with his, I ought to be able to handle one big rudder pedal."

Chesty shook his head. "I guess you will, Jack. I wish I had your assurance that things will be all right."

"It's always worked that way for me."

*****

Doctor Jennifer Setterdahl: 9:15 PM, their new home on Willard Street, Galesburg, logistics

"When are you leaving in the morning?" Keith asked.

"Jackie's picking me up at 0500. She's getting me, Helen's picking up Harmony at the hotel. Then we go to Monmouth, wherever that is."

"About fifteen miles west. I looked at a map. When will you be back?"

"If the weather holds, sometime after dark. But we're coming into Galesburg. Jackie says the new field will be ready by then. We'll land by lights. First landing there I guess. If the weather's iffy we either stay at Pensacola or Nashville. Wain Engineering has some sort of aviation shop in Nashville and they'll refuel us. Quite a jaunt, though."

"Not something people do every day," my husband remarked.

"Jackie said we'd probably set several world speed and distance records tomorrow, even though we won't publicize what we did. This is an ordinary means of travel *uptime*, but not here."

Keith shrugged as we got into bed. "I'll stay here and set up the workshop at Cottage; that's enough excitement for me."

"That's fine," I said, "This is going to be an all-female expedition anyway."

"That oughta rattle a few of the brass down at Pensacola."

I chuckled. "The plane will surprise 'em; then when we step out that oughta knock their puttees off!"

"Do they still wear those stupid things, Jenn?"

"Not after we arrive!"

"Jenn, you're being silly…and I love you! You know, though, it's going to be an awfully short night."

"Longer than the ones who went to the concert. They weren't going to get out till about eleven."

Keith pulled up the covers. "I'm glad you decided to skip it. Wise choice, in view of tomorrow."

"Don says we can hear it in a recording next week, that's enough for me."

"Hey, Jenn, we better get to sleep."

Jennifer looked at her husband. "What's the hurry? I'm not driving…or flying."

"Good point, Hon."

*****

Jackie: 0030, Saturday, April 3rd, 1926, a very short night

"Here we are," I remarked, "Going to bed at the same time as all the concert-goers but we never saw the concert!"

"I guess irony can be pretty ironic sometimes...*Eeep*!"

"Easier to poke when you're undressed, surely."

"Let's not go there, Love," Don muttered as he hoisted the shih tzus onto the bed, "We'll get to hear it, plus Rick and Jeff ran cameras from the sound booth. And Amy's a natural master of ceremonies."

"Amy's always presented herself well," I replied, "and she says she's very satisfied with married life. Elwood has the *knack*, she says."

Don snorted. "Another talent we didn't know Elwood had. And Rick said the sound was good enough for commercial records."

"Think Brunswick will bite?" I asked.

"I've been talking to Bill Brophy," Don replied, "He's sold on our recording methods. That Light Ray process they have is worthless and he knows it. He's still rumbling about selling the business to us."

"Do we really want it?"

"I've been praying about it, Precious. We could use it to help our musician friends and get the public ready for advanced electronics. I'd like to have the equipment out there before the crash."

"That's a topic for later, Love. Right now, I have to get to sleep. Gonna be a long flight to Pensacola."

"I've done that flight. It's very long," Don mused, "How's the weather look?"

"Sherry says unusually good, with a rare tailwind on the return flight. We may make it back nonstop."

"Don't push it, Love," Don said as he crawled under the covers, "I'm glad you had Marisol come in from *uptime* to be your copilot. She'll be fresh for the flight. I wouldn't want to trust Helen this time."

"Oh? Just because she came apart at suppertime and Lucille

had to stick her in their guest room tonight?"

"Exactly," Don said, moving Theodore to the outside of the bed, "She's too whacked emotionally to be safe flying this time. Let her help Jennifer and Harmony in the back. And I repeat, don't play if there's bad weather. The clinic at Nashville can keep Jack stable overnight."

"I know," I said as I joined Don and shut off the light, "Doctor Denton and the clinic staff are alerted in case that happens."

Don snorted. "How did we get docs in the company with such funny names?"

"The Lord's sense of humor maybe," I replied. Then I shivered slightly.

"What is it, Love?" Don asked.

"I think the stress of Jack's accident, the flight planning, and the concert just hit me. Hold me please, Love. I need your warmth."

"You've never asked for that before, come on in." Don opened his arms.

"Thanks, Love. This helps."

"You'll be fine tomorrow, Precious," Don whispered in my ear, "You have Marisol as copilot, Jennifer and Harmony to mind Jack, and Jack for Helen to focus on. Plus a lot of people backing you up with prayer and support. No sweat."

"Thanks, Love, I needed that."

We were still in each others' arms when the Bose wave radio kicked on at 0415.

CHAPTER FOURTEEN

Mimi Conger, Saturday, April 3rd, 1926, 8:05 AM again, her room at Cottage.

"Good morning, Mimi."

"Good morning, Matthew," I replied. My voice was stronger than it had been two days before.

"I'm sorry I wasn't here yesterday, but I was stuck in negotiations and closing for a property lease at the end of North Seminary Street. Don's leased a field so we can fly direct to town, and not have to base in Monmouth."

"Jackie told me when she visited yesterday."

"She visited?"

"Just for a moment. She wanted to tell me where you were so I wouldn't worry."

"Oh...did you worry?"

"No. Did you miss me?"

Matt turned a bit red. "Yes, I did." *Another test*, I thought, *He's coming along nicely.*

"If you will transfer me to the chair please, you can tell me the news while I eat."

"Sure," Matt replied, and the drill began.

Matt unrolled the two-inch-wide webbed belt and put it on the bed. He then grasped my shoulders through the cotton gown and gently helped me sit up in bed and swing my legs over the side. So far, so good.

I braced myself upright with my arms. I hadn't been able to do that the week before. Matt threaded the belt between my arms and body, and carefully positioned it. Since my incision wasn't fully healed yet the belt had to be very carefully placed in a narrow zone over my lower rib cage, above the area of the incision, and below the bottom of certain items I noticed were returning to their normal volume after my brush with death. I saw where Matt's eyes were focused.

"They're still breasts, Matthew," I said with a grin. "I have given you permission to notice them, as long as you don't catch them in the belt."

Matt blushed deeply, as he always did. There was no other way to get me safely from bed to chair at this point, so without a word he placed the belt and tightened it. He grasped the belt to either side of me and prepared to count down for the *stand-pivot transfer*.

"Ready?" he asked.

"On your count."

"One, two,..."

In a transfer of this sort, the two people face each other. They must be as close as possible, to ensure safe lifting and reduce the effect of the other person's weight on the lifting person's back. If they can, the person being transferred wraps their arms around the lifter.

Matt was skilled and very careful. He lifted me with one gentle motion, and I helped balance myself by standing while bearing a little of my weight. The transfer was completely normal...except when I came up to the level of Matt's face, I presented him with what is known colloquially as a French kiss.

Matt's eyebrows rose into his hairline and his posture stiffened. We continued the transfer, in spite of the added detail, while he assisted in the extra activity.

After about thirty seconds we ended the kiss, and Matt gently placed me into the chair. We were both breathing a little heavier than usual. He released the gait belt and sat down on the bed. We looked at each other.

"That's an interesting grin on your face, Matthew," I remarked.

"I see you are also grinning," Matt replied.

We sat quietly and caught our breath.

"Why?" Matt finally asked.

"It seemed like a good idea at the time," I replied

"Does it still?"

I could feel my cheeks flush. "Oh yes, it does."

I prayed for my Cream of Wheat and poached eggs, then dug in. By this time I was able to eat by myself unless the meal was long.

Matt told me about the injury to Helen's fiancé, and his return to Galesburg today. He described the concert and the preparations for the long flight to Florida.

We seemed to be just a little hurried in the meal but took our time with my transfer back to the bed, now that we had something extra to look forward to.

*****

Jackie, 10:35 AM, approaching Nashville, Tennessee

Marisol Baughman checked her instruments again. "On course, forty miles out, TACAN knows we're here."

"Nothing like a good 'old uptime tactical air navigation system," I chuckled, "Shall I give 'em a shout?"

"*Si*," our designated pilot in command replied, "perhaps we will catch them dozing."

"Nashville base, Wain three calling company, over."

Marisol and I looked at each other. "One ringy-dingy," I muttered.

"Wain three, Nashville base. Reading you loud and clear, Over."

I winked. "Nashville, Wain three four zero miles out. Angels eight, speed one forty, fuel forty percent. Request approach clearance, over."

"Wain three, company. We have you on radar and TACAN. Altimeter three zero point zero zero, wind north at eight, CAVU. Ground temperature fifty-three degrees. No traffic in the area, cleared for approach, runway seven five, length twelve thousand. Over."

"Wain three, thank you. ETA fifteen minutes. Request refuel per flight plan, over."

"You got it Big Bird, call at five miles. Nashville out."

"Thank you, Wain three out."

I turned to Marisol. "A little lax in their radio discipline."

Marisol grinned. "What radio discipline? We are the only ones with radios, much less air traffic control."

"We'll have rules next year if Herbert Hoover gets his way—and he usually does." I pulled out the before landing checklist.

"*Pobre Herbert*, poor Herbert," Marisol replied, "All the power he has as Commerce Secretary will go *poof* when he becomes President and the Depression hits."

"Yeah," I replied, "never know what hit him." I flipped the intercom switch. "You ladies awake back there?"

"Where are we?" a groggy voice replied.

"About to land in Nashville, Harmony. Be down in about fifteen minutes. You three OK back there?"

"May I take the landing please?"

"No, Helen, you may not," I replied, "This trip you're the designated morale officer for Jack!"

"Oh, ok an' phooey!"

"That's the spirit, Helen," I said with a chuckle, "How about you, Jenn?"

"I'm still amazed at the view from up here," Doctor Setterdahl said, "could use the facilities though."

"You didn't use the porta-potty?"

"Not unless we have to, Jackie!"

"Perfectly safe, guys. Just not private."

"How will we use it when we get Jack in here?" Harmony asked.

"*Yo recomiendo* either Helen smothers him with kisses, or you cover his head with a bag."

Marisol beat me to the answer.

*****

Helen: a few minutes later.

"Nice place," Jennifer remarked.

We had a half-hour to kill while the dash-3 was refueled and checked over for the flight to Pensacola. We used the facilities in the main hangar and picked up our box lunches sent over from the cafeteria.

Why is this hangar so huge?" Harmony asked.

"We have uptime transport aircraft coming in here at night," Jackie replied, "They bring stuff that's too big to send through the transfer rooms. We need to keep them out of sight in the daytime. They taxi in one end of the hangar and out the other."

"People hear them come in and leave, but do not see them," Marisol added.

As we headed back to the plane we stopped at a disassembled form in a corner of the hangar.

"What is all that?" Harmony asked.

Jackie stopped, looked, and grinned. "The first of our new aircraft from Germany, ladies!"

The airframe sitting on a large framework with wheels looked like a larger F 13. A radial piston engine sat on a wheeled cart next to the plane, and various wheels and tubes sat on the floor under it.

"So that's the W-34?" I asked.

"Yep. Larger than the F- 13, higher gross weight. We're setting it up to bolt on a series of engines. This one's getting a Pratt and Whitney Hornet radial from uptime to start."

"Aren't we consulting with them?" I asked.

Jackie nodded. "We're reviewing their Wasp design and making suggestions for improvements. They're just about to test the first completed engines. They don't know how much we know."

I snorted. "Bet they find out eventually." Jackie smiled at that.

"What's with the wheels?" Jennifer asked.

"We're putting in retractable landing gear, good for about thirty miles an hour more airspeed. We're taking them from the Grumman F6F fighter of the next war. Strong and simple."

"Wow. When do we get it?" I asked.

"First delivery scheduled for June, if flight test goes OK. We'll see."

"I'm confused," Jennifer remarked.

"I'm impressed," Harmony said.

"I'm impatient! Let's get going! I want to fly the next leg." I declared loudly.

"No!" the others shot back, "You're the morale officer," Jackie added with The Look.

CHAPTER FIFTEEN

Jack: 3:15 PM (Eastern Time), NAS Pensacola ramp, waiting for a lift home

"You ready to go, Gunny?" the doctor asked.

"Ready as I'll ever be, Sir," I replied.

"How're you draining?"

"Fine, Doctor. Both ways."

I lay on a stretcher, wrapped in blankets. Clipped to the outer blanket were two bottles with rubber tubing coming out of them and snaking under the blanket. One led to a drain at the end of my former left lower leg; the other led to a nifty device called an indwelling catheter. Both bottles were collecting what they ought.

Commander Towers came out of the operations hut. "They're about ten minutes out. Glad Don Wain called us this morning. They really *do* want kerosene for fuel. Gunny, what kind of motor does that airplane have?"

"Sir, all I know is it is very experimental. I've never been allowed to see it." I told the absolute truth. I wasn't about to explain they wouldn't let me see it so I'd be able to dodge that question!

"Say, Gunny," Chesty said, "please let me know when you're getting married. I'd be honored to be in the swords with you and the others."

"Sure will, Lieutenant. Helen will let you know if I can't."

Major Vandegrift looked over at me lying on the stretcher. "Gunny, I'd like to come out for that too, if you wouldn't mind." "Of course, Sir, I'd be honored to have you join in." *This could be an interesting swords detail,* I thought.

"Me too, if I can shake loose," Commander Towers added.

"Of course, sir," I said. *Very interesting swords detail.*

"You gentlemen may not get swatting position, though," Chesty commented. "Sergeant Barlow has The Medal, and that trumps rank. Plus, I'm sure Captain Heckel from Galva will be there if he's well enough. He got The Medal at Cold Harbor."

"Civil War? I'd love to meet him!" Major Vandegrift said.

"I'm sure he'd be happy to talk with you, sir," Chesty said, "I learned a lot from him at Luther's wedding."

"You also got some cooking lessons, Lieutenant," I added, "I hear Deborah Kittridge and Pastor are now at Chambers Street Baptist in Galesburg, where Helen goes."

"If she does another dinner, I'm in!" Chesty replied. "I learned how to make puff pastry from her."

"Talking food at a time like this. I like the way you gentlemen think." Commander Towers observed.

"What's that whining buzz?" Major Vandegrift asked.

"That's the Wain aircraft, sir," I replied.

The anticipation of seeing my betrothed overrode the pain from my leg.

*****

Jackie: a few minutes later, time to phone home

"Hey, Precious, how's it going?"

"Just fine, Love. We're on time, fuel consumption is as predicted, the weather's fine. We're grabbing some box lunches and using the facilities. They're feeding us kerosene. A couple of senior officers really want to see under the cowling."

"Don't let 'em, love," Don replied, "Tell 'em to come up here and we'll brief them on the experimental engine. Cowl locks are your friend."

"I'll do that, Don. By the way, the officers are Jack Towers and Archie Vandegrift. Chesty's here too but he's staying by Jack and Helen."

"Three big names from the next war. I think they'll show up here eventually. But how's Jack?"

"Jenn says he's doing remarkably well considering what happened to him yesterday. Vitals are good, only a little seepage. She hasn't looked at the wound yet. The leg's wrapped up like a mummy."

"Good, Love. And before I forget, confirm you'll be flying into the North Seminary Street field. The grass is fine, and I have temporary lights rigged up. Runway thirty-six hundred feet and laid out at three hundred degrees magnetic. Please call in early and we'll give you more details."

"OK, Love, we can do that. Figure about nine local this evening I think, a bit later if Nashville slows us."

"What did you think of the W-34?"

"Too early to tell. May still use this bird for fast trips."

"Understood. We need to get the dash 3 in for a retractable gear install sometime. We'll see how it goes."

"And now we gotta go. Love you, Mister Wain!"

"Love you too, Precious! See you!"

"Bye."

*****

Jackie: shortly after takeoff

"You're on your way home, Love!" Helen said over the intercom.

"I am very glad, Sweetheart."

"Remember you two, we can all hear you!"

"Thank you, Harmony, for that little reminder," I said, "Flaps up please."

"Flaps up. Trimming ship. *ITT* muy bueno."

"Thanks, Marisol. And away we go!"

Marisol and I had traded seats in the cockpit and I was now pilot in command. We rigged a headset/microphone on Jack as he lay on the mattress and board crammed into the cabin. I wasn't worried about the weight or balance, but we'd have a hard time getting out of the plane in a hurry. The three ladies in back could reach the patient to check on him, and crawl over each other to use the porta-potty. I was sure that thrilled them no end.

I keyed the mic again. "Ladies…and Jack, we'll start out cruising at eight thousand again. Sherry and the Weather Bureau predicted a strong southeast wind at that altitude, which would help our speed. We'll still plan to land and refuel at Nashville, but if we catch the right winds Marisol and I might reconsider that. Dish out the box lunches whenever and use the porta-potty as needed. Jack, please close your eyes while they do that."

"Right," Jack remarked.

"Who brought the paper bag?" Jennifer asked.

"Hey! I'll shut my eyes!" Jack's voice was weak but insistent.

"Remember, Love, you're badly outnumbered," Helen added.

"Yes, Dear."

I had to explain why Helen and I broke out laughing. The others had never seen AP Kittridge's schtick.

Two and a half hours later Marisol and I engaged the new autopilot while we calculated some flight data. I used the venerable celluloid *whiz wheel* calculator while Marisol tapped numbers into an iPad. We scribbled numbers on a pad in our laps.

"Switch?" I asked.

"Si," Marisol replied, and we swapped instruments. Another couple of minutes and I set the iPad down and scribbled on the paper pad.

"What've you got?" I asked.

"Fifteen percent iPad, fourteen percent whiz wheel."

"I got the same," I replied, "Fifteen percent isn't much of a fuel reserve, but it's consistent and we know the tank gauges are accurate."

"And the kerosene they gave us is clean also. No water," Marisol added.

"Yeah. Trying to burn water would ruin our whole evening." I glanced out at the setting sun off to our left. "You feel comfortable going non-stop?"

"Si, Jackie," Marisol replied, "Everything looks good, tailwind is adding forty miles per hour to our speed. Alternate airfields?"

I grinned. "Peoria, or Monmouth...or a well-elevated farm field."

"Dios no lo quiera! God forbid!" Marisol replied, "We should do well with a lighted airfield."

"Concur," I said, "Please let Nashville know, and have them call in our revised arrival time."

"What's going on up there?" Helen asked.

"We just decided to fly straight through to Galesburg. The winds are helping us, and we'll save nearly an hour."

"Good enough for me, Jackie," Helen replied, "Does that suit you, Love?"

"Not as much time to nap, Sweetheart."

"I'll give you a nice long knuckle nap, Mister!"

"And he loves you for it."

"Thank you so much, Jennifer!"

*****

Jackie: shortly after 9 PM central time, over central Illinois

"Wain 3 calling Company Galesburg, over," Marisol spoke into the radio.

"We're sixty miles out but they might hear us," I remarked.

The reply came, a bit scratchy but understandable. "Wain 3, this is Company. Reading you three by. How far out are you, over."

"That's Don. Please take the ship, I'll talk to him. Copilot's airplane."

"Copilot's airplane," Marisol repeated.

I picked up the microphone. "Company, Wain 3, Six Zero miles out, bearing from you about one seven zero. Altitude eight thousand, speed one sixty, fuel twenty percent. Five pax and one patient patient on board, over."

"Roger, Big Bird, Top Chop actual, and I caught that last remark, over."

Our passengers could hear the exchange and I heard giggling.

"On the ball, Top Chop. Request conditions at Galesburg, please, over."

Don answered, all business this time.

"Wain three, altimeter two niner niner four, wind one five zero at thirty, gusts forty. Temperature thirty-eight degrees. Visibility eight miles with slight haze. Temporary beacon at center of field; other lights will come on at your word, over."

"Wain three roger. Any known traffic?"

"Negative, Wain three. Nobody knows we're here yet."

"Roger, Company. Now over Peoria at angels eight. Will start descent past the city. Which corner of Galesburg should I aim for again, over."

"Wain three, the northeast corner. Field is west of both Q lines coming out of northeast corner of town. East border of field is on the west side of the Q Rock Island line, over."

"Roger, Company. Northeast corner. Will check in at five miles. Three out."

"Company out."

"OK, everyone, make sure your seat belts are snug, all the gear is stowed, especially the porta-potty!"

"Everything's fine back here, Jackie," Jennifer announced.

"All gear secured," Harmony added.

"Patient impatiently waits for landing."

"One poke, my betrothed! Hey Jackie, do you realize I haven't flown as a passenger since Slim Lindbergh brought me home after that DH4 crash?"

"Let's pray you never need to be a passenger for that reason again." I pronounced, "One bale-out in a career is quite enough."

"You know that from experience," Helen added.

"Amen," I said, "Starting descent, one thousand feet per minute, to one thousand feet. May I take it please, Marisol?"

"*Si*, Jackie. Pilot's airplane."

"Pilot's airplane," I repeated.

A few minutes later the lights of Galesburg appeared on the horizon off the nose of the plane to the left.

I nodded to Marisol. "Company, Wain three. Five miles out, angels one. Speed one forty. Request runway lights."

"Wain three, company. Lighting up now, Marisol."

A moment later lights glowed to either side of the runway path. The entire grass runway was bathed in a cool white light. Lines of red lights marked each end of the strip, and two flashing lights marked the designated starting end.

I picked up the mic. "Company, Wain three. There we have the longest extension cord setup in the world. Or the longest string of Christmas lights ever!"

"Both, Love! Please bring the present in. we're ready for him!" I knew what that meant.

We made one circuit of the field, then slipped over the few houses in the area and touched down smoothly on the grass runway. I put the prop into reverse for a few seconds, then taxied slowly over to where the spectators were gathered.

Several lights on poles around the parking area came on...and so did a lighted sign. I heard the others start to cry as they looked out the windows. I knew what the sign said:

> *Welcome Home Gunnery Sergeant Sewell!!*
> *We all love you very much*
> *(but not half as much as Helen does!)*

CHAPTER SIXTEEN

Jack: Easter Sunday, April 4th, 1926, 1 PM, Cottage Hospital operating theatre one, Man of the Hour

"Happy Easter, Darling," Helen whispered into my ear.

"Never spent an Easter like this, Love," I whispered back, "I feel like a pincushion, or maybe an insect pinned to a board."

"I'll pin you, Love on our wedding night!" I don't think anyone else heard Helen's whisper, but I did!

I lay on a table in a room with white tile walls. I couldn't remember ever being in a room lit so well, and so evenly. The room was chilly; the blanket covering some of me helped but didn't make me comfortable.

Several serious-looking men and women gathered around my table. They pointed, poked, and talked. The focus of their attention was the part of my body formerly occupied by my left lower leg. The area was unwrapped and seeped onto a towel. It hurt some, but they'd given me medication to ease the pain, so I was pleasantly fuzzy.

The talk around the table was laced with long, strange words. I understood the jargon well enough. They were figuring out how to cut and shape the remains of my lower leg into a stump the prosthesis would fit on. The outcome was well worth the discomfort. They also paid a lot of attention to my knee, poking and feeling around it. I figured the swelling was part of the injury.

For fun, I counted the professionals who were examining me. Doctors John Bohan and Jennifer Setterdahl. Gloria Hodges and recent arrival Harmony Ives also watched the proceedings; from time to time, Gloria would whisper in Harmony's ear, and she'd write on a tablet she carried. Doctor Setterdahl's husband Keith watched closely; he would make the prosthesis to fit the stump the doctors would build.

Jackie stopped in as our party began; she said she had an appointment with Doctor Bohan and he'd asked her to join us. And finally my favorite examiner, Helen.

After several minutes of hushed discussion, the group gathered around the foot (my foot) of the table. Helen stayed by my head and stroked my hair. She knew how to put me at ease.

"We'll wait for a moment while the couple enjoys this tender moment," Jennifer said with a grin.

"OK, we're ready now," I finally whispered.

"Not quite," Helen said and kissed me again.

"Now we're ready," she finished as the others chuckled.

"All right," Doctor Setterdahl shifted to her clinical voice. "Here's what we're going to do tomorrow. We'll smooth off the remaining bone, put a fold of skin, thick as we can make it, over the end of the remaining bone. We'll shape it to give you the best protection we can, then let it heal. When it's healed, Keith will take a mold of the stump and build a prosthesis to fit it. We'll work on getting the fit and function as close to perfect as we can make it. Our goal is to have you be able to function just like Luther."

I couldn't resist. "I'll be able to play the organ...Eeep?"

"Thanks, Helen, he needed that," Doctor Setterdahl said, then she frowned. "We need to tell you about what else we've found. Your knee is very close to the start of the injury. We think it may have also been damaged when the injury occurred. In particular, the anterior cruciate ligament may have been severed. That ligament makes your lower leg bend forward and backward. It's very important because if it's destroyed your mobility with the prosthesis will be reduced."

"Can you tell if the knee itself is damaged?" Jackie asked.

"No, and that's a problem," Jennifer replied, "There's too much swelling for the X-ray machine to see through the knee. We're going to have to open up the knee during surgery to see what's in there."

"Could he lose the knee?" Helen asked.

"Yes," Jennifer replied, "if it is too damaged to repair, or has osteomyelitis, bone infection, it'll have to go. That would make the recovery, and your ability to walk, much more complicated. We don't want to see that."

"Doctor Setterdahl," Jackie interrupted, "May I see you, along with Jack and Helen, privately after we're through here?"

"Of course, Jackie," Jennifer replied, then gave a quick wink, "Any more questions?"

"Seriously, how long do you figure I'll be healing before I get the prosthesis?" I asked.

Keith spoke softly. "Depending on how that knee turns out, if everything goes perfectly and you heal without infection, figure at least two months. I have heard of people getting them sooner. But getting the stump safely healed is the first priority. If I were you, I'd concentrate on other things—like getting married—and let the healing come as it comes."

"Read your mind, did he?" Helen asked.

I just smiled.

A couple minutes later Helen was pushing me down the hall on a narrow bed with wheels. Jackie helped guide the front of the contraption; Doctors Bohan and Setterdahl brought up the rear, still discussing my case, I guess.

At a corner, the table lurched as we almost ran into a large man pushing a thin woman with dark curly hair in a wheelchair.

"Well, hello, you two!" Jackie spoke first, "So glad to see you up and about, Mimi."

"Afternoon, folks," the man remarked. "Mimi, I don't believe you've met Doctor Jennifer Setterdahl, orthopedic surgeon, and Gunnery Sergeant Jack Sewell, USMC, the fellow lying down on the job. This is Mimi Conger, a...good friend."

"And the man pushing her is Matt Plotczyc of Wain Engineering," Helen added. I thought I'd seen him before.

The folks shook hands, except I just waved and smiled.

"I've wanted to meet the man who stole Helen's heart," Mimi said. "And I'm pleased to meet you, Doctor Setterdahl, and witness something I've heard about but never experienced."

"What's that?" Jennifer asked.

"A paradox."

I'd never seen two doctors laugh so hard.

*****

Helen: a few minutes later, sorting out

Doctor Bohan left us at the door to Jack's room. Jack and I, with Doctor Setterdahl and Jackie, entered the room. Jackie helped transfer Jack to the bed.

"I'll only stay a minute," Jackie announced, "but what I have to say John Bohan shouldn't hear. I gather there's a real possibility Jack may lose the knee too, right?"

Jennifer looked at Jack as she spoke. "That's right, Jackie. Jack, I don't have a good feeling about your knee. I think it sustained internal damage when the leg came off. I'm not sure we can repair it if it's damaged. We may have to remove it."

Jack moved his mouth around. "So you're saying I might have some sort of trick knee put into the prosthesis? I've seen those before. They're hard to get used to."

"Before you answer that, Jenn, I need to say my piece," Jackie displayed the sort of frown I'd seen before on Marine officers, "I think you need some help. At our facility in Hoople, we have an orthopedic surgeon named Bob Meister. He retired there from uptime, but he's fully trained in this stuff and would be happy to lend a hand. We also have a selection of artificial joints, again from uptime. We could have one installed, either with the lower leg stump or on the prosthesis. They're not perfect, but they usually work quite well. What do you think?"

"Artificial joints?" Jennifer's eyes widened, "We've been trying to develop those for decades! They never work. And yours do?"

"Yep," Jackie replied, "May we call Doctor Meister in for a consult? He can bring a selection of joints along and be ready if needed."

"Won't Doctor Bohan see what we're doing? And can you get Doctor Meister here before tomorrow?"

Jackie nodded. "Yes, to both. We'll tell him it's experimental, and he'll believe us. So far he's kept his suspicions about us to himself."

"Jack, what do you say to this?" Jennifer asked.

"Love, may we go ahead with the doctor from Hoople?"

He knows to ask me, I thought to myself, then replied, "Yes!" and kissed my broken Marine.

"Let's do it," Jack said when we came up for air.

"All right, kids," Jackie announced, "Jenn, let's go over to my office and make a few calls, shall we?"

"Lead on! We'll let you know what's happening when," Jennifer said as she followed Jackie out the door.

I sat in the chair next to the bed. Jack put his hand in mine. As I sat there, I began to feel very strange. I felt light-headed, almost dizzy, then my stomach started to dance. I jumped up and barely made it to the bathroom before my stomach turned inside-out and I deposited its contents into the commode.

"What is going on, Love?" Jack called, "Should I hit the call light?"

"No, no, not yet," I muttered between deposits, "I think I know what this is."

A few minutes later I flushed the commode and washed my hands. I passed a wet paper towel over my mouth and another one around my sweating face. I looked in the mirror. *Bad, but not sick,* I thought, *I've done this before.*

I walked slowly back to the chair and sat down. Jack looked at me with a frown of worry. "What is wrong, Dear? You look really sick."

"It's not that kind of sickness, Jack," I replied softly, "I do this when something is really bothering me and I'm not sure what's going to happen. Usually happens a couple of days later, when I've had time to think. It'll go away when I talk about it, when the Lord gives me peace it'll be taken care of. This is the third day after all this, your accident, the flight happened. It's coming out now."

Jack took my hand again. "OK, Love, spill it. It's the accident, isn't it?"

I thought for a minute. "No, sweetheart, that isn't it. I think it's me afraid you won't be able to stay in the Marines if the surgery runs into problems. We'll go to your next base, then they'll let you go and neither of us will have a job. I don't think I can handle that!"

I was crying now. Jack couldn't take me in his arms, but he took my hand in both of his. "We're not going anywhere, Love. This injury means I will be retired with a pension from the Marines. With this kind of injury, that's automatic. I'll be a civilian, guaranteed!"

I stared at my husband to be. "You know that? Already? And you're not upset?"

"Sure, Helen, and I'm really not upset. Listen, when I got shot up at Belleau Wood, I had to face this possibility. My leg took months to heal, then I got appendicitis and was really sick. I could have been retired for disability then…but I wasn't. And I worked it through in my mind, the Lord helped me to understand He was calling the shots, and He wanted me to stay in the Corps."

"I'm not sure I understand. You knew this could happen to you?"

"Yes," Jack replied, "Then when I got shot out in San Pedro I didn't know if I would live or die for a while there. Again, I took a long time to heal. I could've been retired that time too…but I wasn't. And that time I thought through what would happen to me if I got retired. I didn't have you then, of course, and I didn't have the flying I could do in civilian life, but thanks to Luther's pa I knew I was set OK for money, and I figured I could find something to keep busy. But the Lord let me stay in the Corps again."

Something occurred to me, finally. "So…if you are retired you can stay here instead of going off to duty someplace." As I said that the whole business clicked into place. "And you can stay here. I can stay here. We can get married and," I cried harder, "I can keep my job at Ayers and not let anybody down!"

I buried my head in Jack's mattress and cried. I felt Jack put his hand on my hair, stroking it.

"I thought you understood all that, sweetheart," he whispered near my ear, "You seemed so normal, so matter-of-fact, I thought you'd figured all that out and it didn't bother you. I should have known that was you holding it together for me. Now it's all come down on you at once! Let it out, Love, but know we're together like we said we'd be, just here instead of at some base out in no man's land. I'm here, Helen, and I'm staying."

I don't know why I remember what Jack said, seeing I was crying my eyes out at the time. But I do remember…and eventually I stopped crying and looked up at my betrothed.

"My stomach's not upset anymore, Love," I remarked.

"Good," Jack replied, "but now I have to use the bedpan."

We laughed as he pushed the call light button.

*****

Matt: same time, different room.

"Good friend?"

I winced when Mimi said that, and my stomach started the long descent to my toes. I knew as soon as I introduced her that way. She would call me on it...with good reason. It was the first term that entered my mind when we almost collided.

"That's a baseline, Mimi."

"Is there more?"

My reply to her question didn't sound any better than the introduction.

We looked at each other.

The question we had both tiptoed around the last few weeks now appeared: imminent, pressing, and incredibly important.

On Amy's face, questioning for sure, maybe fear, maybe love. I couldn't tell.

On my face,... what? Uncertainty? Fear...fear of what? Commitment? All of the above, I thought.

Suddenly I remembered what I must say to this incredible woman.

"Mimi, I remember the last time I talked with Grace, before I left Washington to go sort out *Cyclops*. She was bedfast, in great pain,

We had hired help, and Pam Wain, Don's late wife, stepped in too. Despite her pain, Grace spoke to me clearly."

Amy just looked at me, face impassive. I plunged on.

"She said, 'Matthew, by the time you get back I will be gone to Jesus. Let me tell you what will happen. You will grieve long and hard. You will take the offer the Admiral has made, retire, and go to work for him. And someday...you will meet someone you can help, and you will marry. You are so sweet, Matthew. You won't smother the woman, just like you have not smothered me. You will know who this is when you meet her.'"

Mimi's face remained frozen, unmoving. I was an emotional wreck; I had no idea how much of it showed. *You're in the pot now*, I thought, *Lord, please see me through!*

I staggered on.

"I haven't found any woman who affected me enough to make what Grace predicted to happen. Until now." I noticed my hands were shaking as I took a breath. "Mimi Conger, will you marry me?"

"I might."

"What?" I blurted that one word out before everything in my mind froze. I could feel a pounding in my ears, my head spun like it did when I had to climb the mast of the old *Monongahela* at the Naval Academy.

"I might," Mimi continued. She crossed her arms over that wonderful chest as I felt the floor tilt then right itself. "You might have noticed I live in two different worlds. A teacher and Principal has to be calm, logical, incisive. It's a good disguise," She gripped the arm of the wheelchair, "for when I feel overwhelmed. Nobody knows I'm making it up as I go along."

She sniffled and reached for a tissue. "Underneath my veneer, there's the *emotional* me. Up to a few months ago a proposal like you just made would have put me curled up in your lap instantly. I'm not sure how to go about romance now that I belong to Christ, but I do know things are different."

I sat, heart in my throat, as Mimi spoke.

"Here's some history I haven't told you. My father walked out when I was six. My mother worked two jobs to keep us afloat. I worked as soon as I was old enough. I got a scholarship to attend Lombard and worked like a dog to keep it. My mother died in the influenza—by then I was Principal at Silas. There wasn't much time for affection when I was growing up, and I was used to being alone. But I dreamed of having someone to love me and who I could love back. I found I could flirt with men... and sometimes I got a response. So when I was away from the school, the town, I would practice my skills. That creep who got me pregnant was the first one to accomplish that...but not the first one who could have. I was looking for love in several wrong places."

I remembered something from years before and snorted before I could catch myself.

"Something wrong, Matthew?"

"No...yes...I just remembered something from when I joined the company and went uptime for orientation."

"I see. We'll discuss it later," Mimi said, "The personality I'm talking about is emotional, sensory, acts on the feelings of the moment. That's how I am deep down, Matthew. I had to suppress, work around all that when I became a Principal. But now," she took a tissue, "I'm not a Principal anymore. But I have to act like one to make sure I never give my heart away to someone who will use me and break it, ever again. Like you, Matthew, I must execute my *due diligence* calmly, objectively, in order to protect myself. Do you understand me?"

"Yes, Mimi, I do," I shifted to my *Naval officer* persona, "I lived the same way, but more openly in the Navy. Until I trusted Christ I behaved like the typical sailor, a girl in every port, and I knew how to make the rounds." I knew I was turning red.

So did Mimi. "I see your embarrassment, Matthew. And this changed when you met Grace?"

"It changed over the months after I trusted Christ," I said, "I met Grace about a year later. She wasn't beautiful on the outside, but she was amazing on the inside. I fell for her like I'd never fallen before. Even through the illness, the pain, the stress of moving away from her culture to strange towns, and stranger people, she showed how perfectly she was named. And I could never put anything past her, nor did I want to. Does any of this make sense? I feel like I'm just rambling."

"It does," Mimi replied, "and now I have a question to ask you. You know what the Lord had to do to drag me to Him. I would have kicked and screamed but I was too sick. I could do nothing but decide, ask, and trust."

I'd never heard the conversion experience summed up like that before...and she was right. I almost missed her question.

"So how did it happen for you? You were in the navy, living like a sailor, officer type, lost like me. How did He finally get you?"

I got goosebumps all over as I remembered that blessed, horrifying day.

"OK, Mimi, you asked for it. I'll try to skip some of the details. Naval officers tend to hide in their details."

"Is that what they call your skivvies?"

I snorted so hard I had to reach for a tissue. "Mimi, you got me again! This is serious."

"Oh, I know," Mimi smiled, "but I never can resist a good straight line. Back to your story—I'll stop you if you get too wordy."

"How I know," I tossed the tissue in the wastebasket. "I was assistant navigator on the battleship *Oregon* at the battle of Santiago de Cuba in the Spanish War. At the end of the battle, we ran down the Spanish cruiser *Cristóbal Colón.* Her captain beached her on one of the islands and surrendered. Our skipper wanted to pull her off the beach and take her home as a prize. He detailed me and twenty men to go aboard the ship, check it over, and try to relight the boilers. We rowed over to her and climbed aboard. While the others were working topside I volunteered to go below and check out the machinery. OK so far?"

"I'm still with you. Go on."

"OK. I'm down in the boiler room, hot, dark, dripping. All of a sudden I felt the thing move. Another ship had come up and her skipper wanted to help. They got a tow line attached to the stern of the ship and pulled her off the sand without giving us time to get off! I guess everyone thought she'd float, but she was more damaged than we knew. She promptly rolled over and floated, bottom up. Then she started to sink."

"And you were still in there."

"Yes. The rest of the salvage team were topside, and they scrambled off. Not me. I found myself standing on the overhead...the ceiling...with water coming up around me. I'd have to swim underwater to get out. I couldn't find a way through the ship upside down. I knew I was going to die. I was alone like you, and not ready."

Mimi nodded and reached for the box of tissues. She offered me one, and I took it.

"I'd heard the Gospel when I was a kid. Like so many others figured I didn't need it. I was young, strapping, and had appetites. I wanted to live for the moment, learn my trade in the Navy, and have fun. The fun was over. I was trapped, alone, and going to die in a couple of minutes."

"So was I, Matthew," the dark-haired beauty in the wheelchair said, very softly.

I nodded. "Some people hear the Lord's voice when they're in that spot. Ask Luther how it happened to him. I remembered what I'd been told in Sunday School long ago. The water was rising quickly, the air compressing in a bubble above me as I treaded water. I knew I had to choose. Forget this life, it's done. Eternity...I remember exactly what I said: 'Lord Jesus, I'm lost! Take me and save me. I'm yours!'"

I started to cry. Amy handed me another tissue and I wiped my eyes. She did the same as I continued.

"It seemed like the air in that bubble glowed like the inside of a light bulb. I felt total peace come over me, and I knew I'd meet Jesus myself in a few seconds. Then I heard a slosh, and a narrow face with a coal-stained beard popped up beside me. It was Bull Reeves, my closest friend on the ship. He gulped in air, then said, 'Gotcha! Don't just float there like a buoy. Take a good breath and follow me out!'"

I just sat there a moment, basking in the memory as Mimi wiped her eyes again and blew her nose. Her chest heaved,... and what a heave it was!

"I did as Bull said, and we swam out through a crack in the hull. Came up beside our whaleboat and watched as the old *Cristóbal Colón* slipped under the waves. The undertow tried to take us with her, but we held on to the whaleboat and our shipmates dragged us aboard. Bull got the Lifesaving Medal for bringing me back, and I've been the Lord's ever since."

Amy blew her nose again, then threw away the tissue and spoke. "Don didn't say which officer got you out of there when he told me the story."

"What?" *You're fond of that word today, Plotczyc*, I thought as Mimi continued.

"Ever since that day, I woke up your friends have visited me. I asked each one of them the same question. What about Matt Plotczyc? Is he as good and kind as he seems? Can I trust what he says? I asked them not to tell you I asked, and I guess they haven't."

I saw my face in a mirror as she spoke. *Yep, that's how I feel,* I thought.

Mimi continued. "Every one of them sang a rhapsody of your virtues! They told me stories about how they've worked with you over the years, how lonely you've been, and how you've brightened up since you met me. They also told about the Sunday morning you went forward in church and why. Yes, they figured that out too."

"I...I thought I'd hidden that," I stammered.

"You didn't. Not even from me, sick as I was. But I needed verification, assurance that I was sensing things right. My last check was to ask you that question and see how you answered."

I thought I knew the answer, but I had to ask. "How'd I do?"

"Help me get on the bed and we'll discuss it."

I got up and prepared to transfer Mimi from wheelchair to bed. I set the gait belt, grasped it as usual, and counted down.

Amy stood up, and we found ourselves in another one of those kisses. Eventually, we broke the kiss, still standing.

"Does this mean yes?" I whispered.

"Maybe," Mimi replied, and resumed the kiss.

Now, what is that supposed to mean? I thought.

CHAPTER SEVENTEEN

Harmony Twichell Ives: 6:30 PM, The Homestead Room, Hotel Custer, Galesburg, changes

"I'm staying."

I enjoyed watching the surprise on the faces of the other two women at the table.

"You've only been here a week, Harmony," Gloria Hodges stated. "How can you decide to move out here so quickly?"

I smiled at Gloria and Jennifer Setterdahl, my dinner guests for the evening.

"I've learned several things since my Charlie died last month. First, I can make my own decisions. I always knew that, and Charlie never prevented me from doing what I thought best, but I always checked things with him as a good wife should. Now, I'm on my own...and I realize how empty, how unfulfilling, how dull my life out east has been. I have many acquaintances but few friends. I came out here, and everyone has been so nice! And it's not for show. I can tell when it is, just like I could tell which of Charlie's friends were real, and which just wanted something from him. He never could tell, and his illnesses didn't help."

"We'd love to have you stay out here and work with us," Jennifer said, "but how are you going to wrap things up out there and move it all here? Keith and I about went crazy doing that, and we left the house to Mom and the kids until summer."

I sipped my tea. "Charlie and I had no children. I lost our first one and needed a hysterectomy. Mike Myrick, Charlie's business partner, is a fine, honorable man. He's got the business arrangements already made. I told him I wanted out of the business before I came out here. Plus, I have my own financial arrangements independent of the business, and I'll inherit Charlie's part of the estate. I'm very impressed with the banks out here, so I'll move my money when I move me. As for the property, auctions work very well!"

"Have you looked for a house out here?" Gloria asked.

"I've already found one! There's a lovely little house, brick, just built next door to Lucille and Gil Foster, two doors down from Pastor and Deborah Kittridge. It's a dollhouse! I just fell in love with it! I close on Friday."

"Wow! You don't mess around, do you? Keith and I live out that way too, over on Willard Street close to the school."

"That's the school where Sylvia is principal, isn't it?" Gloria asked.

"Yes. The house isn't fancy, but it'll be perfect for Mom and the kids. Easy walk to school, too. Out in Maryland, Mom has to drive them to and from school."

"Speaking of driving," I remarked, "I'm going to need a car. Are there any honest car dealers around here?"

Gloria grinned. "Lee Wright and Rol Allensworth, right over there," She pointed out the window, "Chevrolet and Oldsmobile, but he can find just about anything. Whatever you get, you should talk to Don Wain, or more likely Matt Plotczyc, who we met with Mimi Conger this afternoon. Wain Engineering does wonderful things with automobiles...uptime equipment." She whispered the *last*.

"That would be nice," I agreed, "I'll do that after we get through tomorrow."

"And now we get to meet one of those doctors from Hoople," Jennifer remarked, "Have you had any dealings with them yet, Gloria?"

"Just what Jackie and the others have told me," Gloria replied, "They've promised us new partners a trip out there this Summer."

"Helen's said something about a nurse friend of hers out there," Jennifer added, "drives a souped-up British sports car."

"From uptime?" I asked.

"The nurse, yes; the car, no," Jennifer replied, "She used to drive that sort of car before she came out here. Says this one is way better than those."

"They're coming in about nine tonight, whoever they are," Gloria brought us back on track, "but I want to know about your nursing background, Harmony. You've done fine so far. Were you a nurse back in New York?"

"A long time ago, before Charlie and I got married," I replied, "Even though I wasn't practicing I kept reading in the field. I asked questions whenever a doctor or a nurse would come to visit. In the old days, I did traveling nursing, sort of like social work with a black bag. I'm finding this orthopedic field fascinating! I hope I can be of some help tomorrow."

Jennifer nodded, "Oh, you will be! When I'm operating, I appreciate all the help I can get. That's why I drag Keith in there whenever I can. You'll be very helpful. I've been evaluating you today, and you know what you're doing. Didn't know I was watching you, did you?" she added with a grin.

I could feel myself blush. "No, Jennifer, I had no idea. Logical, though, considering you don't really know me."

Jennifer shrugged. "I think we're still figuring out things. We're both new to this area. But so far, I've enjoyed the experience."

"So have I, I declared, "I think this will be more fun than I've had in a long time."

"Fun for us...not necessarily for Jack."

"I don't know, Gloria," Jennifer said, "I think Jack has the best attitude about this kind of injury I've ever seen. Doesn't hurt he has Helen there cheering him on."

"It's a real blessing to see someone so unconditionally committed to someone in need," I commented, then fell silent.

"Harmony, you did everything you could with Charlie. Sometimes we give it everything we've got...and it doesn't work out. The Lord's doing it, not us. Then our job is to accept it. Your loss is much greater than our job loss, but the Lord blesses us even as we grieve."

I sighed. "Thanks for the reminder, Jennifer. I know that, but it's hard sometimes."

"Grieving, Harmony," Gloria said. "Let it come, give it to the Lord, He'll get you through it."

"I know."

Jennifer looked at the remains of the meal. "Perhaps a little dessert before our efforts tomorrow would be in order."

"Chocolate!" We said together, then giggled.

*****

Anna Gregoris, RN, MSN: 8:25 PM, eight thousand feet above the Mississippi River

"Have you ever been to Galesburg?" the bald older man spoke above the sounds of the rotodyne.

"About a year ago," I replied, "I met some of the company folks, talked to Matt Plotczyc about the mods to my Bentley, and got a tour of that wreck of an auditorium Don bought. Ewww!" I finished with a shudder.

"What was wrong with it?" Robert Meister, MD, FACS, BCOS, Captain, USN (retired) asked.

"What *wasn't* wrong with it?" I replied, "Only the lights in the lobby worked, you didn't dare try to flush the johns, and the night before I visited it rained and most of the ceiling came down! They had the seats out of the thing so they weren't ruined, but that's about the only good thing I saw. I won't comment on the smell!"

"Thanks, Anna, I smelled more than enough when I was in 'Nam."

"You were in 'Nam, Bob?" He insisted on first names unless we were in surgery.

"Yeah. Normally I rode the carrier *Bon Homme Richard* on Yankee Station, but when the Tet offensive went down they flew me into Saigon to help. Stayed there for three months. Never been so scared. Let's change the subject, OK?"

"Sure, Bob," I replied. *There's a subject to avoid*, I filed away in my mind.

"Hey, folks," a voice from the cockpit sounded in our headphones, "We're starting our approach to Galesburg now. We'll be firing up the tip jets in a moment so it will get a bit noisy."

This thing's loud enough already, I thought. The pilot, my friend Dave Sampson, continued.

We'll be on the ground in about ten minutes. Don says they have arrangements all made for your stay, and a late supper if you'd like. He wants to know if you like Chinese food?"

"Fine by me," I said into the microphone.

"Me too, but did I hear this is traditional Chinese seasoned cuisine?"

"Affirmative, Doctor, I know from experience!" Dave replied.

"Tell Don that is great, then," Bob said.

"OK. Keep your seat belts fastened and we'll see if we can surprise our friends from nineteen twenty-six!"

"If they're not awake to see us arrive, they will be when we land," I remarked as the tip jets began their song. The headphones helped tone down the racket.

*****

Don: 8:45 PM, driving into town

"I didn't know we'd be met by a reporter," Dave Sampson

remarked.

"Not just a reporter. He owns the newspaper," I replied, "He's Omer Custer, a good friend. I called him when we found out you were coming in the rotodyne. This is a good way to introduce the ship to the world."

"What were they taking the photographs with? I've seen press cameras, but not rigged up like that."

"It's a Speed Graphic with a special low-light rangefinder," my wife announced, "We set them up with the flashbulb array too. They were using flash powder before."

"Not a good idea around an aircraft," Bob Meister added.

"Only you can prevent *Forest Fires*," Jackie murmured, "You guys saw the film, I assume," referring to the chilling film of the fire aboard *USS Forrestal* in 1967.

"Every other year for my entire career," Dave said, "It alternated with *Plan to Get Out Alive*, that one Frank Field did."

"Close the door," I said in a soft deep voice.

"Close the door," the others echoed.

"Praise the Lord you told us, Jackie, or I wouldn't be here tonight."

"What was that, Dave?" Bob asked.

"Late last year I was flying 747s for UPS," Dave replied, "We had a fire start in the cargo. It was the lithium-ion batteries like you thought, Jackie."

"Figured," Jackie said.

"Things went bad fast. We made it to an emergency landing in Moline, Illinois. Jackie and Helen Smiley were up on a training flight and heard our mayday. She flew wing with us into the field, told us when the hull breached. We just got out the top hatch before the ship blew. She saved our lives—and then invited me and my wife out here!"

"I missed the *Forrestal* incident," Bob added, "but I had more than my share of adventure." He didn't elaborate; I knew where he'd been and understood his reticence.

"So now you have publicity for the rotodyne?" Dave asked.

"Looks natural, only a little contrived," I replied, "By the time the paper hits the streets in the morning it'll be gone. Thanks for staying over while Gil gets some time in the ship."

"My pleasure," Dave said, "I need to go annoy the kids in D.C. anyway."

"Do they have any idea where you two are?" Jackie asked.

"They know we're doing well, and we'll visit every so often. They have been instructed not to ask where. They're obedient children."

"So where is everyone staying?" Bob asked.

"We're putting you two up at the Broadview, across from the Auditorium," Jackie replied, "Luke's bunking with Gil and Lucille so they can both get an early start. Anna's staying with Helen—they're friends and Anna will keep an eye on Helen's emotional state."

"Good idea. I've wanted to meet the folks at Cottage I've heard so much about."

"They've heard about you too," I said, "You'll get a good dose of each other the next couple days."

"I saw the operating plan they've come up with—Sherry sent it to Peter," Bob referred to our class A cyber intelligences. "It looks good. Doctor Setterdahl knows her stuff."

"Agree," Jackie said, "and here we are at the restaurant. Yu Chen is staying open to feed us."

"She must be your friend to do that," Bob remarked.

"You might say that, Bob," Dave said before Jackie could respond.

Yu Chen promised me no seafood platter tonight, I thought with relief.

CHAPTER EIGHTEEN

Jack: Monday, April 5th, 1926, 10 AM, Cottage Hospital operating theater one.

I was surprised to still be awake when they wheeled me into the operating theatre. Every other time I'd had surgery I was either brought in unconscious or been knocked out while I was still on the ward.

I found myself in the same well-lit room I'd been in the day before. The same group I'd seen in there before met me, less Helen. She insisted on teaching to keep her mind off things... *right,* I thought.

I'd met the uptime doctor and nurse earlier that morning. Everyone wore gauze masks, but I knew who was who.

I decided to have fun while I could. "Is this a stick-up?"

"Yes. Give us all your money." Doctor Setterdahl replied.

"But I'm just a poor Marine, have mercy on me."

"You'll have to give us an arm or a leg then," Doctor Meister retorted, "Let's make it a leg."

"Everybody wants to be a comedian," Doctor Bohan remarked.

"In a moment Harmony is going to put a mask over your face too," the new nurse, Anna intoned, "This mask, though, will have a mixture of oxygen and ether coming out of it. It will put you under so we can do the job on your leg. When you come out of the ether you will be..."

"The ether bunny!"

"Told you the lad was sharp," Gloria remarked.

Doctor Setterdahl continued, "All right. Remember, Jack,

things might not make much sense for a bit when you come out of the anesthetic. Don't panic, or try to flail around—just relax, and you'll be back with us shortly. Got it?"

"Got it, Jenn-er, Doctor."

"I answer to either, Jack. Just don't call me Shirley. OK, Harmony"

I remembered groaning at the old chestnut as Harmony put the mask over my....

*****

Jackie: same time, same place, different room

"Thanks for coming to see me, Jackie," Mimi Conger said, "I wasn't comfortable asking anyone else."

"My pleasure, Mimi," I said as I sat down next to her bed, "What's up?"

"He asked me, as you predicted."

"What'd you tell him?"

"Maybe."

I nodded. "I thought you might do that. How'd he take it?"

"I don't think he knew what to say. He told me about the day he surrendered to Christ, what you said, more detail. We kissed, he asked me if that meant yes, I said maybe again. We talked about other things, then he left."

"Did he get angry?" I asked.

"No...just confused, I think. What do I do now, Jackie?"

I looked straight at the dark-haired woman. "What do *you* want, Mimi? I mean *really* want?"

"A bottle of olives nobody takes away from me."

I determined not to be surprised by anything this complex woman told me. "Had that happen?"

"All the time growing up," Mimi replied, "Mama thought they weren't good for me. They were a lot better for me than the booze she put them in!"

"Olives are just fine," I said, "and anytime you visit my house you're welcome to your own bottle. What else do you want?"

Mimi frowned. "I want a hot sauce that is on fire, not that insipid store-bought stuff. I want a chance to manage something that does not have classes attached to it. And...I want Romance, not a fantasy dressed up in flesh. Had way too much of that."

"You want a real love, not the kind that only wants to peel your panties off."

"Got that right!" Mimi's eyes flashed, then filled. "I've had too many of those. Especially that last one. I can't afford to be hurt like that again, ever.'

"A lot of dating is projection, what you think you want. That falls apart in real life."

"And nothing does that faster than getting pregnant," Mimi spat out, then gasped, "I can't believe I said that!"

"You didn't tell me, but I figured it out. Nobody's said a word, and I surely won't, even to Don. Who else knows?"

Mimi's mouth moved. "Doctor Bohan and Gloria know. they saw the evidence during the surgery, Gloria told me. Matt knows. He figured it out too. Nobody else that I know of."

"It doesn't matter to me", I replied, "Now that you know Christ, His is the real Love. Everything else comes within His love."

I took Mimi's hand. "You're Christ's and He's put your sins as far away as east is from west. Now, what do you really want?"

Mimi wiped her eyes with a tissue. "Nobody's ever asked to marry me before. Ever. I want to hear it, wallow in it. I want him to keep asking me. I want to hear it even after we're married, just to remember how it felt. That's what I want."

"What you want is something real. But you also want romance —the real thing. That about cover it?"

"Yes, Jackie, that does. Is Matt the one?"

"What do you think?"

"I think so, Jackie. I'm almost sure...but I want to *hear* it."

I smiled. "I know Matt pretty well. He's a very thorough Naval officer and manager for us. But he's also tender-hearted, emotional, caring, down inside. I think he'll keep asking you until you say yes...and afterward too. So, are you going to say yes?"

"Maybe, yeah, I don't know, he's got dreamy eyes."

"OK, Mimi, but I suggest you don't string him along too much. He won't give up, but too much angst will leave him with a tiny doubt in his mind, and that could fester. You don't want that."

"No, I don't," Mimi squeezed my hand and let go. "Thanks for the advice, Jackie. I needed someone to talk to about this before I act."

"I understand, glad to help," I replied.

Now to my next appointment—I love it when a plan comes together! I thought as I left the hospital.

*****

Jackie: twenty minutes later, the Auditorium office.

"OK, Matt, what's up?" I said with my best deadpan expression.

The big man sat across the desk from me. I noticed his hair was graying more. *I wonder why*, I thought with an inner smirk, then he spoke.

"Here it is, Jackie. I asked Mimi to marry me and she said maybe. We talked about how I got saved in the capsized *Cristobal Colon*, then we kissed. I asked her again, and she said *maybe* again. What am I doing wrong, *Captain*?"

"Let me ask you a question, *Captain*," I started with my Commanding Officer persona, "How many times do you think someone's asked her to marry him?"

Matt's Commanding Officer persona shriveled a little. "Er...

maybe five times, not counting mine?"

"How about zero, negat, nada times?"

"What?"

His situational awareness is substandard, I thought, *Gotta be careful here.* "Matt, Mimi's never been proposed to. Ever, until you. I talked to her a while back." *Like a half hour ago, but he doesn't need to know that*, I added in my mind.

"All those other boyfriends?"

"Just wanted to have sex with her. Nothing more, no commitment. Especially that last one—the one who got her pregnant."

Matt turned beet red. "You...you know about that?" he stammered.

"I guessed it, she confirmed it, we tell nobody else," I replied, "You are the first honorable man to ever ask her to marry him. How do you suppose that makes her feel?"

I watched Matt's reaction. Wide eyes, deep raspy breath in, then exhaled through his teeth with a slight whistle. *Never seen him do that before*, I thought, *He's got it bad.*

"I think...no, I hope and pray she felt happy and wants to say yes. But why does she keep saying *maybe*?"

I smiled. "You know, I think she just wants to keep hearing you ask her. Savor it, wallow in it maybe. She wants to hear it enough times that she believes it. She's been hurt a lot of times, a lot of ways. She gave herself to a man this last time and it all but killed her. I think she wants to be sure of you, and sure of herself. *Shuōdétōng?*

"What?"

Good, he's listening. "Oh, sorry, I popped into Chinese for a second. That means *Does this make sense?*"

"Oh, okay, I get it. Yes, I think I understand. She wants to hear something she's wanted to hear all her life and never heard it before. So, I should keep asking her?"

"I frowned. "I do believe that's the general idea, Matthew. If you don't ask her at least three times every time you're with her I'll have you flogged! And while you're at it tell her you love her. Have you ever come out and said that to her?"

Matt looked like I'd slapped him. In a way I had. "No, Jackie, I don't think I have. How could I be so stupid?"

You're a man. Need I say more? I thought, then revised my reply.

"I don't know, Matt, but that's done and gone. She still wants you. I'm sure of it. Just tell her you love her and ask her. That is what you want, right?"

Matt's eyes started to fill. "Yes, Jackie, like I've never wanted anything since I met Grace. I'll do what you say. Is there anything else I can do to prove myself to her?"

I thought a moment. "Besides what you already do to help with her care, maybe some sort of food item she craves. She loves olives, hasn't had them for a long time. And hot sauce. Plus, there's always chocolate."

"She's mentioned hot sauce before, but not the others. Where can I get them?"

"I think I can help there. I get olives from uptime, and there's a local hot sauce in Galesburg I really like. Don can't even taste a drop. We can also get some premium chocolate..."

Sherry's voice interrupted. "I have already messaged Kathy Trainor *uptime.* Her staff will buy a sampler from as many types of olives as they can find at your favorite Olive Bar in Peoria. I have also asked her to procure two bottles of *Dave's Gator Sauce,* and a selection of *Godiva Chocolates* from the store named *Calico Cat.* She says the items will be included in the supply shipment arriving Thursday morning. She also advises the bill for all this will appear on Matt's tab, not yours. She says it will not be cheap."

Matt stifled a groan as I replied. "Sherry, you did it to me again! You had those things ordered and on the way before I even finished my sentence!"

"I believe I have mentioned before that I read minds," the Cyberintelligence observed with a chuckle, then the speakers clicked off.

"And once you get these items, keep them coming daily in small amounts. Especially the chocolate."

Matt and I stood up. "Thanks for explaining it to me Jackie. I'll keep asking, and telling her I love her, because I do."

"Good," I said as I shook his hand, "And by the way, keep asking and telling her even after you're engaged, and married. She may act like it's a running joke, but every time you do it you'll remind her of the joy you've given her. That means a lot to a woman."

Matt picked up his hat. "Thanks again Jackie. That's what I needed to hear."

Bet your sweet bippy you did, I thought as he left the office. *Lord, please take care of them like you took care of Don and me.*

And prepare Don for his next little surprise, I added with a smile.

*****

Lillian: 11 AM, her office at Ayers Primary School

"Come in," I called.

A tall young woman with an elongated face and pleasant smile stepped into the office. Leila Guidinger exuded competence and caring wherever she went. I always enjoyed seeing her back in the classroom.

"Did I hear right that you're throwing Helen out of her own classroom?" Leila never did mince words.

"You heard right, Mrs. Guidinger," I replied with a smile of my own, "Helen thinks she can teach effectively while her betrothed is having major surgery on what's left of his leg. I disagree, and that's why I called you in. I asked her student teacher Dorothea to keep me informed; she reports Helen's not herself this morning. Her students are enjoying the departure from the norm."

"Only Helen. What a mess. I can't believe she thought that," Leila replied, "If George or one of my children were ill I couldn't be away from them. That's why I can't teach full time. Maybe when they're older."

"George?"

Leila snorted. "You know what I mean, Lillian! And by the way, please thank Don for sending Marcella out to mind the little darlings again. She's first-rate."

"I will do that, at the same time I tell Don what he arranged and hand him the bill."

"He doesn't know?" What if he refuses?"

"He won't refuse me, and if he did Jackie would override him. You've never met them, have you?"

"No, but you said he's seen me somewhere."

"So I remember," I remarked. *You'll be his first-grade teacher a long time from now in another universe,* I thought, *but you don't need to know that right now.* "I'll be sure to introduce you when we see them, at my retirement party if not sooner."

"Thanks, Lillian," Leila said, "I've already eaten and I'm ready to take over."

"Shall we go rescue the class and send Helen packing?" I asked.

"What if she won't leave?"

"You've never seen my catapult on the roof," I replied.

*****

Jack: mid-afternoon, how time flies when you're unconscious

I opened one eye. I felt like I was floating in another well-lit room. Two women I did not recognize tended me, and two other people in nearby beds.

Shirley said I might see things when I woke up, I noted, *but everything's normal here.*

"Jack! How do you feel?"

I looked at the one who asked that question.

The face was Helen's, of that I was sure. The voice also sounded like Helen. From there things got...interesting. This apparition's hair was dark like Helen's, but much longer. She (*definitely a she,* I thought) was dressed in a very revealing, skin-tight bathing suit. I felt my face start to heat.

I looked down and saw she was wearing shoes with impossibly high heels. I snapped my eyes back up to stare into her face. Her face was framed with a bow tie at the neck...and large floppy ears on top of her head!

As I beheld this figure, *And what a figure*, I thought, I managed to come to two conclusions. First, I was indeed feeling the effects of the anesthetic. Second, I positively identified the one standing before me and called her by name.

"Hello, Ether Bunny!"

"What? Oh. You're hallucinating! Let me help you snap out of it!"

With that, the vision bent down and kissed me. She definitely kissed like Helen! We finally broke the kiss, and she stood back upright. There stood Helen, normal. Still the best real vision I'd seen all day!

"Thank you, Love, I needed that," I whispered, "Tell you how much later."

"What did you think, I had rabbit ears on the top of my head?"

"Well..."

CHAPTER NINETEEN

Mimi: Tuesday, April 6th, 1926, 6 PM, dinner at Cottage with a guest

"I want to go to church this Sunday, Matthew."

Matt looked up from where his eyes had wandered. "Are you recovered enough? Do you have enough strength to make it, even in a wheelchair?"

I returned his gaze. "I think so. My incision is healed and I am gaining strength. If you will help me get there, I think I can do it. I want to see that church, hear your Pastor, and go forward. Gloria has described that process to me. Will you help me?"

Matt's eyes brightened. "I will be honored to help, Mimi! One thing I can do is give you a more comfortable wheelchair than those hardback chair ones they have around here. It'll fold too, from uptime."

I swallowed the last bite of my tasteless casserole. "Can you get one here before Sunday?"

"I'm sure I can," Matt replied, I believe I will have the chair, and a few other surprises, by supper Thursday evening. We can try the chair out then, OK?"

"What other surprises are you talking about?" I wasn't going to let him slip that one in without challenge.

"Oh, a few things you might enjoy. That's all I can say right now."

"Some combination hot sauce and paint remover?"

"You'll see. Now, may I escort you back to bed?"

I smiled. "Did I drop something on my gown, Matthew?"

"Er, huh?" Matt looked down and up.

"Do you like them?"

"I..uh...," he began, then looked me in the eye, "Yes, I do," he said firmly, even though he turned beet red.

Good. He still blushes. I bet he didn't even realize he was staring at them, I thought as he fumbled with the gait belt. *I wonder if he'll ask me a third time this evening?*

As Matt helped me up with the gait belt, he whispered, "I love you, Mimi. Will you marry me?"

"Maybe. And I love you too."

I hadn't intended to say that. Is that what I really mean? And how long can this charade go on? Is it time, Lord?

I lay awake for a half-hour after Matt left, pondering that question before another need interrupted me and I pushed the call light button.

*****

Jack: same time, different room

"I brought a few guests," my betrothed remarked as she opened the door to my room, "They want to tell you about your leg before they go back to Hoople."

Behind Helen stepped Doctor Meister, Anna the nurse, Doctor Setterdahl, and Gloria. *Crowded room,* I thought.

"You're leaving tonight?" I asked.

"Yeah," Doctor Meister replied, "They don't want to fly the rotodyne down here in daylight yet, and I have surgeries tomorrow."

"They tell me I have to get back to unscramble the nurses' schedule, and my cat isn't feeling well," Anna added.

"Tell him your cat's name," Helen said.

"Hittie...full name Mehitabel Le Plume," the curly-haired nurse with the pug-nose replied," She's fourteen, had her from a kitten. My baby."

Anna reminded me of one of my Marine boots when I was a

drill instructor. He put a brave face on things, but I knew his mother was dying back home. *The cat's her baby and she's dying,* I thought.

"Ok, we need to explain some things to you before they leave," Jennifer said, "First, reshaping your leg went as we planned. You should have a good stump to put the prosthesis on."

"But I still won't be able to play the organ…Eeep!"

"Good shot, Helen," Gloria remarked.

"Unless you practice," Doctor Meister continued, "Your anterior cruciate ligament was damaged, as were the insides of the knee itself. You would have had to have it amputated, but fortunately we brought along the equipment and were able to repair it. It should be good as new when it heals; if it isn't, we can always put in an artificial knee later."

"Attached to the prosthesis?" I asked.

"No," the doctor replied, "inserted instead of your current knee. What's left of your lower leg is good enough to support the artificial joint."

"But we don't think that will be necessary," Jennifer added, "I can't believe all Keith and I have learned since Sunday! I feel like a whole different doctor now."

Doctor Meister smiled. "You were an excellent Orthopedist before, Jenn, Keith is the most skilled prosthesis maker I've ever met. I'm just giving you a few more tools and materials to work with."

"And Keith and I are so grateful for the new toolbox," Jenn continued, "Especially the therapy appliances for Keith."

Doctor Meister grinned. "We had spares, so we brought 'em with us. And Jack, you will get to try them all out during your rehab."

"What kind of appliances?" I asked with a fake waver in my voice.

"You'll see," Doctor Meister replied, "It's odd, but most of them seem to be derived from the medieval rack."

The laughter from the others eased my mind. "That's a joke, right?"

"They're laughing, because *they* don't need therapy," Anna said with a wink.

"Thank you so very much," I replied. I was happy to take her mind off the sadness back home.

"I'm surprised he hasn't asked this yet," my betrothed said, "but when do you think I can take him flying again?"

Doctor Meister raised an eyebrow. "I wouldn't take him up in an open cockpit job for a while. The Junkers will be fine as soon as he gets his prosthesis. If Don would spring for an *Ercoupe* you could fly just as you are."

"A what?" I asked.

"Ercoupe, spelled like it sounds," Doctor Meister said, "Designed in the late '30s, they fly nicely without rudder pedals. Amputees and paraplegics have flown 'em ever since. I'll put a bug in Don's ear to get one. No, I'll put it in Jackie's, it'll get *done*. Knowing those two, they'll probably have Hugo Junkers start *building* the things!"

"Thanks, I think," Helen said, "He will be able to fly our normal planes, won't he?" She's worried, *I thought,* "Lord, please have your will..."

"Absolutely!" Doctor Meister declared, "and while we're on the subject here's a book for you." He pulled a book out of his briefcase and handed it to Helen, who handed it to me. I looked at the title...*Reach for the Sky*.

"This is an *uptime* book about Douglas Bader, a fighter pilot before and during the next war," Doctor Meister began, "He crashed...crashes...in 1936 and loses both his legs. He got prostheses, invented his own therapy, and the RAF let him back in when the war started. Became an ace in Fighter Command, Group Captain, then a prisoner of war for several years. I think you'll find his story interesting, and not just for the medical stuff."

"Thanks, Doc," I replied, "Is this your only copy?"

Doctor Meister laughed. "Not hardly! I keep a shelf of these things, hand 'em out as needed, have for years. Familiarity does *not* breed contempt." He ended with a serious expression.

"Thank you, Doctor," I said, then stopped as the room door opened. "I hope I'm interrupting something," the tall spare man in a cassock remarked with a smile.

"Hi, Father," Anna bubbled, "Let me introduce you." Her voice dropped to a whisper, "This is Father George Doubleday, retired Navy chaplain, Pastor of Corpus Christi Catholic Church, Chaplain of Saint Mary's hospital, and incognito partner in Wain Engineering." She said the last so quietly I didn't quite catch it.

"What kind of partner?" I asked as I shook the elderly man's hand.

"Incognito," he replied, The Church is unaware of all kinds of things. I'd rather keep it that way."

"Pardon my asking, but why are you still in the Catholic church?" Helen asked what I wanted to ask.

"I was ordained as a Catholic priest many years ago," Father Doubleday replied, "Then I spent a career as a Chaplain in the Navy. While I was there, let's just say Someone changed my heart. He's told me that my ministry is here at Corpus Christi until He chooses to change my address. Here or *there*, I serve at my Lord's pleasure."

"Me too," I remarked.

"I heard of your circumstance," the elderly priest said, "and I am sure Our Lord will bless you for what you did."

"He already has," Helen piped up and kissed me.

"With that, I need to wander off," Father Doubleday said, "I have a few more folks to visit here before I sleep."

As he turned to leave Anna touched his arm and spoke quietly. "Father, you need to come out and visit us. You missed your time in the tank last year, and things can happen if you go too long."

The priest nodded and smiled. "I know, Anna, and I will try later in the summer. Right now, our Bishop has just suffered a stroke, and I fear things will be a bit chaotic until we are settled down again."

"Don't let it go too long, Father," Anna said softly, "Some of us enjoy your company," she finished with a warm smile.

"I will remember, Anna," he replied, "And now I must be off, but you all knew that." Father Doubleday touched his hat and walked out the door.

"What was that all about?" Jenn asked.

Anna snorted. "He's got the driest sense of humor of anyone I know! He always cheers us up when he comes out to Hoople."

"Getting away from the stress back here," I remarked.

"That's quite a place the Lord's stuck him," Doctor Meister remarked, "We all pray for him regularly. He's close friends with Father Wilcox, our Chaplain."

"We've met him," Helen added, "Now we'll have someone else to pray for."

"A great thing to do while I'm engaged in pain and…er, P.T."

"Best not let Keith hear you say that," Doctor Setterdahl said, then laughed with the rest of us.

When the others had gone Helen sat down next to my bed. Our hands found each other as usual.

"Did you catch Anna's expression as she talked about her cat?" I asked.

"I did, Love," Helen replied, "What's going on?"

"The cat's her baby, and she's dying. Anna's trying to work

through her worry and grief and not quite managing. I saw the same thing in one of my recruits at Quantico. In his case his mother was dying and he couldn't be there."

"And she's out there alone, no old friends, no man, just Hittie," Helen said, "We'll pray for her situation. Speaking of situation, what now for us?"

"I see four things, my love," I replied, "First, we see how therapy goes and when the Setterdahls think I can leave the hospital and go home somewhere. Second, we pray and keep our eyes open for a house in good shape we can buy. Remember, I have money so we can buy it when we find it. Third, we talk to Don and Jackie about when we can get married. I think another patient around here is going to get married before she goes home."

"Mimi?" Helen asked.

"Right, Love," I replied, "I think they'll get married in the Auditorium—no stairs. I think they'd let us do that too, eventually."

"OK. And the fourth thing?"

"Ah—oh, never mind—I'm all right now."

"Ewww!" my bride-to-be remarked as she pushed the call button.

CHAPTER TWENTY

Marcel Dupré: Wednesday, April 7th, 1926, noon, a small restaurant on the left bank of the river Seine, Paris

"So, tell me about these people you are going to visit," Louis Vierne remarked after the waiter left with our orders.

I met Louis and his *amoureuse*, Madeleine Richepin at Notre Dame when I stopped to borrow some music for the Saint Sulpice choir. I treated them to lunch at one of our favorite bistros nearby. I drove as I wanted to show off my new automobile, and because Madeleine's driving terrorized even the insane drivers of Paris!

Madeleine guided Louis to a table and read him the menu. She expanded the usual meaning of *amoureuse* from *lover* to caregiver and protector. Louis could not function without her.

After we ordered we chatted as we always did. Then my friend dropped his surprise question. I thought a moment about what I could and could not say.

"Let me see...Donald Wain is the owner of the company I worked with during my visit. He bought a rundown theater and rebuilt it, adding the most amazing organ I have ever encountered."

"Greater than our instruments?" Louis asked.

"Not greater, but different in ways I cannot describe," I was not about to let slip about *Allen and Hauptwerk* organ electronics, "The method of register changing is very simple, and the power of the instrument is amazing."

"But you asked about the people," I continued, "They consult with governments and business at the highest level of technical brilliance, yet are the kindest, most giving people I have ever run across. Jeannette and I have made many close friends in that small town, and I look forward to working with them to retrieve those precious Barker machines. We will share with Notre Dame, of course."

"We are very grateful for that, Marcel. And they will charge you nothing?"

"Not a *centime*, my friend! They are not Catholic, but Donald and the others share our love for the instruments of old Aristide."

The server set our food in front of us. Madeleine took Louis's hand and touched each item on the plate with it, describing the food as she did so. She then placed his spoon in one hand and touched his wine glass with the other. *His blindness is even worse. She never had to do that for him before,* I thought sadly.

We began to eat. After the first bite of quiche au fromage Louis took a sip of wine and set down his fork. "I want to come with you to America."

I stopped cold with my fork halfway to my mouth. I never dreamed I would hear that statement from him. "Why?" was all I could ask.

"Madeleine and I have been talking," he began, "Affairs at the Cathedral have weighed on me more than usual lately. I am weary of the endless intrigues, and I believe a visit to this Galesburg place will refresh me. If you'll take us along, we'd like to come."

I thought of the travails Louis had endured to come to this point. Jeannette and I had prayed for Louis often since we had been reborn. Yes, he needed refreshment all right—the sort Our Lord meant when he said, "Come to me, all you that labour, and are burdened, and I will refresh you."

(Matthew 11:28, Douay-Rheims version)

"I am sure Donald and the others would love to have you visit them! I will cable Donald Wain immediately. I need to ask him when to come over anyway, and I will mention your request. I assume you both will make the trip. Would that be agreeable?"

Louis and Madeleine nodded; Louis added a grin.

I was surprised again. *That's the first time I've seen him smile in ten years!* I thought, *Thank you, Lord, for this opportunity.*

*****

Mimi: Thursday, April 8th, 1926, 6:15 PM. her room, Dinner

"What's in the box?" I asked as Matt levered his way through the door to my room.

"On top is your supper," Matt replied. He set the box on my bed and placed the covered tray on my rolling table, "The box is something I promised a couple days ago."

I sat up in my chair and contemplated the tray. "I guess I ought to see what I'm sentenced to this evening," I remarked, and lifted the cover.

"Ugh," I groaned, "sentenced is right. Salisbury steak...dead petrified *maybe* cow. Creamed peas on toast. Half-cooked mashed potatoes. And for dessert," I stared, then started to laugh.

"What's funny?" Matt asked.

"That," I pointed, "Lime Jello to start with. The white stuff embedded in it is cottage cheese and marshmallows. The orange is shredded carrot. Meaning this is," I took a breath, "Lime Jello Marshmallow Cottage Cheese Surprise!" I giggled again.

"Sounds like a song title," Matt remarked.

"It is! Jackie was here at lunch one day when they served that. She brought in a funny song from *uptime* and played it on the laptop computer. It's a scream. Maybe I'll sing it for you someday."

"I'd like that, Mimi," Matt said, "Perhaps the contents of this box will help you tolerate the meal."

I opened my eyes wide and smiled. "Yes! Anything to help this poor patient's supper would be greatly appreciated."

Matt opened the box. I gasped, then began pulling out small bottles. "All these different olives! Where did you get them?"

"I didn't. Jackie had our uptime staff go to a large grocery store, (they call 'em supermarkets) and visit what they call an olive bar. They got samples of all they had, and here they are."

I looked at the rank of small bottles. "I know the green and ripe ones, and I've tried kalamata olives, but I don't know what the rest are."

Matt pulled out a book. "Jackie loves olives too. She said this book will explain the types and show some recipes."

I looked at the book. "I haven't been able to afford olives for so long," I sniffled, "Thank you, Matt, this is wonderful!"

"I'm glad you like them, Mimi," Matt said, "and here's something else for you to try." He pulled out a tall tapered bottle filled with light green liquid.

"What is this?" I asked, then read the label. "*Dave's Gator Sauce*. That's a cute picture of a running alligator. Is there a real gator in this?"

Matt chuckled. "No gators were harmed in the making of this sauce. I'd say it's hot but see for yourself. I had one taste, then had to drink about a quart of water." Matt shivered.

"Then I'd say it'll be just about right. And where did they get this from? What's an autobody?"

"A place where they fix wrecked cars. Around here the dealerships do the repairs, but uptime they have specialized shops. I guess the owner came across this stuff and liked it so much he markets it."

"Strange, but let's see." I opened the bottle and put a bit on my finger. I tasted it. Tasted it again, then shook the bottle all over my hospital food, including the Jello!

"Are you sure you want that much?"

"Oh, yes, Matthew! It's been so long since I've had a good hot sauce. This is the best I've ever tasted! Would you pray please so I can dig in?"

"Sure," Matt said, and prayed.

As I feasted on the ordinary hospital meal, made special by the amazing sauce and the olives, I realized how much the Wain folks cared about me...and cared about Matt, to help him supply these wonderful items I'd been without for so long. I decided.

I finished the last of that Jello salad, flavor masked by the gator sauce. I wiped my mouth and looked at the man sitting across from me. "Ask me," I said.

"What?"

"Ask me!"

"Ask you what?"

"Ask me!" *Talk about dense,* I thought, *Lord, please let him remember what he needs to do!*

Matt jerked back like he'd been slapped. "Oh, I'm sorry! Mimi, I love you. Will you marry me?"

"Bend over here and I'll answer you."

He got up and bent over me.

"Yes, Matthew, I will marry you. Thank you for asking. I'm ready now. Fool me, you kiss!"

"Huh?" he began, but I reminded him of the proper response.

"Uh oh," I whispered as we broke the kiss, then launched into the loudest, longest belch I could ever remember!

Matt stood back up, grinning. "Greetings from the interior," he remarked.

"I think my sinuses are cleared forever!" I said, then wiped my mouth again. "So, can we get married when I get out of here?"

"I think so, love," Matt replied, "Let's check with Don. It would be easier on us if we did it in the Auditorium."

I couldn't resist. "I'd rather we did it in our bedroom, dear. But how many people do you expect to come to our wedding? Do we need that much room?"

Matt turned red…then smiled. "Yes," he whispered, "We'll need every bit of that room."

This is going to be fun, I thought, *Thank you Lord for these blessings..and Matt....and the olives! He's nice, isn't he, Lord?*

And then Matt brought out the chocolate!

*****

Don: 9:15 PM, at home with Jackie, the trifecta of phone calls

Jackie hung up the *company-only* phone. "That was Matt. She said yes."

"Wooed by a persistent Captain. And all those olives," I remarked, "First the call from Helen about their wedding, then the call from Sherry reading the cable from Marcel, and now this. Gonna be a busy day tomorrow. Did he say what pushed her over the edge?"

"I don't think I'd put it that way," Jackie said with a warning look. "Matt says she loved the olives, but the *Gator Sauce* sealed the deal. She put it on everything."

My stomach took a lurch. "Everything? I can hardly stand to smell that stuff! Reminds me of a combination of this Christmas salad relish my mother made and burnt jet fuel."

"You have a sensitive system, my Admiral," Jackie resumed her place on my lap, "He said she had to jog his memory to get him to ask her again. He finally caught on, and she said yes."

"Matt's a genius, but every so often he needs a poke, as we all do." I moved to parry Jackie's fingers, but she didn't try.

"They want to get married when she can leave the hospital," my wife continued, "and they want to use the Auditorium."

"Good idea," I said, "no steps. And he tells me she wants to come to church this Sunday. Can he get her and a wheelchair up the steps?"

"He has an uptime lightweight wheelchair coming in tomorrow's shipment. It had to be ordered. He says he'll carry her up and down if someone will get the chair."

I had another thought. "Does she have any idea what our service is like? Won't be anything like the Universalists."

"I've explained things to her, and Gloria's been telling her about it from the viewpoint of a recent arrival. Mimi's just glad she won't have to listen to baseball scores from the pulpit!"

I chuckled. "That's more common than you think, Love. The Pastor of the first church I went to after I got saved did that. That and stuff from Time magazine. Nice guy, I think he knew Christ, but he couldn't preach his way out of a paper bag."

"I grew up in my parents' church in Taiwan," Jackie said, "My dad always made sense, and his Taiwanese assistant did too. Dad turned the church over to his assistant the year before he died."

"A good missionary always works himself out of a job," I remarked, "I hope we can do the same here."

"Me too, Love. Although I don't know. The Lord has made it clear things will be different in this universe."

"Yeah. We never know when He's going to send us the proverbial curveball." Jackie shifted off my lap to my side, "We just have to be flexible and wait on Him. That's why I had Sherry send Marcel the cable agreeing to have them start over next week. Sooner the better."

"Agreed, Precious," Jackie said, then frowned. "Love, I'm not feeling so well tonight. Something in the digestive system."

"Too much seafood platter?" I asked as a joke, then saw her face, "Do we need to call the Doctor, Love?"

Jackie got up from the couch slowly. “No, Dear, I think I’ll be OK. Let’s just go to bed. I’m not up for playing tonight.”

“OK, Love, sure,” I replied. I made a note in my mind to watch her closely.

CHAPTER TWENTY-ONE

Luther: Friday, April 9th, 1926, 9:05 AM, the Auditorium office, more fun

"Thanks for coming in at short notice," Jackie said as I stepped through the performer's entrance. They'd given me a key and I used it.

"I think I've figured out two of the three subjects for this meeting, but I'm stumped on the third one."

"Helen and Jack's wedding, and now Mimi and Matt's wedding. That's what he *thinks* we're discussing. The third one is what we should be talking about. I'll let Don explain it." We started walking up the aisle of the Auditorium. I noticed Jackie wasn't moving as quickly as usual.

We stepped into the foyer. "You got called too?" Deborah Kittridge asked.

"For my sins, I guess," I replied, "Where's Pastor?"

"Out visiting," Deborah said, "Then he's having lunch with an old Navy friend of his. He's retiring and thinking about coming out here."

"Do we know him?" Jackie asked.

"Commander Rich Martindale. Chaplain out in San Diego. His wife's a nurse."

"AP could use an assistant," I commented.

"You noticed?" Deborah winked, "It took a while to seep into AP's brain but now he agrees. We'll see how the Lord swings it though."

Jackie opened the office door and we stepped in. Dick and Amy occupied their usual desks with Don. Jackie sat down at her desk and Deborah and I took the love seat.

"You've run out of room, Don," Deborah observed.

"I know, but we'll have plenty of room when we get the Bondi Building built."

"When's ground-breaking?" I asked.

"Late this month, early next month," Don replied, "Depends on the site clearing and some of the stuff we're going to talk about."

"Get to it then, Admiral," Jackie sent Don the look.

Don picked up a yellow pad. "OK, here goes. You've probably figured out a couple of these items. First, we need to decide when we can have Helen and Jack's wedding."

"No."

Don stared at the lithe blonde at the next desk. "What did you say?" I heard his voice rise in pitch with steady volume.

"I said no," Amy replied, quiet as always but with an edge. "Who decided when Luther and Sylvia got married?"

Don frowned, "They did."

"And Lucille and Gil?"

"They did."

"You and Jackie?"

"We did. *Think*, Admiral," Jackie also stared at Don. He started to sink lower in his chair.

Amy pointed her finger, "And who decided when Elwood and I got married?"

"You did," Don whispered.

"Very well," Amy leaned forward toward the shrinking Don. "We can host those weddings in the Auditorium any date they choose—our contracts say we can reschedule events. So we will meet with the couples this afternoon and let them decide... them, not us! Otherwise, we're just a bunch of talking heads pretending to decide about things we have no right to decide!"

"I thought I was in charge," Don mumbled.

I noticed Amy's normally pale face shone red as she continued to speak.

"Not of this! I did not retire from the Navy, travel to another universe ninety-three years in the past, and marry the man of my dreams just to be a talking head in some third-rate science fiction novel!"

"Hear, hear!" Dick announced. "Amen," Jackie and Deborah said. I just sat there watching Don. He looked like he was going to cry.

"I want at least second-rate," Amy added.

When we were more or less composed again, Jackie spoke. "So what are we going to do this afternoon, Admiral?"

"We'll schedule a meeting to talk to the couples about when they want to get married," Don whispered, "and I'm sorry."

"Yes, you are, but they love you anyway," Sherry's contralto voice interrupted, "You meet with the couples and others in the Cottage training room at two this afternoon. You're welcome."

After a moment of contemplation Don lifted his head from his desk. "May we continue now?" He asked.

"We'd better," Jackie replied, "This next matter is serious, and I'm not sure what to do about it."

Don picked up a telegram flimsy. "I want to read this telegram from Marcel Dupré to you, then Sherry will fill in some details and we'll discuss it. Ready, Sherry?"

"What? Oh, pardon me, I dozed off," the Class A Cyberintelligence said.

"Right," Don coughed, then began. "'Planning spring activities. Need to know when I may come for the B machine job. Can start the journey next week if desired. Also, Louis Vierne and his amoureuse, Madeleine Richepin, wish to accompany me. Jeannette is unable to come this time. I believe their coming is an answer to prayer; will explain when I get there. Please advise. Warm regards to all, Marcel.'"

"Does *amoureuse* mean what I think it does?" Deborah asked.

"It does," Sherry interrupted, "but she is much more than just a lover. Louis is virtually blind. Madeleine helps him perform almost every task of daily human living. Without her, he is utterly helpless, especially in an unfamiliar environment."

"I never got to meet him when I was in France," I remarked, "Marcel said he was getting medical treatments. Both Charles and he filled in at Notre Dame while Louis was gone."

Don started to speak but Sherry stopped him. "I will add the details. Louis' life up till now has been the same as it was in the uptime universe. He started out nearly blind, and surgeries over the years have only made it worse. He was hit by a vehicle on a Paris street twenty years ago and almost lost his leg. His brother and only son died in the War."

Jackie tapped a pencil on her desk. "Let's stop here. We have a man coming to visit us who is dependent on others to function, and he's coming to a place he knows absolutely nothing about. How are we going to keep him safe everywhere he needs to go?"

"It's not that hard," Don began, "We give him a close escort, arm in arm, if he'll take it. We watch out and give verbal cues to let him know if there's a step or uneven ground coming. We...."

Jackie turned on Don, eyes blazing. "You think that's easy? When did *you* ever have to mind a blind person? Oh, my! I'm so sorry!"

Now Jackie looked like she was going to cry. Don just sat, motionless, staring out. I wished I were someplace else.

"Peace, you two," Deborah spoke softly, "You have both been reminded of what you forgot. You both love each other; you both loved Pam. Leave it at that. Let's take advantage of each other's experience and build on it. Agreed?"

Don and Jackie both nodded. They looked at each other; both stood up and they hugged.

"That's better," Deborah continued, "I have a question for the group, but let's finish this part first. Do any of you know anyone else with experience working with a blind person?"

"Me," Amy said, "I was married to Pat for eight years. He was blind from birth, so he'd learned all the tricks before I met him. I still watched out for him, but quietly so I wouldn't embarrass him. I wanted him to get a seeing-eye dog, but he refused, said he'd learned to hear and feel his way around. He didn't want to be responsible for an animal. He was amazing. I think we'll find Louis has his ways to get by. Remember, blindness is not a blanket disability. We just need to learn how Louis operates and make sure any of us working with him learn the tricks too. And never, ever, discount what he says because he cannot see."

"Thank you so much, Amy," Dick said, "I've worked with the blind a little, but nowhere near as much as Amy and Don. I think we'll manage, and remember he'll have Madeleine with him."

"Right," Don said. His color was returning, as was Jackie's. "I think we also need to think about the relationship between Louis and Madeleine, and how we respond. I know Sherry's going to interrupt me, so just go ahead."

"You are finally learning," Sherry remarked, then began. "Louis was married. His wife ran off with Charles Mutin, the successor to Cavaille-Coll the organ builder. So far as I can determine Louis was not the one at fault. The Catholic Church allowed their marriage to be annulled but forbade Louis to marry again. This is not logical from what I understand of the Bible."

"No, it's not logical," Dick Meriden added, "but we're talking *The Church*, not logic."

"Indeed," Jackie replied, "and if The Church ever decides to take official notice of him living with Madeleine they'll fire him. They have Louis over a barrel."

"And they created the need for that arrangement," Don said, "What a bunch! Anything else, Sherry?"

"Not at this time, Admiral. Have a nice day," Sherry said with a chuckle, then clicked off.

Don sighed and looked at his yellow pad. "So we know we have Company partners here who can help Louis function and enjoy his stay here. Since Madeleine is the expert in caring for him and she's coming with him we may only need to support them." Don looked from side to side and hunched his shoulders. "Now, how should we handle Louis's situation with his amoureuse?"

"That's a good question, Love. None of us are going to take your head off. This time," Jackie added softly.

"For Madeleine and Louis, we don't say anything derogatory," Deborah began, "As they're just visitors, their life isn't anyone else's business. Don't you have some uptime word to call someone who keeps a person from crashing and burning?"

"Wife?" I couldn't resist.

"Besides the obvious, Luther," Deborah retorted.

"Administrative assistant," Dick offered.

"Caregiver," Amy added.

"Private nurse," Jackie said.

"Or...," Deborah paused, "We ask Madeleine when she gets here. She's learned discretion in a lot more toxic environment than ours. The one thing we don't do is condemn them for the arrangement. If you have to blame something, blame the fallen world and the system they are in. They deserve our prayer and support.

"I concur," Don said, "From what Marcel implied, and what we know from uptime, it sounds like the two are religious, not reborn. We can arrange a few recitals for Louis, and let the Lord do what He wants. How's that sound?"

"I think that will work," Jackie replied, "He's had a rough go in life. Let's be kind, warm, and see what happens."

"And a recital in the Auditorium, for sure," I added.

"Everybody cool with that?" Don asked. I wasn't exactly sure what he meant by cool, but I nodded like everyone else.

"OK," Don picked up his pen, "Then this afternoon we talk to some people, all together."

Jackie looked at Don, who looked back at her.

"We talk to some people," they both said at the same time.

The rest of us looked at each other; Dick and Amy rolled their eyes.

Don saw them. "You're just miffed you didn't think of it first."

"I guess irony can be pretty ironic sometimes," Amy said, then the four from uptime started groaning and giggling.

"Sometimes these people are just weird," Deborah observed.

"Sometimes?" I countered.

*****

Luther: 2 PM, Cottage Hospital training room

"The Wain Engineering Wedding Planners meeting will come to order," Matt said with a grin.

"You want to lead this one, Matt?"

"Oh no, Don, I just want to see how you sort all this out. You were the logistics genius; I just drove the boat."

"See what you're in for, Mimi?"

"I'm looking forward to it!" the dark-haired woman in the new wheelchair said.

"Right. Besides, Jackie's going to chair the meeting," Don replied, then bowed to his wife. "Precious?"

Seated around a table in the staff training room at Cottage Hospital were Don and Jackie, Pastor and Deborah, Mimi and Matt, Jack and Helen, and me.

Don said he needed my help to make sure the building was ready for the weddings; Jack asked me to help arrange the out-of-town guests for the arch of swords. Either way, I was stuck.

Harmony Ives happened by just before we started. Jackie dragooned her in too.

Jackie sat next to one of the windows. I thought her face looked flushed, and not from embarrassment. She looked at her yellow pad and began.

"Thanks for taking time to meet with us today. Here's the situation. We have a number of things happening in the next three months, including a couple of weddings. We need to know when you want your weddings so we can schedule around them."

Our two engaged couples nodded.

"Before we start picking dates, here's a new twist," Jackie continued, "The organ at Chambers Street is going to be taken apart for rebuild sometime in the next month. The sooner we get started the sooner it's done.

"We'd like a last recital before it leaves, if we may," Pastor remarked.

Don opened his mouth, but Jackie spoke over him. "Count on it, Pastor, and it'll be a good one. Marcel Dupré is coming back from France to help disassemble the organ and escort the old Barker machines that control the machinery back to France. And he's bringing along another master organist to help. Louis Vierne, the organist at Notre Dame Cathedral, and his assistant. Two of the most famous French organists will be here. This'll be fun!"

"I know Louis!" Harmony exclaimed, then blushed. "He and his wife spent two months with Charlie and me in 1908. We introduced him to our musician friends, and he performed several recitals. Charlie and I followed his career and travails."

"Then you know his needs due to his lack of vision," Jackie said, "We want to give every support to Louis and his assistant while they're here. We have several partners who have assisted someone with low vision."

"I did that for Louis during his visit," Harmony added, "Charlie was working, and Louis' wife was unwilling to spend much time with him. We worked together well."

I saw a kaleidoscope of emotions flit over Harmony's face as she spoke. *There's a connection here,* I thought.

"I'm sure we'll ask for your help," Jackie replied. She looked at the paper in her hand, took a breath, and continued.

"Matt and Amy, Helen and Jack, you want to have your weddings in the Auditorium, correct?"

The couples smiled and nodded. "Yes, please," Mimi said.

"OK, just tell us when you want to do them, Please decide today if possible. Next," she checked off an item on the sheet, "Within the next week we will have an elevator connecting the stage, Green Room, and basement. That will remove the last physical barrier in the building."

"About time," Matt remarked, "Sirius Cybernetics finally come through?"

"Yep," Don said, "It's only taken six months for Hoople to re-engineer the thing. Good for us it was cheap."

I hope that elevator is safe, my engineer's mind thought.

"Next, we'll have parking available on the lot across the Square until the Bondi Building gets started. And..." Jackie grinned, "Then, on April 20th, we close on the Broadview across the street."

That's a surprise, I thought as a chorus of cheers filled the room.

When the noise died down Don spoke. "We're not giving company discounts in the dining room…"

Cheers turned to raspberries and a few boos.

"…but we will give a special price for catering wedding receptions."

"How much?" Mimi asked. Giggles bounced off the walls.

Jackie snorted. "Always cut to the chase, Mimi! Let's talk later. I have an idea."

"Hopefully not an arm and a leg," Jack added.

Don explained, "Seriously, we want to develop a catering and conference hosting business using the hotel foodservice operation. Nobody does that in this area, and we think it will be a good addition, one that can continue while we're rebuilding the actual hotel. We will start by doing these two receptions, if you folks don't mind, for free."

More applause, and the two couples engaged in a not-too-short kiss.

Jackie looked like she was getting tired; so did Jack. "Now, the real question: When?"

The room got very quiet.

"Could we continue this in my room please?" Jack sounded like he'd run five Marine miles, "I thought I could do this but I can't. I need to get back in bed now!"

"Adjourn to Jack's room," Jackie announced.

Ten minutes later a subset of the first group met in Jack's room. We collected several chairs, and everyone sat except Jack, who had gotten back into bed.

Jackie looked at the yellow pad resting on her lap. "I know you were talking while we dug up the chairs. Did you decide anything?"

Matt grinned. "For us, Saturday, May first, at the Auditorium. Reception at the Broadview. No arch of swords, but we'll try to get my old friend Bull Reeves in as best man. Will that be OK, Boss?"

"Fine by us," Don replied and wrote on his pad.

Mimi looked at Matt. "You said I'm getting married? To *him*?"

Matt grinned. "I could ask George to be grooomsman."

Mimi stared, then turned bright red.

"I don't think George will be interested, unless we're serving mice at the reception."

"What are you talking about, Jackie?"

"Tell you later, Love. Need to know."

Don snorted, then put up his hands. "Never mind."

Jackie sighed, then turned to Helen and Jack. "What about you?"

"Saturday, May 29th, at the Auditorium," Helen said, "We'll have the Arch with the usual suspects if we can get them. Luther, may we count on your help?"

"Sure. Jack, you said some folks you worked with at Pensacola want to come, right?"

"Yes," Jack whispered after Helen nudged him, "We'll look at the list...tomorrow."

CHAPTER TWENTY-TWO

Sylvia: Friday, April 9th, 1926, 3:45 PM, Silas Willard School, teachers' meeting.

"So, really, what's happened to Mimi Conger?" Mary Fitch asked.

The teachers of Silas Willard School had gathered in the second-grade classroom. The event was partly an informal teachers' meeting, but mostly we just craved a little time to relax and unwind after the long school week. I'd brought the coffee pot from my office anteroom, and we were working hard to drain it.

"You knew she was still ill, didn't you?" I asked.

"Every time any of us called her she said she was fine and sounded normal. She'd never let any of us come over to see her though, and when her phone was disconnected, we didn't know what to think. Next thing we knew she was in the hospital about dead!"

Mary Fitch was one of the young teachers in the building. Since she was married to a city fireman, her situation was unusual. She had a reputation for competence and plain speaking. Her students loved her.

"That's about it, Mary. She finally made it over to Lillian's house that Friday evening and Lillian acted to get her help. Doctor Bohan came out, took one look, and got her to Cottage. I've had the kind of surgery she had; it's a miracle she lived."

"Never did trust Doctor Sandburg," Helen Wasson, another of the teachers remarked. "I started with him but went to Doctor Bohan after my first visit."

"Well, I guess he won't be practicing around here anymore," I remarked.

"Or anywhere," Mary observed.

After the situation with Mimi, Doctor Bohan had launched an investigation by the Medical Society. As a result, the Society had recommended his medical license be suspended, and the State agreed. The week before Doctor Sandburg had ingested a little too much cocaine, something the investigation found he had a fondness for, and had died.

"So how is Mimi now?" Hattie Saaijenga, the third-grade teacher asked.

"Haven't any of you visited her in the hospital?" I asked.

The other teachers turned red and looked at each other.

Finally, Mary Fitch replied. "I could tell you we were so busy we never got around to it, but I'd be lying," She took a tissue from the box on the table, "We talked about it, but we all felt so embarrassed that we didn't just barge over there and insist on her seeing us, we haven't worked up the collective courage to face her."

"When we needed correction Mimi never minced words," Hattie added. Given what Mimi told me about Hattie I figured she had first-hand knowledge.

"Remember, ladies, Mimi kept you all at arm's length. She realizes that was wrong now, but it happened and it's over. I'm sure she'd love to see you."

The other teachers sighed and nodded. "How is she?" Mary asked.

"Slowly recuperating," I replied, "She can feed herself most of the time now, She's able to be up in a chair and pushed in a wheelchair. Gonna be at least another month before she's recovered enough to live on her own. But I don't think that's going to be necessary."

"Not necessary?" Helen asked.

I grinned. "Nope. It seems one Matthew Plotczyc, retired Navy Captain and department head at Wain Engineering, has asked Mimi to marry him, and she has accepted!"

The ladies around the library table displayed varying degrees of shock.

Mary spoke up. "I'm amazed! I always thought Mimi was too independent to ever marry someone. I don't think she ever even had a suitor."

Mimi sure had them fooled, I thought to myself.

"Kind of hard to have one of those and be a building principal," Helen remarked, "And she has such an impish streak about her!"

Evelyn had kept quiet through this exchange, as befit the very junior member of the group. Now she spoke up.

"I know Matt, the man she's engaged to. He's a big man, graying hair, with the strangest sense of humor I've ever seen! He's the *jokester* of Wain Engineering, and I've never known him to be without an outrageous and funny comment. And the pranks he's pulled!"

"Speaking of pranks," I interrupted, "Lillian told me Mimi would occasionally pull one around here. I asked, and Mimi suggested I mention *George*."

The other teachers looked at each other and giggled.

"OK, who wants to tell about George?"

"Not me!"

"I can't even think about it!"

"You go ahead, Mary. You could actually stay in the same room with it."

"Right, Hattie," Mary Fitch said, then turned to me.

"A couple of years ago all the grades were studying animals in science class—it just turned out that way. Mimi had a herpetologist friend over at Lombard College."

I started to smile. I thought I knew where this one was heading.

"Anyway, without telling any of us, she arranged to borrow George for the afternoon. George is a python, about three and a half feet long, probably longer now."

I noticed the looks on the others' faces, except Evelyn. She just listened intently. Mary Fitch continued.

"So right after lunch one fine Thursday afternoon, Mimi comes in with a covered birdcage. She puts it in her office and comes out with George wrapped around her waist. This has an effect on the students…and the teachers."

I started to giggle. "I can just imagine," was all I could get out.

"One august faculty member in this room who shall remain nameless…—"

Hattie Saaijenga turned bright red before Mary even finished her sentence.

"…headed straight for the furnace room and would not come out until George was off the property."

"My student teacher could handle that classroom perfectly well without me!"

"Yes, I did," Helen Wasson commented. "Go on, Mary, this is fun."

"Right. Mimi came to my classroom first. I wasn't up to holding the thing, but I found I could at least stay in the classroom with it. The children loved it. Many touched it, a couple even held it. Great teaching moment!"

"Sure was," I remarked. "So there was some *teacher migration*?"

Mary giggled as the rest of the teachers, except Evelyn, blanched. "It turned into something like deer fleeing in front of a forest fire! The teachers would abandon the room before Mimi and I came in—or rather, Mimi and George and I came in. They'd flee to one of the other classrooms, and one of them took over my class since I was with Mimi and her guest. When we were about to change rooms, I'd go warn the teachers in that room, and they'd scoot to the next room. It looked like a Marx Brothers routine!"

"I suppose I should confess I like the Marx Brothers."

"You do, Syl?" Evelyn spoke up. "I do too! Mom puts up with them; I think Don would bring them to the Auditorium again if he could get away with it."

I wondered what the other teachers were thinking of Ev and me about then.

"We finally finished showing off George," Mary continued, "and Mimi took him back to his home at Lombard. The children talked about it for weeks; we teachers just tried to forget."

"Did George make any trouble?" I asked.

"Not really...but he did crawl into Mimi's blouse at one point. The children howled, and Mimi giggled as she pulled him out. She's a trouper. The funniest part, though, came right at the beginning. Flora Potter hadn't heard the commotion and came breezing into my room to ask me something. She came in like this," Mary strode across the classroom, "and then she saw George, and...she executed the smoothest about-face and retreat I've ever seen."

Mary imitated the turnabout, then stopped. Tears started to dribble down her face. Several of the others reached for their handkerchiefs.

"I'm sorry, Sylvia, it just hit me all of a sudden there."

"I understand, folks. Grief does that. I know from experience. Let it come. Use the tissues."

A moment later I could continue. "Now, was there anything said from higher up about this little *event*?"

"One school board member heard about the business and went to Lillian, demanding she discipline the teachers and fire Mimi. Lillian told him she hoped, if Mimi did something like that again, she'd tell her so she could come meet the *guest* herself! The board member was not amused...but we don't have to worry about him any more."

"The one who was killed in the shootout in Peoria?" I asked.

"Yes," Hattie pronounced. "Good riddance! He even tried to have Flora's son Jeff committed to Lincoln State School! Someone proved he could learn, though, and that was stopped."

Now my eyes started to well up. I glanced over and saw Ev was doing the same. Time for the rest of the story.

"Confession time, ladies. I was the one who found out how Jeff learns and communicates, and we're catching him up under special tutelage. He has done extraordinarily well, and," I looked over to Evelyn, "You finish it, Ev."

"When school is out this year Jeff and I are getting married!"

The other teachers showed variations of surprise and shock on their faces. After a moment Mary spoke again.

"We know we can trust Lillian's decisions. You are both excellent teachers, we could tell. And we're so glad you're both here!"

The other teachers crowded around Ev and me, hugging us, shaking our hands, crying. It was another fifteen minutes before we were all composed enough to find our cars and go home.

*****

Sylvia: later that evening, in bed

"So, I guess you and Ev are accepted, Love," Luther remarked.

"Guess so, Sweetheart. We were OK before, now we're part of the team."

"A good place to be."

We were discussing the day in our usual location. After the marathon teacher's meeting, I came home to Luther preparing a light supper of our signature peanut butter and fried egg sandwiches, with some canned vegetable soup. The meal hit the spot.

"How did they take Evelyn being betrothed to Jeff?" Luther asked.

"They were stunned, Love. They had all met him. He doesn't show how brilliant he is at first glance. They accepted Lillian's decisions and the coming marriage. Now I think we're building the team again."

"That's just what you want to do, Love," Luther replied, "Mimi had them working as a team; then she fell out and Flora took over. It's never quite the same when the leadership changes. Then Flora is taken away, and Lillian drops you in there...with Ev for good measure! No wonder they were shaky."

I stretched and rolled into my love, a pleasant collision.

"They got the job done through it all because they're professionals, and ultimately they answered to Lillian. Now, I guess they've accepted me as the leader, even though I didn't come up the way they did."

"Even more reason to keep your situation in prayer. The Lord's made a bunch of changes in our lives in the past six months —six months already? I'm glad He knows what He's doing, because sometimes I don't!"

"So we take it one day, one revelation, at a time, my Love, and in the meantime...we keep each other company."

"Something like that," Luther replied.

*****

Marcel Dupré: Saturday, April 10th, 1926 5:08 AM, their apartment

I woke up with a start. *Did I just hear the phone ring?* I wondered as my fogged mind started to clear. The sound did not repeat. I opened my eyes and realized Jeannette was not in bed with me. I could hear her voice out in the hallway by the telephone but could not understand what she was saying.

I turned on the bedside lamp and looked at the clock. *Who could be calling at this hour?* I wondered.

A few moments later I heard Jeannette ring off. She walked into the bedroom with a smile I could see without my spectacles.

"I get to travel to America with you!"

"What?" I sat up in bed.

"That was *Directeur* Latecote. He begged me to go with you. He said he had a vision."

I stretched, "This is great news, *Cherie*, but a vision? I wonder which angel informed him of this."

"He said he did not ask, but he suspects it was Saint Gabriel."

"What?!" I turned to my love.

"You are too fond of that word, my love," Jeannette replied, "Directeur Latecote said a shining being appeared in his bedroom. He said the being implored—his word—him to let me travel with you, that I was needed for the plans of Our Father and Saviour. The Directeur agreed, and the being disappeared. What do you think it means?" she ended.

"First off, it means you come with us," I replied, "When I mentioned an angel I spoke in jest. But for real?"

"I've always thought Latecote tended toward the mystic," my wife said, "but now I wonder if he has been reborn, as we have?"

"Or he is hallucinating," I said with a snort, "Either way, the message is clear. Our Lord is cooking something up for this trip, and we get to be sous-chefs!"

I began to tick off items on my fingers. "We will hasten to the CGT office as soon as it opens and arrange for your passage." CGT, the *Compagnie Générale Transatlantique*, is the main French shipping line.

"Then to the railway office for the same," I continued, "I must let Monsieur Widor know about this development, and call Louis and Madeleine, probably after Mass. And cable Donald Wain...what's so funny?"

The love of my life continued laughing for a full minute. When she could, she spoke.

"There is my husband, planning every detail of our trip and its preparations, bustling about like Martha before Jesus! Let us stop to thank Our Lord for His provision in this matter, pray once again for our two friends, and then get another few hours of sleep! We have the entire day to make these arrangements, so let us put first things first!" She ended with a decisive nod and a kiss.

"Correct as usual," I mumbled through the kiss.

CHAPTER TWENTY-THREE

Mimi: Sunday, April 11th, 1926, 8:45 AM, her room at Cottage, show-time

"Are you sure you're up to this, Sweetheart?" Matt asked again.

"I am quite sure, Matthew. And that's the third time you asked me. Why are you so worried?"

My insistent betrothed bit his lower lip. "I...I really don't know. You've met the Company folks and they all love you. The other church folks know you from school. I know I can carry you up and down the stairs. I think I just don't want anything to happen to you."

"Afraid my sordid past will catch up with me?"

That stopped him. He looked right at me. "Absolutely not, Love. We all have that sort of past, one way or another, and we've been forgiven and redeemed. It's over. So there!"

Matt bent over and we kissed. "Besides, anyone says anything mean and I'll...."

"You'll be very nice to them and correct them. I'll have no broken heads during my debut!"

Matt turned red. A nice color on him. "Yes, dear," he said softly.

"And I know about the pull chain," He turned redder. "Now, if you'll help transfer me to the wheelchair, we'll get outta here."

Matt positioned the color-coordinated gait belt at the proper place and counted for the transfer.

"And you will notice I am wearing a bra this morning. Lillian thought of everything when she brought the clothes over."

I was ready in case he dropped me, but he didn't.

We gathered our coats and wits and prepared to leave.

Matt turned to me. “And may I say you are the prettiest young lady I’ve seen in many years?”

“You'd better say that,” I shot back.

We wheeled out past the front desk.

Gloria looked up as we passed. “Be back by two or Matt turns into a pumpkin!”

“Good one,” I snickered, “See ya!”

We rolled out the door and down the ramp to the parking lot.

“Is that the fabled Roach Coach?” I asked.

“It is, my Love! It befits my august station in life.”

“Looks like a ride in an amusement park!”

“You’re too proud to ride in it?”

“I didn’t say that. Jackie called it the *Ensign-mobile of your old age.* What is it really?”

We rolled up to the right-side door. I noticed I was about as tall as the car, even sitting in a wheelchair.

“If anybody asks, this is a Duesenberg Model A coupe with a custom body by Budd Manufacturing. It has the Duesenberg engine, but the car is a Jaguar XK140 from 1956 *uptime*.”

“Is that the whole story?”

“No, dear. Let me help you in and I’ll tell you the rest.”

I was able to pivot with Matt’s help and drop into the seat. “Beautiful wood dash,” I remarked, “but how do you fit in it?”

“Watch,” Matt replied, and after he folded the chair and put it in the trunk, he opened the door and folded like a jackknife. “See? Easy!”

“Now here’s the real story,” he continued, “I bought a wrecked Duesenberg model A last year. I wanted to rebuild it but all I could salvage was the motor. We were working on the Bentley Anna the nurse from Hoople bought at the time and I asked her what I should get. She suggested an uptime Jag. That’s what these are called."

He started the car. "I love that low rumble," I said.

"So do I," Matt replied, then continued as he got the car moving. "I got hold of our Export Director, Doctor Art, and asked him to find me one of these with a bad motor. I wanted to put my motor in it. He found me three inside of an hour! I bought all 3 and built this from the parts."

He pulled out onto Losey Street and headed east. "This is neat, Matthew! Could I drive it sometime?"

"Sure, Love. I'll build you one if you want! This is my summer car; I buy a couple of odd cars a year to drive in the winter, then pass them on to Art. Anything from this time goes for a mint uptime."

"I thought the car I had before was fun, but this is a ...*whee!*" I squealed as he took the corner at Chambers street way too fast.

"What did you have?" Matt asked.

"Bet you've never heard of it. I had a Chevrolet V-8."

My betrothed snorted. "We have two of 'em in the company! Don bought Luther Barlow's that he got from Pastor Kittridge, then Dick and Estelle Meriden have a heavily modified one. What happened to yours?" he asked as we stopped for a Santa Fe train.

"I sold it back to the dealer in Rock Island when I started to run out of money," I sniffled a bit. "I really loved that car, even though I couldn't get it serviced at Wright-Allensworth. Lee said he didn't have the manual on it."

"I think AP, Pastor, had that problem when he got his. Luther switched a spark plug wire and got it going. Don uses it as a second car now. So, you're OK with a stick shift?"

"But of course," I said, "and my former male acquaintances said I could have been a racing car driver."

"I think we're going to have fun, Love," Matt said as we started across the tracks.

"And not just with the car," I added.

"They'll wonder why you're blushing," I said as Matt pulled into the small parking lot, "I won't tell."

*****

Luther: 10:30 AM, interlude

Between Sunday school and Church this lovely spring morning I found it necessary to use the facilities off the foyer of the church. As I took care of things, I mused how much time John Ward had spent in this little room, and how he must be rejoicing now.

I dried my hands and opened the door.

"Hey, Luther, could you give me a hand please?" Matt Plotczyc called from the landing by the side door. I started to clap, then I saw he had Mimi Conger in a wheelchair at the foot of the stairs.

"Get the wheelchair?" I asked as I carefully walked down the stairs.

"If you could, please, Luther. When she's out of it just pull up on the front and back of the sling seat. It'll fold right up."

"Will do. Hello to you, Mimi."

"Hi back, Luther. Thanks for your help."

"My pleasure. Ready when you are, Matt."

Matt reached down and scooped Mimi up with one smooth motion. He then started up the stairs. I folded the wheelchair and carried it up the stairs. *Made of lightweight tubing of some sort,* I thought, *not steel...definitely uptime.*

We both got to the top and I unfolded the chair again. With another smooth motion, Matt set Amy down in the chair. They stole a short kiss as she settled into the wheelchair.

"Shall we go, Love?"

“Guess we get to make an entrance, Matthew.” Mimi grinned.

I started to follow the couple down the aisle, but people crowded around and stopped their progress. I slipped through one of the pews and came around from the other side.

“What is all that commotion back there?” Syl asked as I came up to where she was sitting.

“Matt brought Mimi in. They’ve been mobbed.”

“Oh, my! He carried her up the stairs?”

“Sure did, Love. I brought up the chair.”

“That’s so sweet. Would you do that for me?”

“Of course, my Love, I would be happy to bring up your chair… Eeep!”

“Easy range mister.”

“We'll have to negotiate this later.”

“You bet. Now, aren’t you supposed to be up on the platform?”

“Yipe! Thanks, Love, I’ve gotta get going.”

*****

Mimi: impressions of church

My first impression as we walked in was pre-empted by a crowd of smiling, chattering women. Some I knew and some I didn’t. Matt tried to introduce them but ended up holding on to the chair for dear life as I was mobbed. *A really friendly bunch. Not like the other church,* I thought as we finally pushed beyond the clump.

We stopped at the third pew on the left, in front of Luther and Sylvia Barlow and next to Don and Jackie. Matt slipped in, leaving my chair in the aisle. We’d decided I shouldn’t try to transfer to the hard pew this visit.

“Switch,” I heard Jackie say, “I’ll switch back when the service starts.” Matt and Jackie squeezed past each other in the pew.

Jackie handed me a folded paper. “Here’s the bulletin, order of service, who's singing, and so forth."

I looked at the paper. "I know Lucille and Luther, but who's singing?"

"Harold Coupland. Deacon, nice tenor voice. He's singing a good one this morning."

Lucille began to play the piano, some sort of hymns I thought. Three men came out and sat in chairs on the stage. Pastor and Donald Wain along with another man. "My mailman," I whispered to Jackie.

"Yes, Ed Joseph, composes music in his spare time. He and his wife Dayle help with the church accounting."

"Oh. Do the members know about the finances? We never heard about that where I came from."

"Sure. Business meeting every quarter with printed financials available. We help them keep good records."

I nodded. Lucille stopped playing and Jackie nudged Matt. They switched places again and my hand found Matt's.

After some announcements and prayer, the congregation stood and read together two verses from the Bible.

As ye have therefore received Christ Jesus the Lord, so walk ye in him: Rooted and built up in him, and established in the faith, as ye have been taught, abounding therein with thanksgiving. (Colossians 2: 6 and 7)

Don then led the congregation in two songs. Matt showed me the songs in the hymnal. I didn't know them, so I did not sing; Matt hummed the tunes but didn't sing either.

"Why aren't you singing?" I whispered.

"Voice like a toad," he replied.

"Needeep," I added. His eyes crossed but he didn't laugh.

After the singing, Pastor Kittridge got up and gave prayer requests. He prayed for the offering, and Lucille played as the plates were passed. That was only part of the service duplicated in the Universalist church!

After the congregation stood for one more song Luther climbed onto the organ and Harold Coupland walked to the pulpit.

"I sang this a little over a month ago," he began, "but Captain Plotczyc asked me to sing it again this morning."

I looked over at Matt. He looked at me, then took a handkerchief from his pocket.

Harold continued, "In Romans five, verses twenty and twenty-one Paul writes:

Moreover the law entered, that the offense might abound. But where sin abounded, grace did much more abound: That as sin hath reigned unto death, even so might grace reign through righteousness unto eternal life by Jesus Christ our Lord."

Luther accompanied Harold as he sang in a mellow tenor voice, every word clearly enunciated. I don't think I'd ever heard a song like it.

The chorus of the song stuck in my mind:

Where sin abounded, Grace abounded more,
My ransomed soul shall sing it o'er and o'er.
As vile as I could be, in love He rescued me,
Where sin abounded, Grace abounded more.

At the end, Harold repeated the last line of the chorus. The last three liquid notes brought tears to my eyes as I remembered my own story.

I looked at Matt and saw him with eyes shut, tears flowing. I caught Jackie's eye and we both offered him handkerchiefs, which he took and used. Pastor was five minutes into his sermon before Matt finally composed himself. I saw Pastor glance our way and nod. *He's OK with the emotion and so am I,* I thought.

I am embarrassed to report I remember very little of Pastor's sermon that morning. I know he started from those verses the congregation read, and from there wove the most lucid explanation of Christ and his love I'd ever heard in a church. And not a ball score or magazine article in the lot!

The invitation hymn that morning was *I'll Live for Him.* The phrasing of the tune is a bit choppy, but the words say it all. Matt stood up and maneuvered me to the front. Pastor spoke with me for a moment as the congregation continued to sing. He asked if I would allow him to tell the congregation what I had done, and I said yes. He gave a hand signal to Don Wain leading the song, and they stopped after that verse.

Matt turned me to face the congregation as Pastor spoke.

"Mimi Conger comes forward this morning to tell us she trusted Christ the afternoon of March second. Gloria Hodges led her to the Lord in her hospital room. She wants to be baptized, but we must wait until Doctor Bohan clears her after her surgery, and she has regained some more strength."

"Mimi and Matt would also like me to announce they are engaged to be married soon. Details later."

Pastor grinned.

"And now I have the pleasure to announce some interesting upcoming activities! A benefactor who wishes to remain anonymous...but won't get to, since he's standing on the platform behind me..." Pastor hitched his thumb at Don "...has offered to finance the rebuilding of our organ in memory of his late wife, and our dear sister, Pam. The dismantling of the organ will begin in about two weeks. Rest assured the rebuild will sound just like this one now, except for some needed additions and mechanical updating. Luther will be in charge of the project."

I saw Luther's eyebrows raise and mouth open. *I love surprises! Especially someone else's,* I looked at Matt and we both smiled.

"And we will have guests here to help," Pastor continued, "since parts of this organ are badly needed by our friend and Brother in Christ, Marcel Dupré, for the Saint Sulpice organ. Marcel will be coming here from Paris in ten days to help dismantle the organ. He is also bringing another famed organist, Louis Vierne of Notre Dame Cathedral in Paris, and his assistant, to help. Don promises me the organ at the Auditorium will get quite a workout while they're here!"

The congregation laughed at that. *They must know their organs. Even I know who those two organists are!*

"Now, Don and I have asked Luther to play something by Marcel as you are leaving this morning. Luther will announce the piece after we pray; there will be no last song this morning. Thank you for your attention, folks, and now let's pray."

While Pastor prayed Matt wheeled me back to our place. I was amazed again, as his prayer complemented his sermon. *These folks mean what they say,* I concluded, *and so does my Savior.*

After Pastor prayed, Luther spoke. "I'd like to play the *Prelude and Fugue in B major,* by Marcel Dupré. I'm still working on this, so it might be a little rough in spots."

He got up on the bench, pushed a button on the console and let fly.

Luther's hands flew over the keyboards as his feet flailed at the pedals. I had no idea Luther could play like that. About seven and a half minutes later he finished at the organ's full cry. He limped coming off the stage, but if he hurt his leg it never altered his playing. Syl met him as he came and held his arm. I knew that team would manage my former school very well. I felt one tear form and then it was gone. Silas Willard was the first part of my life; here came the next part, and I understood better the term *blessing*.

As I rolled slowly through the crowded foyer Syl beckoned us over to where she stood with Luther and an elderly couple. "I want you to meet our surprise guests," she bubbled, "This is Doctor Carl Christian Christensen, F.A.G.O, Luther's organ teacher, and his wife Marie Heath Christensen. Guys, here is Matt's betrothed, Mimi Conger."

Carl and I shook hands, then Marie hugged me. She was so short she didn't have to bend down to do it.

"Are you two going over to New China?" Luther asked.

Matt looked over at me. "Love, are you up for it?"

"Real food? Let's go!"

Luther started to applaud.

"Why are you clapping, Luther?" the tall elderly gentleman asked.

"Does that mean you're going to take the wheelchair downstairs for us?" I asked.

"Oh! *Give me a hand*...old theater joke, lame in the '70s," Marie added.

"I'll handle the wheelchair," Syl said, "Your stump's not happy." Before Luther could protest Syl took hold of my chair and wouldn't let go until she had placed it at the bottom of the stairs.

"Thank you," I said as Matt lowered me into it.

"No prob," Syl replied, "That chair's lighter than a basket of laundry. And I know why," she added in a whisper.

As Matt helped me into the car to go to the Chinese restaurant, I had a question for him.

"Love, why did you cry when Harold sang that song?"

He started the car before he replied.

"I never forget."

"Forget what?" I asked.

"Everything."

CHAPTER TWENTY-FOUR

Mimi: after supper at Cottage, an evening of loose ends

Click clickclickclickclickkaChunk!

Click clickclickclickkaChunk!

Click clickclickclickclickkaChunkkraWhump!

"Are we having fun yet?" I asked the slim blonde figure at the front desk. I was bored after supper and wheeled myself out to see what was going on.

Kristen Delaney, Assistant Director of Nursing and Night Shift Supervisor looked up from her work and frowned. "Loads," she muttered, "Really, I'm glad to have some time to catch up with these invoices. Some nights I don't even get the adding machine out."

"Why do you have to do this?" I asked, "Doesn't the hospital have bookkeepers?"

"Exactly two," Kristen replied, scratching the back of her head through her white-blond hair, "They're buried with payroll and patient billing. These invoices are for medical equipment and supplies. I'm supposed to know what comes in and check 'em for accuracy."

"Can you do that and take care of us too?"

"Most of the time. John Bohan says patients come first, and he means it. We need a better system though; if Jackie Wain hadn't gotten us this adding machine we'd never keep up!"

"Wish there was a better way," I offered. I knew there was a much better way. Like the laptop computer in my room. But Kristen wasn't a partner and keeping books by computer was very uptime, so an electric adding machine was the best Jackie could do.

I shifted in the wheelchair. "Good that it's this boring tonight, except for pesky patients who keep interrupting you!"

"Oh, you're not a pest! Glad to have the company. I…."

Kristen froze, lifted her head, and turned. She stood up suddenly and called down the hallway, "INCOMING!"

As two nurses and two aides came running, I heard the roar of automobiles passing by the side of the building and into the parking lot. "How'd you hear them?" I blurted out.

"I dunno, just do," Kristen said, then. "Sarah, open up exam one. Gail, stand by with the gurney."

"Right," the nurses said as the door burst open. In strode Gloria, followed by Doctor Setterdahl and her husband. Keith carried a tall, spare elderly man. It was Carl Christensen, I'd met him that morning. Bringing up the rear were Harmony Ives and Carl's wife Marie. I backed up against the station half-wall to watch the show.

"What've we got, G?" Kristen asked.

"Carl Christensen, middle seventies. Collapsed and fell off the organ bench at church just now," Gloria's staccato delivery continued, "Vital signs OK but some odd bowel sounds, obvious pain. We need Doc Bohan, and we need him now!"

"On the phone, here in ten," Sarah the nurse called out.

"Got it thanks. I'll take the triage, K. Sarah, let's get him into the exam room."

The group followed the gurney into the exam room. Kristen and I just stared after them.

"Is it always like that, Kristen?" I asked.

Kristen grinned and winked. "Naah, sometimes Gloria gets excited."

Forty-five minutes later Matt showed up at my door. He swept me out of my chair for a suitably steamy kiss, then set me gently back down. “Good evening, sweetheart,” he began.

“What happened with Carl?” I countered.

“Huh?”

“Good evening, Matthew, I love you, what happened with Carl? I have to know before my mind can move on.”

“Uh, I don’t understand.”

“No, you don’t, but you will. Whenever something happens that I don’t understand, my mind can’t get off the topic until I have enough information to sort it out. I’m sorry, but that’s just how I am. Used to drive my teachers nuts, but they learned to tell me what I needed to know so we could take care of it. So, tell me the story please, Love.”

Matt sat down on the bed. “OK, Dear, I get it now. I just have to shift to my Naval Officer brain to tell you. Grrrrrindd!!” he finished.

“Cute, Love, feel free to do that as needed. Now spill it!”

My betrothed squared his shoulders; I don’t think he realized he did it. “Luther talked Carl into playing for the offering tonight. He played an arrangement of *Saved by Grace*. If they recorded it I’ll play it for you later. Anyway, the offertory was beautiful…I could tell that even with my tin ear. The end was so quiet…and then he just toppled off the bench. His foot hit one of the pedals, and it honked as he capsized. If this had been Luther or someone younger, we might have thought it was a joke. Not this time!”

“Then what?”

“Gasps, talking, no screams. The medical people and Marie ran up to the platform They checked him over, then Keith picked him up and they all hauled off out the door.”

“And I know the rest. Thanks for the details, Love. What happened to the service?”

“Three of the Deacons prayed for the situation, then Pastor

said he'd keep the sermon short...fifteen minutes instead of thirty."

"Did he?" I had to know.

"Yes! Fifteen minutes on the dot. I've never known another Pastor who could do it."

"Me neither," I added, "or any who would try. Everyone in the Universalist Church was in love with his own voice. Thought they were the reincarnation of Edward Everett."

"I know who that is," my betrothed said, "Spoke before Lincoln at Gettysburg. I hear tell old Abe did better."

"Did he ever," I said, "Anything else new?"

"Yes, Love. Don and Jackie want to see you down at the Auditorium Thursday morning. They want to give you a tour of the place and discuss a job possibility with you."

That got my attention. "A job? Doing what?"

Matt shrugged. "They won't tell me. Say it's a secret."

"I will not clean bathrooms or windows!"

"Mimi! We have an uptime cleaning service to do that. They're good and secure."

"I winked. "I figured that, Love. I just wanted to twit you a little."

"Right," Matt replied, "and I have another little secret that'll wait till Thursday."

"My ring?"

"Wait till Thursday, Love."

His neck started to turn red. I'd guessed right again.

*****

Sylvia: around nine, the Cottage waiting room

"We need to get some cushioned chairs in this place," Don observed.

"You buying?" Kristen the night shift supervisor asked.

"Just might. We keep spending hours in here like this, might pick up a few hide-a-beds too."

"There's a thought," Jackie finished Don's comment for him.

Don and Jackie, Luther, Marie, and I waited for word of Carl Christensen's condition. Kristen held court from the front desk.

"You're going to feel this tomorrow, Love," Luther said to me.

"Don't worry, Sweetheart, I'm still vertical. Wouldn't want to make this two nights in a row, though. Are you OK, Marie?"

"I am," the elfin lady replied. "Carl and I have discussed this sort of situation often. We know how old we are, and what can happen. We're together until the Lord takes one of us, whenever. I was more nervous the evening little Dorothy Templeman was born."

"I remember that," Luther said. "Did you know she's due again, late May or early June? Estelle said Agnes told her this was absolutely the last one."

"Then she'd better figure on tying something in a knot," Marie said softly.

"Marie!" I sputtered.

Marie grinned. "Agnes used to laugh for ten minutes straight when I said something like that. If Charlie had been there he could have defended himself, but he never was. I pray for them daily, even Charlie."

Marie had lived at the Templeman boarding house with Luther while he went to Bradley. She had trusted Christ the year before and had met Carl shortly after. Charlie was Agnes' rarely-seen husband.

I noticed Don chuckling softly and shaking his head.

The elevator door opened, and Doctors Bohan and Setterdahl came out. They both looked exhausted.

"I don't know what it is about organists and bowel problems," John Bohan opened. "First Marcel, then Carl. Too much pedal work or sitting down on the job, something."

"I don't know," I remarked, "You also had to do that to Mimi Conger and me, and we're not organists."

"Yours wasn't a...never mind. There are other punch lines but I'm too tired. Marie, your husband's gall bladder was almost ruptured. We got it before it spilled bad things into his peritoneum. The appendix was inflamed too, so he got a two-for-one operation. He's resting comfortably, his heart is strong, prognosis optimistic. And Jenn here was a great help!"

"Easier on the back than sawing bones," Jennifer added.

"I wonder if what we had for lunch had anything to do with it?" Marie asked. "We ate at New China Café."

"I don't think that had anything at all to do with this," John replied. "I think those two organs had been acting up for months. Tonight, one just started to let go."

Marie put her finger to her nose. "Now that I think of it, he's had to take more naps after meals lately. I wonder if things were bothering him then?"

"Wouldn't he have said something?" I asked.

"I don't think so, Syl. We've talked about how stolid he is before. He never complains of pain or feeling ill. I guess tonight it finally took him down."

"Well, he is quite healthy otherwise for his age, and I think his prognosis is good," Jennifer added, "Do you have any other questions, Marie?"

Marie reddened. "Yes, Doctor, I do have one, but I'll whisper it to you."

Jennifer leaned down and Marie whispered. Jenn started to blush, and thought a moment.

"Yes, Marie. Give him time to recover, and I believe I may say his *vigor* will return."

Don groaned. Jackie and Luther chuckled, I snorted, and John looked puzzled.

CHAPTER TWENTY-FIVE

Marcel Dupré: Tuesday, April 13th, 1926, 8 AM, their apartment, Paris

"Are you ready, chérie?" I asked my wife.

"Still stunned, but ready," Jeannette replied. "I still cannot believe the Director is letting, no, begging me to go!"

"We will accept this gift from Our Lord through unusual means. As Donald wrote, *take it and run*!"

"However it occurred, we've had a merry time since," Jeannette remarked as she brought another suitcase down the stairs to the foyer.

"Our Lord was in it, though, chérie, right down to the special deal we got for your fare. Makes CGT appear generous."

CGT, the *Compagnie Générale Transatlantique*, is the main French shipping line.

Jeannette checked another item off her list. "When they get some free dining music for the voyage, they can afford to seem generous."

"Louis and I figured they would want to make an arrangement, and if you travel free of charge as a result, I'm perfectly happy to play a little for them."

"Is Madeleine traveling free too?" Jeannette asked.

"No, Louis had to pay her passage. She is unattached legally."

"I have to admit that's fair, Love—although I pray the Lord does something about that situation."

"So we have prayed, chérie. Let us see what He does...besides arranging for you to come with us!"

We stopped to kiss, then carried the baggage out to our car. We loaded the car, locked the door of our house, and started over to the apartment of Louis and Madeleine.

We parked the car and walked up to the first-floor apartment. I rang the bell twice.

"Hmmm...no answer," Jeannette remarked, "This is unusual. I would have expected them to be standing on the curb, except the weather is so damp."

I tried one more ring. "Three rings of the doorbell should have roused them, chérie. It is time for the alternative plan."

I fished in my pocket and pulled out a key. "The cost of being his closest friend, I suppose," I said as I turned the key in the lock. The apartment door opened, and we walked in.

"Who is there?" A voice from the back bedroom.

"Marcel and Jeannette, Louis. What is wrong?"

"Come and see."

We walked through the apartment to the bedroom. Louis Vierne sat in his shirtsleeves on his bed. Empty suitcases stood in the corner, open drawers in the dresser, and the half-empty closet.

"We have to meet the train for Le Havre. Where is Madeleine?"

Louis held out a paper. On the bed next to him sat a larger paper, with dots imprinted in it...Braille.

I took the paper from Louis and read. I handed it to Jeannette and she read. She took another look around the room. "Do you think the Cardinal Archbishop really threatened her with excommunication if she went with you?"

"I... I don't know," Louis wrung his hands, "but it does not matter now. I emptied my bank account to pay for the tickets. We pooled the rest of our money to live on in America, and she has taken it all. Now I have nothing!" He sniffled and reached for his handkerchief.

"And this also leaves you without a caregiver on this trip," I observed, then realized I had just made things worse. At that moment I had an idea, and it was not from my own addled brain.

Louis wiped his eyes. "Marcel, what am I to do? I can barely function here without help. I cannot even get to the cathedral without someone to guide me. I am undone!"

Jeannette and I looked at each other and nodded.

"Here is what we will do, my friend," I said softly, "Jeannette and I will collect your things, and tend to your care needs. We will meet the train this afternoon as scheduled. Tomorrow, we will leave for America aboard the *Paris* as scheduled."

Jeannette smiled and nodded in agreement as I continued, "We will travel to Galesburg, Illinois, as scheduled...and see what happens from there. You might as well come with us, you have nothing here except your organ, and since the Cardinal Archbishop has chosen to take notice of your living arrangements you may not have that. Will you still join us?"

Louis started to cry. He wiped his eyes again before continuing.

"How...how can you be so kind to someone like me?"

"I will be happy to explain that on the voyage. It might take a while, but we will have time. Will you come?"

"Yes, Marcel. Do with me what you will." Louis put his head in his hands.

"There is Someone you should say that to, my friend, but it is not me. Now we will get busy!"

I sent a cable to Donald before we boarded the afternoon express for Le Havre.

*****

Jackie: 10:15 AM, the Auditorium office

Harmony Ives bustled into the office out of breath. "What is it, Jackie? I got over here as soon as I could."

"What are you talking about?" I asked before Don could get refocused from the paper he was studying.

“Sherry said you needed me down here ASAP.”

“That is what I told Harmony; thank you for arriving so quickly,” our cyberint said through the hidden speakers, “I thought it best Harmony be here to learn of the cable we received. I am sending it through the printer.” The camouflaged laser printer in the corner spat out a sheet of paper.

“This had better be good to bring Harmony rushing down here,” I said. I retrieved the paper. I read it quickly. “All right, it’s good,” I added, sitting back down, “How long have we had this cable?”

“Just as long as it took Harmony to get here,” Sherry replied, “I have already replied in my name to Marcel in Le Havre.”

“Do you understand them, Harmony?” Don asked.

“If you don’t then I certainly don’t,” Harmony replied, sitting down on the love seat with a sigh.

“I guess I’d better read this. Thanks, Sherry, for handling this.”

“My pleasure. And you’re welcome too, Donald,” she sniffed, and the speakers cut.

“OK, it’s from Marcel,” I began, “quote, ‘Some changes. Through a miracle, Jeannette is coming with me. Madeleine has left Louis without warning at the behest of the Cardinal Archbishop. Still bringing Louis, we are taking care of him, he will need more help there. Please pray he is reborn, and some work may be found for him while we are there. Embark tomorrow noon aboard Paris. Warm regards to all, Marcel.’”

Harmony spoke first. “Who is Madeleine? Was she his assistant?”

“Madeleine Richepin,” Don said softly, “We called her his assistant to keep the tongues at church from wagging. She is—was—his *amoureuse*.”

Again, I saw several emotions flit across Harmony’s face. “Oh, I understand now. He certainly needs someone to help him function, and it makes sense for her to become his lover. But he was forbidden to remarry, even though his wife was at fault, not him." Her expression hardened, "Oh, yes! The Church overlooked the relationship until it became advantageous to notice it."

"Looks like that to me," I said, "You, Love?"

"Concur," Don replied, "This makes it easier and harder. We don't have to explain Madeleine, but Louis is used to having help. Marcel and Jeannette will mind him for the trip, but they can't keep it up."

Harmony smiled. "I think we can help out here," she said, folding her coat over her lap, "Let's see what the Lord does. Let me do some checking in the meantime."

"Thank you, Harmony," I said, "but he's not a Believer, far as we know."

"I know, but remember I've also met the Lord's Providence lately, up close and personal. We'll see what He does this time."

*****

Marcel: at sea

The CGT liner *Paris* was completed in 1921. She was the largest liner in the fleet through much of the twenties and plied the North Atlantic between Le Havre and New York year after year. I knew that she was not the largest, or the fastest liner on that run, but a trip on her would be pleasant, relaxing, and reasonably speedy. She also held the reputation for the best cuisine in the CGT.

By the time we settled into our adjoining second class staterooms (No sense paying for amenities we don't need), the ship had been nudged from the dock by her tugs and was heading through the crowded estuary toward the sea wall and the English Channel.

The weather was forecast to be sunny and clear for the voyage; we knew from experience what that meant and were correct.

Storms and heavy seas marked the entire voyage. Fortunately, none of us suffer from seasickness.

Louis and I alternated playing the piano in the first-class dining room for an hour each main meal. In exchange for this service, Jeannette traveled free of charge, and we ate in the first-class dining room. We were happy to oblige as it also allowed us to keep up our practicing.

Jeannette and I knew the time would drag after the evening meal. We had a plan for that time. I explained it to Louis that first night.

"I know you are getting bored already, my friend," I said as we sat in our perambulating stateroom. "Here is an idea. Jeannette and I want to read the New Testament through in its entirety on this voyage. May we read it aloud, and would you like to hear it?"

Louis sat for a moment in thought. "You know, that might be a good idea. I have never heard the Bible read like that. This is approved, isn't it?"

"Of course," I replied, "It is complete with the *Imprimatur* and the *Nihil obstat* on the second page." I noted the irony of requiring the written permission of The Church to read God's Own Word.

Louis thought a moment, then decided. "Yes, Marcel, I would like to hear that. Please go ahead."

So, beginning with the Gospel of Matthew, that evening we began to read.

CHAPTER TWENTY-SIX

Don: Thursday, April 15th, 1926, 10:55 AM, the Auditorium office, tour with a tail

"Well, what do you think?" I asked the dark-haired woman in the wheelchair.

"I think...I think I'm in love, and not just with Matthew," she replied, pulling Matt over for another kiss, about the fifteenth that morning.

"How so?" Jackie asked.

"Well," Mimi began, then shut her eyes, to think I guess. "This is the most incredible venue I've ever seen or dreamed of. You have room to stage any play or even an opera on that platform. The acoustics are beyond belief. I understand now how you do that, with Sherry and the speakers. And you can record what goes on any way you want, in a quality we've only had before in a live performance. And why are you doing this again?"

I started to reply but Jackie shushed me. "We want to improve the recording technology of course. We'll broadcast direct from here too, for whatever network we can set up. But we also know listening to good music helps the brain organize itself, and promotes mathematical, analytical thinking."

I just had to add my two cents' worth. "Music helps reorder people's minds to increase their understanding. It helps bridge the two halves of the brain. If you're interested, we have several good books on the subject from uptime you can read."

"I'm very interested," Mimi replied, "I have my own theories on how children learn. I synthesized them from my studies. I think we'll agree on how music organizes the brain."

"And I'm pleased to note," Jackie's grin turned vulpine, "That it even works on the Admiral here."

"Hey!" I exclaimed, knowing resistance was futile.

Jackie snorted, "We also want to give the Lord a chance to put the musical *bug* in the minds of people who listen and watch. Music helps them understand His world better, ultimately drawing them to Himself, not us. And get all this going before the Depression hits if we can. Make sense?"

Mimi nodded, eyes moist. "Yes, Jackie, you both make sense. How may I help?

May I answer her?" I asked Jackie.

"Go ahead," both Jackie and Sherry answered, "We'll fill in the details," Sherry added.

I suppressed the urge to roll my eyes and continued. "I just love setting up the programs for concerts here and booking the artists. It's been the most fun I've ever had, but I can't keep it up and also keep track of all the other company projects. Several of the folks around here, and the Lord, have been reminding me of this lately."

I paused as a snort and laughter came from the speakers. "Was that really necessary, Sherry?"

"It was," Sherry replied with another chuckle, "I suggest you get to the point before Jackie stuffs something in your mouth. I've heard a sock works well."

"Thank you oh pesky cyberint," I said in my annoyed Admiral voice. I turned back to Mimi. "What we would like...."

"You're welcome. Don't mention it. I won't." Sherry intoned and clicked off.

This time I did roll my eyes. "Anyway...Jackie has told me stories about how you ran Silas Willard. You had that place jumping. The children learned and had fun at the same time. The place was much more staid when I went there."

"You went to Willard? It was only built in 1912!"

I saw the shock in Mimi's eyes. "I'm sorry, Mimi, I should have worded it differently. I went to school there from the fall of 1959 to the spring of 1965. In another universe. It was pretty quiet, except for sixth grade, but that's another story."

"It sure is, and you're not telling it now," Jackie interrupted again, "What the old geezer is trying to say...and wipe that look off your face!...is you kept that school turning out kids who excelled in high school, and had fun doing it. You learned how kids learn, and you ran an amazing school because of that. We think you can do the same job with a place like the Auditorium. Have you ever managed a performance venue before?"

Mimi blushed. "Matt doesn't know this, but when I was at Lombard, I managed all the incoming speakers and musical groups. I booked them, got them fed and housed, sent out the publicity. They wouldn't let me have an assistant, so I did it all myself. And graduated with honors," she finished with a flourish.

"Why didn't you tell me that, Love?" Matt asked.

Mimi looked up at him with a beatific smile. "Ancient history. You never asked."

"What the Admiral here was getting to before he got off track," Jackie jumped in again, "We'd like you to take over as manager of the Auditorium as a performance venue. I have a salary in mind. it comes out about three times what you made as a Principal. Plus all the usual company benefits. When Doc Bohan releases you, will you take the job?"

Mimi looked up at Matt, and he nodded. She glowed as she turned back to us. "Yes, yes, I would be honored to accept that position!!"

I shook Mimi's hand, Jackie hugged her, and she and Matt kissed again.

"Well, that's settled," I began, "Now about lunch..."

A warbling tone from the speakers stopped me cold. I knew what the tone was. We'd set it up when we established Sherry in the basement. But she'd never used it before.

Five seconds later Sherry spoke. "*Flashlight,* everyone in the auditorium."

"The code word for an overriding emergency," I said quickly for Mimi's benefit.

"I have just been informed by Kathy Trainor that Notre Dame Cathedral is on fire uptime," Sherry intoned, "She suggests anyone who wants to should come uptime quickly to watch the event unfold. She says it looks bad."

"Notre Dame when?" Mimi asked.

"Uptime," Jackie replied, "In that parallel universe, time is running exactly ninety-three years later than here, moment by moment. The fire is burning in twenty nineteen in our old universe."

"Oh, all right, I think I understand," Mimi said, her brow wrinkling.

"Would you like to come with us?" Jackie asked.

"I will call Gloria and tell her you will be late, and why," Sherry added.

"Who'll mind the store here?" I asked.

"We will," Amy said as she and Elwood hurried through the office door, "We don't need to see this. You four just go and sort it out in your minds. We'll cover with Sherry here."

"Rather remember as it was," Elwood added.

"Thanks," Matt said, "Love, will you come?"

"Yes," Mimi replied, "but what an introduction to uptime!"

"You said it," I added, "To the transfer room!"

"Right, Batman," Jackie shot back as we headed for the door.

*****

Mimi: Monday, April 15th, 2019, 11:25 AM, a certain building in Gales-

burg, Illinois, introductions

Don opened the other door to the transfer room and we stepped in—rather, they stepped in and I rolled in after them. We were met by a stocky woman of indeterminate age wearing nondescript clothing. She looked very ordinary until one looked in her face. I have rarely seen anyone with such lively eyes.

"Howdy," the woman said, extending her hand, "I'm Sarah Wade, Kathy's assistant. You must be Mimi! We've heard a lot about you."

"Who from?" I had to ask.

"Amy and Elwood mostly. They like you a lot. And you got a good one in this guy," she pointed her thumb at Matt.

"I think so," I replied, looking around, "Aren't you going to greet the others?"

"Naah, they know me. We've got the TVs going upstairs. Let's go!" She took off down the carpeted hall toward an elevator.

"Don't mind her," Matt whispered in my ear, "She's unique and great at her job. She's got her own way with folks—you'll get used to her."

"I like the way she operates," I said, "but her pants look like a feed sack," I whispered as we followed Sarah.

We got in an elevator at the end of the hall. "So is this building in Galesburg in 1926?" I asked.

"Yes," Don replied, "Big warehouse building from the late teens, blends in so you hardly notice it. It was vacant here, nobody knew what to do with it. We bought it and remodeled—some things people see, some they don't."

The elevator opened on another hallway, wider this time. "This is where we train new people heading back our way," Jackie said, "It's like a small hotel with classrooms. We're on the top floor.

We came to a door labeled *Media Center*. "If this room's disorienting, we can go to a smaller one," Sarah said as she opened the door.

We entered. "Wow!" was all I could say.

Two sides of the room were tinted windows looking out over downtown Galesburg. I never paid much attention to the layout of downtown but even I saw great gaps in the rows of buildings. "Where did the buildings go?" I asked.

"Every hole has a story," Don replied, "Fires got a lot of 'em. Wear and decrepitude got others. Some came down because of stupidity. *We want new* they'd chant, and another landmark bit the dust. There have been some nice exceptions, and we're in one of 'em. One of us will be happy to give you a tour of the town when you're able."

"I might talk Matthew into that eventually," I remarked, then turned my head to the inner wall and gasped. The entire wall was a giant screen, like the one on my laptop computer but huge. That was not the source of my gasp, however.

On the screen displayed a streetscape of Paris. In the distance, the cathedral of Notre Dame lay wreathed in smoke and fire. Every moment the flames rose higher in the spire at the center of the roof, itself being consumed by roiling flame. People were standing in the street watching, pointing, talking. Large red fire trucks moved toward the building, two-note horns howling.

I closed my eyes for a second and swallowed convulsively. "I'm glad I've watched my laptop, otherwise this would just overwhelm me," I remarked.

"All of us, Mimi," Jackie said, "Anybody here ever been to Paris?"

"I took a tour about fifteen years ago," Kathy Trainor said, "but we saw so much so fast I can't remember much of it."

"I spent the summers of 1922 and 23 there," I said, "I was studying theories of learning with Maria Montessori, Jean Piaget, and Théodore Simon. Ended up using parts of their theories to help mentor my teachers."

"I know of the first two, but who's Simon?" Don asked.

"He worked with Binet to develop standardized intelligence tests. We've been thinking about using them here but haven't even started experimenting yet."

"Oh-OK," Don nodded, "Besides developments of the Binet, we have quite a few other tests available here. And they're still nothing more than a fair guesstimate of real intellect."

"I came to that conclusion too," I said, then pointed, "Look at that spire flame up."

"It's gone," Matt stated, "and it's been there what, nine hundred years?"

"No, Matt, only since around 1840," a mellow baritone voice interrupted, "It was erected when the cathedral was restored after the French Revolution."

"Oh, thanks, Fred," Jackie said, "I don't believe Mimi Conger has met you. The voice is Fred, our uptime class-A Cyberintelligence.

"Happy to meet you, Fred," I said, "I just met your associate Sherry."

"Ah, yes, we keep busy trying to keep these humans out of trouble. Donald, please explain the source of my name."

"Oh, all right," Don said, "When I was Disbursing Officer on the old *Lexington* we were testing a payroll system using first-generation micro-computers. It worked great but, as usual, the bureaucrats decided to use a much more expensive, clunky system. They called our test rigs *FRED*—Fleet-Responsive Electronic Disbursing. The sailors called it something else, ending in *ridiculous electronic device*."

I giggled. "Do you mind being called that, Fred?"

"No, I understand the joke. I leave it to my associate Sherry to pay Donald back for that indiscretion."

I started to reply, then choked up as the flaming spire of the cathedral fell into the pyre of the roof.

"This is Holy Week," Kathy remarked, "I hope everyone got out OK."

"Bad day to find bodies," Matt added, "Been there, done that." I looked over at him and saw how pale he was.

"I'm sorry to bring it up at a time like this," Sarah Wade said, "but y'all haven't had lunch yet, have you?"

"No, we haven't," Jackie replied, "Could we order out?"

"Sure! What's your pleasure?" Sarah asked.

"Nothing for me," Matt said, pointing at the screen, "This has my stomach churning. In fact..." He let go of my hand and bolted out of the room.

"What's that all about?" I asked.

"Matt was in the Spanish war and the Philippine Insurrection. He saw a lot," Don said softly, "Every once in a while something triggers him. He'll be OK, but maybe he'll hang out somewhere else for a while."

"Glad I saw this now, so I know if it happens again," I said.

"Yeah," Don replied, "Now if we're still talking food, how about Pizza House?"

"They have Hawaiian pizza: ham and pineapple," Kathy said.

"That's one of those round flat crusty things with stuff on it, right? Yeah...I'd like that!" I replied, "Do you have Gator Sauce?"

Don groaned but Sarah grinned. "Sure do! I heard you like it too. I use it on everything!"

Don coughed, "I'd like my usual, please: medium mushroom, thin crust." He looked over at the screen and winced as another section of roof fell in.

It seemed incongruous to discuss food while the cathedral

burned in detail on the screen, but we managed.

Sarah left to get lunch. We continued to watch the inexorable march of fire across the roof of the cathedral.

"Fred, do you think they'll be able to stop the fire before it's completely destroyed?" Don asked.

"To a degree," the cyberint replied, "The wooden roof is gone. The wood is so old and dry nothing will stop it once it is burning. However, the parts of the interior at floor level might survive in a damaged state. We will see. If the firefighters can make a stand at the towers, items inside that part may be saved. The roof of the tower area is stone, not wood. Everything will be damaged, of course."

"Where is the organ in that building?" Jackie asked.

"At the tower end of the structure," Fred replied, "not underneath the wooden roof. It may survive, but it will have to be disassembled and cleaned, and no doubt the electronics will need rebuilding."

"Electronics?" I asked, "When I visited, they talked about the complex mechanical action, built by Cavaille-Coll."

Don scratched his head. "As I recall, sometime in the early 1960s the Barker machines were replaced by electro-pneumatic action. The old console is in a museum in the crypt. Then in the '90s the controls were computerized, just like our organ. Even if that doesn't burn it'll have to be rebuilt. What a mess."

So, we spent the afternoon munching pizza and watching the disaster as it happened. Matt came back in shortly after two.

I had a question. "How can we receive the video of this as it's happening? Paris is over four thousand miles away across the Atlantic."

Jackie waved Don off, "Many man-made satellites orbit the earth like the Moon does, only closer in. Signals are transmitted up to the satellites and retransmitted down on the other side of the earth. Then the networks beam their signals to other satellites that send them to all the local stations. There's a second or so delay as this happens, but we can't see the delay. Sammy Allen can explain this better—he used to design the equipment."

"When did he do that, Love?" Don asked.

"He did it for the Navy his last tour. All the big companies wanted him when he retired, but he came with us instead."

"I never knew that," Don said, "He could have made millions working for them."

"You know how it is," Jackie replied, "Working for those people you make lots of money, but don't have a life. Sammy decided he wanted a life with Mary Beth and the kids. So he came here."

"And what a life," Don added.

About four o'clock I looked at my watch and startled. "Hey, I need to get back! I'm due for my afternoon meds. Gloria will have a fit if I'm late."

"I don't think so," Fred's voice burbled from the speakers, "I suggest someone return to the basement to meet the incoming party."

"On it," Sarah said and headed for the door. Ten minutes later she returned with Gloria in tow. She carried a small bag with my meds.

"Ah, there you are," she announced, then looked to her right. "Whoa! Is that the cathedral?"

"Yes, but uptime here, not back there," Jackie replied, "They're trying to save the towers right now. No idea yet if they'll succeed."

"That's awful," Gloria said, "You're not going to tell Louis Vierne about this when he gets here, are you?"

"Not if we can help it," Don said, "This may never happen there, but we all know anything can happen if the Lord allows it. Fire, war—Notre Dame survived the Second World War in this universe, but just by a hair. We're not guaranteed anything temporal in this world."

"Amen," Matt intoned.

Matt and I finally got back to Cottage about eight that evening. Our good-night kiss lingered much longer than usual.

"Oh, wait, Love. I almost forgot!" Matt said as he pulled a box from his pocket.

"Ah, the ring! Let's see it," I said. Matt took my hand and placed the large diamond on the third finger.

I kissed him, then whispered in his ear, "Love, you put it on my right hand."

Another test. he's fine! I thought as he blushed deeply and put the ring on the proper hand.

"It's the most beautiful ring I've ever seen!" I got a little carried away, but the kiss which followed suited the occasion perfectly.

CHAPTER TWENTY-SEVEN

Sylvia, Saturday, April 17th, 1926, 6:15 PM, dinner and more

"A rhetorical question, Pastor, if I may," Harmony Ives began.

Five of us sat at the table in the dining room, letting my pot roast, potatoes, and asparagus start to digest before tackling the pieces of apple pie in front of us. Besides Luther and me we had invited Pastor and Deborah, and Harmony. We'd also invited Paul and Edna, but they were at the hospital sitting with one of her students who'd had surgery.

Although the conversation sparkled as usual, Harmony seemed distracted during the meal.

"Of course, Harmony, fire away."

"In your knowledge of Scripture, is there any permitted reason for divorce, and if so what is it?"

"That's a heavy topic for the dinner table," Deborah remarked.

Harmony started to redden around the neck. "I know, but it's a question that's been on my mind. I know what I've read, but I want to check it with your knowledge."

Pastor swallowed. "Matthew 5:32, offers a reason: *fornication*, which is taken to mean infidelity with another than your husband or wife. There's some disagreement among theologians whether that's what He meant, and how far one should go with the definition, but that's our best understanding."

"Thank you for your honesty, Pastor. I have a follow-up question."

"Of course, Counselor...er, sorry, I thought I was talking to Maggie B. there for a moment."

"Who?"

"Margaret Rawalt Bailey, Maggie B. for short," Deborah replied, "Lawyer in Chicago, company partner, and counsel. A real tiger! I just love her! And don't pay any mind to AP's remarks, Harmony. I'll sort him out later. Please go on with your question."

"Thanks, Deborah, and no offense taken. I get to speaking formally when I'm digging through something like this. Here's my question: Would you perform the wedding ceremony for a couple, if one of the parties had been divorced; and if so, what would be the circumstances of the divorce which would allow you to so act?"

"Great question, Harmony," Luther couldn't resist. "If I phrased one in that detail, Syl would give me a Eeep!"

"That's *an Eeep*, Love. Our pokes must be grammatically correct,"

"But not wordy," Deborah added.

"Right," I replied, "Pastor, what do you say?"

Pastor bowed slightly in my direction. "Thank you so much, Syl! OK, the answer: This one is in two parts; please don't throw anything at me till you've heard both."

Deborah smiled, "Notice where my foot is, AP."

Pastor glanced down. "I know, Deborah, and I'll keep it short."

"Yes. you will," Deborah countered, "Relax, Harmony, this one has a happy ending."

"So I hope and pray. Your answer?"

Pastor fiddled with his napkin as he spoke. "I've thought about this one for many years, and I have to go with my personal conviction on it. I cannot in good conscience perform the ceremony for anyone who has been divorced, for any reason. I'm sorry, but I cannot risk it for my testimony. It's just how the Lord's led me."

Harmony's face froze, except her lip quivered slightly. Pastor saw it too.

"Part two," he continued, "If I believe that this divorced person is not at fault, I call in Sylvester Sanford to perform the ceremony. He's an old friend and fellow Pastor. He shares my view about divorce, but he does not share my conviction about performing the ceremony for the innocent party. Does that answer your question, Harmony?"

Harmony's features softened. "I think it does, Pastor, and thank you for your honesty and forthrightness. That's something good to know."

"Louis needs to trust Christ first."

Harmony's mouth dropped open, and she stared at the speaker.

"Welcome to life with Deborah Kittridge," Pastor grinned, "She has the uncanny ability to cut to the *root of the matter* like no one else I've ever met! That's why she drives me crazy and I love her so much!"

"Jackie Wain's right up there with me, in case you haven't noticed. Seriously, though, you're thinking of Louis Vierne, aren't you?"

Harmony blushed and put her head down for a second. Then, she raised her head and spoke.

"Yes, Deborah, I am. I remember what he was like when he and his wife visited us in 1908, stayed with us for two months. I would never leave my husband, but I thought Louis the sweetest, most lovable man I'd ever met except Charlie. And now, after all these years, I don't know what to think!"

Deborah spoke softly, directly.

"Harmony, what you are thinking of may come to pass. Louis has not been *Born Again* though. Without that change, you're letting yourself in for a heap of trouble. You and Charlie shared an unequal yoke. You'll want a Christian husband."

"I loved Charlie," Harmony said.

"Yes, but was it easy to live a Christian life around him?"

Harmony pulled out her handkerchief. "I don't know that I wanted to hear that, but I think you're right."

"I know, Harmony, but God leads us to greater joy than we can imagine. Remember, even if he has trusted Christ, he also has to want your company. You wouldn't want to push yourself on him."

Suddenly all you could hear was the fan overhead.

Deborah continued, "Although I don't think you'll have any trouble knowing whether he wants your attention if the rest of it falls into place."

"You can't sculpt the future," Pastor added, "Our Lord does a much better job of it."

*****

Louis Vierne: Sunday, April 18th, 1926, five minutes past midnight, aboard SS Paris, in the Atlantic.

I had never experienced anything like this.

I lay in my bunk in my stateroom, stared out at the light and shadow, and pondered. The roll and pitch of the ship I could tolerate without getting sick. I had memorized the route to the bathroom and could navigate it by myself. These were not my problems this night. My *life* was the problem.

I have an excellent memory—some would call it eidetic. This night I remembered in crisp detail every wrong turning, every missed opportunity, every soured relationship, in my life. I wanted to blame something or someone else for my failings, but I found I couldn't. Madeleine had indeed betrayed me and taken everything from me. But she had been my choice. All along, I had been allowed to choose my way. The effects of those choices sickened me.

I felt on the nightstand for the ashtray and my pack of Baltos but stopped. *A cigarette will not help me now,* I mused, *and if I fell asleep I would die in the fire. Would that be so bad?*

That I would even consider that scared me even more, and I pulled away from the ledge. I began to consider the other half of the matter.

She hadn't betrayed me. I had betrayed myself, over and over again. I chose a miserable path and I was miserable. Was that my fate? Was I born to be dashed against hard rocks and emptiness?

Marcel and Jeannette had been reading the Bible to me over the past several evenings. I had never imagined the Bible said such things. All my life I had been taught to observe the Sacraments, make my confession, and let the priests tell me what I ought to do. What my friends read me was a revelation, so far removed from the constructs of The Church as to be in a different universe!

I knew how people tended to change things over time; I had done so with my compositions. But I had believed one religion to be much like all others. The difference between what was said at church and what they had read me was astounding!

I had put my faith in the sacraments Christ had established and in the Church for supplying those sacraments. The Bible stripped that down to something much simpler and still much harder. *Jesus wants me to trust Him, not just the sacraments He set up,* I thought. *Was there something within the sacraments themselves, or merely remembrances of Him?*

For all the replay of my memory, the answer still eluded me. My *life* was my sin. What was certain to me from the Scriptures, and the memories of my actions, was that I was a *Sinner*, with a capital S. No penance, no Rosary, no amount of good works, was going to change that. Ever. And I knew it.

So, what am I to do? The final question I could not answer.

Another voice joined the discussion in my mind.

> *"Come to me, all you that labour, and are burdened, and I will refresh you." (Matthew 11:28, Douay-Rheims version.)*

But how? That's too simple, I asked in my mind.

"For if thou confess with thy mouth the Lord Jesus, and believe in thy heart that God hath raised him up from the dead, thou shalt be saved." (Romans 10:9, Douay-Rheims version.)

Is that all? What about penance, the Sacraments, Canon Law as the priests applied it? I started to weep.

> *"For by grace you are saved through faith, and that not of yourselves, for it is the gift of God; Not of works, that no man may glory." (Ephesians 2:8-9, Douay-Rheims version.)*

There was nowhere to turn, nowhere to run...and I knew I must choose.

I chose.

"Lord Jesus, I am undone! Save me and do with me what You will."

I didn't realize I said the words aloud, but I knew I meant them.

I continued to cry, but the *motivation* of the weeping changed. From that moment I felt like I was bathed in cool light, and I felt myself *altered.* Alive, for the first time in my life. I could only describe the difference empirically, by the effects on me. And I *knew.*

The door between the staterooms opened. "Louis, are you all right?"

"All right like I have never been in my life, Marcel."

We did not sleep that night. Marcel said he would send a short radiogram, despite the expense, first thing in the morning.

*****

Don: Sunday evening, April 18th, 1926, Chambers Street Baptist Church.

"Before the prayer and postlude tonight, I want to give you an update on the journey of our esteemed guests, who will arrive sometime next week. Please leave next Sunday afternoon open, as I think we may have a musical program here then, and you're all invited to come listen."

"This afternoon I received a radiogram from Marcel Dupré. He, his wife Jeannette, and Louis Vierne are still at sea, due to arrive in New York sometime tomorrow or Tuesday. The radiogram reads as follows, quote: 'Badly need copy of Bible in French, in Braille. Louis trusted Christ shortly after midnight last night. Please rejoice with us. Warm regards, Marcel'. Unquote."

"We praise the Lord for His saving power once again. And I think we have located one of those Bibles. Now, let's pray."

As I prayed, I heard someone sobbing heavily near the front of the sanctuary. As I finished and Lucille began to play, I noticed my wife comforting Harmony Ives. I had no idea why she was upset.

CHAPTER TWENTY-EIGHT

Don: Wednesday, April 21st, 1926, 9:07 AM, the Auditorium office, logistics again

"Great, Bull! Send us the list and we'll have something for you when you get here. Send Eleanor my love when you write to her. See ya!" We could hear Matt's voice as we walked in the Auditorium door. By the time Jackie and I walked into the office Matt had hung up.

"What's that all about?" I asked as I took Jackie's coat.

"You aren't going to believe this," Matt began.

"I've never heard you say that since I've known you," Jackie announced, "You, Love?"

"Huh? Oh, not me either," I sputtered, "Sorry, my mind wasn't in gear."

"Situation Normal," Sherry added through the speakers.

"Why is it you always have to comment on my confusion?" I asked.

"Because you're so much fun to predict," our *cyberint* replied, "Do you want to know what you'll say next?"

"No! I just want to hear what Matt has to say."

"Right again! Have a nice day," Sherry purred, and the speakers clicked off.

"Don be quiet, so Matt can tell us his news," Jackie gave me The Look.

"Yes, Dear," I squeaked, then added the necessary "*Eeep*!"

Matt chuckled, then sobered.

"You know I wanted to get Bull Reeves to be my best man at the wedding."

"Right," I replied, "You weren't sure where he was."

"I did some checking and sent him a telegram to call me when he could. He's been out on *USS Langley* and just got back last night."

"*CV-1*, the first carrier," Jackie said, "Is he her skipper?"

Matt shook his head with a grin. "Nope. He's *Commander, Aircraft Squadron, Battle Fleet!* Like he was in your universe."

"OK, now it makes sense," I risked a comment, "He saved your life on the old *Colon,* right?"

"He did. And Jack Towers just came aboard as Executive Officer of *Langley.* Helen and our Jack called him Sunday and told him when their wedding was. Towers is coming for that. Then when I told Bull I was getting married that really made his day! And he's got an idea."

"Which is more than the Admiral has at the moment," Sherry remarked with a sniff.

I rolled my eyes but kept silent at the dig.

"What's Bull's idea?" Jackie asked.

"I guess he's friends with Billy Mitchell, and Billy wrote him about us, mainly you, Jackie. Jack Towers talked to Hap Arnold back in DC about you too."

"Word gets around," I remarked, then skittered away from Jackie's fingers.

Matt continued, "Bull's trying to figure out aircraft carrier doctrine from scratch, using *Langley* as a school ship. That is why he dragged Jack Towers out there to be XO of the thing. Bull wrote down a bunch of questions about operating carriers that have got to be answered before they can be truly combat-capable. He's sending us the list and he wants to pick our brains when he comes out."

"Pick *your* brain, mostly, Precious," I said, "So he's coming here for your wedding. Does he want to bring his wife too?"

"Eleanor? He wishes he could," Matt's smile faded, "She spends almost all her time in France. Comes back maybe once every other year. He sends her a stipend."

"Not much of a marriage," Jackie remarked, "You suppose she's stepping out on him?"

Matt chuckled. "That's a quaint phrase for it, Jackie. He doesn't know. She's never asked for a divorce."

"Don't jostle the meal ticket," I said, then changed the subject. "Will he be coming out for Helen and Jack's wedding too?"

Matt nodded. "He says he has to pester the folks in D.C. a bit. *Langley's* having work done. She won't go out for a few weeks. He'll visit us on his way there and back."

Jackie picked up a pen and pad. "Matt, did you say Bull's a Believer?"

Matt sat back in his chair. "Yes. Trusted Christ three months after I did. We used to go out into the barrios in the Philippines and do things for the people. That's how I met Grace," he finished softly.

"And now the Lord's provided you someone again," I said, "and Bull will get to rejoice with you."

"We all will," Jackie added, "and I guess I'd better bone up on my carrier doctrine."

"I don't even think Bull's gotten that far," Matt said, "He's still trying to figure out how to move planes around on deck without sailors walking into the props."

Jackie groaned. "We're gonna need more than me on this. Time to round up all the carrier sailors in the company and get them to help."

"Starting with Dave Sampson," I said, "Sammy too."

Jackie scribbled something on her pad. "Let's not go off half-cocked. We'll wait until we get his questions before we start working on this. We've got another project ahead of him."

"That organ?" Matt asked.

"Yep, and our friendly organists," I replied, "and Jackie and I dreamed this morning. We bring Louis in."

"Even if he and Harmony don't get together?" Matt asked.

"Right," Jackie answered, "In the dreams, she was there when we told him, but neither of us could tell if they were a couple or not."

"She's going to be disappointed if they're not," Matt remarked.

"Yes, but I've had a chat with her. I think she'll get over it if that happens." Jackie winked, "I don't think we'll have to worry about that though."

"Hey, can we get some help out here?" a voice called from the lobby.

"Coming, Amy!" Matt said, and we all trooped out to the front door. Amy and Elwood stood at the door, bracing an American Railway Express cart with boxes on it.

"Is that the Braille Bible?" I asked.

"Lunch for five hundred," Elwood replied, "but you have to like fiber. Yes, it's the Braille Bible."

"All those boxes?" Matt asked.

"Yes," Amy said, "This one's thirty-seven volumes. It fits on six feet of bookshelf space and weighs 68 and a half pounds net. No idea of the cost."

Jackie smiled. "This one came from the San Francisco Association for the Blind—they'll become Lighthouse for the Blind *uptime*. It was free if we paid for shipping. We sent them a five-hundred-dollar donation. Ruth Quinan, their director, was stunned and grateful."

"But where's the truck?" Matt asked, "you took one of the Macks."

Elwood wiped his brow. "Down at the Santa Fe freight house. I went to start it and it ran away. Had to pull the big red knob."

"Did what?" I asked.

"The trucks have *uptime* Detroit diesel engines in them," Matt said, "If something goes wrong, they just keep going faster till they blow up. The red knob shuts off the air. Nothing blew, did it?"

"Don't think so," Amy replied, "Let's get these boxes in and you can take the cart back and check the truck. We're pooped!"

"OK," Matt said, and we started hefting the boxes.

*****

Mimi, 6:15 PM, her room at Cottage

"Matt! What did you do to your hand?"

My betrothed set the box of goodies and my supper tray on the table before turning to kiss me.

"Explain first, then kiss!"

Matt looked at his bandaged hand. "Short version or long version?"

"True version, buster. Spill it!" He looked embarrassed but I didn't care.

Matt sat down in the chair. "We had one of the diesel engines in our trucks act up this morning. I towed it back to the shop and was working on it. The truck hood came down and caught my hand."

I looked at the bandages. "I see splints. What's the damage?"

Matt reddened more. "Two broken fingers, bruises, a couple of cuts. Doctor Setterdahl fixed me up."

I smiled. "That's your right hand. How are you going to *wipe*?"

He turned red. "Carefully," he ground out, "It'll be better by the wedding."

"I'm sure it will," I replied, "but we'll work around it."

Matt's jaw dropped. "Mimi, you'll say anything!"

I grinned. "You got it, my Love. Now about that kiss."

Once he found my lips the damaged hand did not affect his kissing.

"I'm glad it wasn't worse," I said when we finished, "I had to double as the school nurse at Willard. I've seen plenty."

"So have I," Matt said as he tried to open the box with one hand.

"I've got it," I said, and stood up to open it. "Oh, more olives and Gator sauce, thank you! I'm about halfway done with the chocolate."

Matt stopped. "Love, should you be standing like that?"

"Yep! Keith Setterdahl and Gloria have been working with me. I'm up to five minutes standing unsupported! I may even stand for the wedding."

Matt sat back down. "Safety first for the wedding, dear. By the way, I love you! Will you marry me?"

"Yes, Matt, and I love you too," I said, then smirked, "And don't worry, my betrothed. I won't be standing on our wedding night."

I was glad his circulation was unaffected by the injury.

I started to eat my patty of mystery meat and mixed my mashed potatoes and brussels sprouts under a film of Gator Sauce. Matt told me about the Bible for Louis, the phone call from his friend Bull, and the load his request put on Jackie.

"Jackie said something about that this afternoon. She had an appointment with Doctor Bohan and came by to check on me."

"I hope she's OK," Matt said, "I didn't know she had an appointment."

"She said it was a checkup. She's fine," I replied. I knew why, but he did not have *need-to-know.*

Matt saw the two books in plain jackets on my bed. "What are those?"

I picked up the books and handed them to him. "A couple of books Jackie dropped off. They're from uptime."

Matt looked under the covers. "Who's Oliver Sacks?"

"A Neuropsychologist from uptime," I replied, "One book's clinical tales from his practice; the other talks about how music affects the brain."

"You're interested in that stuff, aren't you?" Matt asked.

"Sure am. I'm not just a teacher, I'm an *educator*."

"What's the difference?"

"I teach people to think."

"Students?"

"Teachers too," I replied, "And while you're digesting that, Jackie thinks these books may help me do my new job better. I just started them before you came."

Matt handed me a wrapped chocolate. "I'm not any good at the musical part of our operation. I hope you like it once you're into it."

I popped the chocolate into my mouth. "I think I'll love it. I have a lot to learn about the music and musicians besides how to book acts. People are people though; they don't change."

"It'll be fun to watch you take over for Don. We need him to be more involved in our other projects. You'll take quite a load off him."

"I'm looking forward to it, Love," I replied.

CHAPTER TWENTY-NINE

Louis Vierne: Thursday, April 22nd, 1926, 10:15 AM, C.B.&Q. Depot, Galesburg, a day of transitions

"It looks much different with leaves on the trees," Jeannette Dupré remarked.

I turned my head toward the open window. "It smells of wet earth and lilac blossoms. Only a little smoke."

"It helps to be at the rear of the train," Marcel added.

"How do you feel, Louis?" Jeannette asked.

"More nervous than before a long recital," I replied, "I have the hope of the reborn, as you said, but I do not know what is coming to me next. I prefer routine, certainties—this arrival is anything but."

"I am sure Donald has today all planned," Marcel said, "You will not be left to your own devices." *He sounds very sure of himself. That is one of us,* I thought.

Another question loomed. "I'll need a helper. I can't function without a helper. Who will be able to help me in this place? I get disoriented in unfamiliar places."

"Donald says they have several in the company who have lived with folks who could not see," Marcel replied, "One woman's late husband was blind, and she knows how to help without intruding."

"I am sure your needs will be provided for, and not just by us," Jeannette finished.

I felt the train slow steadily. "We are coming to the station?" I asked.

"Yes," Marcel said as I heard him bump against the ceiling to reach for his hat, "Now, to use a phrase Donald taught me, just *hang in there* and everything will turn out fine!"

"Hang? Why am I supposed to hang?"

"Marcel will explain himself later," Jeannette said as we drew to a halt, "Here is your hat and cane. Just hold on to my arm when we get up and walk toward the light."

"I have been doing that since last Sunday," I remarked. I stood up, positioned my cane, and walked with Jeannette toward the end of the car.

I stepped carefully to the ground, guided by Jeannette and the porter, and we followed the footsteps of Marcel. "Brick walkway, uneven," she said softly.

Amid the noise of the platform, I heard footsteps approaching. Marcel halted as we stood next to him. I heard him speak in English, and a man replied. The man spoke and Marcel translated.

"Monsieur Vierne, I am Donald Wain, of Wain Engineering. With me today is my wife, Madame Jacqueline Wain."

I shook the couple's hands as they were offered to me. We all murmured suitable pleasantries as Marcel translated.

"Who else is with you, Don?" Marcel stepped back as the other man spoke.

"*Maintenant je vous présente Le veuve du compositeur Charles Ives,* Harmony Twichell Ives."

I managed not to laugh at Don's mangling of the French language. Then I realized what he had said. *Could it be?*

I heard small footsteps from behind the group and someone took my hands. Before she spoke, I knew who she was, and would have known without hearing her name. I know people by smell as much as by voice. As she took my hands, I detected the odors of clothing starch, a mild aura of lavender—and *woman. One particular* woman. We conversed, as always, in French.

"Louis, I am so happy you have come! How are you?"

"I am overwhelmed but in a very good way," I replied, "but you are a widow?"

The hands squeezed slightly. "I came home to find Charlie dead the last day of January. I had been out of town. His heart gave out."

"Pushed along by his other medical issues no doubt. I am so sorry for you! How can you cope?"

"It's been hard. Mostly by making changes. I quit New York and moved here, to Galesburg," Harmony replied, "I love the town and my friends here, and I am helping in a medical practice. But what happened to your assistant?"

Harmony knew almost everything about me from our earlier time together. I saw no reason to hide or dissemble. "She was my assistant, but also my *amoureuse*. She was to make this journey, but she left me the morning we were to leave. She left a note that the Cardinal Archbishop would excommunicate her if she went with me."

"Is that true? Would he do that? Would she?"

"The prelates are a hard lot. He could have, but it does not matter now. I cannot...and will not...go back."

Harmony moved closer and spoke softly. "I understand, Louis. They would take notice of your living with her and fire you. You are now reborn. Our Lord guides you as he opened the doors for me to move here."

I smiled. "Yes, Harmony, that is true. I am still finding my footing in the new situation. Will you help me?"

Harmony giggled. "I was hoping you would help me! Everyone is kind, but no one knows me the way an old friend does. I was hoping on bending your ear. Now, let me escort you into the station—the others have already gone inside. We'll get your baggage and go to your hotel, then to lunch. After lunch I must pick up my new automobile down the street, then Don and

Jackie want to meet with you at the Auditorium. Afterward, you will meet that organ you have heard so much about."

Harmony entwined her arm with mine and we started along the walkway. "I am very happy to find an old friend here! Marcel and Jeannette are dears, but our relationship is more professional than intimate."

"I am very happy you are here too, Louis. We'll all help you get where you need to be."

She put her head close to my ear as the train pulled out. "But I want to help you most," she whispered.

*****

Luther: shortly after noon, Simmons Street and Coney Island: lunch with a twist.

"Hey, Luther!"

"Hi folks! I had to be in town today, and figured you'd land here."

I met the new arrivals as they piled out of Don's Wills in front of the Library. Parking was hard to find at noon on a weekday; I had to park in front of the Free Kindergarten in the next block. I was walking toward Coney Island when I spied the distinctive Wills.

"Luther, you know Marcel and Jeannette of course. The gentleman connected to Harmony is Louis Vierne. Harmony, you go ahead and introduce Luther, please."

"Sure, Don." She spoke a couple sentences in French to the middle-aged man in the homburg on her arm, and he moved to shake my hand. I shook, gave the bow, and 'happy to meet you sir' in French. He returned the bow. I guess he could sense my movement. Nobody giggled at my verbal train wreck.

The man spoke and Harmony translated. "Louis says he has heard much about you, Luther. He looks forward to hearing you play."

"Please tell him I am in awe of meeting yet another of the composers I play regularly."

Another exchange. "He thanks you for the kind words but is happier to meet you because of your…," Harmony hesitated, "testimony, I think. He wants to understand how you show Christ to those you work with. You have a reputation for your witness."

"That's very kind of him," I replied.

"We'd better go if we want to get seats," Jackie reminded us.

We walked past the white stone Carnegie library and the Post Office, Harmony and Louis several paces ahead.

"So, they've hit it off?" I asked Don quietly as we walked.

"Big time," he replied. "I predict a wedding tomorrow or Saturday. Those two won't wait."

That statement bothered me. "I'm all for quick weddings with the right people, but isn't that too fast even for us?"

"Maybe," Don replied, "but I think it's been simmering since 1908. Marcel said they took up when they met as if it was only a couple of days since they'd last seen each other! They'll move fast."

"Be careful what you assume, Admiral," Jackie whispered.

Don looked at his wife and smiled. She answered with The Look.

"Can you stick around a while after lunch?" Don asked softly, "We're bringing Louis in."

"Sure," I replied, "He's going to have one big day, that's for sure!"

We crossed Cherry and Simmons streets to the restaurant. As usual, it was jammed with the noontime crowd.

"Reminds me of a café on the Sorbonne," Jeannette remarked with a smile, then repeated herself in French.

We found a small table, enough for all but two of us.

"No problem! We'll sit at the counter." Harmony steered Louis over to adjoining round stools at the lunch counter. She set him down and went to order their food, as did Don and I.

"Would Louis stay here?" I asked as we waited.

"I think so. Marcel said Madeleine cleaned him out, and he thinks she'll ice the cake by going to the Cardinal Archbishop and confessing it all formally. They'll fire him if she does that. But I think we have a job for him here if he wants to stay. Besides the obvious." Don looked over to where Harmony was introducing Louis to Coney Dogs.

"Will Sylvester perform the ceremony?"

"I'm sure he will. I called Sherry on my cell phone and asked her to invite him and his wife to supper tonight at New China. We should have some idea of the time frame by then."

We got the food and returned to the table. *I wish Syl were here to join in the festivities,* I thought, *but she'd have to sit on my lap—not a bad idea.*

*****

Harmony: orientation training

After lunch, Don took Marcel and Luther to visit the organ project at Chambers Street Baptist. Jackie and Jeannette stopped at the Broadview to set up the adjoining rooms before the meeting at the Auditorium.

Louis and I set out towards Wright-Allensworth to pick up my car. We walked arm in arm and Louis used his cane. We took our time.

"May I orient you as we walk?" I asked, "I'm pretty new here myself but I'll do what I can."

"That is fine, Harmony," Louis replied, "I enjoy walking arm in arm with you wherever we may go."

"So do I."

We walked slowly, enjoying the spring air. "We are walking

past a hotel, are we not?" Louis remarked.

We stopped and I looked up. "Yes, the sign says Central Hotel." How did you know?"

"I could smell the rooms being aired out in the pleasant weather. It is not a high-quality hotel; the linens have not been washed lately."

"That's interesting. I could not tell any of that," I said.

"You can see. As I cannot, I have developed other senses." Louis lowered his voice, "And this part of the building once housed a tavern, and there is still one...you call it a speakeasy...in the building."

I looked back. "You're right about the first part. I see traces of a beer sign on the bricks. But the other?"

My charge leaned in toward me. "I smelled stale beer and cigar residue. Then, the tinge of fresh beer and spirits. Easy."

"You are an amazement! I...."

Louis stopped me before we stepped off the curb. "Wait. Running feet and large motors starting. What is happening?"

I looked to my right and saw a red glow over the large building across the street. "It is the city fire brigade, and they are coming out. We are safe here."

Across the street, the doors opened. With the roar of engines and scream of sirens, the building disgorged three pumpers, one towed ladder truck, and the chief's car. They crossed Simmons Street and blasted up Boone's Alley right in front of us. They headed west on Main Street and were gone.

"That was interesting," Louis remarked. May we proceed?"

"Sure," I said, and we crossed the narrow street. "I think you are orienting *me* today."

"We use the abilities we have been given, Harmony. We do what we can and receive help for the rest. My sense of smell has improved since I ceased smoking."

I stopped and looked at my escort. "I forgot! You used to smoke! When did you quit?"

"The night I was reborn. I reached for a Balto and decided a cigarette would not help me in my turmoil. None since."

"Didn't you have cravings for one?"

Louis shook his head. "No, not at all. Why are you gasping?"

It took a moment for me to catch my breath and respond. "Louis...smoking is one of the hardest addictions to quit. Only alcohol and opium are worse. I've never heard of someone just quitting without issues! That is a deadly habit...causes cancer and heart disease among other things. I am really glad you've quit."

"So am I," Louis replied, "and here we see yet another of Our Lord's blessings, one I was not aware of until now."

We resumed our slow walk. I held Louis' arm a little closer as we strolled.

"This is nice," Louis said.

"I agree," I replied.

We passed the Weinberg Arcade and crossed Prairie Street. "Furniture store," Louis remarked.

I looked at the sign. "Rae's Furniture. How...."

"Fresh wood, oak and walnut, and sized cloth. Upholstery. This is fun."

"You are amazing," I breathed.

"As are you, in a different way," Louis added.

We walked past another building. "Another speakeasy."

I looked at the sign. "Revere House. Looks vacant."

"It is not," Louis replied, "Sidewalk to a door at the side, correct?"

"Yes, but...."

"Line of increased light heading off to the left. Smells of footprints with liquor on the shoes."

"The sun is glinting off the sidewalk. I am in awe."

"Aren't we in Galesburg?" Louis asked with a grin. "And now we have grass, with thyme and roses. First I've smelled on this walk."

"That is the Hotel Howe, so the sign says. Maybe a boarding house. Ivy around the porch."

"This is a lovely town, Harmony. I have not yet smelled animal or human waste."

"Paris has that, doesn't it? I remember from visiting there before the War."

"Paris is full of it, and I do not miss it. The sewers are incredibly old. We have arrived at our destination, judging from the grease and oil smells, and the poorly-running automobile I hear."

I looked at my remarkable friend. "You are correct again! You don't need me to get around here."

Louis enfolded my right hand with his. "Yes, I do. My senses only carry so far. It is difficult to orient myself in new surroundings. Will you please continue to help me?"

"Of course, I will, Louis!" He couldn't see the tears forming, "I will give you whatever aid you require."

"Thank you! You need not shed tears over me. I can tell—the salt in tears gives forth a distinctive odor. I have shed enough to know. But not today."

"So far," I added as I wiped my eyes before entering the dealership.

CHAPTER THIRTY

Luther, 2:15 PM, the Green Room, fine entertainment

"Harmony and Louis have just arrived at the Armory parking lot. They will enter the Green Room momentarily."

"Thanks, Sherry. We're ready for them," Jackie replied, "Hidden cameras watch the entire property. Uptime we call it surveillance," she added.

"Can't be too careful," Don added.

Jackie turned to Don. "Admiral, you will *not* ask Harmony directly if they are engaged. Whether they are or not, it is none of our business and very embarrassing to ask. Got that?"

Don reached for the pull chain by his side but was pre-empted. "*Eeep!*" he commented.

Marcel chuckled. Jeannette silenced him with her look.

Three others descended the stairs: Amy, Elwood, and Jeff.

"Hi folks! Elwood and Jeff both wanted to watch the unveiling. They won't tell me why," Amy said.

"Sure, come on in," Jackie said, "They'll be down here in a moment."

They found seats but before they could sit down Harmony and Louis slowly descended the stairs.

"Hi folks! How'd it go?" Don asked.

"Fine," Harmony replied, "The car is just what I asked for. Thank you for finding it for me."

Don squinted one eye. "Sure, there's nothing else new ... *yeeowlp!*"

Jackie moved her foot away from Don's. "I told you not to ask that question. Now let's introduce the others and we'll get on with it."

Soundlessly Don limped over to the table and sat down. Jackie and Harmony winked at each other, then Amy took over.

"Louis, I am Amy Lansdale Foutch. This is my husband, Elwood Foutch, and Jeff Potter, who is staying with us. Jeff studies with Elwood and is betrothed to Jackie's daughter Evelyn."

Louis shook the newcomers' hands, then paused. He stared with sightless eyes at Elwood and Jeff, who stared back. Then all three nodded slightly.

"Jeff has trouble speaking," I think Harmony whispered to Louis in French. Louis whispered back, something about *can*, and Harmony's mouth dropped.

"Explain later," Elwood said, "Everybody sit."

We all sat.

Don asked me to pray for the meeting, and I did, Harmony translating for Louis. Then, Harmony read from a paper in French, describing the nature of Wain Engineering and when they came from. Several of us had worked on this written statement, trying to make the amazing news consistent without causing the hearer to faint or run screaming from the room. So far, no one had.

Harmony finished. Jackie spoke, "Thank you Harmony, Louis, do you have any questions or comments so far?"

Harmony translated. Louis appeared much calmer than I had after I heard this speech. He made some sort of a statement, and Harmony sat back in her chair with a thud.

"Louis says, quote, "This explains my dream then."

"What dream?" Don asked.

Louis and Harmony spoke for a moment; Harmony made notes on a yellow pad.

"Louis says," Harmony began, "He had a dream at the hotel in

Chicago last night. He says he can often see in his dreams; since he had some vision in his younger days. He dreamed he was in a room much like this one, and people were telling him he was now part of a group not originally from this time or place. He could not see the people's faces, but," Harmony sniffled, "he knew I was the one translating for him. He figured I was a memory of friends past; he never dreamed I would actually be here."

Louis said something else, and Harmony squeezed his arm. "Louis says one particular detail of the dream has not yet occurred. He does not want to recount it until the end of the afternoon."

As I sat and digested this new twist, Don spoke. "You know, that makes sense. Harmony, please tell Louis that. We are guided by these dreams we speak of, and the Lord has used that method of communicating repeatedly, as He has since Bible times. Why shouldn't the person being brought in have the same sort of dreams? Please stress to Louis we are honored to hear of this event in his life."

Harmony translated, and Louis said something with a chuckle. "He says thank you, and please get on with the meeting as he is eager to meet the organ!"

"So we shall," Jackie took up the tale, "We normally have a moving picture, called a video, we show at this point to further explain who we are and what we do. When we heard you were coming and were reborn, we had the sound for this video re-recorded by our company's French representative. If you don't mind, we'll play it for you now on a screen against the far wall of the room. I don't think Marcel and Jeannette have seen this video yet either, have you?"

"No, we have not," Marcel replied.

Jackie pushed the buttons on the remote and the video started. We all watched the production, narrated in a melodious female voice. Along the bottom of the screen an English translation appeared. The professional-looking production lasted ten minutes.

The French speakers talked among themselves for a few seconds, then Marcel spoke. "We know the speaker! She is Denise Luton, correct?"

"On the money," Don said, "I guess you would know her, seeing her cover job is musical instrument dealer in Paris."

Louis spoke and Harmony translated. "We three have dealt with Denise many times. She is the most honorable seller of instruments in Paris. I never suspected she was anything more, did you, Marcel?"

"No, never," Marcel added, "although I always thought there was much more to her life story than she would recount."

"Oh, there is," Jackie said, "We cannot divulge any of it without her permission. We will ask her what we can say to you. Now, would you like to meet the organ?"

Louis grinned broadly. "Would I? Would I!" Harmony translated, then slapped his arm as he said something else. "The rest is part of a crude joke I will not translate."

We looked over as Elwood and Jeff guffawed and Amy glared at them.

Five minutes later we stood before the console of the organ on the stage. The group had dwindled to Louis and Harmony, Don and Jackie, and me. I flipped the switches. The indicators turned an agreeable green. Louis sat on the bench with Harmony to steady him as I explained the differences from what he was used to. Louis thanked me, and I retreated to the front row where Don and Jackie sat.

Louis ran his hands around the bench, keyboards, and drawknobs.

He spoke to Harmony, then began pulling drawknobs and playing a couple of notes to hear each voice. He worked rapidly through the rows of drawknobs.

I heard Jackie whisper to Don, "We will need short movable ramps to either side, wrapping around. Sturdy padded back on the bench. Safety."

"I'll get Elwood on it," he whispered back.

Don put on a headset with a microphone. "Right, Rick, please record everything." He whispered, then paused. "Thanks, Sherry, we'll tell him what you're doing too."

At the organ, Louis began pulling drawknobs and depressing foot pedals. He spoke and Harmony translated, "Louis has a set of three improvisations he likes to play to test organs he is introduced to. He wonders if he may play them now."

"By all means Louis, please do, and *Merci!*" Don replied.

I saw Matt come down to sit with us as Harmony spoke. He carefully rested his bandaged hand on the arm of the seat.

Louis spoke again. "He says the improvisations are entitled *Marche Episcopale, Meditation and Cortege,*" Harmony said.

"Please proceed when you are ready," Don replied loudly, then whispered, "I know those works! Maurice Duruflé will transcribe them in the early fifties."

"Shhh," Jackie hissed, "We'll transcribe them right now!"

Louis turned back to the keyboard and launched. The three pieces lasted about ten minutes in total. They were in truth a small organ sonata, and surpassingly beautiful.

We clapped and cheered when Louis finished. Again, he turned and bowed from the bench. As the commotion died down another voice raised.

"*Monsieur,* I am Matthew Plotczyc. My fiancée Mimi and I are being married in this Auditorium on May first. I wonder if I could impose on you to play those beautiful pieces at our wedding: the first as the processional, the second at the sand pouring, and the last as the recessional? I'll pay whatever you ask."

"Belay a moment, Captain, please," Don interrupted Matt. Matt stopped and stared at Don.

“Harmony, please have Louis hear me out before he answers Matt, okay?”

“Of course, Don,” Harmony replied, and said something to Louis. He nodded and spoke. *“Oui?”*

“Louis,” Don spoke slowly so Harmony could translate. “This organ is a remarkable instrument, but we have no-one on staff who can play and manage this instrument as it needs to be managed to get the most good from it. Our organist friends are excellent, but they all have other responsibilities they cannot ignore. You, sir, are a master of these instruments, and it occurs to me you might have some free time.”

Harmony grinned as she translated that last statement for Louis, who also smiled.

“Therefore, I am offering you today the position of Titular Organist for this instrument, on the Wain Engineering staff as a Vested Partner. You would receive all the benefits of a Partner. You would also receive a percentage of any sales of recordings made by you on this instrument. The music you write remains your property in every event.”

Don took out a paper and scribbled on it, then walked up to the organ. “You may also instruct on the instrument, although we recommend you use the Wicks console for that. And finally, you would receive an annual salary we feel is appropriate to the work you would be doing here.”

Don gave the paper to Harmony. “I asked Marcel what you made at Notre Dame, and figured accordingly. Harmony, that’s the dollar amount; perhaps you can convert it to Francs for him.”

Harmony took the paper and nodded. She turned to Louis, read him the figure on the paper, and spoke a sentence.

She then had to hold Louis on the organ bench, as he almost fell off it in a faint. When he could speak, he spoke several sentences in rapid-fire French, then put his head in his hands and sobbed.

As she held Louis, Harmony translated.

"He says this was the last part of the dream he had last night, except for the salary. He says he is beyond astonished, as that amount is four times more than he has ever earned in a year, from the Notre Dame position and his recitals together! He is beside himself...actually, he's beside me...but he accepts. He'll be honored to play for your wedding, Matthew!"

We crowded around the organ and helped Louis off the bench. We shook Louis' hand and the ladies hugged him.

"One more thing the Admiral forgot to mention," Sherry's contralto voice filled the hall, "Rick and I have recorded those three improvisations, and I have already translated them into sheet music. Louis need only proofread the copy for errors and make changes as he wishes."

Sherry then repeated herself in French. "You can do that?" Louis asked, wide-eyed.

"They can't, but I can," Sherry replied in French and English, "Another little service we provide."

"*Merci, merci beaucoup*!" Louis' exclamation needed no translation.

"Now, if we may, let us take you up to the organ loft and recording studio. You might find it slightly interesting*Eeep*!" Don remarked.

Louis said something to Harmony. "He says he was unsure of the significance of the Eeep sounds but has now figured them out. He concurs."

"Wonderful," Don grumped and dodged away from Jackie's fingers.

*****

Louis, 8:15 PM, the Hotel Broadview sitting room, epilogue

"This is the parlor of the hotel," Harmony said, "May we sit here until Jeff arrives?"

"That would be fine," I replied, "I have a few things to ask you while we wait."

"And I have one to ask you. May I start?"

"Of course, Harmony. What?"

"How are you and Elwood able to communicate with Jeff? I don't understand it."

I sat back on the comfortable couch. "I don't understand it either, but I just do. I understand what they are thinking, and I guess they understand me too. Jeff says he also communicates with his betrothed Evelyn that way. Is this odd?"

"Well, yes, it's odd," my escort replied, "but I've seen Ev and Jeff do this often. I'd say take it as a gift from the Lord and run with it."

"That I've determined to do," I said, "and Jeff was certainly helpful when I needed to visit the water closet at the auditorium."

Harmony giggled. "I guess so! I'm glad Don offered to help you before Jeff stepped in. Don used to help his late wife Pam that way."

"She must have been quite a woman," I remarked, "and Jacqueline is no amateur either. Did I hear she flew from ships at sea *uptime*?"

Harmony started to speak, then coughed. "Pardon me, the stale smoke caught in my throat. Don's only owned the hotel for two days. He says they're cleaning this room over the weekend to get rid of the smoke smell, then they'll start working on the HVAC."

"What is HVAC?" I asked.

"Heating, ventilation, and air conditioning. He says when they finish this hotel's air will be as pleasant inside as the auditorium."

"I noticed the atmosphere there this afternoon. Perfect temperature I thought. Now, about Jackie and flying?"

I felt Harmony lurch next to me. "Oh, I'm sorry!"

"You need never say that phrase to me, Harmony...ever." I knew my words bordered on an endearment, but I had determined to speak them and see what happened. "You were saying?"

I sensed Harmony blush. "Jackie was in the Navy uptime. She flew cargo aircraft on and off airplane carriers. She achieved the rank of Captain."

"No mean feat in any case," I said, "Now, may I ask my questions?"

"Of course, Louis. Shoot."

I thought of commenting on her choice of verbs but decided against it. "Which of the priests, er, pastors, at the dinner this evening is from the church you all attend?"

"I could feel Harmony relax her arm as she held on to mine. That would be AP Kittridge. His wife is Deborah."

"Ah, the lady of the razor wit," I remarked, "and the other gentleman?"

"He's Sylvester Sanford, AP's old friend. He's an evangelist, and is pastoring AP's old church in Appleton, about twenty miles east of here."

"And he is the one who would perform your wedding to a divorced man?"

I reached out to catch Harmony as she started to fall forward.

"How...how did you know that?" I had never heard her stutter.

"I suppose I must confess," I began, still holding Harmony up, "I am an educator. I have worked with young people from England and the continent for many years. Some from this country also. We try to talk. They pick up a little French, and

I some of whatever their language is. I find I understand more English than I thought, although I am not ready to try to speak it yet. I understood the significance of Don's questions when we arrived this afternoon, and I knew Jackie had stepped on his foot. Madeleine occasionally did that to me." I stopped to acknowledge the sadness.

"You are correct, Louis, and I see your grief. Take your time."

"Thank you," I said, then continued, "I also heard the conversation among the pastors, and with the Wains during the meal. Evidently, Donald was told not to press about you and me and disobeyed his wife."

Harmony took a deep breath. I relaxed my hold on her, but she put her hand on mine. "Right again, Louis. When I heard you were coming, then heard you were alone, I started imagining what could happen. They thought I was going to ask you to marry me at the restaurant this noon."

The question in both our minds. That one that had never left my thoughts since the depot. "I asked Elwood about the marriage talk, and he explained to me what Our Lord said about remarriage after divorce. I remember Marcel reading those words from the Bible on the ship."

"Yes, that's right," Harmony said in a whisper, "What do you think about it?"

I turned to face my escort. "What do *you* think about it, Harmony?"

"I don't know what to think! I want it to happen, I pray it will happen, but then I remember Charlie and I just don't know what to think!" I felt her fumble for a handkerchief and gave her mine.

"What you are feeling, Harmony, is grieving. I am intimately familiar with its workings; you are facing your first loss, a great one to be sure. You will work through the grief, but it will take time. You can try to shorten the time, but the result will leave you confused, unsatisfied, and taint your further relationships. Does this make sense?"

Harmony sniffled. "Yes, Louis, it does. When will I work through this enough to enter another relationship?"

I sat back on the couch. "I don't think there is a set amount of time. It's been different for each of my friends, and different for each of my losses. I think you'll know when you've worked it through. As for me, I'm still coping with the loss of Madeleine. There's an element of anger in it, but it is grief nonetheless."

"I think you have an understanding of this I'm just learning," Harmony said, "How should we conduct ourselves then? I mean, knowing that our relationship may develop, or it may not?"

I smiled. "I think we should carry on as we have today, if we may help each other learn this strange new world we have both fallen into. I will say I truly enjoy your company, and I hope you do mine."

"I do, and I believe we can continue on that basis," Harmony said, "Let's just see what happens."

"And keep Donald guessing," I added, "He need not know how much English I understand. But I have one more question, if I may."

"It's almost eight-thirty, but what is the question?"

"As a person with medical knowledge, what do you make of Donald's claim that their company ophthalmologist may restore some of my sight?"

I noticed Harmony rubbing my hand with hers; I suspected she didn't realize what she was doing. "I think," she replied, "you would do well to let the doctor examine you. I have met two of their uptime medical people. They are the Orthopedist who helped with Jack Sewell's surgery, and a very capable nurse, both from their facility in North Dakota. If *Iggy the eye guy,* as Don called him, is half as skilled as Doctor Meister and Nurse

Anna were, he can improve your vision if anyone can."

"I have been through so much pain, so many dashed hopes with my vision. Nevertheless, I believe I will take your advice," I said, "and I thank you for your honesty. Now I believe Jeff is just walking through the door."

"I don't see him yet. There he is! How did you know that?"

I just smiled at my friend as Jeff entered the parlor.

CHAPTER THIRTY-ONE

Don: Friday, April 23rd, 1926, 1:40 AM, sleep is overrated

"Precious, are you awake?"

Only one of the other three occupants of the bed opened an eye to that question.

"I am now. It is the middle of the night. What is the major malfunction, *Admiral?*" Jackie growled the last part.

I sat up in bed. Jackie just looked at me with one eye; the shih tzus by our feet in the bed didn't even do that.

"I woke up about an hour ago and couldn't get back to sleep. I prayed, thought, even counted shih tzus."

"One, two. Go to sleep," my wife mumbled.

"Right. Nothing helped this time. My mind kept going back to something A. M. Bondi said at the Broadview closing this week. Do you remember him talking about another property they have for sale?"

Jackie scooted up in the bed. Melissa looked up when her legrest moved, sighed, and put her head back down.

"That closing was so complicated I barely remember signing the papers. If Amy hadn't been there keeping things on track I don't know how long it would've taken. What property?"

I raised a finger. "It's half of a long block with the northern border on Dayton Street, Jefferson Street to the east, and Monroe Street on the west, whenever they get it extended that far. It's on the edge of nowhere right now, but the city will expand past that right after the war. It's flat, sits on an aquifer but that's manageable. All the utilities are within a block and can easily be extended that far."

"I think I can picture it," Jackie said. "But what do we want that for? It's going to be a residential area, probably a wealthier neighborhood. We don't do land speculation, my love."

"How about a church?"

Jackie opened her mouth to speak and stopped. She looked at me, then suddenly bent over and kissed me.

"What was that for?" I asked when we finished.

"For listening to the Lord when I wasn't!"

"Thanks for the thought, Precious, but it took Him an hour to get through my thick skull."

Jackie nodded. "But He did. They'll have to change the name, you know."

I smiled, "Yeah, but I think that could be arranged about the time Terry Fensterer is convinced we need to move...1950."

Jackie laughed. Terry Fensterer, a Deacon on the Chambers Street board with me, was renowned for coming down on the side of delay when dealing with otherwise timely issues. I hoped I never again had to declaim the *dead parrot sketch* to him like I did the night after Pastor Ward's death. At least we'd changed Terry's mind. Since then he'd reverted to form.

"I hope it'll be sooner than that, Love," Jackie added.

"Don't bet on it, Precious. The price AM quoted me is about thirty percent less than the average price of similar plots for sale here. We can just hold on to it quietly until the Lord has need of it. What do you say, Chief Accountant?"

"Of course we *can* buy it," Jackie replied with a frown, "If any of our church friends ever knew how much money the Company really has, they'd either fall over in a dead faint or run screaming in circles!"

"So you approve of the purchase*Eeep*!"

"Do shih tzus have luxury beds?"

"Are you suggesting we make them find out?" I asked with a

smile.

Jackie suddenly looked like she was going to throw up. "Not tonight, dear. I don't feel so well."

With that, she got out of bed and darted to the bathroom. *What's with throwing up at this hour?* I wondered.

Don: 3:05 AM, round two

I snapped awake. I remembered the dream as vividly as those when the Lord told us to bring someone in to the company. I also noticed I had not put my CPAP mask on. I wondered if the one brought on the other.

"Now what?" Jackie asked from the other side of the bed, "you jerked so hard you woke me up. This better be good."

"I'm sorry, Precious, but I have to tell you about this dream."

"You didn't have the CPAP on, did you?" Jackie asked.

"No, but I don't think that made any difference. This dream was vivid."

"The stars you're going to see will be vivid. Get on with it."

I took a breath. "I was walking up a slanted sidewalk toward a church. I got the impression we were on the property I was talking about earlier. I can see the front of the church like it was a photograph!"

"What did it look like?" Jackie shifted into her Naval officer persona.

"Light brick, angular—it reminded me of a church in Galesburg *uptime,* out on Academy Street. Chambers Street church will become that church after they move from the old building in nineteen-fifty-five, I think. Anyway, this building was about double the size of the one I know, big enough to have a balcony."

"Show me a picture later, OK?

"Sure will, Love. Anyway, I walked up the sidewalk. Standing at the door was AP Kittridge, in some sort of vestments like George Wilcox uses. Nothing like he'd wear normally. He greeted me with a smile, grasped both of my hands, then gently moved me out of the doorway so a bunch of other people behind me could come in. I could see the large auditorium just beyond the foyer, with organ pipes at the front. Then I woke up."

Jackie frowned. "That doesn't sound like an ordinary dream. What do you suppose it means?"

"I don't know, Precious. Thinking about that property, maybe. Underlying worry about the church being overcrowded. Everything going on right now. Just odd."

Jackie rested her finger on my chest. "Or you're being alerted that changes are coming."

I nodded, "Could be, Love. That's happened to me before when something really serious went down in my Navy career. Guess I'd better take it seriously."

"So, what do we do about it?"

I thought for a moment. "Keep doing what we're doing with the organ. That's why I'm having it built in modules, so we can move it easily. I'll call the Bondi brothers this morning and tell them we'll take that land. And keep alert to the Lord in case He leads with something else. That sound OK?"

"And sometime this morning, make a drawing of the church you saw in the dream," Jackie added. "That might come in handy down the line."

"You're right, Love! I'll go do that right now." I moved to get my legs over Theodore and sit up in bed.

"Good. Now maybe I can get some sleep," my bride replied and rolled the other way.

Jackie: 6:45 AM, third time's a what?

The scene in front of my eyes faded, and I opened my eyes to the filtered light of a cloudy morning in Galesburg.

What a lousy night of sleep, I thought, then the replay of the dream reminded me of my duty. I reached to the nightstand and took the pad and paper. I looked over at Don as I sat up. *At least he got the blower on this time.* I wrote the dream down and folded the paper.

Don's eyes snapped open. He mumbled something through his mask, then reached over and shut off the CPAP. He removed and stowed the mask before he spoke. "You got the dream too?"

"I did. Here," I said, handing him the pad and pen.

He rubbed his eyes, then wrote on the pad.

"Just give me the pad. Here's mine," I said.

We read each other's papers. "So that's Bull Reeves?" I asked.

"Can't be anyone else. Nobody else I know in the Navy wears a beard like that anymore. Captain's birds, wings on his chest."

"Not pilot's wings," I added, "Aviation Observer. Which he is. But who is the other man?"

"I don't know, Love," Don replied, "He's wearing the uniform of a chief steward, but Bull talks to him like he's his chief of staff. And do you know anyone who looks like him?"

I nodded, mouth open. "Yeah...Dave Sampson. Dave's said one of his ancestors was in the Navy about this time. You don't suppose...."

"We can find out. When we get the papers from Bull, I'll call to confirm we got 'em, and see if he wants to bring anyone else. Dave will be here for the meeting next week anyway. He might just get a surprise if that man's his relative."

"They'll both get a surprise, I think," I smiled, then grimaced as my gut started to undulate. "And now, it's off to the loo again!"

As I deposited into the porcelain throne, I wondered if Don had figured out what was going on. *Probably not. He's never had to watch this,* I concluded.

****

Luther: 9:50 AM, the auditorium office, loose ends

I wandered into the office that morning looking for Marcel. We were going to meet with Pastor, Sammy Allen, and Elwood to start planning the organ removal. Jackie waved and pointed; Don was on the phone.

"We'll be happy to see you next Thursday morning," Don was saying, "We'll have a room reserved for you. And you'd also like to bring your chief of staff? What's his name?" A pause. "We understand, glad to have him. Walter Sampson, eh? May I ask what his wife's name is? Ah, Rose. The reason I ask, I have someone working for me who might be related to them. Please don't say anything about that to the Chief, in case it doesn't work out. We'll have a room for the Chief too."

Another pause. "Absolutely not, Bull! He'll get the room right next door to yours...You'll find we do things a little differently around here." Don looked over at Jackie and gave a thumbs up.

"Let Matt know the train number and we'll be sure to meet you. I think you'll have a pleasant and profitable visit here."

Jackie giggled at that.

"OK, Bull, I'll tell Matt you've confirmed. See you next Thursday morning. "Bye!" Don hung up and took a deep breath.

"First, Bull knows we got the package of questions. He will be here next Thursday morning. We'll meet him and his chief of staff and do our usual. You heard what the chief's name is."

"Sure did," Jackie replied, "There can't be another one in the Navy with those names."

"Excuse me," I said, "but what are you talking about?"

"Let me explain this," Sherry interrupted, "Retired Commander Dave Sampson from uptime flies for us. Captain Reeves' *de-facto* chief of staff is Dave's great-grandfather in this universe."

"We don't know that for sure yet," Don muttered.

"You don't, but I do," the cyberint replied, "Get a clue, Admiral." With that Sherry clicked off.

"And you said something about questions?" I asked.

Jackie picked up a thick sheaf of papers from her desk. "These. Bull calls them his 'thousand and one questions'. Everything about aircraft carrier operations and tactics he wants to know." Jackie set the papers down with a thud, "and he admits he doesn't know *anything*."

"OK, I understand now," I said, "but can we help him?"

"I think so," Don replied, "We have access to all the accumulated knowledge of the next ninety years of carrier operations, and can supply him with the distilled information, both from books and our own first-hand experience. We can feed him as much as he can digest, at the rate he wants it, and can implement it on *Langley*."

"We also don't want to leave him more confused. We'll help him ask the most relevant questions," Jackie added.

"But won't he guess where you learned all that?" I asked.

"Won't have to," Don said, "We have orders to bring both of 'em in. If they couldn't deal with what we tell 'em, the Lord wouldn't have set it up. This'll be a real challenge for them and us!"

I nodded, then looked over as our contingent of French organists walked in, Harmony and Louis arm in arm.

"Good morning everyone," Marcel pronounced, "Luther, we are heading over to the church to start planning the dismantling, correct?"

"Yes," I said, "If you'd like, we're due to meet Elwood and Sammy Allen over there. They'll be our team leaders for the event."

"Excellent! Donald, are you coming with us?"

"Not right now, Marcel," Don replied, "Jackie and I have a lunch date *uptime*. We'll be back mid-afternoon and I'll come over then."

Louis spoke, and Harmony translated. "He says good morning to all. While you deal with what is to come, he will be working on what *is*. We'll be getting further acquainted with the organ he is to mind here."

Jackie grinned. "Very good, Louis. Spend all the time you wish with the organ. You have the key to the place."

Louis murmured something and Harmony snorted. "He says he has ranks of keys now, but he will hold yours close."

"So, I guess we'll be off," Don said, getting up from his desk.

"You know you are," Sherry said softly, "I will contact you if anything happens," she added.

I didn't recognize the dig until we were outside.

CHAPTER THIRTY-TWO

Don: Tuesday, April 23rd, 2019, 11:05 AM, Landmark Café & Crêperie, Galesburg, working lunch

"It's nice to finally get out in the spring air," Jackie remarked as we sat down, "A pleasant walk, and here we are."

"We had snow last week in D.C.," Dave Sampson remarked, "Didn't help the cherry blossoms any."

"I bet," I commented, "How're the kids?"

"Fine," Dave replied, "Walt's still in the Justice Department. Karen just got a new job, assistant to a senior lawyer in the EPA. Says she's a joy to work with. She sings opera in her spare time!"

"Karen sings too, doesn't she?" Kathy Trainor, the fourth in our little party asked.

"Not opera!" Dave laughed, "She grew up singing solos in church choirs. Then she picked up a music minor beside her pre-law major at BJU."

I was confused. "Did you say Bob Jones University?" I asked.

Dave grinned. "Yeah. Surprised? Doctor Bob the third finally eliminated the last vestiges of institutional prejudice about twenty years ago. Karen had a great college experience!"

"I'm so glad, Dave," I said, "I have this little dream that maybe we could help Bob Senior stand away from institutional segregation when he starts the school in the other universe. We don't have any contact with him now though."

"Be careful what you wish for, Admiral," my wife intoned as our server approached.

A couple of minutes later we continued talking quietly as the place filled up with the lunch crowd.

"Don, your message said we're going to educate someone about carrier aviation," Dave began, "Who are you talking about?"

I decided to fill him in gently. "We have that opportunity. What do you know about the early days of the carriers: the *Langley* and the *Lexingtons*?"

Dave grinned. "Oh, just a little. My master's thesis at Naval Postgraduate School analyzed carrier operations in the twenties. I picked apart Admiral Bull Reeves' *Thousand and One Questions,* then traced the development of the answers he got."

We stopped talking as the server arrived with platters of food. Jackie took one look and clapped her napkin over her mouth.

"Jackie, are you OK?" Kathy asked.

"What's wrong, precious?" I added, reaching for my pale, wobbly wife.

Jackie waved me away. "I'll be OK. Kathy, come with me please."

"Sure," Kathy took Jackie's arm as the two of them got up and headed for the bathroom.

"What did I say to upset her?" Dave asked with a frown.

"Nothing, Dave, you just surprised her." I lowered my voice, "We got those questions in the mail this morning. Bull Reeves is Matt Plotczyc's closest friend, and he's coming in for Matt's wedding on the first. He's heard about us and wants to pick our brains. Mostly yours and Jackie's."

Dave sat there, mouth open, staring out the front window. "I… see," he finally said, "This is beyond incredible. Do you know I have a family connection to that man?"

I smiled. "Yes, Dave, we figured that out. Oddly enough, he's bringing his chief of staff slash chief steward with him when he comes out for the wedding."

The retired commander just sat, motionless. A tear started down his cheek. "How will I ever keep from telling him who I am?" he finally asked.

"After we bring them both into the company you won't have to," I declared, "Jackie and I got the dream last night."

"Oh....wow," Dave breathed, "Will he be able to be a company partner and still serve in the Navy?"

"Oh, yes," I replied, "I was, after I was fed into the Navy back there. I had the Lord's prep work to do, but I still performed my Navy duties well enough."

Dave nodded, still a little bewildered. "Yeah. Well enough to become Chief of the Supply Corps."

"A mere bagatelle," I said with a snort, "Anyway, we'll bring the two of 'em in, then launch the conference by having you come in as one of our panel of experts. I expect you to be well-received."

As I spoke the ladies returned to the table. Jackie was pale but composed, Kathy grinned from ear to ear.

"Have you told him yet?" Jackie asked.

"He has," Dave answered, "and you'll notice I haven't run away screaming."

"Good," Jackie said, "The Admiral will ask the Lord's blessing on the food and our discussion."

We returned to 1926 around 2:30.

*****

Don: 3:05 PM, Chambers Street Baptist Church pastor's study

"Hi, folks," I raised my voice as the sound of Louis' loud improvisation on the organ followed me through the study door.

The occupants smiled and waved as I shut the door. "Louis is enjoying himself," Marcel remarked.

I looked at the coverall-clad men around the room. "Looks like you all had fun too. Did the respirators work OK?"

"No problem, Don," Luther replied, "They're like the ones we had in the war but much easier to wear."

"Good," I said, "Everyone working on this project will have one. Be sure to swap out the cartridges for new ones every morning. Safety first."

"Waited for you to brief details," Elwood said, "Luther will tell what you miss."

"Who says I'll miss anything?" I mock grumped.

"We'll see," Elwood shot back.

"OK," I said, pulling out my notebook, "We start this operation at zero eight hundred Monday morning. We expect to be done by Friday. We decided Sammy's team would work on the console and Elwood's team would dismantle the Barkers. Does that still work?"

"Gotta have another team pullin' an' taggin' pipes," Sammy Allen stated, "Luther says he'll mind 'em."

"Will we have enough people to do the job?" Marcel asked.

"We'll bring our service and cleaning team from *uptime* to help," I replied, "Also bringing a team in from Hoople by Rotodyne Sunday night."

"I think we're in for interesting times," Luther added.

"Allow me to change the subject, please," Marcel said. "What is the plan for preparing the organ parts for shipment?"

"You want to start, Don?" Luther asked.

"Sure. The teams will dismantle the organ case, then remove the tracker arms, Barker machines, and associated actuating machinery. Everything will be marked to precisely match where it came from, and color-coded by Barker machine. We have a bunch of packing and tagging materials coming. Luther's done this before."

"I've never saved and packed all the old mechanism like we're doing here," Luther interrupted, "I'm not sure how much room all this will take."

"I wish I could enlighten you," Marcel said, "but I have never dismantled one completely either."

"Take all the room you need," AP said, "If we have to we'll have Wednesday prayer meeting in the basement."

"Thanks a lot, Pastor, for your flexibility on this," I said, "When we get the Barker machines tagged and wrapped, we will load them into twenty-foot-long steel shipping containers from up-time. We'll call 'em Freight Crates here. People will think we built 'em, and we could eventually.

"Start a new business. Just what we need," Elwood said to chuckles from the group.

I looked at my pad and continued. "Anyway, they will all be trucked to the railhead. The Barkers go to New York to be loaded and shipped on the liner with you, Marcel. The pipes and empty console will head to Highland for John Wick to re-build. He wants the wind chests too, so don't smash 'em if you can help it."

"Aww, Don, you're no fun!" Pastor piped up to more guffaws. I motioned to Luther to continue.

"The organ blower will stay in the basement," Luther began, "but we'll probably replace it with a new one. So, by the end of the week, nothing else will remain of the organ but some lengths of wind pipe and a dingy back wall. We'll put curtains up to hide that until it's time to reshape the area for the rebuilt instrument."

Marcel cleared his throat. "At the risk of drawing one of those noises you call 'raspberries', I think this is going to be great fun!"

I grinned. "You're right as can be, Marcel. Fun. You've seen how dirty you'll get. Keep the coveralls we gave you but don't wear good clothing underneath 'em!"

"This is much cleaner than I am used to. We have a community of rats behind the organ screen at St. Sulpice."

Luther and I groaned.

"Wait one," Elwood interrupted, "Pastor, you need to clear out the study. All the dirt we stir will ruin your things, especially the ship," Elwood referred to the large model of *USS New Jersey* on the credenza behind Pastor's desk.

AP looked confused for a moment, then nodded. "You're right, Elwood. I hadn't thought of that. Deborah and I will move it all out by Monday."

"You pack, we move. Call when ready."

"That's very kind of you, Elwood. Thank you," Pastor replied.

"What I do," our brilliant gnome added.

*****

Mimi: Saturday, April 24th, 1926, 7:30 AM, one week till the wedding

The first kiss of the morning was pleasant. "Good Morning, Matthew."

"Good morning, my—did you transfer yourself?"

I grinned. "I certainly did! I had Gloria watch me just in case I missed the seat, but here I am, no damage!"

"That's wonderful, sweetheart! You're making real progress."

Matt set the breakfast tray on the rolling table and scooted it up to me. I lifted the cover. "Ah, no green eggs and ham! And real bacon—the kitchen is finally getting the idea."

"Green eggs and ham?" Matt asked as he sat down on the side of the bed.

"A literary reference, Love. Title of a children's book from uptime. Amy Foutch brought me several from that author. Show you later."

"OK. Since I'm from here I don't get some of the uptime things they talk about."

"More the fun of discovery, dear," I murmured, "Now sit down and tell me what's going on."

Matt prayed for the food, and I dug in.

"So far Louis and Harmony haven't said anything about marriage?" I asked when Matt finished his news report.

"Not a word," Matt replied, "if they've talked about it they've kept it to themselves. They're arm in arm every time I see them though."

I squirted another five drops of Gator Sauce on my English muffin. "They act like a married couple long enough and they'll want to make it official. The sex makes it more fun."

Matt's attempt to take a sip of water dissolved in a spray out his nose. "Mimi! I don't think they're doing that!"

"Not like us a week from today?"

Matt blushed but spoke clearly. "No, Dear. I think they're waiting until they know each other better in this environment. I think it's going to sneak up on them and they'll be surprised at the timing."

I swallowed. "Yes, Matt, I think you're right. Louis has been through a lot in what is it now, three days? Not even you were ready to pop the question that soon!"

Matt rested his bandaged hand on his lap. "You know, Love, I thought I was ready to ask you that first night you were awake after you'd trusted Christ. I saw how it could go and wanted to hurry things up. Maybe it's working with folks from uptime that's made me want to jump like that. I don't think I was that way in the Navy."

"Glad we waited?" I asked, noting where his eyes focused.

"Now I am," Matt replied, "I can see where waiting until we both knew what we wanted was best. I'm sorry I tried to hurry you along. And by the way...I love you! Will you marry me?"

I bent over my tray slightly and looked at Matt. "I will marry you, my love. And they're glad you're still watching them."

I'm loving a man with healthy circulation, I thought as Matt looked up into my eyes and blushed again.

CHAPTER THIRTY-THREE

Don: Saturday, April 24th, 1926, 9:07 AM, the Auditorium office

"Thanks a bunch for calling, Chesty. Let me talk to Helen and Jack and see if they will change the date. I'll call you back at this number later this afternoon no matter what. We can call the others from here too. That OK?...Great, see you." I hung up.

"Plan B?" Jackie asked.

I nodded. "The Marines want to change the date. Chesty couldn't tell me where they're going, but I'm sure it's Nicaragua. This is about when they went down there in our universe. Affects Chesty and Archie Vandegrift both."

"So, when can they make it?" Amy Foutch, the other occupant of the office asked.

"The way the deployment's shaking down, the only weekend they can blow in here is Saturday, May fifteenth. They can get in the thirteenth, gotta leave Monday morning the seventeenth."

"Three weeks from today," Jackie muttered. "Can we do it?"

I ran my hand through my nonexistent hair. "We can. I don't know about anybody else. I need to call Cottage and set up a..."

"You and Jackie meet with Helen and Jack at ten in their room," Sherry interrupted, "I've also called Luther and he will be there. I explained the situation to all parties so they can be thinking."

"You're too doggone efficient," I grumped.

"No, Donald, just efficient enough. And while you were talking to Lieutenant Puller I received a call from Norman Coke-Jephcott. He's coming to the service and concert tomorrow and bringing a surprise guest."

"Who's he bringing?"

"Now really, Donald, I said it was a surprise. Here's a clue: he's not bringing a *Woogie*," Sherry snorted and clicked off.

"What's a *Woogie*?" Amy asked.

"I'll explain," Jackie replied, "But we gotta go to the ladies' room to do it. Don gets nauseous even thinking about 'em!"

"Jackie, I do...." I started, then put my head down and shut my eyes.

"He'll be OK if he's caught himself in time. Let's go make a pit stop." I heard Jackie and Amy get up and leave the office.

Why we have solid trash cans, I mused, then thought about baseball to avoid thinking about other things.

Five minutes later the phone rang, and the Bondi brothers accepted my offer for the property in the northwest part of town.

Now in the cool of the morning, the whole idea seems less certain, I thought. *Well, if we don't move the church I guess we could put baseball fields out there. Call it "Dreams Field." If we build it they will come,* I finished with a snort.

I could hear laughter from the ladies' lounge.

Forty-five minutes after that I was sitting with Helen in Jack's room. Jackie begged off the trip saying she didn't feel well. Luther stepped in as I finished explaining Chesty's call.

"Well, what do you think, Gunny Mine?" Helen asked.

"I'm fine with the change if you are, Love. What about you, Don. It's your auditorium."

"We can do it," I replied. "Chesty gave me numbers to reach him and Major Vandegrift."

"I've got the rest of the numbers," Luther added.

Jack raised his finger. "And Homer Wallin's written and says he's coming too. We could end up with an odd number."

"I'm sure you'll end up with a number of odd folks," I quipped, then turned as the door opened. "Speak of the devil—hi, guys!"

"We were out strolling and heard you talking, thought we'd stop by," Mimi said as she stepped into the room. Matt hovered around the walker but did not help her.

"Great to see you walking, Mimi!" I announced, "Here, sit down. I'll sit on the bed."

"Thanks, Boss," Matt said as he stood by while Amy maneuvered her walker around and sat in the vacated chair.

"So, what's up?" Mimi asked.

"Our Marine friends are getting deployed, and we have to change the wedding day to May fifteenth," Helen announced, "We're talking about rounding up the rest of the folks for the Arch."

Matt stood next to Mimi. They looked at each other and winked. "Gunny, Don, and I would like to be in the Arch for you."

"We WHAT?" I blurted out my first reaction.

"Why not?" Matt shot back, "We both have our uniforms up to snuff from your wedding, just have to get them cleaned. Wouldn't you like to help expedite that marathon kissing party?"

Jack and Helen giggled as I took a deep breath. "Matt, you know how rusty I am with a sword! They don't need an old geezer like me out there."

"I'll get you back into shape," Matt replied, "or Sammy can do it. Or Jackie."

"That I'd like to see," Mimi said with a smirk.

"We'd love to have you in the Swords," Helen declared, and Jack nodded vigorously, "We'll have Captain Heckel and Bull Reeves, and Commander Towers plus all the others. Not a geezer in the lot—including you!"

I felt my defenses crumbling. "Jackie will have a cow," I muttered.

"I've already talked to Jackie," Mimi piped, "She says she won't let you get out of it this time."

"All right, I'll do it," I finally gave in, "but we need to get our uniforms over to Joe's to get 'em cleaned." I had a thought, "Maybe pay a visit next door to the Little John Coal Company."

"Sherry says the new man got there last week," Matt said, "So far he seems on the up and up."

"Will you be safe over there?" Jack asked.

"Why not?" I asked, "He won't know us, and Luther and Paul won't be with us."

"Thanks, Don, I was wondering," Luther spoke quietly.

*****

Louis Vierne, 8:15 PM, Hotel Broadview sitting room, another chat with a friend

"The hotel kitchen seemed unusually busy tonight," I observed.

"How could you tell?" Harmony asked.

I turned my head toward the woman sitting close by my side. "Normally the kitchen is quieter in the evening since they are only preparing individual orders. Tonight, the noise is much louder. The smells tell me they are preparing a number of foods. *Side dishes* I believe you call them. And the master chef is here when he normally is not. He sounds stressed."

"You have it exactly!" Harmony replied, "The kitchen chef is John Wright. He worked with Don in the Navy. Don asked him to cater the noon meal after church tomorrow, and forgot to ask him until this afternoon!"

"Like being informed of a special Mass a half-hour prior to its start," I said, "I wonder if Donald did that to test his staff?"

Harmony shifted her body slightly toward me; she may not

have noticed what brushed against my arm, but I did. "Jackie says he's done that before, but this time he just didn't think about it until this afternoon. He forgot to ask Pastor too. Sherry had to call all the members who have phones to tell them not to cook Sunday dinner."

"Did Sherry say something about that?"

Harmony laughed. "Not a word! She made the calls, but Jackie made Don do the talking."

I chuckled and then changed the subject. "Harmony, thank you very much for helping me at the church organ this afternoon, and for taking note of how Marcel and I changed the presets."

"You're welcome, Louis. I wanted to make sure I understood the changes so I could explain them to others who will play it tomorrow. Certain other organists could be surprised."

I grinned. "I am sure they would do the same for me, were they to have the chance. I am very happy the Auditorium organ is so easy to alter while playing. At Notre Dame, my leg would remind me of its old injury every time I stepped on a preset pedal."

Harmony's arm held mine closer. "Do you miss the other organ?"

I sighed. "Yes, some. But I am becoming more and more enamored of its replacement." I looked over at Harmony.

I smelled the beginning of tears. "Yes" was all she said.

I heard the side door to the hotel open. "Here comes my night minder, with others," I remarked.

Harmony turned. "Jeff, and Amy and Elwood. What brings you over tonight?"

"Elwood's going to check on tomorrow's meat for the church lunch," Amy replied, "and see how the new warming cabinets fit in the pickups."

Harmony translated for me. "Warming cabinets?" I asked.

"Stainless steel, roll," Elwood pronounced, "Keeps hot hot and cold cold."

I nodded, then noticed Jeff staring at me. He was communicating without words, and I understood what he asked me. I replied in our way, and Jeff spoke the English word, "Soon."

"What was that all about?" Harmony asked when they had gone to the kitchen.

"I was just asked when I would ask you to marry me," I had to tell the truth.

"And how did you reply to Jeff?" Harmony asked. I felt her hiccup, as I did when I cried.

"I told him soon, and he repeated the word out loud," I said, "When would you like me to ask you?"

"Let's think about that," Harmony replied. She then brought my face to hers and kissed me. She kissed like no other woman I could remember, or wished to remember.

"We appear to be progressing," Harmony remarked when we finished.

"So we do," was all I could think of in reply.

CHAPTER THIRTY-FOUR

Luther: Sunday, April 25th, 1926, 10:35 AM, Chambers Street Baptist Pastor's study

"It's wall-to-wall organists out there," I said as I stepped into the study for the pre-service meeting.

"Who all's here?" Terry Fensterer, the Deacon of the Day and the only other occupant, asked.

"Let's see...Louis Vierne and Marcel Dupré, and several friends of mine—Norm Coke-Jephcott, Virgil Fox, and Chuck Simmons. Plus Doctor Jennifer Setterdahl, our new Orthopedist also plays."

"That's a crowd," Terry said, "Healey Willan couldn't make it?"

"No, he had teaching commitments in Toronto," I replied, "How did you remember him?"

Terry chuckled. "Despite what I lead Don to believe, I do know what's going on. I met Healey at church last time he was here. Grand fellow, wish he could come down more often."

"I hear he's coming for a month this summer," I said, "We'll be putting the organ back in the building by then, I hope."

"We'll see," Terry replied, "I watched Hook and Hastings install it back in '99, fascinating. I hope you're ready for lots of little parts all over when you take it apart."

As he spoke, I noticed Terry was wearing the hearing aid Don had found for him *uptime*. "We're going to be very careful, so Marcel can take the Barker machines back to Paris. I hope we have enough room to sort it out."

Terry grinned. "Oh, I think you'll manage, although we may have to have a street meeting Wednesday night instead of a prayer meeting."

I started to reply then the rest of the team walked in: Pastor and Lucille, with Don bringing up the rear.

"Chock-a-block crowd today," Pastor remarked, "Everything ready for the lunch, Don?"

"Ready to go," Don replied, "a couple of our trucks will deliver the food just before twelve. We'll see how our new catering gear works. And Elwood says the meat will be good."

"Always is when he does it," Pastor said, "Lucille, what's up with the music?"

"I've got the prelude and the first songs. Luther's taking the offertory and the last song. Harold's singing and I'm accompanying. I've got the invitation and Jenn's got the postlude."

Pastor nodded. "I won't remember all that, Luce, except you've got it covered. Anything for you, Terry?"

Terry winked at me before he spoke. "Why are all the organists here?"

I could see Don start to flare, then he choked it off somehow. "Come back after lunch this afternoon and you'll see, Terry."

"Why? Is there an organ recital?"

Don would have been fun to watch, except I knew what his blood pressure was doing. *Is Terry saying those things just to yank Don's chain?*

"All right, folks, let's pray. You, Luther, then I'll close."

Just before my offertory Pastor rolled out the grenade.

"Doctor Norman Coke-Jephcott, the master examiner for the American Guild of Organists, is visiting us today and has something he'd like to say before we pray for the offering. Doctor?"

I felt like the mouse at a cat convention.

Norm came up to the platform. "Good morning, Ladies and Gentlemen. Normally I have the Pastor make the request I'm about to make—"

Here we go again. Lord, please keep me from doing something stupid in front of all these people, and these organists!

"...but AP told me he thought Luther was on to our little game and asked me to make the request myself. I'm most pleased to do that."

Syl's down there grinning...and so are the rest of them! And I'm swinging in the wind...

"What I'm about to ask is a little test I give to organists I'm examining for the Guild. Luther passed this test with flying colors in 1921, but I've asked it of him several times since, just for the sheer joy of hearing him play."

That's high praise from Norm, I thought, *now here comes the payback.*

Norm continued, "Luther, after Pastor prays, I would like you to improvise on the last song before the special music. The usual rules apply, except there will be no time limit imposed by me on your improvisation today. Pastor tells me he will turn off the blower at the fuse box if you exceed fifteen minutes."

The congregation laughed, and I had to chuckle, too. *A new twist...and I can't cry up here, so might as well laugh.*

"Do you understand what you are to do, Luther?"

"May I scream before I run out of the building?"

More laughter. "Screaming is optional, but I suggest you run fast. Mister Fox says he can catch you."

In the second row. I saw Virgil turn bright red. *So he can be embarrassed!* Then I caught the pun and laughed myself.

"I believe I have done enough damage to decorum up here. Pastor Kittridge, thank you for letting me speak, and now back to you."

Pastor returned to the pulpit, stifling a last giggle. "It is good to laugh, folks, and thank you, Norm, for giving us the opportunity. Now, let's pray."

Again I checked to see what I was improvising on this morning. Hmmm...

I Am His, and He Is Mine. The one that brought Syl and most of the congregation to tears at Galva a few months ago. Stinker knew that was the last song. Here we go again! Lord, please guide my playing in this one, one more time.

As Pastor finished his prayer I pressed preset number four, the gentlest of the reed choruses in the swell, as I kept it set up. I opened the swell chest halfway, placed hands and feet, and paused.

The prayer ended. I opened my eyes and pressed the first chord.

As my fingers were starting to go down I remembered something. The afternoon before, Marcel and Louis had altered several presets to prepare for the concert this afternoon. Harmony called to tell me what they had changed.

They had changed preset four to full organ, everything coupled, swell doors override full open. I had forgotten.

Oops!!

The organ let forth with a blast that would have rattled the windows had we already installed the new pedal ranks.

Now what?

All my prior planning, experience in improvisation, and preconceived thoughts about this song were blown away.

After the mighty crash, I began to play a melodic line on the great manual and pedals. That gave me a few seconds to think. But I *couldn't* think, and I realized I had no idea how to go on.

Out of time and out of ideas. Except...*Lord, I don't know what to do! Please take over. I can't get out of this!*

At that moment I had the clearest impression of the Lord's nearness to me that I'd experienced since that day at Belleau Wood. A peace like I had that day came over me, and I had the sense of the Lord whispering in my ear, again.

I was waiting for you to ask. Fear not, and listen.

The improvised melodic line streamed forth but began to take a shape, a form. I had no idea where we were heading, but we had *purpose.*

As we progressed, I noticed the development owed something to things I'd heard in Charles Ives' music, and other constructions reminded me of the sort of riffs jazz musicians played. They didn't sound 'blue' like jazz riffs, but they definitely were related. Benny Goodman and Glenn Miller would have been impressed; I certainly was!

The improvisation gradually quieted from the inadvertent full organ blast. I began to hear snatches of the melody we were heading toward...and an entirely different melody, one I did not recognize at all. The two tunes played with each other, chasing each other as if through a meadow. The effect was beautiful—and, as usual, I wasn't planning it.

Finally, I heard the Gospel song *I am His and He is Mine* clearly stated in the eight-foot diapasons. The other melody came in and wove a delightful counterpoint with first song. Gradually I took off stops, eased the swell chest closed, and the music resolved to a gentle restatement of the main melody, and...the other melody murmuring in the sixteen-foot pedal Bourdon stop. The effect was amazing...more so to me, who was not plotting anything.

The improvisation over, I switched to the mid-strength preset and played the song once through straight. Don came to the pulpit, the congregation stood, and we sang the song.

I managed to slither to my seat as Pastor came up to preach. Syl grasped my hand and smiled at me. The smile of the love of my life completed my transformation into a melted lump of gratitude. I don't remember anything of the rest of the service, just the Lord's Grace and my wife's smile.

*****

Jackie: 10:30 PM that evening, their house on Broad Street

The vid on the wall-mounted screen ended. "Yep, that's the tune," I remarked, "Thanks for finding that, Sherry."

"You're welcome," our cyberint replied through the speakers, "Once I reviewed the recording of the improvisation it was easy to trace, despite Donald's lame attempt at humming the tune."

"I tried," Don grumped as he sat on the bed getting undressed.

"Yes, you did," Sherry purred, "a worthy interpretation as conceived by John Cage."

"Isn't he the guy who wrote so-called music for a burning piano?"

"That was someone else I cannot determine, not Cage. Donald, I suggest you stick to your day job. Nighty-nite all!" The speaker clicked off.

"So, it was a Glenn Miller rendition of *I Know Why*, from the movie *Sun Valley Serenade* of 1941," I declared, "but when did Luther ever hear that tune?"

Don sat on the bed with a frown, then he snapped his fingers. "I know! The day Luther rehearsed the Chicago Symphony for the April second concert. After he called out Benny Goodman for a rogue riff in the middle of *Bartered Bride Overture*, he talked to the three of 'em, Goodman, Miller, and Artie Shaw, about managing a band of pranksters. The rest of that day I was humming tunes from those guys that I knew uptime. I had to have thrown that one in. But how did he remember it?"

"Like Luther said," I replied, "The Lord gave him that improvisation. He brought that tune to Luther's mind, then combined 'em."

"For sure, Precious," Don said, "and that was just the first piece of this incredible day of music. Sherry says we got it all, and

Rick wants to make a demo pressing for Bill Brophy of Brunswick."

"Think he'll try to market it?" I asked.

"I think so," Don replied, "Bill loves our stuff. I think he'll use it to talk the Brunswick board into selling us the record business."

I started to undress. "Do we want that, Love? Who'll run it? Not you, Admiral!"

Don looked over at me...and kept looking. "No, not me for skippy. If the Lord wants us to have it, He'll come up with someone. Look at how He sent us Mimi to run the Auditorium."

"Right. And could you believe Louis with that postlude tonight?"

"I guess Norm Coke-Jephcott likes Louis' improvising as much as Luther's. But asking him to do a *sortie* on a Christmas carol?"

"Well, Louis sure rose to the challenge," I replied, "*Adeste Fideles* the way he played it was incredible! I bet the folks didn't see the kiss Harmony gave him at the end. And are you ogling me, Mister Wain?"

Don turned red but kept staring. "I can't help it, Love. You're even more ravishing than on our wedding night."

"Flattery will get you...somewhere," I said as I slipped under the covers, "but I'm feeling a little off tonight. Could we just...?"

Don only hesitated a second. "Of course, Precious," he said as he put his hand somewhere I greatly appreciated.

As we wound the spring on our favorite activity I found myself thinking. *After all these hints he still doesn't understand! And I can't bring myself to blurt it out. What's wrong with me? He's gonna freak out if I don't break it to him easy, but how on earth do I do that? I'm supposed to be an expert at sharing information—except now.*

I had a thought, not from my own jangled mind. *Yes, Lord, I get it. I'll talk to her tomorrow morning.* Then other sensations took over my consciousness.

CHAPTER THIRTY-FIVE

Don: Monday, April 26th, 1926, 10:47 AM, the Little John Coal Company office, Galva, visiting time

Matt glanced over at me and turned the knob. The door opened noiselessly thanks to our ministrations a few months before, but the person in the office heard the latch.

"Hello, who's there?" a voice from the back.

"Hi, we were hoping to meet the new coal company manager," I replied hopefully.

"Come on back," the first voice said.

We gathered our wits and whatever leftover military bearing we could scrounge and entered the back office.

A thin, middle-aged man of medium height and sandy hair stood up from his desk and came around to meet us. He wore horn-rimmed glasses and a thoughtful expression.

As we walked in, I saw an Army cap with tarnished gold braid hanging on the coat tree and decided to open in that line. "We have a wedding in our organization in three weeks, and we're both in their arch of swords. Our uniform tailor is right next door."

The man grinned. "Oh? I'm still in the Reserves, and I have to find someplace to get mine cleaned before the next drill weekend. I didn't know he did uniforms."

"None better than Joe," Matt added, "He cleans ribbons too."

The other man stood appraising us. "I wonder if you gentlemen might be from Wain Engineering?" he asked.

"I'm Don Wain, of the company you said, and this is Matt Plotczyc."

"Plotczyc...pronounced just like it's spelled," Matt said with a grin.

"And I'm Richard Boeke, pronounced 'Bo-Kee'. Friends call me 'Dick'."

So far, so good, I thought as we shook hands.

The new manager of the coal company returned behind his desk. "I have wanted to meet you and discuss some of what's happened around here the last year. Please, sit down. Can I get you anything? I brew a pretty good cup of coffee."

"That would be fine, thank you, Dick," I said as we sat down in the wooden armchairs.

While Dick bustled around producing the cups of coffee, Matt and I scanned the office. We were familiar with the office from the surveillance video but hadn't seen it since Lex's demise. Now, a recently snuffed cigarette smoldered in the ashtray on Dick's desk. The ashtray and the rest of the office showed evidence of cleaning. On the wall behind Dick hung a crucifix between two pictures. On one side hung a hand-colored family portrait: Dick, a blonde woman, and four young adults. On the other side a photo of Dick in Army uniform, on crutches, receiving...*Ah, that changes things*, I thought.

Dick produced the mugs of coffee and refilled his own. He sat back down behind the desk.

"I see you have *The Medal,*" I began.

Dick nodded without smiling. "Mexican campaign, 1916. A little incident involving a bridge over a river."

"Still bothers you, doesn't it?" Matt spoke before I could.

Dick's left eyebrow twitched. "It does. Not even the worst of the Great War came close for me. But let's change the subject. I can tell you were both military. What were you?"

"I retired as a vice-admiral, Navy Supply, er, Paymaster Corps," I replied, "Matt retired as a Captain, Navy line.

"Vice-admiral in supply?" Dick repeated, "You must have run the whole organization."

"Yeah, I did," I replied, "Matt skippered supply ships, then helped me in D.C."

Dick took a sip of his coffee. "*And the rest is logistics*. Heard that one plenty in the Corps of Engineers. We can swap stories later; now let's get down to business."

I sent my mind to *general quarters* as Dick continued.

"First I want to apologize for what happened when Lex Sherwood came out here and took over. I don't know if you are aware of the power structure within this company."

"Luther and Paul have briefed us," I remarked.

"Then you know there are two factions: one interested in taking care of the farmers and the land, the other only profits, and damn everything else, pardon my French."

Why do they always call it French? I thought. *That's an insult to my French friends. Besides, all those words are easy to say, unlike anything French!*

"Where do you fit into the equation, Dick?" Matt asked.

Dick snorted. "I am the only partner in the company who is not a born Sherwood. I married Lex's sister Sharon. May I say her personality is nothing like his!"

Dick smiled at that thought, and we nodded.

"For some reason at the moment, I am the only manager both sides trust enough to take over this operation after Lex nearly destroyed it. When I found out what he was going to do to the farmers in this area, and who he brought up from Herrin to help him, I was physically ill. I had to throw away the rug beside my desk at the home office."

Matt and I looked interested, concerned. We were also frantically analyzing Dick's statements and his body language as he spoke.

Dick continued, "I knew he'd gone backward in his chair the morning he fired Paul and Luther quit. He left the old chair in the back closet. I almost crashed in it myself! I can understand how that bump on the head eventually killed him—that's what the autopsy found. As a good Catholic, I recognize the Hand of God." He made the sign of the Cross as he said that.

"We certainly agree as to the Source of that event," I chose my words carefully. "How do you propose to run this branch of the Coal Company, sir?"

Dick looked at us, then sighed.

"I do not have permission to set aside the topsoil for over-covering when we are done. If the topsoil is found to be *recoverable* when we are through, that is coincidental, or so I'll tell the home office. I have not been given the budget to engage in public works projects for the other residents of the area. However, I must keep the roads and railroad right of way we use in good repair so our vehicles may pass safely. Our purposes may therefore *coincide* at some points."

Matt and I nodded.

"One thing I have latitude with is in my relations with the farmers whose properties abut ours. Unlike my late brother in law, I would permit...no, I would *welcome*...the legal representative of your company to sit in on any discussions we have with the neighboring farmers, particularly if it involves possible land purchases or right of way permissions. I want to give fair compensation, and not coerce our neighbors in any way."

"Our Legal officer is attorney Amy Lansdale Foutch," Matt said, "and I'm sure she would be pleased to assist the farmers out here. Don and I know most of them personally."

"She would be welcome," Dick replied, "My wife has made it her life's work to rid me of any prejudice against professional women! She's a pediatrician back home."

"We appreciate your attitude very much," Again I chose my

words carefully. "We operate under the principle that what you do with your property is your business, as long as your actions do not affect your neighbors, or damage their land or water, or risk their person. The actions your brother-in-law was planning offended these principles in multiple ways."

"How did you know what actions Lex was going to undertake?"

Crunch time. Matt and I looked steadily at Dick, who looked back with the same expression. I spoke.

"We knew. I cannot divulge how."

Dick blinked and shrugged. "I do not need to know. His intentions were dishonorable, and he died before he could carry them out. I can assure you I will not so behave. You will see."

Matt spoke. "We believe you, Dick. We can work with you within these parameters." I nodded my assent.

Dick sighed. "I am glad of that, gentlemen. Sometime I would like to meet Luther and his wife, and my nephew Paul. I hear he is married too. We need to restore some sort of family relationship. I am forbidden from hiring them back, unfortunately."

"They are both doing other things now," I said. "Let me see what sort of a meeting I can arrange. I have an idea in that regard. Let me do some plotting. The next month is going to be extremely busy for us, though, many projects at once."

"Oh, I understand," Dick replied. "I have to get this operation producing coal by the middle of June. That is going to take all my time and energy. I will never understand why Lex would want to squander his resources and the goodwill of his neighbors just to get a little more gain. He would have had nothing left to build the business with!"

"He seemed like a lost soul," Matt said.

"I agree, Matt. I will try to avoid that sort of behavior."

"So will we," Matt added.

"And now," I said, "may we take you to lunch? We know a very good little restaurant within walking distance. And I have an idea about that topsoil—I think we can save it without getting you into trouble."

"The Friendly Café? I haven't had a chance to try it yet. I'd like that," Dick smiled and stood up. *Mission accomplished,* I thought.

*****

Matt: later, driving home

"Been a while since we had a meeting like that," I remarked as I accelerated the Jaguar out of Galva.

"You said it, Matt. I thought it was going to get a little tense there for a bit." Don's brow wrinkled like when he was worried.

"Understatement. You think he was straight with us?"

"I think so ...*whee*!" If Don hadn't been buckled in he would have hit his head on the car roof. "This thing sure likes bumps!"

I laughed. "Mimi thinks it's more fun than a roller coaster! She says she has a lead foot and can't wait to show me."

"How's your wedding gift coming?" I asked.

"Doctor Art's sending it through the paint booth tomorrow," I replied, referring to our uptime car broker, "Won't have to do a thing to it, he says. Plus I was able to pick up that other car I told you about."

"You're going to really surprise her with that second one," I said, "Gonna tell me what the one from uptime is?"

I downshifted the modified XK140 for a curve as we turned toward Altona. "Mimi sees it first, Boss. Until then, it's a secret. But your take on Dick's honesty?"

"Oh, yeah," Don leaned back in the seat. "Paul's told me how Dick operates, and this was true to form. He's no Lex, not even close."

"Concur," I pronounced. "That was quite a question he delivered, about our knowing what was coming."

"I couldn't say any more than what I said," Don replied. "He's figured out we have some confidential sources, but he won't be able to trace anything. I don't think he'll try. If he does, we'll know it."

"I don't think he's going to," I said, "Folks with The Medal seem to have different priorities."

"As *you-know-who* is going to find out. I got a telegram from Bill Leahy at BuNav this morning—it's been approved."

"Amazing," I said over the whine of third gear at the Oneida corner, "How many markers did you have to call in to pull that off?"

"Every one I could find," Don replied with a sigh, "Worth it though. And now Dick's gonna get to watch our little ambush."

"I'm pleased to get him for the Arch of Swords. He'll fit in fine with that bunch of gold-braid yahoos! Are you going to tell Paul he's joining us?" I asked.

Don frowned as he grabbed the roof handle for another bump. "No. Anticipation will eat on Dick. It can't be helped. Paul and Edna need blissful ignorance before it happens, I think."

"Like Bull and his Chief?" I asked.

"For sure," Don said as we squirted out the other side of Altona next to the railroad embankment. "Coming in on Thursday, right?"

"Right, on the Santa Fe Chief, about 9:30. When are we bringing them in?"

"We'll have their gear dropped off at the Broadview," Don replied, "Might as well do it first off. Maybe 10:15. Harmony and Louis can witness the event."

"They haven't gotten engaged yet, have they?" I asked.

"No, and I'm beginning to wonder if they're playing with us," Don said, "Louis has a sharp wit I hadn't read about, and they sure are acting like a couple. Guess we'll see."

"Could just take them a while," I replied, "Look at Mimi and me."

"Oh, yeah," Don replied, then pointed to our left at a double-arched brick viaduct in the railroad embankment. "That's still there uptime. It's prettier here. Not so overgrown."

My response was drowned out by the whistle of an express train overtaking us.

*****

Mimi: 11:45, her room at Cottage, lunch meeting

"Anybody home?" Jackie asked through the half-opened door.

"Come on in," I replied, "my glorious lunch has just been delivered."

"Yes, it has," Jackie said as she carried a large sack through the door, "I had a craving for a certain uptime fast food and thought I'd share it with you."

"It can't be any worse than this," I said, pointing at my covered tray.

"Don't be so sure," Jackie said as she pulled up another tray table.

Jackie took two smaller boxes and several small packets out of her bag. "These things don't seem like much at first, but they grow on you."

"Like fungus?" I asked, then opened a box. "What *are* these things?"

"Chicken nuggets," Jackie replied, opening one of the packets. "Pressed pieces of *sorta* chicken, fried in a batter. Eat them with your fingers and dip them in your sauce of choice." She pointed at the packets, "Honey mustard, sweet and sour, ranch, marinara, and toadstool."

"Wha—"

"Sorry, couldn't resist," Jackie said, "That one's buffalo habanero."

"The animal?"

"The city. Supposed to be super spicy. I've never tried it."

"Guess I will," I replied. I took one of the misshapen chunks and dipped it and its successor in each sauce in turn and tasted. "Pretty dull, even that Buffalo one. Hand me the Gator Sauce please."

"Figured you'd say that," Jackie smiled and handed me the bottle.

I drizzled the sauce on one nugget and tried it. "There, that's the ticket. May I eat the whole box?"

"Sure, but the cardboard won't taste good," Jackie replied.

"Snot!"

"Thank you."

I anointed the strange chicken parts in the box and dug in.

"Ah, much better," I offered as I chewed, "Have you told him yet?"

"I wanted to talk to you about that." Jackie's mouth formed a frown.

"He hasn't noticed anything different?" I asked.

Jackie wiped her hand with a napkin and placed it on her belly. "No. The cravings, the barfing, my belly. He hasn't noticed any of it!" She pressed her hands to either side of her breasts, "He's noticed these, but hasn't asked why they're expanding. It's maddening!"

"I thought Don understood so much in this world," I offered.

"He does, but not this," Jackie's voice broke, "I'm so afraid he'll just melt-down when he hears I'm pregnant that I haven't gotten up the nerve to tell him. What's wrong with me?"

I was surprised this supremely competent, experienced, bilingual woman was brought to this point. But then I remembered how I had been brought to my knees by my own behaviors. Jackie's problem wasn't like mine, and I thought I saw a way to help.

"Well, you're human to start with," I began in my Principal voice, "Hasn't he seen a pregnancy before with his late wife?"

"No," Jackie replied, "He and Pam were married for many years. He says thirty-five but I'm sure it was longer. But she never got pregnant. Wasn't for lack of trying," she snorted, "With her physical problems it's just as well she didn't have to deal with it. I'm sure Don thinks it was his problem."

"I'd say not," I remarked, "but aren't you a bit old to get pregnant?"

Jackie took another nugget and chewed on it before replying.

"I'm fifty-four. That's not too old if you're still putting out the eggs. And I am. Plus I'm told the treatments of the tank do things to fertility and pregnancy. The far time docs aren't sure how they'll affect someone from back here since our genetics are slightly different. I guess I'm gonna be the guinea pig."

"Were you afraid to tell Don until you were sure it'd take?" I asked.

Jackie's mouth opened wide, then the tears started to flow. "Wow! I think that's a big part of it, now that you bring it up. Even uptime, the older you are the more risky the pregnancy. I didn't want to get Don's hopes up, and then lose the baby." Jackie's mouth twisted, "Guess that could still happen."

I fought back my grief and kept pretending to be logical. "That's right, but as I recall you telling me a while back, we're under the Lord's control now, and He calls the tune. Right?"

"Right," Jackie said, then she saw where I was heading and nodded, "and nothing happens to a Believer without His Will, active or permissive."

"Permissive, meaning it's not what He wants but you get what you want, and learn from the consequences," I said, "That's starting to make sense. So, what is the conclusion for you?" I returned to my Principal's voice.

"You're still a Principal, Mimi," Jackie said with a chuckle, "OK, it means I tell Don I'm pregnant, no later than the afternoon of your wedding. I promise. I'll let the Lord keep the old geezer together!"

"My eyebrows raised. "You call him that too?"

"Yeah," my visitor said, picking up the remains of the sauces and sticking them in the bag, "Don loves humor, and he'd much rather be the butt of the joke than make a joke at someone else's expense. Jokes can be the unkindest cut of all."

"I know," I said, "I never, ever made fun of a student or teacher, far as I know. Although," I added with pursed lips, "if my old teachers got to meet George the python again, I'd enjoy watching it."

"Noted," Jackie said and changed the subject. "Are you ready for the wedding and what comes after?"

I looked from side to side, then spoke in a whisper. "I see Doctor Bohan and Gloria on Thursday for a discharge physical. I'll get detailed instructions of what we can and cannot do, probably from Gloria. I don't think even John could tell it to my face."

I looked Jackie in the eye. "As for the wedding night, I'll make sure Matt finds it hard to walk straight the next morning!"

Jackie laughed so hard I thought she'd lose her nuggets.

CHAPTER THIRTY-SIX

Luther: Wednesday, April 28th, 1926, 10 AM, Chambers Street Baptist Church, surprise

"Hoo-boy, we're gonna have to rethink this!"

"Luther, you are the soul of understatement this morning," Don observed.

I stood with Marcel and Don near the front pew on the far-right side of the sanctuary. The dismantling, tagging, and organizing of the organ had progressed as planned, up to this moment.

Pipes, wind chests, frames of Barker machines, and thousands of wooden levers and dowels covered every flat surface of the sanctuary. Only a narrow network of walkways allowed the teams to move among the pieces. The emptied Pastor's study was full of organ parts, and assemblies had begun to encroach into the foyer.

Disassembly was not the problem. Tagging the parts was not the problem. Organizing the assemblies for packing into the shipping containers called freight crates sitting in the small parking lot beside the church was the problem.

Arranging and staging the parts for most efficient loading, and ensuring the fragile wooden parts were properly labeled and wrapped in protective packing simply took time...and space. Lots and lots of space.

"I never imagined so many parts made up a Barker machine," Marcel said as he shook his head. "I cannot praise your people enough for the care they are taking to make sure all the parts are labeled, and nothing gets lost!"

"Our pleasure, Marcel," Don replied. "But I never dreamed we'd need this much space!"

"Me neither," I admitted. "Working with the Direct Electric actions is so much simpler. Everything here is organized, but we don't dare move any of it until we are ready to pack it in the freight crates."

"If we start moving things we will have chaos, and lose critical parts," Marcel added.

"So right. But we can't use the building for church with all this out here."

As Don made that observation, Pastor and Deborah came from the foyer and made their way down the one narrow aisle to where we stood.

"What happened?" AP asked (in his Navy *Command Voice,* I noted).

"The disassembly and preparation are going fine," I replied, "but we very greatly underestimated the number of parts we were dealing with, and space we'd need to do the job. I'm sorry. This just blew past me!"

"Don't worry, Luther," Deborah said. "We'll just hold prayer meeting in the basement."

"Er...basement's full too." Don turned red as he spoke softly.

"Oh, OK," Deborah said. "Ideas, gentlemen?"

We all just stood there, looking at Pastor and each other. Suddenly Marcel spoke.

"Donald, we are having a wedding at your auditorium Saturday. Would it be possible to hold the prayer meeting there this evening also?"

Don theatrically slapped his forehead. "You're right! Why didn't I think of that! Could we do that, Pastor?"

Pastor and Deborah looked around the sanctuary, then at each other. Then they shrugged. "Might as well, and thanks. Can't do it here, that's for sure."

"Our pleasure, Pastor. Now we just have to tell everybody."

Deborah grinned, "I'll go in the study and start the prayer chain —that'll tell most of the families. Then, we leave a sign on the door. We'll start fifteen minutes later at the Auditorium. No prob!"

Deborah looked over toward the Pastor's study, the way to it completely blocked by piles of rods and levers. She turned back to us.

"Prob."

"Come on back to the Auditorium and make the calls from there," Don said, sticking a small object back in his pocket, "Sherry just left a message on my cell phone to get back ASAP. I wonder why?" he finished.

"She didn't call *flashlight* so it's not an emergency," Deborah remarked, "guess we'll all find out when you do."

*****

Jackie: a few minutes later, the Auditorium office

"I don't know what's going on, Love," I said as Don stepped into the office, followed by Pastor and Deborah, "Sherry made the call but didn't explain herself."

"That's unusual," Don said, "Is this some sort of joke, Sherry?"

"Definitely not," our cyberint replied through the speakers, "A cable has just arrived which requires your attention. Also, Fredrick Rentschler called for you five minutes ago and asks you to call him back as soon as possible. I have the number."

"OK, thanks, Sherry," Don said, "Please send over the cable."

"To the printer now," Sherry said, "Recommend you read it before calling Mr. Rentschler back."

"OK," Don said as he walked over to the hidden laser printer.

"We need to start the prayer chain," Deborah whispered to me, "the church building is piled with organ parts and we need to have prayer meeting here tonight."

"Sure," I replied, "Use that phone on Dick's desk—it's a separate line."

"Thanks," Deborah said and pulled a membership list from her pocket.

"Hmmm," Don said as he walked back to his desk and sat down, "Hugo says Ernst Heinkel wants to buy whatever part of the business Hugo wants to sell him. Since Junkers Aircraft Company is leaving Germany for here Hugo asks how much of the firm he should sell. Ernst is willing to pay good money, and that would help the transfer."

"I'd say his engine business at least," I declared, "Any of his aircraft designs smaller than the F-13 as well, since we're going to feed in some uptime ones."

Don scratched his head. "That sounds good, Precious, but what kind of engines are we going to build while we're developing the turboprop line?"

"Pardon me," Sherry interrupted, "but I think you should take this call before deciding. Fredrick Rentschler is holding for you."

"Oh OK, thanks, Sherry." Don sounded a little distracted.

"Who's Rentschler?" Pastor whispered.

"The head of Pratt and Whitney aero engines," I replied as Don answered the phone, "We're helping them get started with their Wasp radials. Great engines."

"Oh, OK," Pastor said.

"They WHAT???" Don yelled into the phone. The rest of us jumped then froze as Don turned red and listened.

"Ten days to sell it or they close it down and scrap the prototypes? That's the craziest thing I ever heard! Did they tell you why?"

Don listened some more. His face turned from red to a pasty white. I'd never seen him react like this.

"Don't they understand that you're ready to bring out the best aircraft engine yet built, not to mention give their company a license to print money?"

"I think we're about to spend some money," I muttered.

"Well, you've got your buyer! I'll take every bit of the project —tooling, machines, the works. We'll set up on our bases, develop them as you planned, help it along. I need to see you and negotiate the details but I'll tell you right now we'll buy it for you."

"You're right," Deborah whispered, "this sounds big."

"Huge," I replied, "If I hear this right, Pratt and Whitney is about to give away the keys to their survival for the next century."

"Wow," Pastor observed.

"OK, Monday will be fine. We're busy here too till then." Don said, then listened, "That's not a problem here. No board of directors, I'm sole proprietor with help from many wonderful people. Old Henry Ford could do this too if he wasn't nuts!"

Don laughed. "Some might disagree with you there, Fred. Couple more things. Please see if George Mead will come with you on the trip, and into the new business. And I want the names *Wasp* and *Hornet*, and the eagle for the logo. We'll call the company something other than Pratt and Whitney of course. And is it OK to tell Bull Reeves what's going on? He's coming in for his best friend's wedding tomorrow."

Don listened some more. "Great! If you told Admiral Moffett about this I bet I get a phone call from him directly. He knows we're helping Bull with Naval aviation... OK, see you Monday then. If anything changes call us right away. And relax! We do things differently around here, not like Wrights...or P. and W. See you!"

Don hung up, took a couple of deep breaths, and turned to us. "Figure it out yet?"

"We're buying the premier piston engine line and its builder for the next century," I pronounced.

"Yep," Don spat out, "The Pratt and Whitney board has decided that aero engines do not fit into their 'business model'. They make tools that build things, not the things themselves, they say. They've given Fred ten days to find a buyer or they close it down and scrap everything!"

"That's insane," Pastor announced.

"I guarantee you this didn't happen uptime," I added, "Where we come from Pratt and Whitney's still the byword for reliable engines: piston, turboprop, and jets."

"Another case of things not going here as they went there," Don said in a quieter voice, "I wonder if this is one of the curve-balls the Lord told us He'd throw at us, to change how things come out here?"

"Definitely," Deborah said, "You didn't go looking for this opportunity, but it sure found you. Now what?"

"We get ready for a meeting with the Pratt and Whitney people Monday afternoon after they arrive. We tell Bull about this, along with all the other stuff he gets hit with tomorrow. And we pray about who we get to manage those two engineers and their product!"

"Not to mention talking carrier aviation with Bull, and that little wedding Saturday," I said, "I love it when a plan comes together."

"Hey, that's my line!"

"Not today, Admiral," Sherry broke in, "and as you predicted, Admiral Moffett is on the phone for you."

"Happy logistics, Love," I said as Don picked up the receiver.

*****

Harmony: 5:30 PM, a pleasant walk to dinner

"Our friends seem to inhabit a kicked-over anthill today," Louis remarked as we left the auditorium by the side entrance.

"Big anthill," I replied, "How could you tell the difference from their usual frenzy?"

"The number of subjects they spoke to each other about, and how quickly they changed subjects. I gather the removal of the organ at church proved more than they bargained for. They are preparing for the arrival of the Naval officer and his assistant tomorrow. I must thank Donald for inviting us to attend their induction. Finally, we have the matter of the aero engines. I could not follow much of that discussion at lunch, only its emotion. Have I missed anything?"

I smiled at my charge...or was he my love? *He leaves me confused*, I thought. "The wedding on Saturday you are playing for, and your assistant seems to be grasping your arm closer to her body."

Louis looked over at me with his sightless eyes. "So you are, my dear. Is there some significance beyond this uneven sidewalk?"

"Maybe."

"Did I not hear Mimi Conger said that to Matthew not so long ago?"

I squeezed his arm. "Yes. Is there some significance?"

"Perhaps we shall find out Saturday."

"Perhaps."

We came to the intersection of Ferris and Cherry streets. Louis put his free hand on my arm. "Stop a moment."

"What is it?" I asked.

"A most interesting confluence of smells, my dear. Breathe in; what do you smell?"

I inhaled. "Ugh. Concentrated horse manure! Marsh's Sale Barn is a block north and the wind's blowing toward us."

"Yes, but what else?"

I breathed in again. "A whiff of very tasty meat, well-seasoned.

We call that barbecue. The other is so strong I didn't notice it at first."

"Ah, the answer!" Louis grinned. We must investigate where that smell is coming from, but not tonight. I do not want to spoil the experience for you since the ambiance is foul."

"You could eat with that other smell around?" I asked.

"Oh yes, Harmony. Paris is a city of contrasts. Exquisite dining coexists with the worst of human and animal output. One learns to separate the one from the other, and cope. I did. But let us move on and save that experience for when the wind blows elsewhere."

"Yes, thank you, Louis. I don't think my stomach could manage it tonight. That barbecue smells better than any I've found out here though."

We continued on Ferris street to Prairie. Louis leaned into me, "Two speakeasies at this corner, plus a church and a residence hotel. Correct?"

I looked around. "We're standing next to the Elks Lodge building. Across Ferris Street, the sign says Galesburg Club. Diagonally is the Presbyterian Church, and across the street is the Annex Hotel. You're amazing!"

"And you are the most desirable woman I have ever known."

Louis spoke those words in French so anyone passing would not know why my face and other things heated.

"Was that a proposal, Louis?" I blurted out.

"Let us consider the possibility, shall we?"

I couldn't think of a smart comeback so I embraced and kissed him instead. Fortunately, the quartet of Elks exiting the building was too busy keeping each other upright to notice us.

CHAPTER THIRTY-SEVEN

Mimi: Thursday, April 29th, 1926, 8 AM, her room at Cottage

"Good morning, my betrothed," I said as the door opened.

"Good morning, Precious," Matt replied as he set my breakfast tray on the table, "I brought you a little breakfast."

He bent down and we kissed, then I removed the cover. "Little? This is the first full-sized breakfast I've seen in a long, long time. Thank you for bringing it to me. Now sit down and I'll pray, then you can tell me the news while I eat."

Matt finished his report about the same time I finished my food and capped the *Gator Sauce*.

"That's a lot," I remarked, "So the company ends up building airplane engines?"

"Right, Love," Matt replied, "and the most reliable ones to boot. We have to think big with production even with the Depression coming."

"Where will you put the plant?" I asked.

"Some in Nashville, most up at Orchard Place outside Chicago. Research at Hoople, maybe here too. We have to wait until we see how much stuff they're offering us."

"So, Don really won't have time to play impresario at the Auditorium, will he?"

"No way, Love. I'm so glad you got that job!" Matt leaned over and kissed me again. I noticed where he was looking, then saw I was slightly disheveled.

"They're eagerly awaiting you," I said softly, then watched Matt turn red again.

I changed the subject. "So, you aren't telling me what Louis is playing at our wedding?"

"No, Love, secret until that day."

"Well, I just think that is..." my last word turned into a large belch. I put my hand over my mouth and blushed.

"Bring it up again and we'll vote on it," Matt observed.

I stuck out my tongue at him. "Matthew Plotczyc, when I get outta this hospital, I'm gonna tickle you within an inch of your life! Among other things..."

Now Matt blushed. "I guess our circulation's OK this morning, Love."

"Seems to be. Now, what is on the agenda for today, besides my visit with Doctor Bohan and Gloria this morning?"

"Bull and the Chief get in around ten. We'll drop their gear at the Broadview and take them to lunch you-know-where. You sure you don't want to come?"

I was sorely tempted to make another insouciant quip but refrained. "No, Dear. I'll eat here and go to dinner with you this evening. I do want to be there for the afternoon if they let me out."

"Absolutely, Love! Pick you up about twelve-thirty if that's OK."

"That's fine, Matt. We three will be eagerly awaiting your arrival."

"Three?" Matt asked, then, "Mimi! Are you going to make me blush like this at our wedding?"

I beckoned my betrothed over for a kiss. "I'll be good as gold during the wedding, not say anything to embarrass you, maybe even at the reception. Beyond that, you'll see."

And he will, too, I thought as we kissed.

*****

Mimi: 12:50 PM, the Green Room, show time

"Hi, Mimi. Glad we put that elevator in here."

"Hi, Jackie," I said as I rolled into the room, "Matt's gone to join Bull and the others. They'll be right down. And that elevator is a little strange."

Jackie frowned. "OK, Mimi, what'd it do?"

"Nothing dangerous, but as the door closed a male voice said, 'Down is nice'. What's that supposed to mean?"

Jackie groaned. "I thought we had all the bugs out of it! That elevator came from far time, and it has a computer built into it that is really flaky. So we blocked it from doing anything, I thought. I'll have Sammy Allen work on it again."

"Is it unsafe?" I asked as the door shut, and it started to whine.

"The mechanics of it are perfectly safe. It just...says stuff."

"Another odd thing around here to get used to," I said as I pulled up to the table, "All set for today's drama?"

"Drama?" Jackie asked, "Oh...we bring Bull and the Chief *in,* then Chief meets his great-grandson at the second meeting."

"Right. You're all set up?" I asked.

"Yep," Jackie replied, "I've got my uniform stashed in the office, I'll go change in the john. Sammy and Dave are waiting in the office with Amy till their cue. This is gonna be fun!"

The elevator started to hum, and music followed it down. Jackie looked up, then put her hand to her forehead. "Oh no! The *Candid Camera* theme! Explain later." She muttered something about *Sirius Cybernetics* as the door opened. I stood up to meet the party.

Don stepped out of the elevator first. I saw his mouth twitch and eyes roll, probably because of the unwanted serenade. Next came a tall, rail-thin man sporting a closely-clipped beard and a stylish suit, followed by a shorter balding African-American man in a suit carrying a briefcase. Their eyes darted around, taking in the green room's decoration and the wall of performer photos. *Sharp men, both,* I concluded. Matt brought up the rear, and I felt my heart melt again.

I must have shown it on my face, for the first man walked straight to me and put out his hand. "You must be Mimi! I saw your face light up when Matt walked in. I'm Bull, and I am so happy to meet you!" We shook hands, then he hugged me.

"Thank you for choosing my friend Matt," Bull whispered in my ear, "I've been praying he'd find you since Grace passed."

"He's everything I've ever wanted in a man," I whispered back.

Matt introduced the rest of the group to Bull and Chief Sampson. The others sat down in the green leather chairs around the table.

"Before we discuss your questions and our answers," Don began, "We have another matter to cover with you. Jackie and I have an arrangement, where if we both get the same dream on the same subject, we take it as instructions from the Lord and act on it. Several mornings ago we both woke up after the same dream, concerning you two. Our first meeting is to act on that dream."

"What are you talking about, Admiral?" Bull tapped his pencil on the table as he spoke, "We're going to get answers about carrier operations based on *dreams*?" He turned to Matt, "What is wrong with you people, Matt? I've figured out the company you work for is different, but this is absurd!"

Matt, pale, opened his mouth to speak, but was interrupted.

Chief Sampson crossed his arms and sat back in his chair. "You're from the future, aren't you?"

Bull spun around in his chair, eyes bulging slightly. "How do you know that?"

The Chief regarded his superior with a half-smile. "I had a similar dream a week ago, sir. We were in this room: table, chairs, photographs on the wall. We were told these folks were from the future, and were going to help us. They showed us moving pictures to prove they were from the future. It troubled me at the time, but here we are."

Bull sat back in his chair and looked around the table. Don and Jackie nodded slowly; I had a big grin on my face.

Bull turned back to the Chief. "Why didn't you tell me about this before?"

"Would you have believed me?"

"No, probably not."

"I've had dreams from the Lord before," the Chief said, "but this one was so vivid I wasn't sure I believed it myself. Now I do."

"You have it, Chief." Jackie added, "And now let us explain how we came to be here."

I held Matt's hand. *This is kinda fun*, I thought.

A half-hour later Jackie excused herself to prepare for the next meeting (and put on her uniform). The rest of us adjourned to the table of drinks and snacks, and made small talk.

Fifteen minutes later we returned to the conference table. Matt helped me out of my wheelchair and into one of the swivel chairs at the table. I wanted to spin around but wasn't sure I could stay in the chair.

"Now for the first of the meetings," Don began, "There's a laptop computer in the briefcase we gave you. It is yours to keep; please show it to nobody except a Company partner, or each other. Instructions for its care and feeding are in the bag."

"What do we feed it?" Bull asked, stroking his beard, "Does it prefer facial hair?"

"Only if you try to kiss it," I replied. Matt was taking a drink of tea; I handed him my handkerchief.

"Ahem," Don continued, "Also in the bag is a copy of your questions, and our preliminary answers. Moving pictures, called videos, on the laptop computer will show much of what we talk about in the meeting. Take out the papers whenever you want."

Both men pulled out the binders.

"Now, we have several folks in the company who served on aircraft carriers uptime. Rather than try to explain what they did I've asked them to wear their old uniforms to this meeting. When I send the elevator up to the stage, they'll return in it."

Don got up and walked over to the elevator. He pushed the up button and sat back down. In a moment the car started back down. I kept expecting the thing to burst into song, but it stayed quiet.

The elevator door opened and four uniformed people stepped out.

"First I'd like to introduce...," Don began, but got no further.

Dave Sampson broke away from the group. He stood in front of the Chief. It was like seeing double. Their faces were so similar, down to the expressions.

"Why do you look so much like me?" the Chief asked, "You could be my brother."

"In a way, I am. My name is David Sampson. My grandfather in the other universe is your son Edward. The stories he told me about you influenced me to join the Navy. And now here you are!"

The Chief stood and stared at him. "I see it. Are you really my kin?"

Dave nodded and put his hand out. The two men shook, then embraced.

I wiped my eyes and handed my handkerchief to Matt again.

"It must be amazing to have family," I said.

Matt put his arm around me. "You already do."

*****

Harmony, 8:10 PM, the Broadview parlor, step by step

"I am sorry we missed the meeting this afternoon, but we

made up for it at dinner," Louis remarked.

We were lounging in our usual spot in the parlor discussing the day. We edged closer each time since that first night until I almost rested on Louis' lap. We were both very comfortable.

"Jackie told me at dinner it went about as she figured," I replied, "She is concerned all the surprises and information will cause an overload for our two guests. She's watching out for that."

"As well she might," Louis said, "I remember that first day I arrived here, just a week ago. Seems like a year—and what a year!"

Louis turned toward me and we kissed. That seemed to be happening more and more frequently.

"We hardly heard a word from either Don or Bull all evening," I observed, "I wonder what they were talking about in the corner?"

"They were discussing the *logistique*—logistics—of the sale of the greatest aero-engine manufactory of the day to Wain Engineering," Louis said, "There is a big Navy contract in the wind." Louis produced a sly grin. "What they do not *think* I understand will not hurt them."

I slapped his arm. "Stinker!" I pronounced, and we kissed again.

"You know, it occurs to me that we have been getting closer to each other physically this past week." Louis' sightless eyes darted back and forth twice, "but we have not talked about where we seem to be heading."

I looked straight at Louis. "You're right. We've touched on taking our friendship further. You know what I dreamed when I heard you had been reborn and were coming here. You seem to have had similar feelings. So, what do we do?"

Louis took his free hand and pinched the bridge of his nose. "I know what we will *not* do," he said softly, "We will not cohabitate without the sanctity of marriage. I have done that, and besides the issue of sin I now see it was, I can tell you forbidden fruit was singularly unsatisfying."

"Despite the good reasons you had, needing help as you did. And the prelates drove you into it."

"So they did," Louis continued, "but that did not make it right. I would not want to be in their position in the Day of Judgment."

"I agree," I said, leaning into him slightly, "and now you are forgiven, and if we wish we may marry."

"Yes, but do we *wish?*"

"That's the question, Louis," I replied, "I think we are both torn with the choice and possibility. *Desire*, of course, is also there."

My comment led to another kiss, unusually passionate.

Now I have a question for you," Louis began when he could breathe, "Are you prepared to discuss *things*?"

"No. I'm not, but let's do it anyway!"

"Brave woman," Louis said, "Question: Did you notice I am blind?"

"Just because you need help doesn't mean you're handicapped," I replied, "I need your help too."

We kissed again, and Louis reminded me he was French.

"Next question:" Louis continued, "If you and I were to marry, what would you desire out of the marriage? Besides what we already accomplish..."

The kiss which followed gave me not nearly enough time to think about the question, but I already had the answers.

"I can think of two things, Louis. First, *stability.* I loved Charlie with all my heart, and I know he loved me the same way. But due to his personality and illnesses I never knew where I stood with him, or what crazy mess I would have to clean up next."

"I can understand that situation; it was the same with my wife. She added deceit and treachery to the mix though."

I nodded. "Charlie never tried to deceive or betray me, but I had to clean up his messes, and not just his socks. I found him dead after I had to go to Chicago. Charlie had threatened Frederick Stock and the Chicago Symphony with legal action if they played one of his works. I convinced Charlie of his error and went to retrieve the situation. I was successful, but what I found when I got home put paid to the whole matter. I came out here for the concert, and stayed."

"That was, as our friends say, *Looney Tunes*," Louis added, "I am very glad you were able to restore harmony and came out here."

"Are you being punny with me? Shame on you!" I said, and gently pulled his mustache.

"I could not help myself," Louis murmured, and his hand brushed someplace interesting, "Please go on."

"What was the question again? Oh," I took a deep breath. "What I want, Louis, is someone who thinks and acts rationally. Someone who won't do and say crazy things. Someone I can count on to behave the same way today, tomorrow, and in the future."

Louis smiled. "I think I may know someone like that. May that someone say funny things and make people laugh from time to time?"

"Of course," I replied, "and I love that you're silly! You aren't sad all the time as you were. If it sounds like we're doing it in a boardroom we aren't doing it right."

"I would rather do it in the bedroom," Louis remarked. When we finished laughing he continued.

"Besides everything else I haven't had fun in ever so long!"

We shared another kiss. "The second thing you want?" Louis asked.

"Freedom," I replied, "Freedom to do whatever work the Lord gives me, and somebody to support me when I do it. Charlie never forbade me to do anything, except talk about the Lord to him. But I never felt free to do anything outside the home and his circle of work and composing. At first, I was trying to be a good wife; then I needed to try to keep his deteriorating behavior from ruining his business and his music. His business partner Mike Myrick understood the need and helped however he could, but I was increasingly called on to keep Charlie from destroying himself. I don't want to do that anymore."

"Do you think I will need your restraint?" Louis asked.

"Flat no," I replied, "The little bit of help I give you getting around here is nothing, nothing at all, compared to what Charlie needed. And Jeff reports your personal care needs are not difficult."

"Your answers were what I prayed for," Louis said, then we kissed again. "And you want me to tell you what I need too, correct?"

"I do, Louis. What do you need besides a warm and willing bedpartner?"

Louis' cheeks flared red behind his mustache. "You never mince words, do you?"

"Never did, won't now," I replied, "Your answer, sir?"

Louis took my hand, caressed it, explored its nooks and crannies with his fingers. He raised his head and spoke.

"I have been given the life and love of Our Lord. I have a job to do and willing helpers to do it. I can compose and not be hamstrung by my lack of sight. I am so marvelously blessed!"

Louis turned his head forward as he continued, "I also crave stability in my relationships with others and those I love. Stability, freedom, understanding, and a chance to laugh and spread good humor. Can you help me with all that?"

I leaned over and nuzzled his ear. "I think I can manage. What else?"

Louis wiped his eyes with his handkerchief. "Someone who

can help me when I need help, but asks first if I want it. Someone who never considers me less than human because I cannot see. Madeleine had a problem with this. Sometimes I felt like I was her pet. I felt trapped. But I needed her help."

"It must have been frightening to be so dependent on someone who treated you like that."

"It was, Harmony. Madeleine wasn't like that all the time, but she never let me forget what a grand thing she was doing for me. That frightened me most."

"I never want to be like that, ever," I whispered.

"Does anybody frighten you?" Louis asked.

"Charlie did at times," I replied, then stopped. "The only other person who truly frightened me was Paderewski, and then not him so much as his wife. They stayed with us for a couple of weeks the year after you did. Helena is a sharp-tongued harridan: an old word but it fits! My stomach knotted every time she came into the room. Nothing we did suited her. She embarrassed me personally several times. Her husband just shrugged and went along with it."

"I have met him, but not her. We don't need to do that, do we?"

"Truly, Louis," I replied, "Now, have we moved the discussion further along?"

"Hmmm...I would say so," he whispered.

I paused, then pressed him into an embrace, "So would I."

We didn't notice Jeff standing in the room until we broke the kiss two minutes later. He was grinning.

CHAPTER THIRTY-EIGHT

Luther: Friday, April 30th, 1926, 8:45 AM, outside Chambers Street Baptist, departures

"Well, that's the last of them," Dick Meriden observed, "Where's this one going?"

We watched as the modified Mack AC truck pulled out of the small parking lot, pulling a trailer with the last of our freight crates shipping containers tied to it. The small uptime diesel howled under the load.

"That one's going to the Burlington freight house, then on a flatcar to Wicks down in Highland." I turned to the other onlooker "Yours are leaving on the Santa Fe to New York this afternoon."

"I am certainly glad my charges are finally on their way," Marcel Dupré replied, "I never thought we would require all those shipping boxes! But I have a question. What are we to do with the boxes when they are emptied?"

"I'll tell you what Don told me," Dick said, "They are officially your property now, yours and Charles'. Our French representative Denise has arranged for them to be stored in a warehouse in Paris until you are ready to load them with your household goods for shipment here."

"You're coming back to stay?" I thought I must have misunderstood.

"Not right away, Luther, but soon," our French guest replied with a smile, "Charles and I are convinced circumstances will draw us to come here. We do not know when, or how. Please keep that confidential as we do not want the prelates to get any ideas before their time."

"I'll keep it quiet," I said.

"Thank you, Luther," Marcel said as the freight crate disappeared around the corner on Main Street, "and please thank Donald for the use of the containers, Richard."

"Will do," Dick replied, "Don and Jackie are over at the Bondi office this morning buying another piece of property."

"Donald mentioned that to me," Marcel said, "a lot fit to put a church building on, he said."

"What church?" I asked.

"Keep it confidential," Dick said, "but Don had a dream the other night suggesting he buy that property and hold it. He thinks this church might eventually move out there."

"We sure could use the room," I remarked.

"We could," Dick agreed, "and here come Pastor and Deborah up Chambers Street. They're going to supervise the church cleaning."

"How will they remove all that dirt we left?" Marcel asked, "it is everywhere."

"Every member with an electric vacuum cleaner is coming," Dick replied, "I do not want to be here when they start to work."

"The dust?" Marcel asked.

"The noise!" we both said together.

*****

Deborah: 9:28 AM, same place

"I don't think I've ever heard this many vacuum cleaners screaming at one time!" my husband yelled.

"I haven't either, but I'm glad they're doing it!"

We were standing in the foyer at the doors to the sanctuary watching the noisy chaos. Every church member with a vacuum cleaner had brought it in to try to corral and remove the incredible dust and dirt spread throughout the building by the organ dismantling. One vacuum cleaner was loud; fifteen were deafening. Since we had hardwood in our house, we used an uptime marvel called a Steam Mop to clean our floors.

"At least the organ parts are outta here," I yelled at AP.

"The organ moaned a bit but it never...," he replied.

"PARTS!! PARTS!!" I yelled in his ear.

"Oh, I get it now!" AP chuckled, then laughed out loud. At least, it would have been out loud if anyone could have heard him above the vacuums.

"Eeep!" he further remarked as I gave him a poke.

Suddenly, the vacuum cleaners all shut off at the same time, along with the lights. The silence was deafening.

"There goes," AP yelled, then stopped himself, "the fuse," he continued softly, "I've been expecting that."

He pulled a small flashlight from his pocket and headed for the stairs to the basement. I stepped into the diffused daylight of the sanctuary to calm the surprised ladies.

*****

AP Kittridge: 10:15 AM, the church basement

"Thanks again for coming over, Sammy," I said to Wain Engineering's electronic genius, "What do you think is wrong?"

"Youse got a real problem here, Paster," Sammy Allen put the volt-ohm meter back in his modified doctor's bag. "T' main fuse is blown but none 'o t' individual circuit fusees went. It's not s'posed t' do that."

He felt the wires leading to the fuse box one by one before he turned back to me. "T' current draw 'o all dose vacs overheated 't wirin' someplace, I tink pretty close to 't box here. Youse got a short in dere someplace, an' that's what's blowin' 't main fuse. Gotta get it fixed, or ya risk burnin' t' place down!"

"Can you trace it and fix it, Sammy?" I asked.

"Not safe t' have me do it. I know electronics; AC wirin's a whole diff'rent animal. Ya need a real electrician, Doc. An that ain't me!"

"Who do you suggest?"

"Hermann Trask's t' only one I'd trust for dis job! Knows 'is stuff, an' he won' quit till he finds t' problem. Let's go up 'an call 'im, if dat's OK."

"Sure, Sammy, let's go," I said as we turned our flashlights toward the back stairs.

A few moments later Sammy hung up the phone.

"Do you think he'll be able to fix this before Sunday?" I asked.

"I'm sure e'll have it teased out tomorrow, Paster. If it's too big a problem t' fix in one day, you'll know that too. Too bad 'e couldn't get here t'day."

"The Lord's timing, Sammy; can't be helped. At least he'll be here first thing in the morning. We can make it here that early, can't we, Love?"

"No problem, AP," Deborah replied. "I'll drive since you won't be anywhere near awake..."

"Right. I'll be wide awake for the wedding. Sammy, do you need to be here for him tomorrow?"

"Naah. I tol' him what he needs ter know. We just leave t' power off an' t' fusee out till then. Dat sign yer made'll do fine, Deborah!"

"I'll let you two take it down to the fuse box," Deborah said, "I put the other signs telling about the outage on the outside doors. That should keep folks out."

"Just fer grins 'n giggles, how many vacuums were dere?" Sammy asked.

"Fifteen, right, Deborah?" She nodded.

Sammy scratched his head. "Yeah, dose things take more juice than y'd think. T' wiring started t' melt to protect t' fusee. Hermann'll find that one."

We chuckled at the backward chain of events.

"Will you let Don and the rest know we've got a little situation here?"

"Sure, Paster. Good thing t' wedding's gonna be at t' Auditorium tomorrow. Be a little hard to do it in the dark here."

"Matt and Mimi can do it in the dark tomorrow evening," Deborah remarked.

*****

Mimi: 5:30 PM, on the way to the rehearsal dinner

"Are you all right, Love?" I asked Matt as we left the Auditorium garage.

"I'll be fine, Sweetheart. The weather's changing, and my sinuses are just howling tonight. I used to feel like this at sea before a storm hit."

"Are we going to get one tonight?" I asked.

"There'll be one somewhere close," Matt replied. "The weather is very unsettled. We may not want to stay out too late. I put a storm cellar in our back yard since the house is on a slab, but that won't help you if something happens tonight."

"Tomorrow, though," I put my hand on Matt's leg.

"Oh yes, Love...tomorrow." He looked over at me and smiled.

My smile faded. "I need to tell you something. This morning while Lillian was helping me try on my wedding dress I told her why I needed that first *procedure*."

Matt's expression didn't change. "How'd she take it?"

I wiped a tear from my right eye. "Really well, Matthew. She agreed she'd have had to fire me if the story came out, but it didn't and she didn't. Just like you, she said all that is forgiven, under the Blood of Christ, and we move on from there."

Matt looked both ways before pulling across Prairie Street. He stopped in the middle of the intersection to let a gaggle of young people cross the street. “Not watching,” he remarked, “and so that matter is settled. I’m glad, Love.” He brushed my hand with his before shifting into second.

My mouth quirked, “She told me about something that almost happened to her on a visit to western Iowa in the early seventies, and how she resolved the matter. I can’t tell anybody about it, not even you, Love, but she wants me to tell the story at her funeral.”

“I’m glad you’ve resolved things with Lillian,” Matt said as we stopped at Kellogg Street, “and I’d just as soon wait many years to hear that story.”

“I guarantee you’ll get a kick out of it,” I replied, then snickered, “She also asked my permission for something. She *might* bring a covered birdcage to the wedding. Picture of a python in it and a sign. Not the real George. I told her she could. Do you mind?”

“Not at all,” Matt replied, “Aren’t some of your old teachers at Silas scared of him?”

“Yes. One in particular. Lillian said she’s still thinking about it. If we see it I guess she yielded to the temptation.”

Five minutes later Matt walked and I rolled into New China. Yu Chen hugged me, then waved us to the back room.

We sat next to Bull and the Chief on Matt’s side, and Jackie and Don on mine. “Where’s Lillian?” Jackie asked.

“She decided not to come tonight,” I replied, “She was getting a headache and thought she needed to rest.”

Jackie wiped her forehead with her napkin. “We’re all feeling the aches tonight. My back is starting to howl.”

“From when you broke it on the carrier?” I asked.

“Yeah. The bones heal but it’s never right afterward. My *passenger* isn’t helping either,” She whispered the last.

“Tell him tomorrow?”

"Tell him tomorrow, promise." Jackie nodded and winced as she shifted in the wooden chair.

Don stood up and tapped his glass for the prayer to start the dinner.

I'd never been to a rehearsal dinner with this crowd. I also hadn't tried Chinese cuisine in many years. I found I enjoyed both the food and the company.

Forty-five minutes later Don stood up. "Jackie thinks we ought to wrap this up and get home. A nasty storm is brewing."

The other Navy people at the table nodded.

"Pastor, if you'll dismiss us in prayer for our safety in what's coming, we'll bug out and get home."

"Happy to, Don," Pastor Kittridge replied, "but I recommend you give Amy and Elwood a call. They may want to be on watch —Sherry too."

Don nodded. "Good idea, Pastor. I'll call them ASAP."

"OK, let's pray," Pastor said, and began.

After he prayed the party broke up. We were the last to leave. Don paid the bill while Jackie told Yu Chen about the wedding. They walked out of the restaurant with Matt and me, along with Bull and Chief Sampson.

As we stepped or rolled out the front door the party stopped. The Navy people looked around, heads up, and sniffed the air like a herd of antelope ready to bolt from a predator.

"Not good," Matt said flatly.

Bull scratched his head. "Barometer's dropped, wind's shifting aimlessly, smells like added ozone in the air. Bad news."

I looked up to see the bottom of the clouds scuttling over.

"About now we'd be rigging the lifelines and telling the cooks to snuff the stoves and serve sandwiches," Chief Sampson observed.

"Yep." Jackie didn't waste words.

"And we don't have a Doppler radar set up here yet," Don muttered, "I let it slide and I shouldn't have."

"What did you say, Don? Doppler something?" Bull asked.

"Whoopsie, Admiral," Jackie chuckled.

"No, Love, he's a partner so he's cleared," Don replied, and turned back to Bull. "It's called radar. Radio direction finding and ranging. It'll tell us where something is in the air and how fast it's going. It was invented in the middle thirties in our universe; we'll introduce it sooner here. We can hide an uptime rig of it in the top of a tall building, and I've got one in mind. But we don't have it tonight."

"I want to hear more," Bull said, "but right now we need to get under cover."

"So right," Don said, "I'll arrange a briefing on radar for you two before you leave."

Matt put his hands on my shoulders. "Feels like we're about to start sprouting Saint Elmo's fire from our hair! I don't like this one bit, Don."

"Me neither, Captain. Let's get outta here and see what happens."

"Will you be able to get Mimi to the hospital before it cuts loose?"

"I think we'll manage that, Chief. I'll keep you safe, Mimi."

"Correction, Sweetheart," I said as Matt opened the car door for me. "The Lord will keep us safe; you just get to help."

"So right, Precious. Later, folks!"

"G'night, you two. Don't get zapped!" Jackie had the last word.

CHAPTER THIRTY-NINE

Terry Fensterer: Saturday, May 1st, 1926, Midnight thirty, his home on North Chambers Street, the curtain rises

Everyone needs a hobby. Mine is meteorology.

After my wife Aldine passed in 1915, I kept myself sane by working too hard in my insurance business until 1923, when I decided I had enough money to retire.

So I did. Besides my work at the church, I plunged into the study of weather. I'd always wanted to pursue it but never had the time. With the help of my friends Jackie Wain and Elwood Foutch, I learned to collect the data and make forecasts. I compared my forecasts to the official Weather Bureau ones. I found I was right more than they were.

To help me pursue this hobby I allowed myself an extravagance. I installed a direct telegraph line to the Weather Bureau, the only such line in town. At any hour of the day or night, the *Morkrum-Kleinschmidt* model 14 teleprinter on my office desk would pound out whatever the Weather Bureau wanted to tell people.

I knew as clearly as anyone in the town, maybe the state, what the weather was going to be, but I had no outlet for my forecasts. I did, however, know when to take an umbrella on my walks.

I predicted the February blizzard the day before it hit, and called my contact at Wain Engineering. Sherry said she would inform Don and the others of the threat, and she did.

I knew how the prophets felt, knowing what was coming but not having a chance to tell anyone officially. This was beginning to bother me, and I'd asked the Lord to give me a venue to help the town's residents. Maybe I could help at the new radio station Jackie said Don was going to start; we would see.

This evening, however, we were due to see something most unusual. I sat on my front porch and waited for the show to start.

All thunderstorms have to start someplace. We see them approach, feel their fury as they hit, and watch them move on, but where do they come from? Tonight we would see.

This night, the point of birth of a line of severe thunderstorms lay in the atmosphere above Galesburg, Illinois. I predicted the storms would form in sequence over the city, then move like cars of a train east and slightly south, until a line of connected severe storms a hundred miles long would stretch into central and eastern Illinois from their beginnings over Galesburg. The storms would keep forming until almost dawn that first day of May.

Earlier in the evening, I called Sherry at the Wain offices. She said Don had already called in a warning of the coming storm, and Amy and Elwood were monitoring. I promised to call back when I knew more.

So I lounged in my glider on the front porch, glass of tea on one side and pad of paper on the other, and settled in to watch the show. I expected a lot of lightning, but that did not worry me. I had installed lightning rods on every peak of the house and garage, and in the tops of all my trees. I did not expect to be struck, but the current would be sent to ground if I was.

Around ten, the lightning started, first in the roiling clouds, then from the clouds to the ground. Thunder boomed through the streets, louder and sharper. Thanks to the hearing aids I could hear everything. Don presented them to me, but I knew Jackie procured them. I was so happy to hear clearly again.

Aside from a few drops of rain in the eastern part of town, the city stayed dry all night. The storms saved the rain, along with hail and several tornadoes, for towns southeast of us. Winds swirled, but generally came from the western half of the compass rose, inflow to the storms as they left the Galesburg area.

What we got in abundance was lightning: bolts constantly lighting up the town like a sputtering arc lamp. Roughly three times per minute solid spears of lightning shot from cloud to ground all over the city. Occasionally one hit close enough that I flinched.

As there was nothing more I could do to protect myself, I sat back and waited for something to happen.

I happened to be looking toward the church across the street a hundred feet north when that something occurred.

The flash was unusually large and bright, and I heard a buzz rather than a crash, along with a tingling feeling. I instinctively squinted as the flash registered on my mind.

Like liquid fire the bolt hit the steeple of the church, not at the peak but on the large square framework of wooden slats facing south on the steeple. The slats filled the openings of the steeple where a bell would have been hung had the congregation cared to spend the money. The bolt shattered the slats and blasted through the empty belfry.

I saw flashes of light through the windows of the darkened building. I knew the power was off in the building after the incident with the vacuum cleaners. As I watched, the flashes stopped, but a growing glow shown through the windows. Smoke wafted out of the shattered steeple. *Not good,* I thought.

I ducked inside and called the Fire Department. The dispatcher thanked me for calling but said all the engines were out on other fires the lightning had started. He would send a truck as soon as he could. He told me to call again if the fire threatened nearby houses.

I'll be calling back in five minutes, I muttered as I hung up. I needed to let Pastor and the other deacons know quickly, so I called Sherry and told her. She promised to get hold of the others immediately. *All I can do...Lord, have Your will,* I prayed as I returned to the porch.

Now, four minutes after the strike, smoke billowed from the hole in the steeple, and in the flashes of lightning, I could see smoke coming from the eaves. In a normal thunderstorm, the rain-soaked wood of the building would tend to slow down the spread of the fire. This time there was no rain, and it hadn't rained for almost three weeks. Everything was very dry, and nothing hindered the spread of the fire. As I watched, the top half of the composite front window shattered and fell outward, showing more smoke and an increasing glow from within. The wind blew the smoke toward the house just to the north.

I looked at my watch as I hustled to call the Fire Department again. *Six minutes,* I thought, *Time for* plan B.

Thirty minutes later a somber group of men sat on my front porch.

"This everybody?" Pastor Kittridge, AP to his friends, asked.

"Yes," Harold Coupland replied, "You, me, Don, Terry, Elwood, Ed, and Gil. Quorum."

As Harold spoke the remains of the north wall and the north-east corner stairwell fell in on itself and joined the giant bon-fire in the basement. Two fire trucks, one from Galesburg and one from Monmouth, played streams of water on the nearest houses. The fire had not spread beyond the church itself. The church had been beyond salvage within two minutes of the lightning strike.

We resumed our silent vigil, immersed in our own thoughts.

"I suppose nobody remembered the marshmallows."

The others stared at me, then exploded in laughter. The silence broken, life resumed.

"What now, gentlemen?" AP asked after a moment.

Don raised his finger. "First, we'll tell everyone at the wedding this morning that church will be at the Auditorium until further notice, if that's all right with the rest of you. I can open up some of the meeting rooms at the Broadview for Sunday school, and have a unified adult class, or put one in the balcony, whatever. We can also run the prayer chain, and I'll have my people make a sign we can put in front of the remains here, directing folks to the Auditorium. Will that do for now, gentlemen?"

"So we can count on your organization to help us here?" Harold asked.

"Absolutely," Don declared, "One less thing any of us have to worry about. We've got this."

That's what he thinks, I thought, then spoke. "I know I'm the one always counseling caution in matters of the church, but I can't do it this time."

I saw Don start to roll his eyes, then half-close them. I'd seen him paste a vacuous smile on his face when he was trying to mask his real thoughts. *True to form*, I thought and continued.

"So, what do we do about a new church? I know we can't build on this property. It's way too small."

"Good question, Terry," Pastor replied, "Any ideas, gentlemen?"

Don raised his finger again. "Not praying for our food yet," Elwood remarked.

Don put his finger down and sighed.

"Gentlemen, you don't know this. I haven't even told Pastor. But a week ago the Lord impressed me to buy some land that was available in the northwest part of town. It's a half-block bordering on Dayton, Jefferson, and Monroe whenever they extend it that far. I got a very good deal on it...and the Lord showed it to me as a possible church site. I closed on it yesterday. If the board approves, I'll donate the property."

Ed Joseph spoke just loudly enough to be heard over the thunder and the fire truck motors. "I move we accept Don's gracious offer of the property."

"Second," said Gil Foster.

Harold looked at the others, then, "Moved and seconded. All in favor say aye."

All were in favor.

"Thank you very much on behalf of the congregation, Don," Pastor declared, "So now we have property, but how do we pay for a building? The fire insurance on that building isn't enough to dig a latrine in the woods."

We chuckled, and I noticed Harold had a smile on his face just like me. *Time to drop the other shoe,* I thought.

"I guess it's a little late, but, Pastor and gentlemen, I need to 'fess up to something. Harold knows this, John Ward knew it, but none of the rest of you do."

I had the group's attention. Harold kept grinning.

"The church built that building when I was on the board for the first time. I was young, and the insurance business was pretty good. I wanted to help, but I was never strong enough to do any of the heavy labor building that thing took. I wondered what I could do to help the Lord's work here."

I took a sip of my tea and continued. "Then my late wife Aldine had an idea. She reminded me the one thing I knew well was insurance. With the Pastor's and the board chairman's approval, I wrote a fire insurance policy for that building. I wrote it high, and put in an escalation clause for future replacement cost increases. I've adjusted it a bit over the years, but it's still the same basic policy. Been paying it myself all these years, nobody knew except the Pastor and Board Chairman. I'm sorry I hadn't told you yet, Pastor. Anyway, it's about to pay off."

I took another sip; my throat was still dry.

"I'm sure the adjuster will drop it a bit because the organ wasn't in there, but the loss payout value of that policy is eighty..."

The others stared, beginning to understand, but not quite comprehending.

"...thousand dollars."

My front porch erupted in tears, shouts of 'Praise the Lord', and general loud rejoicing. Eventually, we said all we could say. We watched the remains of the church burn to ashes.

I got Harold's attention and winked; he smiled and nodded.

I looked over at Don. "Hey, Don—We need more warning when a storm's coming. When are you going to put up a Doppler radar in this town?"

Don continued to watch the fire as he replied, "Monday I'm calling the Weinbergs. Lord willing if the building is solid I'm buying the Brown Corn Planter building. We'll convert the cupola to a radome and stick the radar in..."

Don froze, mouth open. I saw his left eye start to twitch. He mouthed words but couldn't speak. *Great entertainment,* I thought, *but we gotta let him off the hook.*

"Harold, will you tell him, or shall I?"

Harold shrugged "I guess I will. Don, several years ago Pastor Ward heard the still small Voice suggesting we deacons who aren't in your company be told who you are. He went to Jackie and Dick; they prayed about it and concurred. We've known who you are and *when* you came from since 1923."

"And you never said anything?" Don asked in a monotone.

"We agreed to honor your secret unless something happened where we should join in to help you. Tonight's that night. Sherry suggested it was time to tell you when she called us about the fire. We all know about Sherry, by the way."

Don sank into his chair. In the light from the fire and lightning, he looked like a ghost. Finally, he shifted and took several deep breaths.

"All right then," he began, "Welcome aboard Harold, Ed, and

Terry. Please come to lunch at the Broadview Sunday at noon. We'll show you our introduction video in the Auditorium Green Room afterward. Since you know about us you might as well get the benefits of that knowledge. Bring your wives too, of course."

I wish I could, I thought, *Aldine would've loved it.*

*****

Matt: 12:45 AM, his house on Baird Avenue, up to speed

I was awake, of course. Just like at sea I could never sleep when a storm was raging. If I wasn't on the bridge I couldn't relax. I knew not to even try. My watch standers learned to put up with my presence. Once in a while, I was able to do something useful other than doze in my swivel chair.

To make this night extra-special my wedding was in ten hours. I thought of myself as a cool, capable naval officer, and maintained that standard of competence in my current work. Storms, and weddings, brought me back to reality. I wondered if Mimi was awake too.

I sat in my oversized reclining chair, an uptime model with massage, heat, and cool available at the press of a button to soothe my weary muscles. Nothing helped this night.

I was reading a C.S. Forester novel from uptime. *The Good Shepherd* told the story of a destroyer skipper in the next war, battling submarines, the weather, and his own insecurities. *Been there, done that,* I thought as I read. With the storm banging away I had no trouble staying awake.

The special line from the office rang. I put my finger on the chair arm and pushed the button for the speakerphone. I love my labor-saving devices. "Plotczyc."

"Foutch," Elwood's voice overcame the racket outside. "Lightning hit the church. Burning down, can't save it. Going to Terry's house to watch. Copy?"

My Navy persona kicked in automatically. "Roger, copy. Who's minding the Ops Center?"

"Amy and Jeff. No other problems. Call if you need to."

I'd say that problem was enough, I thought. "Thanks for calling. I'll tell Mimi in the morning if she hasn't already heard. Call me if you need me."

"Later," Elwood replied and hung up.

Now what, Lord? I prayed, Thank You for having Don buy that land; please let us put a church on it if it's Your will.

I knew I should be grieving for the loss of that building and all it meant for the folks who'd worshipped there since it was built, but I just couldn't summon the emotion. *Why can't I grieve, Lord?* I asked.

A thought occurred. I was about to experience the most emotional event in my life since I returned to Washington just in time for Grace's funeral. This event was joyous where the other was devastating, but in both my emotions were fully committed. I also knew the Lord allowed this to happen for a purpose and no human could change it. If I could not trust His will in the demise of a building built by humans, how could I trust Him to bless a marriage?

Only one response. *Lord, have Your Will in the church building burning as You are in Mimi's and my marriage. Help me to express emotion where You want me to, and help Your people even without the emotion. Your way always.*

I felt peace at that point, both for the church and our marriage. *Can't ask for more than that, Plotczyc,* I concluded.

I picked up my book to continue reading. But instead, I woke up at 6:30 AM, the first time I could ever remember sleeping through a storm.

CHAPTER FORTY

Mimi: Saturday, May 1st, 1926, 7:35 AM, her room at Cottage, time

"Knock, Knock," a voice at my door.

"Who's there?"

"Dwayne."

"Dwayne who?"

"Dwayne the bathtub I'm dwowning!"

"Older than the hills," I chuckled as Amy Foutch slipped through the door.

"Yes, I am, but Elwood doesn't care," Amy shot back, "Did you get any sleep in that storm last night?"

I squirted Gator Sauce on my eggs and muffin. "I woke up a couple of times. Never heard any rain."

Amy set a shopping bag on the bed and sat in the other chair. "That's because there wasn't any. Jeff and I were in the ops center all night monitoring things. Nothing but lightning and some wind."

"Wasn't Elwood with you?" I asked.

"He was at Terry Fensterer's house watching the church burn… oh, I see you haven't heard!"

"Was it my wide eyes or open mouth?"

"Yes," Amy frowned, "Lightning hit the church about half-past midnight. Burnt to the ground."

I sat back in my chair, breakfast forgotten. "But all the memories! All the stuff!"

Amy nodded, but half-grinned. "Yeah, but we'll take the memories with us. The organ was outta there, nothing left but pews, hymnals, and a mediocre piano. We'll do fine."

"I know I shouldn't worry about this right now, but I am. What will we do?"

Amy crossed her legs. "First, Don bought some land in northwest Galesburg yesterday. Said the Lord showed it to him for a church. Then Terry Fensterer's been paying on a big fire insurance policy since the building was built. Only Pastor and the head deacon knew. They have more than enough to build a building we'll all fit in! Church will be in the Auditorium till the new building's built."

I looked down at the last half of my breakfast. "Too nervous to eat that now," I remarked, "So does the Lord always provide like this?"

"Dunno," Amy replied, "never burnt down a church building before. Anyway, I'm here to take you to your wedding. The bag has a few goodies from Jackie and me."

Amy handed me the bag. I pulled out the contents. "What's this?" I asked, holding up a small box.

"Dreft detergent from uptime. 'It's gentle, washes out the delicate things in the bag. Read the directions."

"Oh, OK," I said, "and thank you for the beautiful unmentionables, but Lillian already brought me a set." I pointed to the bed.

Amy grinned. "Lillian has good taste. And practical like our things. All useful for just as long as they're necessary."

I laughed as I blushed. "You don't mess around! Just like me. Are you ready to play for me at the reception?"

Amy stood up and took the bag. "You're great with that song! You'll have 'em rolling on the floor, which should make cleaning the carpet easier."

I giggled, then thought of something. Amy noticed my face change. "What's wrong, Mimi?"

I looked out the window for a few seconds, then turned back.

I wasn't crying, but I could have. "Amy, I'm worried. Matt is all heated up to marry, and I always catch him looking at *them.*" I pointed and Amy nodded.

"What if we get there…tonight…and something happens and I don't please him? I know he'll be fine, but what if my body gives out at the wrong time? I'm still recovering, you know."

Amy sat back down. Her face wrinkled as she spoke. "Listen, Mimi, I've only worked with Matt for a few months, but I've observed him closely. Jackie and I have talked about you two when he and Don weren't around."

Amy leaned toward me, all business. "Jackie and I have some recent experience with this wedding night stuff. I can promise you Matt will be enthralled with you no matter what happens. You know what to do and how to be careful, right?"

"What to do…no problem," I snorted, "Being careful? Gloria instructed me."

"Then let it happen as it happens," Amy repeated, "worked for Jackie and me, with two very different husbands. And it'll work for you. Promise."

I stood up a little faster than I should have. "Thanks for the advice, Amy! I'll be careful, but not worry about it."

We hugged, then Amy picked up the bag. "Let me put a few of your things in here if you're done with them."

"OK," I said, and started to dress.

"No wonder he loses himself in them," Amy said it so quietly I didn't react for a few seconds. Then, I blushed deeply. "Amy!"

"Yep, Matt blushes the same way, right? You two are made for each other." Amy beamed as I continued to dress.

*****

Lillian: 9:30 AM, the Auditorium stage, details

"Just be sure that stays right where I've put it, Pastor."

"Whatever you say, Lillian. First time I've ever done a wedding with a covered birdcage on the platform. What's in there?"

"I'm not saying, and that's why the sign on the cover says don't peek! Watch the reaction of the bride and groom, and Mimi's teacher friends in particular. I will explain it at the reception."

AP stopped, looked at the birdcage, then at me.

"Wait a minute...Deborah said something about— you didn't —"

I replied with an inscrutable grin. *And I do inscrutable pretty well*, I thought.

*****

Matt: 10:05 AM, the Auditorium stage, more details

"Uh Oh," I remarked as we walked down the aisle.

"What's wrong?" Bull Reeves asked. Out of the corner of my eye I could see him tense.

"Nothing bad, just odd," I replied quietly, "See that covered birdcage on the stage?"

"What's that doing there?"

"Gonna make some of Mimi's friends very nervous. She brought a cage like that with a python in it to school to show the kids a few years ago and scared the other teachers crazy!"

Bull wrinkled his forehead. "A python that little won't hurt anyone. One of those spitting cobras we ran into on Luzon, now that's a different story."

"You said it, Bull! Let's see if Pastor knows anything about it."

We walked up on the stage. "What's with the cage?" I asked.

"Lillian set it there about a half-hour ago," Pastor replied, "said not to peek or move it, and watch our teacher guests. Do you suppose it's George?"

"Either him or a joke on the teachers," I said, "George is the python's name."

"Would Lillian do that to her teachers?" Bull asked.

"Oh, yeah," I replied, "She plays the part of a strait-laced schoolmarm but she's got a wicked sense of humor. There or not, George'll ruffle some feathers."

"If he doesn't eat the feathers first," Pastor added.

"Let's get down to the Green Room," I said, "I'll call Mimi in her dressing room from there. She'll want to have a response ready in advance."

*****

Mimi, 9:50 AM, third-floor dressing room, relaxing before the wedding

"You sure Rick and Jeff won't come breezing out that door?" I asked my assistants.

"Nope," Amy grinned, "They have another stairway to get down if they have to. Nobody but us and Lillian know the code for the elevator. And that's a lock on the outside of the door to the *sound booth.*"

I was relaxing with Amy and Gloria before finishing dressing for my wedding. I wasn't going to put on my dress until just before we made our appearance downstairs.

"Did you say women wear this kind of outfit in public *uptime*?" I asked.

"Yeah," Amy replied, "Swimsuits can look like that—they call 'em *bikinis,* but usually not with that much lace. Not my favorite suit though, even though my friends said I looked good in 'em. You'll be comfortable in the dress with them and a silk slip underneath."

"And later," Gloria snickered.

"Right. And thank you so much for the slip, Gloria," I replied.

"My pleasure," Gloria said, "but more yours," she added.

The telephone on the wall rang. Amy got up to answer it. "Third-floor dressing room." A moment, "No, not yet, but Mimi's here. Wait one." She beckoned to me and I carefully stood to walk over.

"Mimi…Oh, she did, did she?… Whether he's in there or not they're going to react, that's for sure! I think we say nothing, act like we don't see it, and let her have her little joke. Ok with you? OK, Love, and I'll answer that question later. We'll be down directly."

I hung up, snorted, and walked back to my chair. "That was Matt—he wanted to know what I was wearing."

"Figures," Amy said with a giggle, "but what else?"

"Lillian put a covered birdcage on one side of the stage, told Pastor to leave it alone and she'd explain at the reception. Got a 'don't peek' sign on it too. It's either George the python or a fake snake, whatever. You heard what I told him we'd do."

"Sure did," Gloria said as she pulled my slip out of its box and handed it to me, "I'll do the same if that's OK. Doesn't bother me."

"Me neither," Amy added, "met plenty of poisonous snakes in my career. Some of 'em didn't even have arms."

I got the inference right away and laughed with the others. "OK, time to put all this stuff on," I announced.

"And count the hours till the reverse procedure," Amy said quietly.

We were still giggling when the elevator door opened, and Lillian emerged. "Did I miss anything?"

"Not a thing," I replied.

*****

Harmony, 10:30 AM, the Auditorium, countdown

"Hi, folks," Jackie said as we stepped into the Auditorium office, "New suit, Louis?"

I translated. "Yes. My minder here suggested it was time to advance my wardrobe, so we visited The Continental yesterday."

"You have good taste, that one fits you well," Jackie added.

"Her, not me," Louis replied in English before I could translate.

"You understand English?" Jackie asked, "I thought you knew none of it."

"He knows some from his teaching days," I interjected, "but not enough to speak it in public yet. Please don't tell Don."

"I won't," Jackie replied, "What the old geezer doesn't know—"

"Will not hurt him," Louis finished her statement, to chuckles.

"Hey, before you go down to start the music, I need to tell you what I just heard before you came in," Jackie sobered, "Iggy called and said he'd be here for a couple of days at the end of next week. He's giving checkups to Company partners. He wants to examine you, Louis."

"The *Eye Guy*?" I asked, "Will he do surgery here?"

"Not this time. He's set up at our clinic in Nashville and doesn't want to move all the gear. He'll open shop in a few weeks, after he visits the facilities."

I explained to Louis. "So, we will see what I will see?" he asked.

"Might say that," Jackie snorted.

"Have you talked to Don yet?" I asked.

"This afternoon…shhh!" she replied, then, "Hi, Love, everything OK?"

Don stepped through the door and sat down at his desk. Everything's just fine. Now if I can just stay awake…"

"If you go to sleep during the ceremony, you'll regret it," Jackie frowned.

"I won't, Precious," Don replied, "but you may have to drive home. I'm missing my sleep from last night."

Louis spoke and I translated. "Is there nothing left of the church?"

"Nothing but ashes and a half-melted boiler," Don replied, "We'll level the lot out and someone will build a house on it."

"We'd better get down there, it's almost twenty to eleven," I said, taking Louis' arm.

"Ta ta for now," Louis announced in English as we walked out the office door.

We walked down the aisle, dodging the arriving guests.

"The hall is filling well," Louis remarked, "About one third I make it."

"You can tell by sound?" I asked.

"That, and the movement of the air," he replied, "but there seems to be a group on the far side of the hall. Why are they that far over?"

I looked at the stage. "I see why. There's a covered birdcage on this side of the stage. Lillian went through with it!"

"Went through what?"

"In that cage is a sign with a fake snake," I whispered in Louis' ear, "Mimi brought the real snake to school a few years ago to show the children. They loved it but the teachers panicked. Lillian told me she was going to bring the cage as a practical joke on the teachers. That's them on the far side."

Louis smiled. "That is wicked! I must not annoy her."

"I'll keep you posted how they're reacting. She'll explain it at the reception."

We climbed the short steps to the stage. "Hello, organ console," Louis said as he stroked the keys.

"What?" I asked.

"In my youth, I was always told to properly *address the organ console*," Louis replied with a chuckle.

We both climbed aboard, and Louis flipped the switches. "I can manage almost all of the organ by feel now," he remarked, "but I need you to keep me informed of the time and where people are."

"I can do that," I said I sat up against him to keep him balanced (and interested). I would swing my legs out of the way if he needed to use the upper range of pedals.

"Twenty till," I murmured.

"So we begin," Louis replied. He pushed several presets and began to play.

"What is that?" I asked.

"The first movement of Charles Marie Widor's Ninth Organ Symphony," Louis replied, "With the emotions of the congregation after the fire last night it seemed appropriate. I will play the first, second, and last movements before playing what we have practiced. We may talk if you wish."

"OK, but right now I just want to enjoy the music and the organist."

"I just want to enjoy my companion."

We said nothing else as Louis worked through the complex construction of the first movement. In the end, he turned to me. "Time?"

"Ten forty-six," I replied.

"Good. Now the second movement, and a question."

Louis began the quiet, slow second movement, and continued.

"I need your help identifying a piece of music Donald left on my laptop computer. It is from uptime, but I cannot determine how it was recorded or what instruments they used. It is the most relaxing piece of music I have found on that machine, but I cannot figure it out. Can you help me?"

I wondered why he asked this in the middle of the prelude but answered the best I could. "I would be happy to help you Louis, but I need to hear the recording to have any chance of identifying it."

"Ah, a problem," Louis said as he continued to play, "I could sing parts of it, but not right now. And Donald strictly enjoined me not to remove the machine from my room, for fear it will be seen."

I shook my head. "As an unmarried woman, I cannot come to your room for any reason and maintain propriety. That is why we linger in the sitting room."

Louis moved his mouth around as he played and thought.

"I think I might have a solution to this problem," he said softly, "Harmony Twichell Ives, I have always loved you, and now I realize how much I love you. I believe it is time: Will you marry me?"

I kept from falling off the bench by the slimmest of margins. I was still able to reply.

"Louis Vierne, you snuck up on me, you stinker!" I grinned as the tears started, "Yes, I will marry you, Love of my life! I believe I am ready if you are."

"Our kiss to seal this must be deferred a few moments, but the decision seems to have been made," Louis said as he finished the second movement. "Time, Love?"

"Almost ten fifty-one, my darling."

"Endearments...how many years since I have heard or spoken them! Be thinking of when we may do the deed while I finish this up." He then began the last movement of that symphony while I dabbed at my eyes. By the time he finished, I knew when.

"Time now ten fifty-five. And I have a suggestion when."

"Tell me after I start the *Andantino*, Love," Louis replied, then began to play the short work from his new *24 Pièces de Fantaisie,* which Sherry had transcribed for him.

"Marcel and Jeannette have to leave Tuesday. How about we have the wedding Monday? Small, intimate, in the Green Room between Don's meetings."

"I would hate for Marcel and Jeannette to miss the wedding.

They took a great risk insisting I come with them after Madeleine left me. Can we get the paperwork by Monday, and will Father Sanford be able to perform the ceremony on that short notice?"

Since Louis was multitasking, as Jackie put it, I did not correct him on the title. "Yes to both, Love. Pastor Sanford said to just call him anytime, and Amy says with the documents she can make we will get the license in less than an hour! Would that be OK with you?"

"Yes, most acceptable, my Love!" Louis replied, "Donald should be well-toasted by the end of that day, not to mention the news he receives this afternoon."

"Amazing," I whispered in Louis' ear, "Everybody knows Jackie is pregnant except Don."

"Fun to watch," my betrothed added.

Louis came to the end of the short work. "Are they lined up?" he asked.

I peered down the aisle. "Yes, Love, all ready. Hit it!"

"Geronimo!" Louis hissed, then launched his *Marche Episcopale.*

CHAPTER FORTY-ONE

Mimi: wedding observations from the inside

"There he goes. Roll it!" Deborah said to our assembled lineup.

"Rolling," Lillian replied, and two by two we began to follow Pastor Kittridge through the double doors and down the aisle.

Matt had described Jackie and Don's wedding to me. Compared to their wedding party ours was minuscule. Pastor had suggested we all march down at the same time to give it more punch, and we did.

So Pastor Kittridge led our little group down the aisle. Behind him came Lillian and Elwood, standing up with us. Next came Bull Reeves and Matt. Finally, Gloria pushing me in the wheelchair.

"You'd better not wave at the crowd," Gloria muttered in my ear.

"Mind reader," I growled as I smiled.

We arrived at the stage in good time and mounted the ramp. I looked straight ahead as we passed the birdcage.

We arrived at the center of the stage and stopped on our tape marks. We listened as Louis finished his *Marche Episcopale.* I had never heard it before and thought it magnificent. I also noticed Harmony was sitting next to him, beaming. *I wonder if he finally asked her,* I thought.

As the silence surrounded us after the music Pastor prayed for the event, then spoke. "Who gives this woman to be married to this man?"

Bull turned from his spot and held my arm as I rose from the wheelchair. "At her request, I do," he intoned, then he walked me to Matt, kissed me, and returned to his place. His beard tickled.

Matt held my arm firmly through the first half of the ceremony. After the vows but before the rings Pastor nodded, and Matt returned me to my wheelchair. We had experimented during the rehearsal to see how long I could safely stand. We worked in a liberal margin of error by inserting this interlude.

"We will now have a short period of contemplation while Louis plays his *Meditation.*" Pastor's words cued Louis and he began to play. Matt rested his hands on my shoulders and squeezed slightly as we listened.

Louis played one of the most calming, beautiful pieces I'd ever heard. I kept my handkerchief busy as he played. Matt offered me another one, and I kissed his hand as I took it. I noticed Harmony's head resting on Louis' shoulder. *He asked her,* I thought, *and she said yes!*

All too soon the music ended, and Matt helped me up to stand in front of Pastor again. Bull and Gloria provided the rings, and we managed to say the right words and not drop them.

Pastor had Bull pray for us. He prayed in a sonorous voice, yet subdued. I knew he could make himself heard on a noisy, chaotic deck; yet here was a gentleness I found comforting.

Finally, the words we had been waiting for.

"And now may I introduce to you Mimi and Matthew, Captain and Mrs. Matthew Plotczyc! Thirty seconds, you two!"

Lillian told me later we came in at twenty-eight seconds. And a half.

Out of breath from the kiss, I could still whisper, "Hold on to me, Love, I'm walking up that aisle!" He knew better than to argue.

So out we walked, at a decent clip. Matt held on to me, but I'd been saving my strength to do this and we got away with it! The others followed, Gloria behind me with the wheelchair just in case. Lillian brought up the rear…with the birdcage.

I got through the doors, then stopped and motioned. Gloria brought the chair behind me and I plopped into it. "Enough heroics, Madame; let's form the line," Gloria commanded.

We stood or sat as the crowd started to exit and Louis played them out.

And on they came. Lillian and I had chairs, but the rest stood. We shook hands, hugged, accepted best wishes, and made small talk. All pleasant and routine for a wedding.

My teachers from Silas Willard decamped from the far side of the auditorium and began to file past. All but one…

"Wh…why is that cage there?" the short woman pointed from a good fifteen feet away.

"Because I put it there, Miss Saaijenga. Do you have a problem with that?" Lillian smiled sweetly, but her voice was authoritative.

"No…no, Ma'am," Hattie replied. She visibly shook, rocking from one foot to the other.

"I am bringing it to the reception, so I advise you to get used to it," Lillian smiled again.

"Er…yes, Ma'am," Hattie said, then walked quickly away and out the door.

"I'm surprised she came this close to it," I remarked.

"Aren't you curious to know if he's in there?" Lillian asked.

I hugged yet another church member from my wheelchair before responding. "Naah. He and I are friends. If he's there, fine; if not, it's a great prank. Either way's fine with me. What about you, Matt?"

Matt shook another guest's hand and turned to us. "I'm fine, whatever."

Lillian nodded and silently turned back to greet the next guest.

Glad Matt gave me time to set that up, I thought, *Now to watch the fun!*

A moment later a couple I didn't recognize got to the head of the line.

"Captain Reeves! What a surprise to see you here!" the man said.

"So this is where Chaplains go to retire?" Bull replied as he shook the thin, middle-aged man's hand vigorously.

"I guess so," a tall woman with graying blonde hair in ringlets said as she pulled Bull into a bear hug, "Never figured we'd see you here!"

"Introductions, please?" I asked.

"Of course," Bull said when the woman released him, "This is Commander Rich Martindale, just retired Chaplain of *Langley*, and his wife Rowena."

"Call me Ro, please," she added as she shook our hands and I introduced the rest of the party.

"Isn't that Chief Sampson over there talking to AP and that scrawny bald guy?" Rich asked.

"Yes," I replied, "and you'll want to give the bald guy some respect. He's Don Wain, owner of all this."

"So that's him. AP said he was mostly harmless," Rich said, and the couple waved at the trio. They walked over and the Martindales repeated the shake and hug with the Chief, and introductions.

"Did we miss anything?" Harmony asked as she and Louis walked out of the auditorium with Pastor Kittridge and over to our line.

"Just that couple over there. He's a Chaplain, just retired off of *Langley*. They look like fun," I replied.

"They *are* fun," Pastor Kittridge said, "when Deborah and Ro get together nobody's safe!"

I noticed Louis and Harmony had their arms around each

other. "Speaking of getting together," I raised my eyebrows at the couple.

"Yes. Details later," Harmony said softly.

"Oui," added Louis.

"When?" I asked.

"Monday, if we can get the license that fast," Harmony replied.

"Morning, early, no prob," Amy said from behind them, "and I saw Sylvester Sanford in the crowd so you can tell him."

"I love it when a plan comes apart," Louis pronounced in English.

"Together, Love," Harmony corrected him. They stared at each other for five seconds.

"I love it when a plan comes apart," they both repeated.

*****

Jackie: 12:15, walking to the reception at the Broadview

"While we were at the wedding Sherry took a call from Fred Rentschler," I announced as we stepped out the Auditorium door. "He says they'll be in first thing tomorrow morning. They know we have rooms reserved at the Broadview and he hopes they'll be able to attend church."

"They?" Don asked, "I know Fred is a Believer, but I don't think George Mead is."

"Part two," I replied, "Fred says Wright's made George an offer to come back to them, and he's going."

"That should be fun to watch," Don said, "George tends not to get along with bureaucracy, and Wright's has a real doozy of one. So who's Fred bringing?"

"Andrew Willgoos. Bill mentioned he's also a Believer, Dutch Reformed variety."

Don stopped at the curb as the traffic flowed by. "I vaguely remember that name but can't place him. Did Sherry look him up?"

I half-smiled and half grimaced as *someone* annoyed my belly. "She did. Said she had to dig, but found he did yeoman work on the engine designs, especially the R-1830 and R-2800. Very quiet, workaholic, gentle soul."

"He'll be a good counterweight in the organization," Don said as we stepped off the curb, "Fred can get a little worked up at times, and they'll both have to get along with Hugo Junkers. This'll be fun!"

"Speaking of fun," I remarked, "feel the vibrations through your feet?"

We stopped in the middle of the wide street to let several cars pass. "I sure do! I'm so glad we found the tunnel between our two venues, even if it was bricked over and never finished."

"Did you find out any more about it?" I asked.

"Omer Custer asked George Lawrence of First National Bank about it. He's been here forever. George said whoever owned them in the nineties got the idea of a tunnel to connect 'em. Found out it leaked, ran out of money, and gave up."

"Close, but no cigar," I said as we started off again, "I'm glad Dick took that project on. He says it should be finished by the end of the month. The prefabricated casing from uptime will keep the water out."

"Sherry would be very unhappy if she got her feet wet," Don snorted.

We slowly climbed the four short steps to the side door of the hotel. Don held the door for me, and we walked in.

"Nice decoration," I remarked as I scanned the dining room, "and there's the new buffet line, ready for its first use. "We walked over to the gleaming stainless-steel line with sneeze shields and trays of various foods.

"What's the one empty spot?" Don asked John Wright as he passed us at his usual scurry.

The Food Service Manager stopped and turned. "Special dish, Mimi's request. She's going to introduce it before the meal."

"I didn't know about that," Don began.

"I do. No problem, Need to know," I interrupted, "The dining room looks great, John."

"Thanks, Jackie," John said over his shoulder as he resumed his mission somewhere.

"But I own this place! I should know what's going on."

"Not all the time, Love," I replied. *And sometimes you just never catch on,* I thought to myself.

CHAPTER FORTY-TWO

Mimi: 12:30, the reception: another opening, another show

I held on to Matt's arm again as we walked to the head table. The dining room was full as the last of the guests slipped in by the side door.

We sat at the head table, along with our attendants, Pastor and Deborah with the Martindales…and the covered birdcage next to Lillian. I noted my former teachers sat as far away from the head table as they could get, Hattie closest to the exit.

Don walked by and gently laid an object on the table. I picked it up and examined it.

"Microphone?" my husband (let me say that again: *husband!*) asked.

"Yes," I replied, "for my performance before we eat."

Matt frowned. "What performance?"

"You'll see. It's all good."

"And where are you going to hide that thing?"

I smiled—I'd checked this before. I clipped the small microphone to the neckline of my dress and dropped the transmitter down my cleavage. It nestled in the pocket, warm and invisible.

Matt reddened. "You promised you wouldn't make me blush in here!"

I turned to him with my Principal's look. "I promised not to say anything to embarrass you. I haven't said a word."

Pastor Kittridge tapped on a water glass with his spoon, and the hall quieted.

"Thank you all for coming to this reception, on this day of conflicting emotions," he began, "We rejoice with Mimi and Matthew on their wedding day."

Matt looked over and smiled at me. *The smile says it all*, I thought. Pastor continued.

"We also praise Our Lord for what happened overnight last night. Our church building is a loss, a great loss, but the Lord ordained that just as surely as He ordained this wedding today. And He is already making provision for us in miraculous ways, which I'll tell you about after the meal."

Pastor looked around to the buffet line and the elderly Steinway piano where Amy Foutch sat. "After the prayer, the bride has a few things she'd like to say, then she'll dismiss you to attack the new buffet. Please follow the signs and start at the far end. If you've never experienced a buffet you're in for a treat."

A murmur ran through the dining room. Matt said this was the first buffet line anywhere in the area.

"In the midst of all this," Pastor continued, "who should show up but one of my oldest friends, Commander Richard Martindale, Chaplain Corps, U.S. Navy, now just retired; and his wife Rowena—she'd rather be called 'Ro'. Please wave or something."

The new couple at our table waved and grinned.

"I've asked Rich to pray for our food, and to thank Our Lord for His goodness to us. Chaplain Martindale."

"Let's pray."

Rich's voice, melodious, and slightly higher pitch, carried easily in the filled dining room. He managed in about a minute and a half to invoke the Lord's blessing and comfort in equal portions on Matt and me, and the congregation still reeling from their loss. I also knew Harmony and Louis would take the prayer personally, now that they had decided to marry. I prayed the Lord would bless them as He had Matt and me. And I knew the news of the provision of the new building would give these folks a lift they sorely needed. As Amy said that morning, it was just a building, just *stuff*. Replaceable.

I came back to the now as Chaplain Martindale finished.

"Amen. And now, Mimi Conger Plotczyc has something she has been waiting to say. Mimi?"

Showtime! Lord, please let this be fun for all! I turned on the microphone and stood up.

"Matthew and I thank you so much for coming to our wedding today! We hope you enjoy the meal and the entertainment."

Out of the corner of my eye, I saw Matt look up at me, questioningly. I bored on.

"This event reminds me of the PTA luncheons we teachers all attended over the years. To honor those memories, I have requested a special dish for the buffet. John, would you bring out the dish, please? John Wright, Food Service Manager for the hotel."

John stepped through the swinging doors from the kitchen. He wore a white coat, gloves, and a chef's hat. He carried a covered stainless-steel pan made to fit the buffet line. He stepped to my place at the table, bowed deeply, and set the pan down in front of me. He lifted the cover with a great flourish. He held the lid over his head with one hand and held his nose with the other. He marched back to the kitchen trailing giggles from the crowd.

"The substance in this pan is green and translucent," I announced, "Spots of white show through the top and inside of the material. Shreds of an orange vegetable also appear. Allow me to describe it in song."

Jackie approached the table and handed me an outsize decorated hat from twenty years before. I don't know where she found it. I clamped it on my head at the proper angle and nodded to Amy at the piano. She launched the simple accompaniment at speed. The trick to this song was to speak it, not sing it, and move so quickly the laughs built non-stop.

Ladies, the minutes will soon be read today
The garden club and weaving class
I'm sure have much to say
But next week is our culture night,
our biggest, best event
And I've just made a dish for it
you'll all find heaven-sent

It's my
lime Jell-O marshmallow cottage cheese surprise
With slices of pimento.
You won't believe your eyes!
All topped with a pineapple ring
and a dash of mayonnaise
My vanilla wafers round the edge
will win your highest praise."

I loved performing comedy songs like this in college. *Still got it,* I thought.

And Mrs. Jones is making scones
that are filled with peanut mousse
To be followed by a chicken mold
that's made in the shape of a goose
For ladies who must watch those pounds,
we've found a special dish
Strawberry ice enshrined in rice
with bits of tuna fish!

And my
lime Jell-O marshmallow cottage cheese surprise
Truly a creation
that description defies

Will go so well with
Mrs. Bell's creation of the week
Shrimp salad topped with chocolate sauce
and garnished with a leek

The voice, the mannerisms, the diction: all came back to me as I played it up for all I was worth.

And Mrs. Perkins' walnut loaf
that's crowned with melted cheese
Was such a hit last Culture Night we asked,
"No seconds, please."
Now you must try her hot dog pie
with candied mushroom slices
Those ladies who resigned last year,
they just don't know what nice is

And my
lime Jell-O marshmallow cottage cheese surprise
I did not steal that recipe!
It's lies, I tell you! Lies!

Our grand award:
a picture hat and a salmon sequined gown
For any girl who tries each dish
and keeps her whole lunch down.

I'd never seen my former teachers laugh so hard. Even Hattie forgot about George for a moment!

I'm sure you all are waiting for the biggest news:
dessert!
We thought of things in molds and rings
your diet to subvert
You must try our chocolate layer cake

on a peanut brittle base
With slices of bananas
that make a funny face
Around the edges, peppermints
just swimming in peach custard
With lovely little curlicues
of lovely yellow mustard.

I threw in a laugh I'd heard out of over-the-top society matrons before and the audience howled. Now for the punch line.

If all this is too much for you,
permit me to advise
More
lime Jell-O marshmallow cottage cheese surprise
I've made heaps!

I got the inflection of the last line just right, and the crowd stood up as they laughed and cheered. I took off the hat, curtsied, then motioned for the crowd to start for the buffet line. I felt Matt's strong arms under mine and I collapsed slowly into my chair. I hadn't realized how much that performance had cost me, but he did. *Worth it though,* I thought, and kissed my husband again.

"Please take the pan to the buffet, Love," I whispered in his ear. He placed it in the line as the onslaught of hungry guests arrived.

By the time the crowd at the line thinned out I was recovered enough to join them. Matt shuttled the plates from my hand to the table, and we dug in.

"Excellent," I mumbled with my mouth half-full.

"Elwood did the meat again. Perfect!" Matt added.

"So Deborah tells me you were a school principal?" Ro Martindale asked across the table.

I swallowed. "Yes, for eight years. I became very ill and would have died if my supervisor and her friends, and this fellow here," I squeezed Matt's arm, "Hadn't intervened and got me to the hospital. Doctor John Bohan and experimental antibiotic medications from Wain Engineering saved my life." That's all I felt comfortable saying.

"I'm so glad!" Ro replied, "I see so much sorrow from *not-in-time* care in my profession. I'm a nurse trying to help people manage their sugar diabetes. I fail too often."

"You'll want to talk to John Bohan and visit our hospital," Gloria piped up, "I'm Director of Nursing at Cottage Hospital, and John's our Medical Director. I know we need someone with your experience on staff over there."

Gloria was being careful too, since we didn't know if the Martindales would be brought in.

I felt someone come up behind me. "You did great, Mimi!" Amy announced, "and we're going over to pound the piano for a few minutes."

"I looked around to see Amy with Harmony and Louis. "Louis loved your song," Harmony said, "and looks forward to the recording."

"So how did you finally settle your engagement?" I asked.

"Stinker surprised me," Harmony replied, "He has a song he can't identify. Asked me if I could, but I said I couldn't come to his room to listen. He had another idea."

"Can you identify another song like that?" my husband woke up to ask softly.

"Won't have to," Amy said, "He hummed a few bars for me and I knew it right away. It's called *Angela,* written by a jazz musician named Bob James. Uptime," she added in a whisper.

"He wants to duplicate it," Harmony added, "but he says he can't identify some of the instruments."

"We'll figure something out. I'm going to play it now," Amy said, "Then Louis wants to check out the piano."

Louis spoke and Harmony translated. "He says he has never seen a Steinway piano like it. It must have been something special at one time."

"It's been here ever since I can remember," I said, "I don't know where it came from."

Louis put his arm around Harmony. "To the piano before dessert," he remarked in English.

"Have fun," I said to their backs.

*****

Sylvia: during the reception lunch, introductions

Luther and I ate with my teachers from Silas Willard at the reception. Ev brought Jeff along, and the other teachers treated him like the fiancé he was. *She trained them well,* I thought with a chuckle.

"Who is that playing the piano over there?" Helen Wasson asked.

"The man and woman are Harmony Ives and Louis Vierne. Amy Lansdale Foutch is playing."

"Is that the French organist?" Hattie Saaijenga asked. "I've never heard him before this morning."

"You'll hear more. He plays the organ at church like Luther." I got a little catch in my throat as I said that. *Not at that little church anymore,* I thought, "He's the official organist here at the Auditorium."

"Oh," Hattie said and returned to staring at the birdcage across the dining room.

Jackie stepped over to Ev and whispered something in her ear. She smiled and nodded. She turned to Jeff and he grinned. *Communicating without words again,* I thought. *Bet they can hardly wait till the end of the school year to get married.*

"Looks like Pastor's about ready to speak," Luther announced.

"Not yet," I replied, "Deborah stopped him. Louis is starting to play."

"Amazing sound for such an old and ratty piano," Luther remarked.

"Don says it's a Steinway," Ev added, "He says no matter how hard a life it's led it's still a Steinway. He wants Elwood to restore it once they figure out what model it is."

"What is that Louis is playing?" Mary Fitch asked, "I've never heard anything like it!"

"I have no idea," I replied. That was mostly correct—I figured it was something from uptime.

After the impromptu entertainment, Pastor Kittridge stood again and tapped his water glass. This time it did no good whatever.

"Here it comes," Luther said softly as Deborah stood up, put fingers to lips, and let forth with her trademark piercing whistle. The diners shushed immediately.

AP bowed. "Thank you so much, Deborah, you've saved the day again!"

A subdued rumble of laughter rolled through the room.

"First, a few words for our Chambers Street family. We will have Sunday school and church at the regular times tomorrow. Church will be in the Auditorium, Sunday school there and in meeting rooms over here. Stop by the Auditorium lobby and the Deacons will direct you. We'll hold services in the Auditorium until the new church building is finished."

Pastor looked around, grinning. "And there will be a new church building, thanks to two different benefactors! We'll explain all this at a business meeting next Wednesday evening, but one benefactor has donated land in the northwest part of town, big enough to put the building, parking lot, and leave lots of lawn. Then another benefactor has been paying for a large fire insurance policy on the building for years, meaning we'll have enough money to build the building we need! You'll hear the details at the meeting, but the Lord has already provided!"

Cheers and applause filled the dining room.

"And now, Miss Lillian Taylor has something she'd like to say."

Lillian stood. She had no trouble at all making herself heard in the dining room.

"Thank you, Pastor. I know you have all been wondering about who or what is in this birdcage," she intoned. "I think now is a good time to introduce you all to...."

"Wait a moment, Lillian," a clear voice at our table announced. I watched as the teacher most terrified of that birdcage stood up. She stepped around the table and walked over to Lillian and the birdcage. She put out her hand and took the cover.

"Allow me," she said, as she pulled off the drape. She looked down, then up with a grin.

"Thank you. I needed to do that," I could just hear Hattie above the murmur of the crowd. She looked down at the cage again, then turned on her heel and returned to our table.

"He's in there," she announced quietly when she was back in her place.

As I started to get up to go meet our guest I heard Jeff speak into Ev's ear.

"Good one."

She turned and kissed her husband-to-be.

CHAPTER FORTY-THREE

Bull Reeves: 4 PM, his room at the Broadview, sorting out

I stared at the screen of the laptop computer as yet another depiction of uptime carrier operations ended.

I knew the man the aircraft carrier was named for, Jim Forrestal. He was a Navy pilot, now a securities broker for Dillon Reed managing my investments. *He must do something pretty big in the next war to have that named after him*, I thought.

What happened to the ship in the *uptime* video chilled me. One little rocket had fired by accident on the flight deck, and they very nearly lost the immense ship to the fire and explosions. Their fire fighting training on deck was as substandard as the old bombs they were issued. 134 men paid the price. If one of their huge armored carriers could go up that easily, what about the poor *Langley*?

The uptime crew had not followed their procedures. The crew and the officers got hurried, preoccupied with the mission, and perhaps a little lazy. When the worst happened the men were very brave, and very dead.

We can't afford to let that happen to the Langley, not at this stage of development, I thought. We must make *Langley*, her aircraft, and crew as safe and efficient as we can, and make sure the *Lexington* and the *Saratoga* are the same from the first day they're commissioned.

But how? And what first?

Jackie had warned me the sheer volume of information I was given could overwhelm me. I assured her I was used to wading through great quantities of information to extract its meaning.

Was I ever wrong.

Every bit of information I found in the answers to my *Thousand and One Questions* was reinforced by what I saw in the videos. It all made sense for the carriers uptime, even those in the coming war. But where do we start? From the number of wires in the arrester cables to the color of each man's shirt, all was new, vital, useful. *But where to start?*

I wiped the sweat from my beard and took another gulp of cold coffee.

I only knew two things to do at this point, as my head pounded and my mind spun like a top.

First: *Lord, please take over here. I can't do this by myself!*

Next: "Chief, could you come over here a moment please?"

"Coming, sir," a voice from next door, then Chief Sampson stepped through the adjoining door. He carried a notebook binder. Even though he wore a civilian suit he looked like he had just stepped away from a personnel inspection.

"How may I help you, sir?" he asked quietly.

I pointed to my writing table full of papers and laptop. "What do we do? Where do we start?"

The chief produced his gentle smile. *He always does that when he has the answer to something, I thought, but what about now?*

He handed me his notebook, open to about the middle. I saw a line at the top of the page with notes written diagonally against it, continuing for several pages. The half of each page below the line the Chief had written short explanations in his tiny, precise hand. Each entry was keyed to numbers that flowed along above the line.

"What is this?"

"Read the explanations. The numbers are days from the start of the operation."

I read, and I *understood*. "Amazing, Chief! How to set up carrier aviation, broken into digestible pieces and taken in order according to a schedule. Building on each other, nothing too large to make happen. How'd you figure this out?"

Chief Sampson shrugged. "I was just as confused as you, sir. My great-grandson had some long talks with me and showed me how to organize it. He calls it a *plan of action and milestones*: *POA and M*."

Where'd he learn this?" I asked.

"He learned part of it in college. The rest he picked up at Naval Postgraduate School in Monterrey, California."

"Uptime, right?" I asked, "We have the War College now, and the Naval Academy has a postgraduate department, but nobody teaches this stuff."

"Yes, sir," the Chief replied, "This hasn't been invented here yet."

I looked at the diagram again. "It has now, Chief. This document lays it all out, prioritizes what we need to change, and gives us a blueprint to do it. May I have this copy, Chief?"

"Sure," Chief Sampson replied, "We knew you'd want it so we made extras."

"Thank you doesn't even begin to cover this, Chief," I shut the notebook. "Of course you know what the reward for a job well done is."

Chief Sampson smiled. "More jobs, sir."

"Right," I replied, "For right now though two things, Chief. First, you know Don's made us both standing offers to come work for him if anything happens and we need to get out of the Navy. You know the barriers you face in this business. Much as I want to, I can't change them beyond what I've done. I want you to promise me that if things get more than you can stand, or if the Lord calls you, you'll let me get you out of the Navy and go to work here."

"Of course, sir, but I'd rather stay where I am," Chief Sampson leveled his gaze at me, "What I'm doing for you is the best job I could have in the Navy, and I want to keep serving you, the Navy and my Lord as long as I can. That's just how I feel."

I drained my coffee cup. "Chief, your words mean more to me than you'll ever know. We've got a tiger by the tail with *Langley* and the new carriers, and I need your steady wisdom more than ever."

I set my empty cup down with a bang. "Here's my next order, Chief. I want you to stay here while I go to D.C. on Tuesday. I'll be back for Gunny Sewell's wedding in two weeks. I think I'll have a couple of guests with me. While I'm gone you learn everything you can from our friends here. They've invited us to fly with them; I don't have time right now but you do. Have some fun, Chief—and get to know your kin. You've earned this, and then some. *Copy*?" I finished, echoing the term Jackie used.

Chief Sampson's grin lit up the old hotel room. "Copy. Thank you, sir, I'll do that."

*****

Mimi Conger Plotczyc: 4 PM, her new home and husband, sorting out

"I haven't been out this way since the District Fairgrounds closed," I remarked as we passed Whitesboro Street heading out Grand Avenue.

"I wanted someplace far enough out to be private, but close enough for an easy commute. I bought four lots."

I snuggled into my new husband in the bouncing car. "No close neighbors, eh?"

Matt glanced over at me and down. *Even in here*, I thought.

"Oh, I'll sell off a lot or two eventually, but for right now I like the space. Not too bad to mow either. I have a disguised uptime riding mower. You might enjoy horsing it around."

"Get me to do your housework now?" I smiled to pull the sting.

"Only what you want to do, Love," Matt replied, glancing over again, "I have all the uptime gadgets to make it easy."

We turned right at Farnham Street and jogged left just past a small grocery store. "This street is new," I remarked.

"The developer figured one main brick street and the rest chip and tar," Matt added, "I don't know why they named it *Baird Avenue.*"

I smirked, "Because they took out the grandstand and track and left it bare."

I could see Matt start to redden. "I guess so, Love," he replied. *Right on schedule,* I thought, *Just like me.*

We came to the last house on the street and Matt turned into the wide concrete driveway. "Three garage doors? And a drive around back? What is this, a car dealership?"

Matt stopped in front of one of the doors. "Not quite. I wanted room to tinker without splashing around in the mud outside. I think you'll like this." He reached over and pushed a button on the polished wood dash. The door in front of us opened.

"Look to the right as we pull in," he said. I looked and saw a shiny dark blue car, larger than the Jaguar but obviously related. It looked more like a normal car than our little two-seater. And beyond it a familiar form in the shadows. *That stinker,* I thought, then returned to the nearer car.

"What is this?" I asked as he shut off the car and pushed the button again. Behind us, the garage door slid shut.

"That, my Love, is a 1951 Jaguar Mark Five saloon with a Chrysler slant six motor and five-speed transmission!" He got out and walked around to my door. "Do you like your wedding gift? It has a story. Doctor Art outdid himself this time!"

"I do, and I'm sure he did," I said as Matt helped me out of the car, "and I want to hear all about it, but not right now. I need to get in and use the facilities. And I see my old Chevrolet parked next to it. Why did you go find that?"

"When you told me how you'd sold it when you ran out of

money I decided to go looking. I contacted the dealer in Rock Island and found they still had it—nobody wanted it. I did, and now you have it back."

"That was very sweet of you, Matthew, and I'll get reacquainted with it later. Right now though, if you don't want to *see yellow* you'll get me inside to use the bathroom!"

And proceed with other things, I thought but did not add.

"Oh, right now, Dear," Matt said softly as he blushed. He held my arm as we walked to a side door. "One small step, the only one in the house," he added as helped me up it.

He opened the door and we stepped through an airy space with windows front and back. "Breezeway," Matt said as he opened the next door.

We walked into the strangest kitchen I had ever seen. Wood cabinets abounded, a couple of them larger than normal.

"Uptime appliances," Matt said, opening two cabinets.

One was a disguised refrigerator, the largest I'd ever seen, well-stocked. "I remember you like steak and shrimp," Matt remarked.

The other cabinet contained ranks of olive bottles and at least ten bottles of *Gator Sauce!*

"That's amazing, Love! But we can explore later. Right now I need to *skip to the Loo!*"

Matt snorted. "Right, Precious, this way." We walked into the living room. A strange chair dominated the space.

"Never seen a chair like that," I said.

"Large recliner, with heat, cool and massage built-in." He flipped the top of an armrest up, exposing several buttons, "Really helps after a day at the shop. We'll get you measured for one. They're custom-built uptime."

"Thank you so much, Matthew!" I gushed a little, "Now, the bathroom?"

"Here we are," Matt paused at an open door, "There's another one off the master bedroom."

"This will do fine. I'll only be a moment," I said as I closed the door.

The lights turned on before I could find the switch. *What next in this crazy house?* I thought. As I took care of business I noticed a button labeled *Bidet* within easy reach. *Haven't seen that since I was in Paris. So that's how he managed when his hand was bandaged!*

I washed my hands and checked myself. *All in order. Should last for about the next thirty seconds,* I thought, then finished drying and stepped out.

Matt took my arm again and we walked to the room at the end of the hall. He ushered me in. The largest bed I had ever seen anchored a couple of dressers and a mirrored vanity.

We stopped and I turned to face my husband. "Beautiful," I remarked, then executed my plan.

I grasped the bottom third of my dress and pulled up in one sweeping motion. When I tried this in the hospital I had easily pulled off my dress and deposited it on the bed next to me.

Right. This time I caught my slip along with the dress. Somehow the assembly ended up wrapped around my head! I couldn't see, and I couldn't lift the mess off my head. I was stuck in a giant turban! Inside it was hard to breathe, and I started to cry.

"Wait, Love! Let me help," I heard from outside, then large hands started to move the cloth and untangle it. The room reappeared from the gloom, and with it the face of my amazing husband.

"That didn't work," I murmured.

"It doesn't matter," Matt said, then we paused for a long kiss. When we finished I took Matt's hands and gently placed them where we both wanted them to go.

"It opens from the front," I added.

*****

Don: 4 PM, home and wife, sorted out

"So where were the kids going?" I asked as we got into the Wills.

"Amy and Elwood invited them to supper at their apartment. Louis and Harmony are coming too. They're going to talk about Ev and Jeff's wedding in June."

"That'll be the strangest conversation in town tonight," I said as I backed out of the Armory parking place, "They'll all sit in a circle communicating without words and writing on yellow pads."

"Not all of them," my wife chuckled, "Amy said she was going to take Harmony to the Ops center and teach her how to play video games."

I laughed. "And they can read the report later."

"Yeah."

We climbed the Broad Street hill and carefully edged through the intersection at North Street. "You think it's time to pass the Wills on to Doctor Art?" I asked, referring to our uptime export director.

"If you're tired of it I guess so," Jackie replied, "What'll you replace it with?"

"Something smaller, easier to handle on these streets," I said, "We don't need all this room since we've got a Twin Coach bus coming in a couple months."

Jackie frowned. "Let's think about that a bit before we go converting this one back to stock, OK?"

"Sure, you say so," I replied, "I didn't think you liked driving this thing."

"Let's just think about it." I had learned when Jackie became obtuse she always had a good reason, so I let it go.

We got to the house and pulled in the driveway. "Nice to see the yard again after all that snow," I remarked.

"I hope Slim has time to keep the grass mowed, now that we have him working at the airport," Jackie said.

"If he can't I'll just get a rider mower like Matt has."

"Speaking of airports, *Admiral,* Doctor Art's bought us an Ercoupe. He's sending it through the *paint booth* next week. He says he wants to be here when you solo in it."

"Me?"

"You. Besides being perfect for Jack's therapy, the thing is so simple to fly even you can do it! I want you able to take over when we fly places or if something happens to the pilot."

I opened the side door for Jackie, and we walked in. "You know I'll never be proficient at all the details. I don't have the concentration—that's why I never tried to learn before."

"You'll do OK in a pinch—or an Eeep."

"Whatever, Love," I replied as we walked through the kitchen.

"You suppose they're doing it yet?" Jackie asked.

"You want I should call them?*Eeep!*"

"Philistine."

"You started it."

Jackie didn't try to poke me again. "You're right, Dear, I'm sorry. I need to visit the loo—I'll catch up to you."

"Sure, Precious," and she skittered through the kitchen. *Stomach bothering her again?* I wondered.

Theodore and Melissa sauntered into the kitchen. They stopped and accepted my petting, then exited the doggie door to the back yard.

I passed through the house to the den. We had turned the second bedroom into our technology room, closed off from non-partners. We had computer workstations with printers, a decent audio system installed, and our most comfortable recliners. I opened up the sound laptop and turned on the speakers. The extra soundproofing would keep the neighbors from hearing us.

I punched up one of my favorite pieces, *Overture to The Wasps,* by Ralph Vaughn Williams. I did not like the insects, but I loved the music.

I settled into my recliner and relaxed. The orchestra was from *uptime*, but I had suggested to Fred Stock that we program it one of these days. I knew I had to let Mimi manage the programming for the Auditorium, but I hoped she would listen to my suggestions.

I must have fallen asleep. Next thing I knew the music was over and Jackie was standing in the room scribbling on a yellow pad.

"Hey, Precious, what are you doing?"

Jackie turned to me, smiling.

"Just doing some thinking, and simulating in my mind. You're going to have to move out of this room in the next few months. All this stuff can go in the back bedroom down the hall. I'd say you have two months to get it all moved."

My mouth dropped open and I stood up, staring.

"Why on earth would I want to do that? I've got everything organized...all right, half organized, in here, and all the electrical outlets I need. That bedroom's a different shape. It'll take weeks to get it set up like this. Why?"

Jackie set the pad down and put her hands on my shoulders. She turned me slightly.

"Because we will have need of this room for another purpose. Can you guess what that purpose might be?"

I just stared at my brilliant, obtuse wife. "No, love, I just don't get it."

She looked me straight in the eye. “Have you ever changed a diaper?”

“No, I haven’t, Love. What does that...”

Suddenly I understood. Finally.

The light in the room turned red and my knees buckled. I landed back in the recliner where Jackie had aimed me.

The scene changed, and I found myself on the quarterdeck of *USS Lexington* (AVT-16) again.

At least this time it’s good news, I thought as my younger self came out to relieve me again.

ABOUT THE AUTHOR

Donald Bowers

Donald Bowers served as a Naval officer and teacher before spending over thirty years as a Case Manager for adults with intellectual disabilities. He finally got around to writing in his late fifties. He lives in Galesburg, Illinois with his wife, Ellen Anne Eddy Bowers, three cats and three greyhounds.

BOOKS IN THIS SERIES

According to His Purpose
A series of books mixing multi universes, people of faith and Galesburg history. What happens when you change people's lives, one soul at a time, According to His Purpose? Visit the Galesburg that never was and meet more folk Called According to His Purpose.

With Patience Wait

With Patience Wait
1918—Both Sylvia and Luther have had their lives turned upside down by the war and the Spanish flu. But God has plans for them they could have never thought Follow their lives and others as they find their path in His will.

Conformed To The Image

Conformed to the Image
1925—What would happen if we brought technology back from the future to the past? Would it change who people are and what they could do? Would it avoid the horrors of the Depression and War? Follow Don on his mission to help conform the world to His Lord's Image.

To The Praise Of His Glory

To the Praise of His Glory

1926—New year, new challenges in this Galesburg in another universe.

Luther and Sylvia find themselves thrust into new positions of responsibility they did not seek. Don Wain faces the greatest trial of his life in two universes. Jackie Brighthonor must finally face that night in the South China Sea so far in the future. And a fledgling teacher meets her Prince Charming in a Buick. All in the middle of the snowstorm of the century.

Want to Learn More?

With Patience Wait, and all the other *According to His Purpose* novels are inspired by actual historical people, places, inventions, and times. Learn more at Don's web site,

www.acordingtohispurposeweb.wordpress.com

Also check there for information on upcoming books by Don.

www.ingramcontent.com/pod-product-compliance
Lightning Source LLC
Chambersburg PA
CBHW071150250626
47159CB00001B/49

9781732285040